A Long Day in a Short Life

Other books by ALBERT MALTZ

A Long Day in a Short Life

Albert Maltz

Introduction by Patrick Chura

CALDER

CALDER PUBLICATIONS
an imprint of

ALMA BOOKS LTD
Thornton House
Thornton Road
Wimbledon Village
London SW19 4NG
United Kingdom
www.calderpublications.com

A Long Day in a Short Life first published by Calder Publications in
April 1957
This revised edition first published by Calder Publications in 2023

© The Estate of Albert Maltz, 1957, 2023

Introduction © Patrick Chura

Front cover: David Wardle

ISBN: 978-0-7145-5063-3

Contents

Introduction

Albert Maltz's desire to write a prison novel did not begin with his incarceration in 1950 for refusing, during his testimony before a congressional committee, to answer the question: "Are you now or have you ever been a member of the Communist Party?" His interest in crime and punishment was formed much earlier. In 1926, his uncle was convicted on a charge of armed robbery and sent to the Ossining Correctional Facility in New York. For several months young Albert, eighteen, paid him regular visits. Out of these visits came questions about the origins of criminal behaviour and its effects on the individual.

The uncle's case was not a miscarriage of justice: he was guilty. He had not stolen bread in hunger, but had participated in the theft of a truckload of expensive furs. Nevertheless, the root cause was poverty. As Maltz understood, the forty-year-old man was driven by a hunger for more of the world's wealth than society gave him for his labour. Recalling the prison visits decades later, Maltz found it significant that the Saturday-morning train to Sing Sing was crowded with the poor of New York City, almost exclusively the poor.

Maltz's own imprisonment was the second experience that led him to write *A Long Day in a Short Life*. At the height of the anti-communist hysteria of the Cold War, he was one of ten screenwriters and motion-picture directors who were blacklisted, declared guilty of the crime of contempt of the United States Congress and sentenced to a year in jail.

The case became known as that of the "Hollywood Ten". In 1947, Maltz and his colleagues were summoned to Washington for interrogation by the Committee on un-American Activities, chaired by J. Parnell Thomas. The committee claimed to embody patriotism, but was in fact the brutal vanguard of American fascism. Maltz refused to answer its red-baiting questions, and instead read a statement: "The American people are going to have to choose between the Bill of Rights and the Thomas committee. They cannot have both. One or the other must be abolished in the immediate future."

Maltz was committed to the Federal jail in Washington, DC, in June 1950. Although he would serve the main part of his sentence at Mill Point Prison in West Virginia, he remained in the DC lockup for eighteen days. It was there that *A Long Day in a Short Life* was conceived.

By Maltz's own admission, his acclimation to prison life was harrowing. He had not known the meaning of freedom until it was taken away. With twenty-one out of twenty-four hours spent in idleness in a claustral cell, each day seemed endless. After a week he managed to acquire pencils and paper. Over the next ten days he made seventy pages of notes for a novel. Then he learnt that he could not take the papers with him or send them to the outside. The night before he was transferred to West Virginia, he memorized the notes, then tore them up and flushed them down the toilet.

Conditions were better at the rural Mill Point Prison. As soon as he could get his hands on paper and pencil, he rewrote his observations about the DC jail. In a letter to his wife Margaret, he described this second adjustment as "easy" and added that he felt "stronger and quieter and only more solid inside in ever so many ways". He hinted at the project that became his novel, referring strategically to his incarceration: "We'll write it off as ten months of research, as it partially is."

Upon his release from Mill Point in April 1951, Maltz went to work immediately. By the end of the year, he'd finished a first draft. "I had expected it to pour out of me," he recalled, "and so it seemed to come."

A Long Day in A Short Life centres on Huey Wilson, an eighteen-year-old from a poor but striving black family. Wilson works by day, takes classes at night, drives himself hard and dreams of becoming a prominent civil-rights attorney. He is first seen on a picket line leading a demonstration against Jim Crow segregation in the Washington school system in 1946. After the protest, Wilson is stalked and savagely attacked by four white men. He is rescued in the nick of time by a middle-aged passer-by, Tom McPeak, a Georgia-born white who doesn't know Wilson but jumps into the fight and saves the young man's life. Immediately the police frame Wilson for the crime of being black, working up fake charges of felony assault with a deadly weapon, while the would-be lynchers get a slap on the wrist. McPeak is arrested too, but he is offered a deal: he can go free if he will leave town without testifying, thereby allowing the police to clinch the frame-up that will saddle Wilson with a long sentence.

The rest of the narrative takes place in the course of one day in the Washington jail. It revolves around the question of what McPeak will do with his personal ethical dilemma. Initially the white man turns away from Wilson because his plight seems hopeless, a race-based injustice that is "as old as the United States itself, and wouldn't be solved in a day".

But as Wilson and McPeak converse, they find common ground. McPeak is a spot welder in a Ford plant in Detroit. From his experience organizing factory workers and leading labour actions, he has learnt the adhesive power of common interest and shed his racist upbringing. He realizes that deserting Wilson would be exactly like scabbing on his fellow workers in a strike. To him, interracial "unity" is not an abstract word, but the only real tool for achieving justice.

McPeak remembers something taught to him by a black worker during a sit-down strike in the 1930s. When a labourer wants to better himself, there are two keys to open the door. One of them is white and the other black. Wilson understands and finishes the thought. "We're the two keys in this situation, aren't we, Tom?... If we work together, we can open this jail door." For both men, the metaphor of the keys is "a bottom truth".

In early 1952, Maltz shared the draft manuscript of the novel with his friend A.B. Magil, a communist writer and editor of the Marxist journal *Masses & Mainstream* who had followed Maltz's career from its beginnings. Both men were now living in Mexico as political refugees. Magil took in the manuscript eagerly and responded, "The book has impressed and moved me deeply as a work of great truth and superlative artistry."

While Magil found the novel compelling and courageous, he also felt that it contained "ideological errors" in its treatment of race. Among them, the fact that "Huey's awakening comes not from his own people, but from the preachments of a white man" was a serious flaw. "White progressives inevitably move among pitfalls in this area," Magil said, "and often we are only partly conscious of them."

A week later Maltz responded to this criticism in a lengthy letter, reminding Magil that the black liberation struggle would necessarily involve unification with white progressives, and that "it is among Marxists that Negroes will find their staunchest allies".

But the matter was far from settled. Magil had sent the manuscript to other *Masses & Mainstream* editors, including Lloyd L. Brown, an African-American writer and labour organizer. Brown had recently published his own well-received prison novel, *Iron City*, based on his experiences in the segregated cell block of the Allegheny County Jail near Pittsburgh.

Brown read Maltz's manuscript, along with his thirteen-page response to Magil, and was offended by both. He saw the character Huey as an "artistic failure" and was outraged by the book's "utter and illimitable ignorance of the essence of Negro life". The problem was not just that Maltz had written a "white saviour" story, but that his work had displayed a lack of consciousness of the historical burdens of blackness.

In the novel, Maltz had allowed a white progressive to proclaim that American blacks "must and will fight". Brown found it necessary to remind the Jewish American author that millions of African-Americans had been fighting "every hour and every minute for over 300 years" in an "unremitting struggle for freedom and equality". He had also detected in Maltz's writing a condescending set of assumptions about methods of racial liberation as expressed by a "literate progressive" whose treatment of black culture was not based on lived experience.

"The negro is a soldier who never gets a furlough," Brown wrote on 1st June 1953, adding,

> Good God, man, don't tell him that he "must and will fight"!… And don't come up here to Harlem hollering "Fight"! Don't talk like that to Lloyd L. Brown, who first heard that word from an aged Negro woman who had walked a thousand miles barefoot in the snow to Freedom.

The scorching indictment closed with a derisive suggestion:

> Go ahead, Albert Maltz – write about any kind of typical Negro, good, bad, or middling. But first, be wise enough and humble enough to find out something about the Negro people.

The black novelist's rhetoric was potent. Maltz's groping, soul-searching response was, in human terms, also impressive:

Dear Lloyd Brown,
    Reading and re-reading your letter has been a painful experience. […] I will destroy this novel of mine and I never will publish another line before I consciously will do harm to the Negro Liberation Movement, or to the cause of unity between the white working class and the Negro people. […] The fact that I may be without malice, does not excuse ignorance. […] After twenty years in the progressive movement I have certain responsibilities. One of these responsibilities is that of knowing something about the struggles of the Negro people. […] I don't mean that you have the obligation of trying to mend my ignorance. I am seeking criticism.
    I am fighting for a piece of work in whose truth and value I believe.

For the next five weeks, Maltz licked his wounds, studying and reflecting on Brown's assessment. Then on 14th July he wrote again to Brown, informing him of the outcome of his self-examination:

> I think all of your criticisms are sound. My point of view on the book has changed. I believe I thoroughly understand the distortions it contains.
>
> I hope my persisting confidence that I can handle this material with truth is not mistaken. In any instance, I now am preparing for a major re-write, from page 1 on.
>
> I know I have listened; I hope I have learned; we will see the results.

The results were brilliant. The new version of *A Long Day in a Short Life* retained the story of McPeak and Huey Wilson, now changed in ways that realized cultural work rarely accomplished in previous American fiction.

First, Maltz amplified the novel's African-American voices and clarified their role in Huey Wilson's growth. More than McPeak's aid, it is Wilson's personal code of doggedly fighting back against white chauvinism, a legacy from his father and brother, along with the solidarity of other inmates in Huey's segregated cell block, that inspires his struggle.

Second, in the revised novel the interracial alliance is symbiotic rather than hierarchical. With Wilson on his side, McPeak is "stronger than himself", because he is not alone. He envisions a partnership exemplifying "human brotherhood on the highest plane". This is the idea that nudges McPeak towards the selfless act of testifying for Wilson against the police frame-up, a spiritual dynamic that reverses the familiar "white saviour" narrative.

Third, McPeak is now a fully developed and therefore more admirable character. A factor in his rebellion is pure defiance, what Maltz calls "an explosive resentment of arbitrary authority". The thought of the men around him, prisoners black and white, who "stuck together in the face of authority", stirs his pride in humanity.

Simultaneously Maltz added emphasis to the story of a second white protagonist, the thirty-year-old convict Floyd Varney, who is callously abused by a legal system rigged to maintain and serve the hegemony of the elite classes.

At the novel's close, these plot threads come together in a moving representation of racial interdependence. Varney, despairing and devastated by a sentence of twenty-five years to life in prison, slits his wrists in his cell and will die without a transfusion. The call goes out for a blood donor, and the single volunteer is Alfrice Tillman, a young inmate from the segregated fourth tier. Very little of Tillman's life had been calculated to induce compassion across the colour line: "Yet now, somehow, he was sensing the inner heart of this white man with the cadaver's face. [... H]e might be white, he might be a stranger, but his suffering brought kinship."

Interestingly, the scene redeploys a key element of Maltz's 1945 screenplay *The House I Live In*, a film made for the purpose of counteracting anti-Semitism, in which a Jew-to-Gentile blood transfusion figures prominently as an argument for true multicultural democracy.

As this textual history suggests, the development of *A Long Day in a Short Life* demanded introspection and involved substantial creative growing pains for Maltz as a novelist. Yet he persisted and kept faith in his art. These efforts did not make US publishers any more receptive to Maltz's work – or willing to break the blacklist. In 1953, at the peak of Senator Joseph McCarthy's power, Maltz's long-time publisher Little, Brown and Company rejected the novel. That year, the state department banned his 1944 novel *The Cross and the Arrow* from overseas libraries, after which stateside librarians took the hint and began removing his other works from their shelves. For Maltz, horrified at this erasure, it was suddenly as if he had never lived or written at all.

Over the next three years *A Long Day in a Short Life* received a long series of rejections from American publishers while getting sixteen contracts for publication in foreign countries, including the UK. When domestic options ran out, Maltz gave the novel to International Publishers, a New York publisher whose communist affiliations ensured that the book would not be widely read or reviewed – so that at least his friends could read it.

A Long Day in a Short Life sold less than a thousand copies in the United States. Only small-circulation leftist journals recognized its power. In the *Afro-American*, Saunders Redding called it "both tough and tender. Its toughness derives from its truth; its tenderness derives from its deep compassion." In *Masses & Mainstream*, Philip Stevenson observed, "Albert Maltz's first novel in eight years is not only the best of his work; it is one of today's most important novels. It seems almost incredible that eighteen American publishers refused it."

Today, this reception should remind us that there's a price to pay for proto-fascism. *A Long Day in a Short Life* might have had immeasurable cultural impact. Instead, a major novel of the early civil-rights era was effectively suppressed. This new Alma Books edition makes the book available on both sides of the Atlantic for the first time since 1957.

Patrick Chura, University of Akron

A Long Day in a Short Life

To my daughter,
Katherine, with all my love.
In your maturity,
the world will do many things better.

AUTHOR'S NOTE

Since this is a fictional tale, the characters are invented. Any resemblance to living individuals is accidental.

In the centre of all, and object of all, stands the Human Being, towards whose heroic and spiritual evolution poems and everything directly or indirectly tend.*

WALT WHITMAN

You got a right, I got a right.
We all got a right, to the tree of life.*

NEGRO SPIRITUAL

AMONG THE MEN

First Tier

Name	Cell	Charge	Sentence or Status
Hal Jude, Jr.	112	Grand larceny	Awaiting sentence
John Lauter	124	Suspicion of first-degree burglary	Awaiting court ruling on extradition
Thomas McPeak	130	Assault, disorderly conduct, resisting arrest	Awaiting preliminary hearing
Eddie Quinn	102	Grand larceny	1 to 3 years Awaiting transfer
Floyd Varney	124	Second-degree murder	Awaiting sentence

Second Tier

Wacky Mike	208	First-degree murder	Death Awaiting execution

Third Tier

Art Ballou	318	Suspicion of disorderly conduct	Awaiting preliminary hearing

Fourth Tier

George Benjamin	424	Armed robbery	15 years Awaiting transfer
Eugene Finnerty	430	Arson	6 years Awaiting transfer
Isaac Reeves	428	Income-tax fraud	3 years Awaiting transfer
Dewey Spaulding	426	Violation of lottery laws	Awaiting preliminary hearing
Alfrice Tillman	428	Grand larceny	18 months Awaiting transfer
Ben Wellman	426	Aggravated assault	Awaiting trial
Huey Wilson	430	Felonious assault with deadly weapons	Awaiting preliminary hearing

Chapter 1

Floyd Varney

At dawn of this October day in 1946 a muggy fog lay heavy upon the streets of Washington. Since the night was warm, the fog penetrated into bedrooms through open windows and added its moisture to the night sweat of humid bodies. Despite the heat, with easy conscience or bad, most citizens were asleep.

The inmates of the District Jail also were asleep. However, since they were the errant children of their society, their sleep was guarded by a group of trained custodians – by tier guards in each cell block, and armed guards in high turrets on the outer walls, and a night watch in the central control room.

In a narrow sense, the inmates of this particular jail slept better than some of the city's free citizens, who lay three in a bed, five and seven in one room of a rotting slum kennel. The central jail of this capital city was modern in design, sanitary and efficiently administered. Day in and day out it sheltered, fed and supervised eleven hundred inmates in various stages of the judicial process. Some of these were newly arrested men, not yet brought to trial, innocent perhaps, yet confined because they had no funds to pay for bail; others had been tried and convicted and were being held for transfer to a penitentiary; still others, who were doing the work of the jail – in tailor shop and laundry, in kitchen, hospital, office and warehouse – were in residence for the duration of their sentences, which ran from one year to life. And since this jail had been scientifically designed and was scientifically operated, no one escaped from it and few even contemplated escape. For each inmate lived, ate, slept and waited within a series of confinements: within an immense building of stone and steel that was his assigned cell block; within a smaller rectangle of stone and steel that was his assigned wing; within a steel-and-concrete cell that was his assigned burrow. And from this confinement within confinement no man by his own will walked free.

* * *

Inmate 84421, hotel cook and fancy baker, groaned, moved restlessly in his bunk and awakened. His sleep had been broken by a dream that left him with sweaty hands and a pounding heart. He lay still for a few moments, hoping to sleep again, but then sighed and opened his eyes. As he saw the steel bars at the front of his cell, he automatically thought to himself, with wretchedness and indignation, "But it was an accident, it was self-defence, why couldn't they understand?"

This was not a new thought for Floyd Varney, and he scarcely was aware that it had passed through his mind. On many another morning during the six months of his imprisonment, the first sight of his cell bars had evoked the same cry. Actually it expressed something more than protest: his anguished yearning for time to be reversed, his tormented wish that by some magic he could relive the moment in which he had killed a man. But now, as on other mornings, the dull gleam of the steel bars reminded him that time and death never could be reversed, and that a jury had held him guilty of second-degree murder.*

At this hour, shortly before 5 a.m., the cell block was very quiet, seemingly devoid of life. Even though men snored and one coughed in his sleep and another turned over with a sigh, all sounds were instantly absorbed by the cottony hush in the cavernous building, enfolded and lost. Varney felt hopelessly alone, abandoned by an alien universe – and it was this emotion that his dream had expressed.

In the dream Varney had been lying naked on the hard earth of a vast plain, with his arms and legs fastened to iron stakes. A great bird, repellent and vulture-like, with the knowing eyes of a rapacious old man, had been hovering over him. Varney knew that the bird was about to tear at his body with its beak and talons, and that it would feast upon his living flesh with the horrible cruelty of the indifferent – yet he was powerless to defend himself.* He awakened as the bird swooped down.

The dream had been appropriate. This new day at hand would be of no great moment to most people, but it was sentence day for Floyd Varney. An hour or so from now armed guards would transport him to the District Court. There he would be taken before the judge who had presided at his trial, and this man in a black robe, an indifferent stranger, would pronounce sentence upon him. And if the sentence were unfair, as he knew the jury verdict had been unfair, there would be nothing on earth that Varney could do to alter it. It would make no difference that he had been innocent of intention to kill – it would not matter that the man's wife had lied about their relations or that he, Varney, never before had violated the law. Whatever the sentence was, it would be beyond his power to change it.

It was this, his utter helplessness, that oppressed Varney the most. He was thirty years old, and he had been making his way in the world since the age of ten. Through hardship he had acquired the ability to rely upon himself – unknowingly, he also had acquired a congealed distrust of everyone else. Whatever his past circumstances, never before had he been in so terrifying a position as this, where his own intelligence and determination were impotent, and where he was completely at the mercy of others.

Thinking of the moment when he would be standing before the judge, Varney began to stir restlessly in his bunk. From where he lay he could see a small section of the cell block, as though through a camera lens, and the scene was not without a certain cold, sombre beauty. The blend of night shadow and dim electric light, playing over austere lines and polished steel surfaces, over the expanse of immaculate floor and outer wall, had the quality and mood of fine chiaroscuro in a painting. Varney, however, saw nothing in the view except the bleak conditions of his confinement. He saw implacable bars that pinned him in his cell; five feet beyond, he saw a screen of heavy steel mesh that pinned him to the runway in front of his cell; twenty feet beyond this, he saw the stone wall that pinned him within the building. And suddenly, as though what lay before his eyes was too intolerable to bear, his mind slipped into fantasy. Like a small boy with a candy in his mouth, he lay in momentary contentment, sucking pleasure and nourishment from a dream that never would be realized.

Before that awful moment two weeks past, in which a jury had held him guilty of second-degree murder, there had been little time in Varney's life for daydreaming. All of his energy and thoughts had been directed to the concrete matter of his defence. For five months he had discussed his case daily with his cellmate, John Lauter, and with other men at every opportunity, and even with imagined persons when the lights were out and talking was forbidden. There was no grain of evidence that he had not sifted over a thousand times, no argument on his behalf, concocted by a fellow inmate, that he had not repeated to his attorney, no aspect of the law governing homicide that he had not explored. He knew with certainty that he would be acquitted on grounds of justifiable self-defence – or, at worst (by some frightful blunder on the part of the jury), that he would be held guilty of the comparatively minor crime of manslaughter. He knew that he had not wanted to kill, and he felt miserable that he had taken another man's life, and surely the jury would understand that it had been an accident.

The jury had not understood. The verdict had been murder, and from that moment Varney had become a different personality. Except for occasional bitter comments to Johnny Lauter, he had ceased talking about his case. Whereas before he had gone eagerly to Recreation or the Yard in order to meet others, now he emerged from his cell only for meals. For the most part he spent his days on his bunk – stunned, withdrawn and lost in dreams. Without willing it or being conscious of what he was doing, he spent the bulk of his time reviewing the events of his life and weaving from them an endless series of glittering self-deceptions. Out of the memories of his childhood, which were wretched, would emerge a different home, a mother he loved and a fictional, idealized father. Lying on his bunk, he would go to school in a way he never had, enjoy privileges he had been denied, have tempestuous love affairs with beautiful women who adored him, and win success in important professions about which he knew nothing. There was one type of daydream, however, that occupied him most, since it was intimately connected with the disaster that had befallen him. This was his relationship with his sweetheart, Janey, whom he had betrayed, and who had forsaken him. Now, a few hours away from sentence time, Varney was elaborating a satisfying lie about Janey and himself.

He saw a kindly judge on a high bench, he heard a sympathetic voice… "The circumstances of your crime… your splendid war record… your years as a good citizen… all lead me to conclude that you are not a man of criminal tendency, and that you do not belong in prison. For this reason, while giving you the minimum sentence of ten years, I hereby grant you probation. You are now free to leave the courtroom."

Happiness! Spectators applauding! Janey with her eyes shining, her sweet face radiant with love. She would fling her arms around him and cry out, "Darling, now we'll never be separated!"

"Yes," he would reply, "never again separated. You and me, we'll have a home and kids. I'll never look at another woman, I'll love you for ever, my darling."

A jailbird's fantasy – recurrent, compulsive, tortured! Like most of his other dreams, this one too collapsed from its own fragility. Janey would not be in the courtroom this morning, because Janey was finished with him. He had broken faith with Janey, betrayed their good love for a few hours in bed with the wife of another man, and Janey had dropped him from the moment of his arrest. No Janey, and no probation for him either! The law forbade probation in cases of second-degree murder, and there was no way for him to go free this morning – and oh God, how had this ever happened to him?

Varney groaned. With anguish he reflected that in the six months of his imprisonment he had learnt the meaning of the word "freedom". Who beside a jailbird knew what it meant? Talk to the average man in the street and he'd think you meant "freedom of speech" or something silly like that. But talk to a jailbird… Christ! Each day like the one before, like the next and the next – hollow days, grey days, up at the same hour, eat at the same hour, to bed at the same hour. The same walls to look at, the same bars, the same grey faces. Never the sight of a woman, of the living beauty of a woman, or the sound of a woman's voice. Never a child running down a street, or flowers in a garden, or leaves on a tree. The same food, the same flat, horrible meals, the same stone floors, the same line-ups. Nothing in a man's heart but dry dust, nothing but endless hours, endlessly the same.

That was what they took from you when you were in jail – the right to be alive in the only way that living counted. And how many more months and years would he have to endure it?

Another man would answer! A stranger would tell *him*, Floyd Varney, how many years he would have to spend in prison.

Of a sudden, Varney's throat constricted – a tremor, as though from a chill, shook his body. The judge could give him twenty years, thirty years, even more. Ten years to life for second-degree murder, said the law – anything a damn judge wanted to hand out. What would he do if the sentence was twenty?

Varney bit his lip, rolled over on his bunk and told himself to stop being a fool. He had suffered the torment of his trial, of the possibility of a death sentence, without going to pieces. The US Attorney had charged first-degree murder, and for three weeks he had sat in the shadow of the electric chair, and for sixteen horrible hours he had sat in handcuffs waiting for the jury's verdict, yet he had endured all of it. Why now should he be so frightened? The very worst the judge might give him would be fifteen years. He knew he could be certain of this, because he had been offered a fifteen-year sentence if he would plead guilty and waive jury trial. He hadn't pleaded guilty because he was innocent, but they couldn't go higher than that now.

No, he decided, there was little reason to be worried. His past record was so good that the sentence was sure to be the ten-year minimum. He'd be eligible for parole in one third of the time – only forty months. Parole was a certainty, because he'd be a model prisoner. Since he had been six months in jail already, that would leave only thirty-four months in all. They'd be hard, harder than anything he'd ever had to face before, but he'd pull them. He'd be out on the street by the time he was thirty-three.

Thinking along this vein, Varney began to dream again, a familiar jailbird's dream of the best of life as it had been, and the best of life as it would be in the future, honey and roses and sweet lies.

He was back at work in his old job at the hotel. He could smell the hot rolls in the oven, and see his hands covered with flour. Janey was home now, no longer working. They were married, and they had a baby girl with russet hair like hers. And now they were dancing to dreamy music, and now they were in bed, close and happy, tender and sweet with each other, whispering together between kisses, laughing and carefree. Oh, Janey, Janey, he thought, we were good together, I loved you truly, I didn't give a damn about that other woman… Ashes and lies and steel bars before him!

Now, in the bunk below, his cellmate began a soft, sighing snore. Johnny Lauter, the snorer, he thought dismally. A good guy, a decent guy, but he hadn't enjoyed a solid night's sleep since Lauter was committed. Stone walls and other men's snores – this would be his home for a thousand days and nights.

Varney pressed his face into the lumpy pillow, smelling the stale, disagreeable odour of disinfectant. He began to weep softly, wondering why, why the jury had not been able to understand. He was no criminal, he never had harmed a soul in his whole life. What would any man do when another attacked him with a knife? Surely a man had the right to protect himself. He hadn't intended to kill.

It was an ACCIDENT, he wanted to shout to the heavens, but he kept silent. He was inmate 84421, and shouting was forbidden.

It was now 5 a.m. In the west wing of cell block CB1, which housed transient prisoners only, it was time for the new day to commence. On the first of the five tiers, a guard stepped up to a panel recessed in the wall. He glanced at his watch and then began playing his morning roulade with a battery of buttons. Electric light flooded the rectangular cavern between the outer wall and the tiers; a moment later, on the runway before each cell, a ceiling light snapped on – a naked bulb encased in wire mesh; a few moments after this, light flashed within each cell, a wall of light behind unbreakable glass.

In this manner day was pronounced. It had been night, but now it was day. It made no difference that some of the men in the cells yearned to sleep on, or that others, like Varney, were frightened of the day at hand – whether they were ready for it or not, day had been announced; breakfast, dinner and supper would come at an appointed time; the lights would snap off again at an appointed time, and now they had been commanded to awaken.

In cell 102 a man in his late forties, Eddie Quinn, left sleep with an eruptive, powerful desire for a drink of liquor. He gazed at his cell bars for a moment, and then, since he had a sense of humour, began to laugh at himself. He sat up on his bunk, dangled his bony legs over the side and lit a cigarette. After a few moments he inspected the empty lower bunk, then murmured half aloud, "Just like I thought – the wife's still on vacation." He sat smoking, grinning with relish over his little joke, waiting patiently to be relieved of his desire for drink.

On the fourth tier, where Negro prisoners were held in segregation, another man of middle years, Isaac Reeves, was gazing mournfully at the bars of his cell. During the daytime, by conscious effort, Reeves kept his spirits light. Early morning, however, was a hard time for him. He was an expert stonemason, a man who loved work and who was proud of his achievements as the proprietor of a small building concern. The idleness of jail life was more difficult for him to bear than sheer confinement. "Income tax, income tax," he was fond of saying with faint humour. "Where in the Bible does it say a man's gotta pay income tax?"

On the first tier Floyd Varney was out of his bunk and already half dressed. Men like him, who were scheduled to appear in court, were served breakfast earlier than the others. His cellmate, watching his hurried movements, raised up on an elbow, coughed his morning cigarette cough and said quietly, "Mornin', pal. How do you feel?"

Ordinarily a question like this called for jailhouse levity in reply, and to most other men Varney would have responded with a bravura jest. But Lauter was a sympathetic man, and Varney had acquired a measure of confidence in him during their months of close living. He grinned weakly and muttered, "I'm terribly scared, Johnny."

Lauter gazed at him with compassion, but said nothing. Three times in his life Lauter had stood before a judge to be sentenced – he knew in his marrow what it was like.

"I got such a funny feeling in here," said Varney, pointing to his chest. "Like a nerve got shook loose. Look, my hands aren't shaking, but I'm shaking inside. You ever had a feeling like that?"

"Something of the sort, I guess."

"Like in the war, when I went into action. Ten thousand Jap guns on that island, all of 'em firing at me." Varney chuckled morosely. "I'm sure cheerful this morning. Had some bad dreams."

"My snoring keep you awake?"

"Not much. I slept pretty good. I'm just so worried that damn judge'll throw the hook into me."

"It's gonna be all right, you'll see," Lauter pronounced cheerfully, as he had again and again in the week past. "I'd settle right now for what you're gonna get."

Both men were quiet for a few moments. Lauter got out of his bunk and began to dress. Regarding him, Varney asked softly, "How about you, Johnny? You'll hear on your own case today, maybe, huh?"

"Any day now, any week, any month," the other responded lightly. He rubbed a hand over his two-day growth of beard, then turned away from Varney to stare through the bars of their cell. He was thinking not of his case, but of his wife and two children, towards whom he felt a heavy burden of guilt. At this hour they would be asleep still, the boy with his long, long lashes and his milky skin, the girl with her face pressed close to the brown teddy bear, and his wife, his patient, gallant, loyal wife – all of them so entangled with him and his miserable past. "Is Poppa still sick? Can't he come back from that hospital yet? When will he?"

Maybe today, maybe tomorrow, maybe never. The law of North Carolina took a stern view of the crime of first-degree burglary. The penalty for it was death. Lauter was wanted for trial in the city of Durham, and he was fighting a writ of extradition. Maybe today, children, maybe never.

"I don't worry about trouble till it comes," Lauter announced suddenly. He gave Varney an affectionate slap on the arm. "Don't you either, pal. We'll both be all right."

Neither believed it, but jailhouse life, like any other, demanded its proprieties. It was the thing to say on a morning like this.

All over the west wing the silence of the night was being dispelled as men rolled out of their bunks. The noises peculiar to this community began to be heard. The sound of plumbing was the first of these – of plunger buttons that had to be forced hard with the heel of the hand before they would work; of the running splash of water in sinks and the powerful suck of water in commodes.* Presently there began to issue from each tier a wordless murmur that was jailhouse conversation, a muffled sough of male voices that rose from the cells to spend itself in the cavern of the eating range. This muted babble was rarely punctuated by loud talking or by loud laughter, and never by whistling or singing, for even though the latter might be normal in the behaviour of all men, they were forbidden here, and infractions were punished.

Finally, some ten minutes after reveille, there came the discordant serenade that was wholly private to prison life, a metallic clangour that could be heard in other prisons in other cities, but in no other place on earth – the stupendous percussion of steel doors being slammed open or slammed shut. On all tiers except the second, which was the Death Tier, it was time for a number of inmates to commence work duty. Whether a single cell door was opened or whether a number were opened in concert, there was no one in the entire wing who could avoid hearing the heavy iron grind that meant a door sliding open, or hearing the grating din as a door closed. Each man in the wing waited for the peculiar finality with which a door slammed shut, waited for the inner lock to snap fast with a sound like doom, waited for the final harsh echoes from outer wall and roof. A man might be in jail for only a day and find these noises curiously disturbing, or he might be old in the life of prison and accept the sound as familiar, yet no one quite could shut his ears to it, or remove it entirely from his consciousness.

At ten minutes past five two inmates left their cells on the first tier to begin their day's work. These two, Johnny Lauter and Eddie Quinn, had been chosen by the guards for special duty because they were old-timers familiar with jail routine, because they had good records and because they were intelligent. For their part, Lauter and Quinn had accepted the status of tier men not because they wanted to curry favour with Authority, since they were not of that sort, but because they received two privileges in return: the right to take a daily shower bath and the right to have their cell doors open for the better part of the day.

As they met on the enclosed runway in front of the line of cells, the two men launched into a routine of nonsensical talk that both of them enjoyed. As prison veterans they knew how important it was to combat time consciously, to keep time bouncing.

"G'mornin', Mrs Lauter," said Quinn, in an affected, mincing voice. "You rested well, I hope?"

"Bad, dearie, just atrocious. Those rich desserts after a big supper, they never agree with me, especially when they have so much whip cream. Belching all night long, I was."

"An' you with your sensitive stomach – greedy, greedy, greedy!" With finished skill Quinn popped his upper denture loose from his palate, so that it protruded between his lips in macabre fashion; he rattled it vigorously with his tongue, then clicked it back into place again.

They grinned at each other, two men greeting the day in the best manner they knew, fighting time with a chip on their shoulder, knowing that they would conquer or be conquered. Yet each of them already bore on his face the scars of partial defeat, the stigmata of bad days, bad nights and badly spent years. Lauter, the younger of the two, was a man of middle height, who appeared older than his thirty-eight years because of his sallow complexion, his thin hair and his bad posture, shoulders rounded and abdomen sagging. In point of fact, however, he was vigorous in body and alive in spirit, a man of quick intelligence and considerable self-education. Quinn, who was called "Barber" because of his profession, had a face that had been ruined in an automobile accident a dozen years before. The left side of his neck and jaw were scarred by ugly burn tissue, and, in addition, a muscle in his right eye had been severed, so that the eye had swivelled in, comically and unpleasantly, towards his blunt nose. Nevertheless, it was impossible for others to know from Quinn's manner how sadly disheartened he was by his appearance. He was amiable, gay and talkative, and he never whined.

Side by side the two friends walked to the end of the runway, where the officer on duty was standing beyond the steel door, Lauter murmuring the meanwhile, "Oh, it ain't my stomach that bothers me, Mrs Quinn, it's just the phlebitis in my buttocks." Then, raising his voice, "Morning, Mr Simmons."

"Varney in 124 and Jude in 112 go to court. See they're ready," the guard told them flatly and quietly. He was a broad-shouldered, bulky man in his middle forties, wearing a thick black moustache. Whatever he might be as father, husband or citizen, at work he conformed to the code of the Federal prison regulations – that is to say, he spoke to inmates in a quiet tone, he was impersonal and he demanded obedience. Beyond his custodial duties, however, he had no more concern for the men in his charge than a watchman guarding a warehouse of turnips.

"Yes, sir," said Lauter.

"Right," said Quinn.

The two men walked back on the tier range at a brisker pace, Lauter resuming their private conversation as though it had not been interrupted. "Another Monday, Mrs Quinn, another washday. By any chance could I borrow a few clothes pegs?"*

20

"Any time, Mrs Lauter. I believe in being neighbourly, it's Christian. You ain't got a shot of whiskey I can have before breakfast, have* you dearie?"

"Oh my, yes, big or little?"

"Jesus love you, make it big."

Chuckling at each other, the two men parted at cell 112, Lauter remaining there and Quinn continuing on down the range. Hal Jude, known as Georgia Boy, was standing before the washbasin at the rear of 112, washing his powerful naked body with cold water, talking animatedly to his cellmate. The night had been warm, and here on the bottom tier, which was below ground level, it always was somewhat damp. Even though Jude had showered and shaved the night before, a privilege granted to men who were due in court the next day, he had awakened in a sweat. "Sure kaint go to co'ht smellin' bad, kin I?" he was saying to his cellmate with perverse fastidiousness. "Not with a woman jedge a-settin' up there to sentence me. Need t'go smellin' like a lil ol' flower, need t'show respect!"

His elderly cellmate, who was suffering from a bad cold, murmured in a nasal tone, "I hear you, you little ol' flower. Why don't you advise her how to make moonshine liquor? Maybe she'll go in business with you."

"Hey, Georgia Boy," Lauter called, "hurry up. Grab your socks. Boss Man wants you out."

"Bugger Boss Man," Jude replied, half-turning around. "I ain't in no hurry. Nothin' good gon happen t'me t'day. 'Sides, I need t'show respect for that female jedge, need t'go up there smelling like a sweet lil flower." He grinned wolfishly at Lauter and spat into the washbasin.

"OK, so don't hurry," Lauter told him genially. "You're the cracker who'll miss breakfast, not me."

"Won't miss nawthin'," retorted Jude with a grin. "Law says yeh kaint sentence a man less'n yeh feed him first. That's the Law."

"Yah, yah," Lauter jeered, "I hear you!" He moved to the next cell, where a former employee of the US Treasury was standing at the bars. He asked in a routine manner, "You through reading last night's *Star*? I'll exchange you my *Post* later on."

"OK. You got any nail clippers?"

"No, but I know who has. I'll ask for you." Slapping the folded newspaper against his thigh, Lauter sauntered down the runway to see how his cellmate was getting along.

Varney had finished dressing. He was so nervous, however, that he was fussing over his bow tie, undoing it and tying it over. Eddie Quinn, standing outside on the runway, was speaking to him in an urgent, almost tender manner. He liked Varney, and he too knew how a man felt on sentence day.

"That's what I'm tryin' to explain to you, feller. There's some judges who're real human. You think judges don't have feelin's? Every once in a while you'll meet a judge who's real square."

"God, I sure hope this one's square," Varney said tensely.

"Now you got a nice appearance," Quinn continued, "an' that always helps in your favour. You tell him about your war record. You bring out you've never been arrested. You tell him about your old mother – she's dependent on you. He'll give you the minimum for sure."

"My ma's dead!"

"You got an old aunt?"

"I haven't got anybody."

"Then tell him you're an orphan. Get up there and bleed in front of him. Make out you were under the influence of liquor. That can happen to anyone. Judges drink too. Hell, some of 'em are terrible souses. Ain't that right?" he asked Lauter, who had joined them.

"Right," Lauter echoed. "That's not a bad angle to use, Floyd." He entered the cell in order to slip the newspaper he had borrowed beneath his pillow. "There was a sailor in Atlanta with me who'd knifed another sailor. Now, you know there's nothin' tougher than a Navy court martial, don't you?"

"No, sir," Quinn put in. "Tough as they come."

"He was prime for hanging," Lauter continued, "but they gave him only twenty years because he was drunk when he did it."

"You never told me about that case," Varney said eagerly.

"I forgot."

"You see?" Quinn observed. "You swear to the judge you were drunk. It'll help in your favour."

"Are you sure I'll get a chance to speak to him before sentence?" Varney asked emotionally. "By God, I sure want to! I got things to say – I got a raw deal!"

"You or your lawyer always has the right to speak before sentence," Quinn advised him. "Only take my advice, kid – don't 'raw-deal' him. He won't listen to that. He'll say that was the jury's business. You'll do better to point to your war record and such like that."

"God, what awful luck!" Varney exclaimed bitterly. "I'm no criminal – I never stole a nickel in my life. It was self-defence, that jury was deaf, dumb and blind."

"You'll get off light, kid, don't worry," said Lauter.

"How's this bow? Is it even? Do I look all right?"

"You look fine – you look real respectable," Quinn replied earnestly.

Indeed Varney did look respectable, portrait of a successful young man of commerce. He was wearing a smart, tailored blue suit that had been pressed the night before in the prison shop; there was a silk handkerchief in his lapel pocket. Although he was pale with anxiety at the moment, he was an attractive, personable man – blond-haired, sturdily built, with fair skin and limpid blue eyes. There was nothing in his natty appearance to betray his heritage: that he was the neglected, bastard issue of a Tennessee prostitute, or that he had left his mother's hearthstone at the age of ten and thereafter made his own way. He presented as fine an appearance as any man could who was about to be sentenced for second-degree murder.

"You ready, kid?" Lauter asked.

"Ready but not willing," Varney replied with a weak attempt at humour.

Lauter clapped him on the shoulder; they shook hands. "Time for your breakfast," Lauter said, and, with false briskness, both men left the cell and started up front. Trailing behind, Quinn called to Varney, "You got enough smokes?"

"Yeah."

"Take it easy."

Quinn watched them move away, thinking to himself, "What a pair! One might get life today and the other might get the gas chamber. I ain't so bad off with my little old three years, am I?" He paused in front of 112, where Hal Jude was knotting a gaudy tie, and asked archly, "You goin' anywhere, Georgia? What you all dressed up for?"

"Gon get me a honey gal, man, what you think?"

"Georgia Boy," his cellmate put in nasally, "you'll get something today, but it sure won't be that."

All three laughed with relish. Said Quinn, "You ready?"

"Shoh! Tell that Boss Man I'm hot to be sentenced."

"Say, Georgia, what's the least thing in the world?"

"Least? How you mean?"

"The littlest."

"Shoh, I dunno. Fish egg, maybe?"

"Naw – it's a nit on a gnat's ball."

The men laughed again. Quinn called down the range, "OK, Mr Simmons, you can open 112."

"Good luck, you lil ol' flower," said Jude's cellmate.

"Thanks, stinkweed."

From the end of the range came the noise of the chain crank used by the guard when one cell door only was being opened. The steel bars in front of Jude slid back in their groove, and the door clanged loudly against the stop. Jude stepped out, and the door slid noisily back, its percussive echoes ringing from outer wall and roof as it locked fast.

"Say, Georgia," Quinn said confidentially, "if you pick any pockets in the courtroom today, cut me in for a watch, will you?"

"If I pick any pockets in that co'htroom, I'm a bettah man than I think I am." Chuckling, Jude sauntered down the range, waving his hand at the succession of faces behind bars, calling airily, "S'long, you convicts, I done been bailed out by my grey-haired pappy – done mortgaged his cat house to set me free. By the time y'all eat breakfast, I'll be havin' my first beer."

A voice called after him with a jeering laugh: "We hear you, Georgia Boy. Tell that woman bedbug to give you life an' get it over with."

Waiting for breakfast, which was not due for another half-hour, men tried to kill time with conversation. Even though the day was young, time already was a presence in each cell; time sat down on a man's bunk the moment he awakened; time stared at him from the walls.

Killing time, the elderly man in 116 said to his youthful cellmate, "There's one piece of advice I'd give any man who's startin' to pull time: never trust a screw."

"Sure, I know," the other replied. Indeed he had been given this advice the morning before, and the morning before that.

"What kind of a man takes a job in the prison system, anyway?" the older man asked in a dry, monotonous way. "Only half a man! Can't make a livin' on the outside, so he's willin' to get paid for keepin' other men locked up."

"That's sure right."

"Readin' other people's mail! Is that a job for a man?"

"Sure ain't."

"Take it from me... the lowest of the low, that's what a jail guard is."

"You're sure right..."

In 110, a car* thief from West Virginia exclaimed exuberantly, "Man, I'm hongry! Wonder what's comin' for breakfast this mornin'?"

His cellmate, the former employee of the US Treasury, who once had lived comparatively well on his government salary, observed with ill humour, "Whatever it is, won't be fit for a dog to eat."

"Man, you're crazy. A feller can get along on the chow in here. It's not so bad."

"Not bad? I tell you my dog wouldn't eat it!"

"You should've been with me on the Nashville chain gang I just come from. Fourteen months of beans an' stale bread twicet a day. Lost sixty pounds on that gang. Went from one eighty to one twenty, almost died."

"So this seems better to you, all right. But it still isn't fit for a dog to eat."

They argued the question idly, killing time.

Said Eddie Quinn to Johnny Lauter: "How much of a stretch do you think Varney'll pull?"

"He'll get fifteen or twenty years, maybe even twenty-five."

"You're off your rocker. He's a first offender. I say ten."

Lauter laughed in a peculiar way he had, a kind of throaty gargle as though the body of the laugh were being retained in his chest for motives secret to himself. "For second-degree murder, with the corpse a big shot, with the trial on page one of every newspaper? You wanna bet some cigarettes he gets more than ten?"

"Jesus!" Quinn exclaimed. "You think so? Twenty years? If I ever got that, I'd blow my stack, I'd never serve it."

"Why, you been serving it right along, you rummy," Lauter jeered affectionately. "Ten days in for drunk, two weeks out. Thirty days in for drunk, four days out. It's been goin' on like that since you were six years old, hasn't it? Add it up, you've served twenty already."

"You low-down safe-cracker," Quinn retorted. "I was barbering second chair in the Maylor Hotel when you was glad to get eight cents an hour in the jute mill at Atlanta. Anyway, I'm through with alcohol."

"What'll you drink when you get out – shoe polish?"

"Buddy, I've quit solid, didn't you hear me? You're lookin' at a man of character. I got the backbone of my Yankee mother, the will-power of my Irish father and the holy grace of the First Presbyterian Church of Philadelphia, where I oncet was the leadin' choir boy. When I say I've quit liquor, I mean quit!"

"Oh, *now* I get it!" Lauter replied with a guffaw. "You mean you're not boozing for the time being because the government's temporarily restrained you. Isn't that what you mean?"

They argued the question good-naturedly. They were killing time, and they were holding in check the secret, tumultuous flow of their private anxieties, shames and yearnings. Quinn, despite two months of jail abstinence, desperately wanted a drink, and hated himself for his weakness – and wished,

wished that breakfast would come along with a cup of coffee. And Lauter, a man in love with his wife, children and family life, three months separated from them now, kept thinking, "That bedbug is gonna give his ruling today. I feel it! If he sends me back to Durham, I'm a dead pigeon. That trial won't be any better than a lynching. God, if I only was religious, I could pray. But if there is a God, He knows I didn't do that job. He knows how hard I've worked, how much Amy and the kids depend upon me."

"Hey, Johnny," Quinn said, killing time, "did you ever hear the one about the Mormon with the twenty-two wives?"

"No," replied Lauter, eager for a laugh, "what about him?"

Chapter 2

Huey Wilson

During this early morning hour, in the receiving section of the jail, three prisoners were undergoing the ritual purification and processing required for all new guests of the Department of Correction. They had arrived a little before 5 a.m. in the custody of two detectives from a precinct house. With them had come a bit of advice: that all three had been involved in a nasty street fight, and that it would be wise to confine the two white men on separate tiers.

"I don't get it," the receiving officer whispered. "You mean there was a fight, and one of those white fellers was on the side of the nigger?"

"Yeah... that bird there... the older guy."

"How do you like that! OK, I'll pass the word along."

The prisoners, who still were handcuffed, were sitting in an ante-room that was divided by wire mesh from the remainder of the processing area. They had been separated, one to a bench, and the second detective was standing watch over them. All three were slumped down wearily, fatigue visible on their faces. They had been thirty hours in the precinct station, and had been awakened at 4 a.m. of this, their second night in custody. Heavy-lidded, unwashed, they appeared anything but fighting cocks.

Mr Prager, the receiving officer, and another jail guard, entered the ante-room through an open doorway. For a few moments Mr Prager gazed sternly at each of the prisoners in turn. Then he addressed them in a bass voice that had gravel in it, speaking curtly, although quietly. "I hear you guys've been in a fight. That's your business. But in here is our business. There's no fightin' in this jail. A man who fights in here gets thrown in the Hole, but fast. You got that?"

The prisoners nodded, although only one of them knew what the Hole was, and Mr Prager glared at them. He was close to fifty, a heavily built man with cold eyes and a gross face. It was his job to let new inmates know at once that in here Authority ruled, and that in here things were different from outside. He liked his job, and he performed it with relish.

"OK," he said to the detectives, "you can take the cuffs offa them." He strode to the exit door and stood waiting. When the detectives had removed the handcuffs and were ready, he slipped a bunch of heavy keys from a ring on his belt, selected one and opened the steel door. "Be seein' you," he said genially. "Tell the front office these boys'll be comin' up in about thirty minutes."

"Will do... be good."

Mr Prager locked the door, slipped the keys back on his belt ring and spoke curtly again. "All right, you guys, stand up. Take everything outa your pockets. Put the stuff on the bench where you're sittin'. Then turn your pockets inside out so I can see 'em."

The three prisoners obeyed.

"An' make it snappy, if you want any breakfast," Mr Prager added. He stood watching them, one hand hooked in his wide military belt. "Get that inside pocket all the way out," he ordered the young Negro... "All right, now, take off all your clothes except your shoes an' your socks."

As the men undressed, Mr Prager said to his assistant, "Didn't you call CB3?"

"Yes, sir, I did."

"Well, where are they?" He was referring to the several inmates whose work it was to take the photographs and the fingerprints of new inmates, and otherwise to aid in their processing.

"You want me to call again?"

"Yeah."

His assistant, Mr Roche, strode to the telephone, but then paused. At the other end of the receiving room a steel door, which led to the cell blocks, was being unlocked. It swung back – four inmates dressed in jail blues entered, and the door was locked behind them.

"Three commitments," Mr Roche said to them. "Get ready, huh? Here's copies of their papers. Snappy, huh?"

One of the men he had addressed nodded without speaking, the others did not even nod, but all went about their business. They were long-term men, and they had been doing this work for some years.

In the ante-room the new commitments had undressed. Mr Prager, arranging their papers in alphabetical order, asked, "Which one of you is Art Ballou?"

A blond, rosy-cheeked youth of nineteen, who was seated on the front bench, answered, "Me."

"Come along. Bring all your things. You two guys stay where you are."

Rising, Ballou took the opportunity to turn round.* He was a tall, well-built youth, whose good looks were somewhat marred by a pouting, surly mouth. Ignoring the young Negro, he gestured at the middle-aged white man, a childish, obscene gesture of the streets, the thumb of one hand thrust between two fingers. Then, with a small grin, he walked out.

Mr Prager was perched on a stool before a high desk. He pointed a stubby forefinger. "Put your pocket things down here. Put all your clothes except your handkerchief in there."

"In there" was a canvas bag held open by Mr Roche. It already was tagged with Ballou's name and jail number.

"A fine way to treat a good suit," the blond youth remarked. He never had been in jail before, but it was important to his self-esteem to be casual about it. "When do I get it back?"

"When you leave, or if you go to court," Mr Roche answered. He did not add that the clothes would be subjected to a steam bath by which all insect life, if any, would be exterminated, and that when they were returned to Ballou, they would have an odd smell for some time after.

"Over here!" said Mr Prager. "Take your money outa your wallet." He was occupied in listing Ballou's possessions on the required form: a Gruen* wristwatch with gold band; a monogrammed, stainless-steel cigarette lighter; a set of keys; a nail file. Together with the empty wallet, he sealed these articles in a manila envelope. He pointed to the handkerchief and comb, and said, "You take these with you." Next he picked up a half-empty packet* of cigarettes and tossed it expertly upon another desk ten feet away. It was forbidden for new commitments to bring cigarettes into the jail, lest they contain marijuana or other contraband. This, as it turned out, was convenient for Mr Prager, who was a heavy smoker. Finally he began counting Ballou's money.

"Eighty-six dollars and forty-five cents." He wrote the sum on a receipt and said, "Sign."

"Don't we get to keep any money? How does a guy buy smokes?"

"You can draw on this money for canteen. Take your receipt. Now go down them steps an' shower. There's an inmate there who'll give you a towel an' some clothes. Step on it!"

In the several minutes of privacy allowed them, the two prisoners in the ante-room had been carrying on a tense conversation. Although they had fought side by side in a vicious street brawl, they were strangers and, in addition, they had been confined in separate cells in the precinct house.

The moment Ballou departed, the young Negro, a brawny youth of eighteen, burst into hasty speech. At the same time, despite instructions to the contrary, he slid one bench forward so that he was directly behind the middle-aged white man.

"Say, Mister, I don't know how to thank you enough for what you did for me. You sure were great. I guess you just about saved my life."

The other man half-turned his head. He replied morosely, and a bit stiffly, "Well... weren't right what they was doin' to you."

"I'm awfully sorry you got into trouble over it."

The older man grimaced and said with blunt frankness, "So'm I!" Then he added gloomily, "But you're in worser trouble than I am, young feller. Those polices are doin' a job on you."

"What do you mean?"

"They're working up fake charges on both of us. But you're the one they're out to git."

"How do you know?"

"One of 'em told me so, a detective."

"How come he told *you?*" the young Negro asked, with quick suspicion.

There was a moment of pause, and then the answer came with a kind of distant coldness: "Cos they want me t'leave town. They don't want me testifyin'. Said they'd let me go free if I took the first bus home."

"I see!"

The middle-aged white man suddenly began to speak with uneasy rapidity, like a man unburdening himself. "They're out to frame you good. You know that knife this fellow Ballou had? Well, that's disappeared already – none of the cops ever seen it. It seems that feller you sent to the hospital has an ol' man who's got some pull with the polices. That detective said they was gon t'send you up for five years."

"What? That's crazy! They arrested me on suspicion of disorderly conduct, that's all. They can't—"

"That was Saddy night," the older man interrupted. "Yisterday afternoon that detective explained me different. He said that feller you damaged was in the hospital with a busted jaw. He said—"

"Listen," the youth interrupted, "we sure got to get together for a talk somehow, there's no time here. What I need to know right now is what *you're* going to do. You know what that fight was about. Where do *you* stand right now?"

"Shucks, how the hell do I know?" the older man replied with sudden anger. "I don't know where I stand any more'n you do. I come all the way from Detroit t'go to my niece's weddin', an' now look where I am. I wasn't wantin' any trouble."

"Thomas McPeak!" came Mr Prager's gravel voice. "Bring your things. Snappy!"

Watching the older man leave, the youth, whose name was Huey Wilson, thought to himself with instant, erupting bitterness, "Well, here we go, 'get the nigger'. Damn those bastards. They won't get me. Five years – God Almighty!"

He began to tremble with anger, indignation and terrible uncertainty. In the thirty hours past, he had been uprooted as by earthquake from his normal life; subjected to physical violence, hurt and terror; arrested, locked in a cell, held incommunicado. And now another blow – that they were framing him on some serious charge, and that he couldn't be certain if the white man would stand up for him. "How the hell do I know?" McPeak had said. "I don't know where I stand any more than you do."

Except that Wilson knew damn well where *he* stood. One more Negro feeling the white man's boot, a "snotty* black boy" being put in his place.

He sat trembling, with fists clenched.

In a certain sense it could be said that Wilson's arrest was an accident. If he had not gone to the movies* with a girl on the Saturday night past, or if he had chosen another street by which to walk home, nothing would have happened. From another point of view, however, both the street fight and his arrest were as natural to the American scene, and as commonplace, as sky or air or an item of folklore.

The sum of it was this: Huey Wilson was eighteen years old, and he had come to the city to make a career for himself if he could. From his parents he had received inexhaustible love, high goals and faith in himself – but no money, for there was none to give. And so young Huey worked by day and went to school at night, weighed his pennies, drove himself hard and dreamt big dreams. This might be called the first part of a somewhat familiar tale. There was another.

In this capital city there had been a district, one of many, in which no one of dark skin could live, a commonplace matter also. In the course of time, however, changes had occurred in the district, a slow encroachment of black upon white in a quest for living space, a moving out and a moving in, until finally the district had become largely a "black" district – that is to say, one of the several congested areas in which Negroes could live without suffering violence or legal sanction.

31

Yet, as it happened, the high school in this former "white" district had remained exclusively white – or, rather, had been maintained so by the powers that be. Negro students living on the same street as the school were not permitted to attend it. Instead they were segregated in their "own" high school a considerable distance away.

It happened also that the "white" high school had empty seats and a lack of students, whereas the "black" school was grossly overcrowded. Some of the students, like Huey himself, were obliged to travel even farther from their homes to what was called a "school annex" – in reality a converted warehouse. This, to the Negro community, and to some in the white community also, seemed absurd and definitely unfair, and somewhat less than democratic. As a result, agitation began to remedy the situation.

There were meetings and public speeches. There were newspaper editorials, pro and con, and committees of citizens who visited with the powers that be – to no avail. The colour line remained. There was, in addition, a certain amount of familiar violence. A number of Negro youths, passing by the "white" school on the way to their own, were attacked and beaten by groups of students.

Nevertheless, the Negro community refused to accept the status quo, and the agitation continued. So it happened that on the Saturday afternoon just past there had been both a demonstration and a counter demonstration at the school under dispute. Within the yard a number of white people had assembled, both students and adults, all of whom felt passionately that the school must remain as it was. Among them was a rosy-cheeked youth of eighteen, Art Ballou. Outside on the pavement* there was a picket line of Negroes, and some whites as well. These others, with equal passion, felt that the school should admit any students who lived in the district. Since Huey Wilson was one of the picket captains, and a tall, brawny youth as well, he was noticed by Ballou.

There was no violence on this occasion, because the demonstrations were supervised by a contingent of police, who had been instructed to keep things orderly no matter what their own point of view. That night, however, Huey was on his way home from a movie,* and Art Ballou, together with three friends, was on his way to a party, and they met.

Thus, out of a commonplace sore in American life had come a commonplace street fight. It was a familiar thing, part of the folklore, for a Negro to be beaten by white men on a dark street at night and left bleeding or dead. So it might have been for Huey Wilson.

That it had not been so was due to another white man, a squat, middle-aged resident of Detroit who had come to Washington for the wedding of his niece. For Huey Wilson and his career, this man now had assumed burning importance.

Waiting in the ante-room, Huey thought about McPeak and searched his own feelings about him, and nibbled for the inner meaning of the man's every word and look. He was gravely uneasy about McPeak, yet he felt that his uneasiness was partially unfounded. Without even knowing him, McPeak had jumped into a fight on his side, against other whites. It took a truly decent man to do a thing like that. Except... that this morning McPeak no longer knew where he stood.

Why not? And why the marked change in his manner? On Saturday night he had been friendly, seemingly proud of himself for what he had done. Now he was frozen up, stiff as a board, the geniality gone. Yet he hadn't taken the detective's offer, so what did it all mean?

Huey stared through the wire mesh at McPeak. There were things about the white man that reached below thought, into the interstices of his feelings and intuition. The way McPeak talked, for one thing, the unmistakable speech of a southern hillbilly. Huey had picked fruit for farmers who looked and talked like McPeak, who had paid him outrageous wages, and cheated him into the bargain. It was not very sensible, he knew, to come to conclusions about a man from evidence such as this, and yet how many Saturday afternoons down home he had seen McPeak's type come in to buy at the stores – thick-necked, tobacco-chewing peckerwoods* from Albemarle County and illiterate whiskey makers from the Ragged Mountains, so many of them Ku Kluxers and Negro haters. It was no use telling himself that this man had saved him from a terrible beating, or worse. He knew this, and he was enormously grateful, but he also knew that McPeak didn't inspire the confidence he should. It left him with a feeling of deep confusion.

McPeak's voice rose a little in conversation with Mr Prager, and Huey strained to hear. He caught something about a suitcase and clothes, but he couldn't hear the officer's reply. McPeak was looking angry. His lumpy face wore a sullen frown, and he clearly was restraining himself from some outburst. "Man about fifty," Huey reflected, "almost as old as my pop. Told the desk sergeant he works for the Ford Company* – wonder what his job is?"

Mr Prager turned round* and beckoned, and Huey stood up. He scrambled for his clothes, for his frayed wallet with two dollar bills in it, for the comb with several broken teeth. As he approached the desk, Mr Prager left it for a moment to saunter to the head of the stairs that led to the shower room. He bawled out, "What's so slow down there?" A voice came back, "Comin' up now."

"Those damn polices," McPeak whispered to Huey. "They got my suitcase* down at that precinct station with all my bestes clothes, an' they ain't sent it over."

"Have you asked this officer how to get it?"

"He's no damn help. Told me to take it easy an' see if they sent* it."

Ballou appeared on the stairs, dressed now in blue cotton shirt and trousers, his blond hair neatly combed and his face bright from the shower. Mr Prager said, "Over there for your fingerprints." And then, to McPeak, "Down there for your shower... No, wait a minute, I wanna ask you somethin'."

McPeak waited while Mr Prager fished a toothpick from his pocket and began probing between his teeth. There was quite a long silence. Mr Prager was curious about the street fight, but he didn't know how to put his question. His initial interest had been quickened by hearing McPeak's southern speech; it was pricked further now by the sight of the two standing naked side by side. He was thinking that if Wilson had been light-skinned or had sharp features and long hair, a mistake on McPeak's part would have been possible. But Wilson was a rather handsome specimen of a race that Mr Prager considered to be inferior – dark bronze in the colour of his skin, his hair short and close-curled, his features strong and clearly Negroid. Mr Prager simply couldn't understand how McPeak, a white man and a southerner, had made common cause with him.

"You two guys know each other good?" he asked McPeak suddenly.

McPeak shook his head, and Huey could see him stiffen in body and face.

"Where you from?"

"Detroit."

"You talk southern."

"I was brung up in Georgia."

"Georgia, hey?" Mr Prager worked his toothpick for a moment. "How come you got in this here fight?"

McPeak waited for a moment before replying. Then he answered softly, with bland features, "I like t'fight. Most every Saddy night I find me a good fight."

Mr Prager flushed. He jerked his toothpick. "Down for your shower! Make it snappy!" He turned his attention to Wilson. "Put your valuables here, your clothes in that bag there."

Huey said, very politely, "Can I ask you something, officer?"

"What?"

"How do I get to see a doctor in here? They wouldn't call me one at the precinct."

"What's wrong with you?"

"I got hurt in that fight – my tail bone* is awful sore, and I think one of my ribs is broken or cracked."

"You got X-ray eyes?" Mr Prager asked. "How do you know what state your ribs are in?"

Huey's reply came slowly, purged of feeling, as though there had been no malice in the question. "It hurts me some when I breathe."

Mr Prager grunted and asked, "What's them swellings?" He pointed to Huey's middle, which was ringed by large welts.

"They're bedbug bites I got at the precinct."

"I never saw any bites looked like them."

"I'm allergic to bedbugs."

"Well, you sure got a lot of troubles, boy, ain't you?" Mr Prager said with amusement. "Put yourself down for sick call when you get to your cell. Now start moving."

"Will I get to see a doctor this morning?"

An acid, unfriendly look came over Mr Prager's face. "Probably you will, probably, but I don't know an' I don't care. If your kind don't like to get hurt, you oughta stay out of fights. Now stop askin' so many questions an' stuff your clothes in that bag."

For a moment Huey didn't move. His dark eyes blazed. Then he turned away to do as he had been told.

The shower room was very large, immaculately clean. As Huey descended the stairs, he thought wryly, "What a lovely, lovely jail! They let half the coloured in Washington live without a bathtub, but get yourself in here and they offer you the best – hot water, white tile, not a cockroach to be seen."

At the opposite side of the room from the showers there was a bench stacked with clothes and towels. The inmate attendant – a slender, grey-haired Negro – was sorting through a pile of blue trousers in an effort to find some for McPeak. It was not a simple task. McPeak was under middle height, a broad-shouldered, muscular man advancing into corpulence.

Trousers that fitted* the length of his legs were too small for his fleshy, expanding waist. He assumed a somewhat comic pose as Huey approached and said sheepishly, "Looks like I'll hafta spend my jail time nekkid. This beer belly of mine is sure in the way."

Grinning, the attendant tossed him another pair. "Try these. If they fits your middle, you just better roll up the legs." To Huey he said: "Hi, pal, you poor fish. Any man's a poor fish who gets in here. Put your comb and rag down, leave your shoes and socks, an' go bath yourself."

Struggling with trouser legs that were a foot long for him, McPeak said with a touch of amiability, "Wouldn't think, t'look at me, that I oncet had a lean figure like you, young feller, would you? That's what my ol' lady's cookin' has did to me."

Huey smiled at him, feeling a sudden burst of affection for the man. "Give me time. Anyway, I'm looking forward to a lot of good food in this jail."

The attendant let out a guffaw. "I hear you! That's the true reason I'm here. Best damn garbage I ever ate."

"Hey!" came Mr Prager's voice. "Get a move on down there."

Walking towards the shower, Huey thought soberly: "He's certainly different than he was on Saturday night, but I still don't feel any colour prejudice. That's something you always feel when it's there." He began to wonder if his lack of confidence in McPeak was merely his own wariness towards any white man, especially a southerner. McPeak had been magnificent – but even if he were a Negro, he couldn't be happy over landing in jail. Jail was jail, and the man had a right to be upset about it.

The thought left him more at ease. As he watched McPeak walk up the stairs, he wondered if he had expressed the gratitude he felt in an adequate manner. What a debt he owed the man! He'd be in hospital now, or dead, if not for him. It was something to remember no matter how McPeak acted from now on. In fact, Huey reflected, it was one of those lifetime lessons. You could read in a history book that Frederick Douglass* had staunch white allies in the Abolition movement, or you could walk on a picket line with some whites on* your side, but the knowledge went deeper, much deeper, when you had the experience of lying on the ground with fists and feet pounding your body, with a knife flashing and blood lust in a white face above you – and then be delivered by another white man. It was something to store up in mind and heart for the future.

Huey closed his eyes and raised his face to the shower. The hot water was like a balm to his sore, tense body. Relaxing under it, suspending thought, he fell without realizing it into a mood of sudden, dismaying loneliness.

For a moment he no longer was a young man of eighteen, ready to meet the harshness in the world with his own strength, but a boy of eight desperately in need of comfort. He wanted an hour at home with his folks; he wanted to tell them all that had happened, and have their close embrace, and see their loving faces before him.

The mood passed almost at once, and he began to think of his brother, to wonder what Jeff was doing. He had been allowed to telephone his brother the morning after his arrest, and Jeff had said that he would come right down to the precinct house. Surely he had come, yet they had not been permitted to talk. There was something fishy about that: it fitted McPeak's warning of a frame-up. Yet, whatever lies the police had told Jeff, he wouldn't believe them. He surely had spent the rest of yesterday hunting up a lawyer. More than likely he had wired their folks, also, to see if they could raise any bail money.

Huey winced a little as this thought occurred to him. It would be a painful business for his folks, especially his mother! She set such store by the family's being respectable. It was dreadful to think of them going to friends with the news that their Huey was in jail. "Oh, goddamn it," he thought suddenly, "why wasn't I sick on Saturday, or studying or something, so that I never went on that picket line? Everything was going along so good for me. Goddamn that Ballou! What bad luck! And now what? All of a sudden it's five years in prison – but that's crazy. They're only trying to scare me. I don't have to scare so easy, I'm no kid. Christ, I needed this trouble like I need a nail in my head!"

Now, soaping his body, an act so routine to other mornings that it made everything seem normal, Huey had a wistful fantasy: that he was out of jail and home. It was seven in the morning and he was eating his usual breakfast, an orange and some oatmeal and a glass of milk. Propped open against the sugar bowl was his geometry book, or a Spanish grammar, and soon he would tuck the book under his arm and walk down to the bus line. He would ride to North Capitol and H and be inside the Printing Office by eight o'clock. He would have fifteen minutes for study before work started:

"*Dónde se habla español?*"

"*Se habla español en muchos paises, en…*"*

…The voice of the inmate attendant interrupted his thoughts. "Hey, pal, Mr Prager ain't gonna like you. He can't have his breakfast till he runs you through. Neither can I, for that matter. Better finish off."

Reluctantly Huey turned on the cold water, reluctantly left the shower. Drying himself, he became aware that the other man was scrutinizing him with odd intensity. He stared back, seeing grey wiry hair and a gaunt yellowish face, and a long scar on a scrawny neck.

"What's them things?" the other asked.

"Bedbug bites." He began to rub soap on the welts, a household remedy learnt from his mother.

There was a moment of pause, and then the attendant said, with intense, pathetic envy, "You got a good build, pal. You're gonna be able to do things in life. I've always been weak in my body. Guess that's the reason I never got nowhere. I never had no confidence."

Huey gazed at him with curiosity, and didn't know what to say.

"It's hard enough bein' coloured," the other continued mournfully, "without havin' a weak body, ain't it so? I shoulda been born with A1 brains, but I wasn't. Only B or C brains, I guess. God let me down every which way. That's why I quit goin' to church."

Feeling the need to respond, yet not knowing what comment to make to so many scrambled ideas, Huey asked: "How long you been in here?"

"Twelve years, pal. Got eight more if I earn my good time, eighteen if I screw up bad. Been doin' pretty good so far – but you never can tell. A man can't always control his nerves in here. You get mean low sometimes."

Huey nodded, and shivered a little.

"Come over here now, so I can outfit you. Say, pal, what they get you for, what's the charge?"

"I don't know. I was in a fight and they booked me on suspicion of disorderly conduct. But now I hear they're working up some other charges. How does a guy find out what he's charged with anyway?"

"That's easy." He tossed Huey a blue cotton shirt with short sleeves and a pair of trousers. "You ask the feller upstairs who takes your prints. He'll have your papers. He's an ofay,* but he's friendly."

"Thanks, I will. You got a shirt a size bigger?"

"Got 'em all sizes, pal. There's every size of poor fish has passed through here. Say" – he lowered his voice and glanced around to see if either of the officers was watching – "I put you three cigarettes under your handkerchief. Pick it up careful, so they don't drop."

"Thanks a lot. Only, I don't smoke."

"Take 'em anyway, pal. Give 'em to someone else. There's always guys hungry for smokes."

"OK."

"Them clothes fit all right?"

38

"Guess so, sure."

"So long, pal, take it easy."

Huey gazed at the man, feeling the awful weight of the twelve years already served, and of the years to come, and marvelled at the three cigarettes in his pocket and the brotherhood behind them – one black man offering cheer to another in trouble. "Thanks, I will," he said gratefully, and walked up the stairs feeling stronger and less alone.

Mr Prager stood a close watch while Huey's fingerprints were being taken, and it was not until he was wiping the ink from his fingers that he was able to talk to the other inmate. He said softly: "Fellow downstairs told me you might know what the charges against me are."

"Didn't look. Ask that guy when he takes your picture. Go over there now."

The photographer slipped a chain over Huey's head so that a board with inset letters, recording his jail number and the date, would hang suspended around his middle. He said mechanically: "Sit down. Sit up straight. Look at the camera right here."

Complying, although his ribs hurt when he sat stiffly erect, Huey asked about his charges.

"Didn't notice. Hold still now, don't talk... OK, got it! Now turn sideways. Sit straight. Raise your chin a little. Hold it... OK, got it! Go over there. Ask him, he has your papers."

"Like a side of beef," Huey thought with sour amusement, "like a side of beef when Jerry used to hook it, and I'd push it, and Red-Eye would heave it on the truck."

"Sit down, Wilson," said the young, sandy-haired inmate behind the typewriter. "First name, Huey. You got any middle name?"

"No... Say, buddy, have you got my commitment papers?"

"Sure. How old were you at your last birthday?"

"Eighteen... The reason I ask about my papers is that I don't know what charges I'm being held on."

Clicking the typewriter, the other said, "I'll tell you in a minute. What's your address?"

"Four twelve A Lamont Street, Northwest."

The clerk glanced around to locate the guards. It was not necessary for him to do this, since he would be taking no liberty in giving Wilson the information he wanted, yet he did so out of habit. To his right was Mr Prager, lounging against a desk, picking his teeth and smoking one of

Ballou's cigarettes. To his left, in the corridor that led to the cell blocks, was Mr Roche, who was keeping watch over Ballou and McPeak. The clerk tapped out the address, then glanced down at a paper beside his typewriter. "Do you work or go to school?"

"Both."

"They've got three charges on you: intoxication, resisting arrest and felonious assault with deadly weapons. Where do you work?"

Wilson stared at him in disbelief.

"Where do you work?"

"Are you sure you have the right papers?"

"Damn it, tell me where you work, will you?" the clerk said in a whisper. "I got to keep this machine going, or he'll be on my tail."

"Government Printing Office."

"Address?"

"North Capitol and H streets."

"Sure, those are your papers – Huey Wilson, coloured… What job?"

"Messenger… Does it say what weapons?"

"Just weapons."

"That's crazy. I didn't have any weapons."

"A lot of crazy things go on in police stations… What school do you go to?"

"Cardozo High… night school. Say, do you know what charges they've put on the other two men?"

"I'll look in a minute. In case of death, what relative gets notified?"

"My father, I guess."

"Name and address?"

"Thomas Wilson… one six nine Page Street, Charlottesville, Virginia."

The clerk hammered the keys, snapped the form out of the roller and shuffled some papers. He said quickly, "Ballou is disorderly conduct; McPeak is assault, disorderly conduct, resisting arrest." Then he called loudly "OK, Mr Prager, he's ready to go" and returned Huey's nod of thanks with a wink and a smile.

The receiving officer said to Huey "Over there, with the others" and picked up a telephone.

The exit corridor, like the ante-room, was separated from the main receiving area by a steel-mesh screen. Quite deliberately, Huey sat down by the side of McPeak. On the bench opposite them was Art Ballou, and standing at the exit door was Mr Roche.

Rather gloomily, McPeak said to Huey, "That bath made me feel like a new man, but I wisht me and my good feelin's was some-where* else."

"You ever been in jail before?"

"No."

"Me either."

Ballou spoke. Calmly, with satisfaction, he said to them, "There's one of you who's gonna be in jail a long time, maybe the two of you."

Both McPeak and Wilson turned to stare at him. They had stiffened instantly, and their faces had hardened. They had been trying to ignore his presence.

Carefully, with satisfaction, Ballou said to McPeak, "I'm gettin' out of here today or tomorrow. So could you if you wanted to."

"Nobody wants to hear you talk," McPeak answered with cold contempt. "Why don't you shut up?"

"Or maybe you *want* five years, like he's gonna get?"

McPeak said to Wilson, "You ever know this horse's ass before?"

"All right, pipe down, you guys," interrupted Mr Roche. "No more talking."

Softly, but with deep indignation, Ballou asked, "Officer, you keep coloured and white separate* in this jail, don't you? That guy looks white, but I think he's part-nigger."

A shudder of rage swept through Huey Wilson, but he did not move. In the eighteen years of his life he had learnt the discipline of survival, the self-control before malice that was the ancient property of all Negroes. He knew that Ballou wanted to provoke him before a white guard in this white man's jail, and he refused to be provoked, but his body trembled, and an ashen hue came to his face.

McPeak spoke then, not to Ballou, but to the guard. He was in dead earnest, and his tone was ugly. "If that son of a bitch says one more word, I'll ram his teeth right down his throat."

Mr Roche snapped up a warning finger. "You start a fight in here an' you'll be plenty sorry."

"It's up to you then," McPeak responded flatly. "I've told you! If you don't want a fight, keep it level here!"

For an instant, with astonishment and anger, the guard stared at McPeak. Then, assessing the situation in his own interest, he said with the voice of Authority: "The first man who talks goes up for discipline. All of you shut up!"

In the hostile silence that followed, Huey Wilson saw something in McPeak's face that filled him with wonder. McPeak's features were pudgy and gross, and in repose his face was rather unexpressive. But now, as he gazed at Ballou, he wore a look of such eloquent disgust that Huey was astonished. He had assumed that McPeak, as a decent man, had been motivated on the Saturday night past by a sense of fair play. Now suddenly he began to wonder if the man did not have genuine feelings on the race question, and if there had not been conscious thought, as well as humaneness, behind his behaviour.

They sat in silence for a few minutes. There came then the rattle of a heavy key in a lock, and the steel door that led to the cell blocks swung open. A guard entered, followed by half a dozen men on their way to court, among them Floyd Varney and Hal Jude. Varney's face was tense and pale, and he took no notice of the new men, but Jude, passing by, muttered with a grin, "Mohnin', gentlemens, lovely mohnin' for a hangin', ain't it?"

In the doorway a second guard said to Mr Roche, "These the new men?"

"Yeah."

"Let's go."

"OK, let's go," Mr Roche repeated. "You two first." And to Ballou, "No talking."

They entered a long, cavernous passageway, pausing there for a moment while the steel door was locked behind them. In silence they marched until they came to another door. The new guard asked: "Any you guys ever served time before?"

All three shook their heads.

"OK, then, here's the rules." He spoke drily, in the manner of a bored guide in a museum: "You keep your cell neat and clean at all times. When you're in the Yard, don't go near the walls – stay away from the walls. You can talk in your cell, but you can't whistle or sing. It's against the rules to fight with another inmate or to have sexual relations with him. Either of those things can get you a lot more time. When an officer tells you to do something, you do it. Most important is eating! Now, in here you don't hafta eat anything you don't want. When you go to the steam table, tell the man 'light' or 'medium' or 'heavy'. If he gives you more'n you want, tell him to take it back. But remember – anything you got on your tray when you leave the steam table, you hafta eat. We don't allow no waste here. That's very important. You got any questions?"

The three remained silent.

"All right," the guard said, "just obey the rules and you won't get in no trouble. We treat everybody alike in here." He unlocked the door and, waving them on, remained where he was. They passed through; Mr Roche followed; the door slammed.

Now, in the narrow area fronting both wings of cell block CB1, there came a surprise inspection designed by Authority to trap the sharpies. Mr Simmons, chief guard of the west wing, rose from his desk, slipped his fountain pen into his breast pocket and said in a matter-of-fact way: "Any you guys got anything on you that you shouldn't have?"

Huey Wilson felt himself turning hot all over – he had three cigarettes in his pocket. "Oh, that pal in the shower!" he thought angrily. "Twelve years' jail experience, yet the favour he does a man gets him into trouble."

"Well?" Mr Simmons asked. And then, without waiting, "Strip! Everything off! Drop your clothes in front of you. Shoes and socks, too."

Huey's brain raced and got nowhere. He realized with dismay that there was nothing to be done. "That pal sure started me off right," he thought with sour resentment.

When they were naked, Mr Simmons said: "Turn around. Bend over. Spread your* cheeks with your hands."

They did so, and were examined for concealed narcotics. They stood erect and watched as the two guards explored their shoes, scrutinizing each one for false heels or soles, rapping each shoe on the floor to see if contraband was concealed in its toe. Their socks came next, and were turned inside out; their shirts were shaken out, the sleeves and breast pocket examined; their trousers came last.

"Well now," said Mr Simmons, "look what we have here." The two guards stared at the cigarettes, then at Huey. Mr Simmons said, with mixed amusement and irritation: "The world's full of smart operators. That's why so many end up here."

Mr Roche asked: "Where'd you get 'em?"*

"Found 'em." The welts around Huey's waist began to burn like fire.

"Where?"

"On a bench."

"What bench?"

"Where we were sitting before we came in here."

"No you didn't," Mr Roche snapped hotly, and Huey realized that he was impugning the man's efficiency. "I was there, an' you didn't find no damn cigarettes there. One of the inmates gave 'em to you – the coloured guy in the shower room, probably, didn't he?"

"No sir, he didn't."

"OK, feller," Mr Simmons interrupted, "you can stop lying. But from now on you'll be *inside*. You keep your nose clean. All right, you guys, put your clothes back on."

Dressing, Huey saw McPeak's small grin, and returned a weak smile. This, he decided, was as close to trouble as he wanted to come in his jail stay: from now on he would hug the rules.

"Ballou?" Mr Simmons said, consulting a roster sheet, "You go to 318. McPeak – 130. Wilson – 430. Come on."

It was now five forty-five in the morning, and these three men, having been bathed, booked, fingerprinted and photographed, were officially in custody.

At this hour Floyd Varney was sitting on a bench in the receiving room, waiting for the jail bus. Sentence time was moving closer, but for the moment he was free of anxiety. Whereas the others around him were smoking hard and chatting nervously, exchanging the wisecracks and the bravadoes with which men comfort themselves in a time of fear, Varney sat silent and apart, absorbed in a fantasy. He was inventing a pleasant fiction about himself and his sweetheart, Janey Welch. And, as usual with him, his dream was beginning with a measure of fact.

There had been a night, shortly before his arrest, on which he had come close to asking Janey to marry him. He had not. It happened that the rush of tremulous emotion which prompted this impulse was the result of a quarrel between them. The dispute was of no great moment in itself, yet its significance for both of them was profound.

Janey Welch was an attractive young woman, warm-hearted, open in her nature. She had made a wartime marriage that had ended badly, but the experience had not soured her optimism about marriage, or made her fearful of seeking love again. What she most wanted in life was one man to cherish, and the children they would have. She had been deeply attracted to Varney in their first contacts, despite the fact, as she told him with candour, that he was easy to like but hard to know. Quite clearly there were areas of thought and feeling within him that he would not or could not share easily with another. Yet, coming to love him, perceiving his essential decency and sweetness, she was not overly distressed by his reserve. She knew that he was worth loving, and she was confident that in time she would understand him fully, and that he would learn to trust her more completely than he evidently did. Within a few months after they had become lovers, she knew that she would marry him if he asked her.

Wanting this, yet feeling uncertainty in him, she waited. Varney had a way of jesting about marriage that made her realize that he was wary not so much of her, as of marriage itself. He would say about her sister, "What a life! Can't have a night's fun unless she hires a babysitter." Once, referring to Janey's divorce, he said lightly, "I know you don't want *that* to happen again." And sometimes, with a sudden revelation of feeling that to her was as lacking in completeness as it was obviously affectionate, he would say, "Ain't we got fun, honey? Jiminy, I like to be with you. Isn't it fun to be on the town like we are – no responsibilities, just do any damn thing we feel like doing?"

Janey, no less than he, liked the way they played together and were lovers, but she knew that a man and a woman moved closer, accepted ties and knitted bonds, or they had no good future. "Fun" was a word that Varney spoke often, and, as Janey came to realize, it had a meaning for him that it did not for her. She could find pleasure in an evening spent in her sister's living room, dancing to the radio and drinking Coca-Colas, but to Varney an evening like that was humdrum. He had a lust for bright lights and glitter, for nightclubs with noisy bands and hotel floor shows that were beyond his means. Although he earned a good wage for a working man, he was, after all, only second cook in a hotel, and to Janey there was something unbecoming in the relish he took in spending ten, fifteen or even twenty dollars for an evening's entertainment. In order to own several expensive, tailored suits, he lived in a shabby furnished room; in order to have "fun", he frequently had to borrow until pay day.

On Janey's twenty-fifth birthday, which turned out to be their last date together, they had quarrelled over this. Since it was a warm evening, Varney had taken her to the Shoreham Hotel, where they might dine on the garden terrace and dance. There had been a corsage of gardenias, which she loved, and a taxi instead of the usual bus, but then, for Janey, a spasm of uncomfortable extravagance – a bottle of imported champagne costing thirteen dollars. Janey knew how many hours of waiting tables it took for her to earn that sum, and how many years she could wear a sweater that cost no more. She also knew that on the day following Varney would be shy his rent money* and would have to evade his landlord. She couldn't forbear a protest over something so unnecessary to her pleasure and so alien to the real fabric of their lives. "Aw listen, honey," she said, "call that waiter back, for goodness' sake. A beer or a ginger ale will suit me just as well."

"Hey, hey," he replied, "it's your birthday. Relax, have a good time."

"I am, honey, wonderful – but thirteen dollars because there's some bubbles in a bottle—"

"Listen, Janey," he said with some seriousness, "money's just paper. It's no good if you don't get good out of it. So tomorrow I'll get run over by a taxi – what'll I buy with thirteen dollars in a grave? I aim to get a bang out of life."

"But nobody lives thinking he'll die the next day. When you came out of the Marines, you made a plan for the future, didn't you? You went to school so you could be a cook."

"Sure, it was a means to an end – it would get me something, it would get me right where I am this minute. Or maybe you want me to spend my money on some other girl?"

"You know I don't, Floyd." And then, because she was honest, "Listen, honey, I want to ask you something."

"God, you're cute-looking. What?"

"I see domestic champagne on the menu that costs much less – why didn't you order it? Don't you know my tastes by now?"

"Sure, but it's your birthday, isn't it? Only comes once a year."

"Floyd," she said seriously, and with love, "I'm going to say something you won't like. I don't think you ordered that champagne to please me. You didn't even ask me if I wanted it. I think you did it for the same reason my sister's little boy stands in front of a mirror and makes a muscle – because it makes you feel big and important to throw money around."

He flushed with anger over her comment and snapped back with something less than logic: "OK, OK, from now on it's a bag of peanuts and a glass of water – what fun!"

"No, Floyd, I don't—"

"I know just what you mean," he interrupted. "Save your money so you won't go to the poorhouse when you're too old to work. Save your money so you can have eight kids and send them all to college. Only where do *I* come in? I've lived like a damn dog for most of my life – Christ, don't put a collar and a leash on me, don't tie me down with a set of rules... I can't take it, I want some fun out of life!"

She understood something about him then that she had sensed only vaguely before: that behind his independence and his manliness there somehow dwelt a small, unsatisfied, restless boy. And with great sorrow she thought to herself, "He won't marry me – he'll be afraid to tie down. He doesn't really love me – I'm just passing fun, like a bottle of champagne."

The glance she cast upon him then caught at his heart. There was pain and disappointment in it, and sorrow and pity for him, and a deep, close understanding. Something within Varney felt as though it would burst. His throat become swollen, and he wanted to fling his arms around her and press his head to her breast and sob and sob, and say, "Love me, Janey, love me, marry me, don't ever leave me." It was a wild, tumultuous, unnerving impulse, something out of his depths that confused and pained and frightened him. It was not this way a man asked a woman to marry, not with tears like a child... there was something wrong – he was drunk, he needed to think it over. He said nothing.

As much as Varney could love any woman, he had come to love Janey. Yet, whenever he thought of marriage, an uneasiness would rise within him. He would think to himself: "What if it don't work out? I'll be stuck, I'll have to pay alimony." He would ask himself: "How do I know this is real? Maybe tomorrow I'll see another girl and go for her. What the hell – Janey says she loves me, but she thought she loved that other guy, and then they got divorced."

Out of this uneasiness, he had not asked her before; out of distrust for the tumult in his heart, he did not ask her on this night. The very thing he most needed, a woman's unreserved, wholehearted love, he was afraid to take. He left it sitting on a hotel terrace and told himself: "You're drunk, you need to think it over."

Now, six months later, he was thinking it over, but in a quite different way. Janey's face was vivid before his eyes, the same look of pain and understanding upon it, but he felt no confusion, no frightening tumult. Instead he felt the deep satisfaction that can come to a man when he loves surely and is surely loved. Janey loved him, and in some way he had wounded her by what he had said, and this he didn't want and couldn't bear. In his fantasy he gazed upon her, thinking to himself that yes, he wanted her for his wife – this friendly, clear-eyed girl with her open laugh and her neat, braided, russet hair, this slender, graceful girl, always so trim and attractive and clean-looking in the dresses she sewed for herself, so quick and efficient when she stepped into the kitchen to load a tray... and so sweetly soft and exciting when she turned to him in the dark with her eager, responsive kiss, her slender body arching to his...

"Janey," he said in his fantasy, "I love you, my darling. With my whole heart I love you, and want you, and belong to you, and want you to belong to me. Will you marry me, Janey?"

"Oh yes," she said, and there were tears in her eyes, and her eyes were like jewels, and her mouth was trembling. And so they danced that night to the joy of their marriage, dancing close and warm to the pulse of love – and it was all a nightmare that he had gone to bed with another woman – why should he, when he already had Janey?

"OK, you men," said Mr Prager. "Stand up and form a double line."

With the others, Varney rose.

Chapter 3

The House We Live In

Johnny Lauter, fulfilling the duties of a tier man, sauntered down the runway and paused at cell 108. He said "Mail man... parcel post from Momma" and tossed a bar of soap to one of the men inside, who was awaiting sentence for disorderly conduct and assault upon a policeman.

"Thanks, feller. We goin' out to the Yard t'day?"

"Don't know yet, Boss Man ain't told me yet." He continued on to 112, where a slender, elderly optometrist, under sentence of five to fifteen years for carnal knowledge of a female under sixteen, was suffering from a heavy cold. Lauter said "Mail man... registered letter from Momma" and thrust a roll of toilet paper between the bars.

"Thanks, I surely appreciate this, my nose is running like a sugar tree."

"You want me to put you down for sick call?"

"No, thanks. I went yesterday. You wait on line two hours, and all they give you is an aspirin. But I'll be much obliged if you keep supplying me with paper."

"Will do," said Lauter, and turned back to 110 to deliver some nail clippers to the former agent of the US Treasury now under three-year sentence for accepting a bribe. He said: "Ten dollars' deposit an' you'll get your arm broke if these ain't returned."

"You can have 'em back in two minutes. Say, Johnny—"

"What?"

"That bedbug ruled on you yet?"

"I think he's waitin' for me to die of old age."

These errands completed, Lauter sauntered down to 130 to make the acquaintance of the man who just had come in. New men always were of interest: they made fresh conversation and they helped to kill time.

"Mornin'," he said to McPeak. "You got here for breakfast, I see. How do you like your eggs – an' if the kitchen's run low on eggs, would you mind eatin' some chicken?"

McPeak, who was lying down on the lower bunk, stood up with a small grin and came forward. He was the only occupant of the cell. "How's about if there's no chicken?"

"Why, then you'll just hafta eat the usual manure. Lauter's my name, I'm tier man here. What's yours?"

"McPeak. What's a tier man?"

"Guess you never been in jail before?"

"That's right."

"A tier man's the way things get done in here. Like, f'r instance, I see you don't have a blanket or a mattress cover. You tell me, I tell the screw, see? You're a new man, so I'll answer your questions, tell you the rules and give you free legal advice. You wanna borrow some cigarettes till you make canteen?"

"Thanks, don't smoke."

"That's great, that makes life easier on everybody."

"Tell you what I could use, though."

"What?"

"Some matches to chew. It's a habit I took up when I stopped real chewin'."

"Never did understand how a man could chew tobacco," Lauter said, giving him a handful of wooden matches. "I tried it once and throwed up."

"Didn't chew terbakker myself either," McPeak explained. "Snuff was my chew, but it give me stomach trouble." He thrust one of the matches into the front of his mouth, gripped it with his teeth and said: "Thanks, I appreciate these."

"Give you a piece of advice," Lauter volunteered. "Don't lie down on a bunk like you were. Take your shoes off. A screw catch you with your shoes on, you're liable to get written up. Didn't they tell you that?"

"No."

"They tell you the rule about eatin'?"

"Said you hafta eat everythin'."

"They mean it, too. Give you another advice: if you make a mistake and a screw catches you, give him the 'Yessir, yessir' business. Play it respectful, an' you'll make out better. It ain't hard to get along in here."

"OK – say, they told me down at the precinct house I was gonna be tooken before a commissioner. What's that mean?"

"That's for your preliminary hearing. The commissioner's like a judge. In any Federal arrest, he looks over the evidence. Then he decides if you go free or you get turned over to the courts. He sets your bail and things like that."

"But I can't be a Federal case," McPeak protested. "I was in a fight, that's all."

"Here in Washington?"

"Yeah."

"That makes it Federal. If you live in Baltimore and get in a fight, it's a city matter. Here in Washington everything's Federal, see?"

"I didn't know that – I'm from Detroit. So when do they take a guy before the commissioner?"

"Pretty quick. When they arrest you?"

"Saddy night."

"Today, tomorrow. You got a lawyer?"

"No."

"You don't actually need one before a commissioner, but it don't hurt."

"Shucks, I don't wanna spend no money for a lawyer."

"Nobody ever does," Lauter commented with a thin little grin. "But sometimes you pawn your gold teeth for a good lawyer, like I did. What's the charge on you – disorderly conduct, assault?"

"I don't know for sure yit."

"Well, whatever it is," Lauter observed from the vantage point of one who was facing the gas chamber, "you got nothing much to worry about."

"I got plenty t'worry about, plenty," McPeak responded morosely. "I come all the way from Detroit in my vacation time for my niece's weddin', an' now look where I am. My sister's countin' on me, the weddin's this Saddy."

"Uh-huh," Lauter muttered with sudden disinterest, and began to think of his children, whom he had not seen for three months, and of his wife, borrowing from friends and asking for relief* – and knew he had had enough of this man* and his so-called troubles. "Well, be seein' you." He started off.

"Hey," McPeak called.

"What?"

"They got my suitcase down in that precinct house with all my bestes clothes, and they ain't sent it over. You know how I can git it?"

"Did they give you a receipt for it?"

"No."

"You got about a twenty per cent chance of gettin' it back. Those precinct cops are highway robbers. They steal your money too?"

"No."

"Guess you weren't drunk then. They roll every drunk who comes in."

"Jesus Christ, I'm gittin' terrible mad!" McPeak exploded suddenly, with naive vehemence. "I'm gonna raise dirty hell about this. I'm gonna sue the polices for false arrest. I didn't deserve to be arrested nohow."

"That's OK with me, brother," Lauter replied softly. "I know just in particular how you feel." He walked off with an unsmiling face.

Three tiers higher up, Huey Wilson was a centre of attraction.* Six men, all Negroes, all wearing white mess jackets over their jail blues, were grouped around him discussing his case. These six were the sole occupants of the fourth tier at the moment, and the only coloured men in this cell block. Since it was their task to serve meals to the white inmates of CB1, they had been lounging on the runway, waiting for the order to go down, when Huey appeared. To his dismay, he had been confronted by all of them at once.

Huey had not known what to expect of the men he would meet in jail, and he had been wary of falling in with a bad lot. A routine question had been put to him – "What'd they get you for?" – and he had explained a bit stiffly, with his guard up. Immediately, then, to his astonishment, he discovered that he had come upon friends. Whatever those men were as individuals, whatever their conflict with the law, they reacted to his story as his brother would have, or his father, or any other group of Negroes. They were indignant, they were concerned for him, and they were on his side without reservation. Several of them, it appeared, already were acquainted with the fight on the school issue – one, Isaac Reeves, volunteered that his daughter had attended classes in the same warehouse. He was a grey-haired, vital-looking man in his early fifties, who seemed to be much respected by the others. "It's no damn accident they're workin' up phoney charges on you," he exclaimed with feeling and bitterness. "Those white sons of bitches got lots of ways to keep in the saddle. Framin' a coloured boy like you is one way to keep Jim Crow* in the schools. They always got somethin' like that in mind when they frames up a coloured man."

"Uh-huh," another added, by name Ben Wellman, a huge, rugged-looking man in his late twenties, six feet three in height, bulging all over from hard physical labour. "Uncle Charlie* don't crack that whip by accident. He aims it good, straight at your ass like he does to a mule. He knows how he wants you to jump."

It was a conclusion that was obvious to all of these men from the fabric of their lives, yet it was so fundamental that it demanded statement. To Huey it was a guarantee that even here, among jailbirds, he had found genuine allies whose understanding he could trust, and whose advice he might seek.

Inevitably, now, he was plied with questions about McPeak. The motives and nature of this southern white became a source of excited speculation, and not a little dissension.

"I'd sure like to shake his hand," a man named Spaulding exclaimed. He was a husky, somewhat stout man in his late thirties, whose speech indicated northern upbringing and education. "I give a white man like that real credit."

"I wouldn't give no white man the sweat off my behind for credit," another put in tartly, an odd-looking runt of a man. "Likely he was drunk an' didn't know what he was doin'."

"He wasn't drunk, and he knew!" Huey stated.

"Then he's some sort of screwball! All I know is I wouldn't trust no white man till he's dead. I'd trust him good then, ha, ha!"

"Shoot, Benjamin, you're just an old country boy," Reeves said genially. "You don't know what's goin' on in the world. Don't you ever read the papers? Didn't you hear Wilson say there was whites on that picket line with him? We got good white friends."

"Listen," Huey interrupted, "there's something I'd like to know that I can't figure out. What kind of weapons can they claim I had? I wasn't even carrying a nail file."

"You sure talk innocent," Wellman put in with surprise. He gestured with both hands held out, the thick-fingered, powerful hands of a labourer. "They'll come up with a razor or a gun, or anythin' they like. Don't you know yet how the police acts with us?"

"Sure, of course," Huey replied. "I didn't mean it that way. The thing is I'm charged with *weapons* – that means more than one. So I'd like to *know*. It's an important side to my case."

"I'll lay money I know!" the little runt of a man, Benjamin, said with authority. He was in his middle thirties, no more than five feet two in height, badly cross-eyed, wearing glasses. "You kicked one feller in the face an' laid him out, didn't you? Ain't that what you said?"

"That's right."

"You do him any damage?"

"I hear he's in the hospital with a broken jaw."

Benjamin chuckled with triumph and self-satisfaction. "Jus' like I thought. Them police don't need t'frame *you* with phoney weapons. You know what the Law says? Law says if a man uses his feet in a fight, like if'n he stomps on somebody, they's counted as deadly weapons. His fists ain't, but his feet is. On account you kin damage a man with your feet as bad as you kin with a club."

There were exclamations of surprise and disbelief from a number of the men. Huey asked: "Are you positive of that?"

Benjamin, who had spent more of his adult life in prison than free, smiled with superiority and replied: "I ain't only positive, I *know*! Anybody wants to bet some cigs on it, I'll lay him odds – like ten to one, let's say."

Although Benjamin was known to the others as a man who told whopping lies and usually believed them, the offer to bet at such odds was impressive – no inmate squandered cigarettes. There was a moment of silence while the group reflected. Then, suddenly, one of them burst out laughing. He was Alfrice Tillman, a brown-skinned, handsome youth. "Lookit there!" he cried, pointing to Huey's feet. He clapped a hand to his head with clownish awe. "Lookit those* felonious weapons. Why, them's two of the most vicious weapons I ever seen. Bet they's size fourteen – they's pure murderous." He bent over with mirth. "Reckon the Law's got the goods on you, Wilson. You better plead guilty, you're sure gonna serve time."

"Goddamn it, Tillman, you're just a plain fool," Spaulding snapped irritably. "What's so damn funny to you about the frame-up of a coloured man?"

Tillman stopped laughing and answered with surprise, "Nothin'! Only, ain't there somethin' funny about this feet business?" He began to laugh again. "I can see how it'll be in the courtroom. 'Where's the evidence?' the bedbug'll say. 'Where's the weapons?' – 'Why, right here, Judge,' Wilson'll tell him. Then he'll wave those big weapons in front of the judge's face. 'Take those weapons away,' the judge'll say. 'Man, they stink.'"

Several of the others joined in Tillman's laughter, but Spaulding turned away with such marked disgust that Huey, who had not been offended by Tillman's clowning, wondered what else had occurred between the two.

Spaulding asked: "What about this white man, McPeak? Do you know anything else about him?"

"Nothing more than I've told you already. They've kept us separated."

"You better find out if he'll stick with you in court."

"I know that! Only, how can I get to talk to him? Is there any time coloured and white are together in this place?"

"Sure – in the morgue," offered Tillman. "They can't afford two morgues." He opened his mouth wide and laughed soundlessly.

"Where is McPeak?" asked Benjamin, the experienced time-server. "What cell block – what wing, you know?"

"In this one. He's right downstairs on the first tier."

"That's easy then. We'll be goin' down there to serve breakfast. You kin talk to him right away."

"Can I be private with him, have some time?"

"Hell no, but you can pass a few words."

"I need more talk than that!"

"You won't get it in here, Wilson," said Spaulding. He spoke with contempt. "They draw the colour line sharp in here. We eat separate, sleep separate, go to separate recreation and Yard. The authorities are careful to keep us in our place: they wouldn't want us getting any big ideas even in jail – hell no!"

"Except in the morgue," Tillman put in. "Don't forget the morgue."

"Oh, dry up with that line!" Spaulding snapped at him with rancour. "This is a serious matter. Why do you have to crack wise about everything?"

"Man, when I can't laugh any more, I may as well die," Tillman retorted. "You're such a sourpuss – you must be half dead already. Come to think of it, you're lookin' worse t'day than you did yesterday. You're dyin' fast of feelin' so important. The big lottery man, the big wheel – my, my, I'm all broken up for you."

"Up yours!" said Spaulding. "You give me a general, all-around pain in the ass, Tillman."

"I think I know how you might could talk to that white feller." The suggestion came softly, hesitantly, from a man who had been silent until now, and who was standing slightly to the rear of the group, as though he did not quite belong. He had, Huey thought, as sad and tragic a look as he ever had seen. Years of poverty, of failure, of fruitless endeavour, were visible in his tired, liver-coloured face, in the gaping holes of his almost toothless mouth, in the timid eyes behind thick glasses.

"How?"

"On sick call! I've got the bleedin' piles, so I've been goin' to sick call most every day. Sometimes you waits an hour, waits two hours. They sits you down in a big room there, coloured 'n' white mixed. You could talk all you want."

"Finnerty, good for you, you got a head on you!" Spaulding exclaimed with enthusiasm. "I should've thought of that myself: I went only yesterday. You sure can talk to him on sick call, Wilson."

Looking very pleased, the man called Finnerty said, with shy eager-ness: "I kin give you another idea too. When they forms the sick-call line downstairs, there's fellers in the front of the line an' fellers in the back. You tell this white feller t'go to the back of the line with you. Then, when you gets outside the gate, your line gets mixed up with another line there, from the east wing. So right then you gotta fall behind 'n' go to the back end of that noo line. If you do that, then you'll be the last fellers to be called in to the doctor – you'll have good time t'talk."

Gazing at the man, Huey thought to himself that even though he was in jail he was not alone, that black hands already were reaching out to help him. In the shower room it had been a beat-up time-server – now it was a whole group of men including this one, who looked as though life had trampled the spirit altogether out of him. Sad and behind bars, yet not so crushed that he didn't reach out to help a black youth being framed by white police. Feeling deeply moved, he said to Finnerty "Thanks a lot, that's swell advice – that helps me a lot", but wished he could say more – that he could say, "I'm sorry for you, Mister. I don't know why you're in here, but if I could help you, I sure would."

From the front of the runway there came a sudden, loud call: "Tier man! Time to go down!"

"Goin' down!" sang Benjamin, and added in a lower tone to the others, "He's tellin' us it's time. Breakfast must be twenty* minutes late this morning, I'm starvin'!"

"Do I go with you?" asked Huey.

"You sure do – less'n you don't wanna eat. I'll git you a mess jacket from the screw."

"Am I supposed to work?"

The undersized tier man gazed up at Huey with an amazed,* satiric expression. He asked, in a delicately patronizing manner, "What's the matter, schoolboy, you never did no work before? You a little prince of Ethiopia?"

Tillman burst out in a guffaw. "Stand back, fellers, we got royalty here." He held out his hand to Huey. "Glad t'meetcha, Prince."

Ignoring the hand, feeling embarrassed and annoyed, Huey replied tartly to Benjamin, "Now look, I didn't mean anything like that. I just meant I'm new in here and—"

"An' you're allergic to work," Tillman interrupted. "That's OK, Prince, we understand how it is with royalty. Can I wipe your ass for you?"

"Oh, for Chrissakes," Huey snapped, "cut it out, will you? If I'm sup-posed to work, I'll work. Can't a feller* ask?"

"Hey, down there, what's the matter? Get going!" the guard called from the other end of the tier.

Benjamin said, grinning, "I'll git your mess jacket, schoolboy. Start down, jailbirds."

Descending the stairs, Isaac Reeves moved alongside Huey. He said with a smile: "You took 'em too serious, Wilson. In here everybody works everybody else for a laugh. We got mighty little else to do. Somebody tears you down, you just fun him back."

"OK, sure," Huey agreed, but he still felt annoyed and uncomfortable. He had been welcomed so warmly by these men that it had come as a shock to feel their quick readiness to turn malicious.

"They don't mean no harm," Reeves added.

"Who'll show me what my job is?"

"Benjamin'll tell you. Handin' out bread or coffee, nothin' hard."

"Listen," Huey said, "over at the precinct a fellow told me I'd be in a cell block with just us. How come we're in with ofays?"

"The coloured cell block is all filled up," Reeves explained. "We're overflow, so they give us a separate tier in here."

"OK, but how come you got this job – serving meals? Did you put in for it?"

"Shoot, no. They give it to us."

"Did you have to take it?"

Reeves looked at Huey closely. "Reckon we did, lest we were lookin' for trouble – an' jail ain't the best place to look for it."

"If they draw the colour line so sharp, how come coloured don't serve coloured and white serve white? How come we're the ones to be servants for the ofays?"

"That's sure right, but I can tell you why I won't fuss over it," the older man responded. "Because we get good out of it: it helps us get along better."

"How?"

"We get to help ourselves to a little more eats, an' that counts in here. We can take us a shower bath every day, and that's *real* good. But *most* important, it gives us the chance to get out of our cells, to move around a little an' to do a little work. That's the biggest benefit of all. You spend one day locked up an' you'll see what I mean."

"Maybe so," Huey muttered, "but I don't like it to have no choice."

"Neither do I, but I look at it this way: fight the right fight at the right time, an' don't fret yourself over everythin' else that needs doin'. You got a fight with the police on your hands. It ain't good sense to pick one with the jail boss at the same time."

"Maybe so."

"Sonny, it's a long hill us coloured are climbin'. We got to live through while we're doin' it. Like with me now – I got a three-year sentence. I sure want parole at the end of my first year. But if I don't get it, I sure want my eight months' good time. I ain't gonna tangle with the prison system if I can help it. I want out!"

"Sure, you're right." They were on the last flight of stairs now, and Huey asked: "Do I have to watch out for the guard when I talk to that white man? Is it against the rules?"

"No, but don't try it now. Wait'll we finish servin' breakfast in the east wing an' come back. They'll be in a hurry for us now."

Huey wanted to ask "What's a man like you doing in jail? You don't seem like a criminal", but he felt too shy. Instead, with a burst of warm feeling for this middle-aged, friendly man, he exclaimed, "It sure feels good to have friends in a place like this. I'm grateful to all of you."

Reeves smiled a little, and his answer was restrained, but bitter. "I got three grown sons, Wilson – good boys, an' anyone of 'em might be in here framed up instead of you. Us coloured needs to be friends. Ain't it so? Huh?"

At this moment Floyd Varney and Hal Jude, their right and left wrists manacled together, were walking towards the prison bus under the eye of several guards. A dozen other handcuffed men, white and coloured, followed them. "Sure is a fine day t'be goin' to the racetrack," Jude observed loudly. "I got mah winners picked an' mah bets all ready. But why in hell this taxi cab has bars on the windows, I sho' don't know." He laughed jovially and looked to Varney for a smile of appreciation. When none was forthcoming, he nudged Varney with his elbow and said crudely, "Take it easy, bub, you ain't gon t'be hanged – nothin' t'worry about."

Varney frowned and remained silent. As the yard doors opened and the bus swung into* the street, Jude sat up straight and exclaimed with animation, "Now, let's you an' me help each other out, feller. You spy out that side an' I'll spy out this. If'n either of us sees a perty* gal, he tells the other. What you say?"

Varney nodded and smiled morosely. He couldn't avoid thinking that careless desire for a woman whom he had met by accident in a hotel bar, as now he might see another woman equally attractive, had led him to this bus, to these handcuffs, to the terror of this day. He breathed deeply, then sighed. There was a refreshing coolness in the air. The night fog had lifted from the streets, but the sky was still hazy and the early sun had a pale, wintry colour.

"Goddam, nothin' but a milkman so far," Jude complained jovially, after a few moments. "You lookin', feller?"

"Uh-huh."

"Man, I'd sure like to see one pretty gal before that ol' whore of a jedge gives me mah time. A man deserves that much good luck, don't he?"

Varney grunted. His thoughts were elsewhere – twenty years away from this prison bus. His mind had gone back to a June morning when a boy of ten had been walking down a dirt road. Behind him was the two-room shack he had called home and the woman he had called mother – and the faceless men who took off their coats and slapped his mother on her fat buttocks and sent him out to play, or sent him to the back door of the grocery for a quart of white lightning.* He had wept with fear and loneliness on that pale dawn when he ran away from home. Yet even that moment had been better than this, because he had not been helpless. Even the agony of Japanese mortar shells in the Battle of New Georgia* had been better than this – even the screams and the bloody flesh and the arm stumps of his buddy in the same foxhole. Because he had not been utterly helpless!

"Why, looky there," Hal Jude exclaimed suddenly as the bus swung around a corner. "There's a prime female if I evah saw one. Just look at the fat ass on her."

"Damn it, shut up!" Varney cried, and was not aware that he still was twenty years back with a grinning man in the doorway saying to his mother, in terms a ten-year-old boy already understood: "Howdy, mam – I got the right address for some prime beef, I hope?"

This he had understood, but other things he never had, and never would. Knowing his own misfortune, he had not tried to understand his mother's. Even now, in manhood, he could think of her only with loathing. It never occurred to him that his mother once had been an innocent child, or that compassion might be due an illiterate farm girl seduced at sixteen by a boy she loved, betrayed and deserted. He knew his own tears and shame, but he could not measure hers; he knew the sodden disregard with which she had treated him, but he ignored the disregard she had suffered from parents, lover and all of society.

The bus moved rapidly through the quiet streets, and Varney closed his eyes. He began to dream of a kindly judge who would be compassionate and who would understand, and who would set him free.

* * *

On the bottom tier of the west wing the inmates were listening to a welcome sound – a busy, metallic clatter from the other wing of their cell block, which indicated that breakfast was finished there and that the food trays were being stacked. Shortly the group of mess men appeared outside the steel-mesh screen of the eating range with their equipment: a shining steam table; trays laden with bread and tin cups; a wagon with eating platters. Huey Wilson, who was being favoured by the others because of his hurt side, was carrying the small mailbox that accompanied each meal.

Mr Simmons unlocked the gate, and the group passed through. As they pushed and carried their burdens towards the far end of the range, a hundred-foot length, men called to them in subdued tones from cells on the bottom tier: "Hey, what's to eat?... What's the slop?" It was the inevitable, three-times-a-day query, and usually it was answered by a fanciful jest, more or less obscene. This morning, however, breakfast was late, and Benjamin answered "Oatmeal 'n' taters" and let it go at that.

Huey Wilson, walking by Tillman's side, asked, "Where do I put this box?"

Tillman pointed to an open doorway in the steel screen that separated the eating range from the tier runway. "Right there, in front of the last cell. That's where they come out t'eat."

"That's McPeak's cell. Can I go talk to him?"

"Sure, but remember – anythin' you say to him, the ofays in the next cell can hear too."

"Can't I go up on the runway so I can talk low?"

"Hell, no – you step on that runway, you'll get your ass chewed off by the guard. We gotta stay this side of the screen."

"OK, thanks." Huey strode quickly to the open doorway and set down the mailbox. McPeak was at the rear end of his cell, with his back turned, washing his hands. The two inmates in 128 were standing at the bars, watching the preparations for breakfast. "Hey," Huey called in a low voice, "Mr McPeak."

Turning round,* McPeak smiled rather formally and came forward, still soaping his hands. With a restraint that Huey noticed, he said: "How you doin', young feller?"

"OK, how about you?"

"Sure don' like bein' caged up. Gives me the creeps."

"Yeah... You know that hurt in my ribs? I expect to see a doctor this morning, when sick call rolls around."

McPeak nodded.

"About your headache," Huey continued, "why don't you go on sick call, too?" A puzzled expression came to McPeak's face, and he started to reply, but Huey interrupted. "This whole cell block goes to sick call at the same time, my tier same as yours."

The uncertainty on McPeak's face was supplanted by a thin grin. "I git it."

"Will you tell your tier man you need to see a doctor?"'

McPeak nodded. "Reckon so."

"Fine, see you later." Feeling very good, Huey walked off quickly to the steam table. McPeak's manner bothered him, but the important thing had been accomplished. Moreover, this willingness to meet him was evidence that McPeak still was an ally.

"How'd you make out?" asked Isaac Reeves, who was stacking some platters.

"Made out OK. He'll meet me."

"That's real good. That's a white man I'd like to know. Say, why do you keep scratching yourself, son? You got body lice?"

"No. I got some bedbug bites in the precinct station – they're all swollen up. They itch like fire."

"Scratchin'll only make it worse."

"I know that, I'm trying not to. But I scratch without realizing it. Are there any bedbugs in here?"

"No, sir," Reeves answered with a small grin. "This is a fine, sanitary place – this place is as clean as a funeral parlour. Well, here we go, here comes the mess officer."

Before each jailhouse meal, by order of the Administration, it was required that a short rite be performed. At the last table on the eating range were two wooden boxes. In one of them there were fifteen large condiment shakers, salt and pepper blended in the same container, and it was the duty of Mr Fuhr, mess officer for this meal, to count them. With Benjamin waiting at his side, he proceeded to do so. He had counted them before and after breakfast in the east wing – he would count them still another time at the end of breakfast here.

In the second box were tin tablespoons, the only utensil allowed in eating. These Mr Fuhr dumped on the table. He checked them off by fives, wrote the total on a pocket pad and returned them to the box. He nodded to Benjamin, who picked up both boxes and carried them forward to the steam table. Mr Fuhr then gestured to Mr Simmons, the tier guard. Since grace had been said, Federal nourishment could proceed.

Instantly the cell doors of the first tier ground back in howling concert, and twenty-six men stepped out on the enclosed runway. A great burst of life surged out with them. All at once an air of festivity enveloped the tier, as though here were a group of men about to depart on a picnic. Most of them were dressed in prison blues, but a number wore their own clothes. The latter were men who had been out on bail during the process of trial and conviction, and now were scheduled for quick transfer to a penitentiary. All of the men, however, were identical in appearance in one respect: they were uniformly unshaven. Shower baths, and the opportunity to shave, came twice a week only.

For a few moments there was rapid movement on the runway, louder talk than usual and seeming confusion as the men shifted about, walked forward and began forming into a single line. Friends who had been separated since lock-up time the night before, a period of twelve hours, manoeuvred to reach each other and exchange a few words. There was good-natured horseplay and gay laughter. But then the cell doors slammed shut, the line began to move forward and the men became more quiet. Once they stepped out on the eating range, conversation would be forbidden.

At the head of the line, exercising their privileges as tier men, were Johnny Lauter and Eddie Quinn. The line wound through the doorway in the runway screen and curved back on the floor of the eating range. Men with letters to mail, like Lauter, dropped them in the box by the doorway, and those without letters, like Quinn, wished there was someone to whom they could write. As Lauter reached the steam table, he took a steel platter, a tablespoon, a tin cup and a tin bowl. With the apathy of one who knows in advance the taste of a meal he has eaten many times before, he said "light" to Isaac Reeves and held out his tray for a serving spoon of fried potatoes. He said "medium" to Dewey Spaulding and received an appropriate dipperful of oatmeal in his tin bowl, followed by a splosh of skimmed milk from Alfrice Tillman. He said "one" to Finnerty and received a slice of white bread, and "no" to Huey Wilson, rejecting a pat of apple butter. The last man, Benjamin, poured the hot liquid called coffee. Quinn, in his turn, whispered quickly to Alfrice Tillman: "Is that grade-A cream? Is it sanitary? Is it pasteurized?"

"Hell no, but the flies in it is," Tillman retorted, also in a whisper.

The two grinned at each other, and Quinn, passing on, clicked his false teeth.

McPeak, following behind, was not aware that every mess man behind the table was scrutinizing him with interest. Coming to Finnerty he said "four slices", because he was a heavy bread eater, and was surprised to see this Negro stranger shake his head. "Bread's awful heavy – you better don't," Finnerty whispered. He held out two slices and looked quickly to Huey at his side. Huey, handling the apple butter, nodded his agreement.* McPeak whispered "Thanks", took the slices* and, wondering about it, followed the others. Under the vigilant eye of Mr Fúhr they filed into place behind one of the narrow-topped steel tables and sat down on the snap seats attached to the table in back of them. McPeak spread apple butter with his spoon on one of the pieces of bread, took a bite, chewed, swallowed… and understood. "Did me a good turn," he thought gratefully, and realized why.

Shortly the cell doors ground open on the third tier. There was the sound of many feet, and a burst of conversation as the inmates up there formed into line and stared down through the wire mesh to see what breakfast offered thirty feet below. On the range floor the men of the first tier did not look up. Humped forward over their platters, they ate quickly and hungrily, five men to a table, five spoons, five bent heads. The line from Tier Three clattered down the several flights of iron staircase, and then, quieting, filed over to the steam table.

George Benjamin, stepping behind Huey Wilson, whispered softly: "Spot the guy you had the fight with." Huey half-turned, nodded and continued serving. Benjamin remained by his side. Shortly Huey murmured, "At the back there, blond-haired, very bright-skinned."

"Behind the short one?"

"Yes."

Quietly, unobtrusively, Benjamin moved from Finnerty to Spaulding to Reeves, whispering to each one: "The blond guy with bright skin, behind the shorty." There was no need for him to say more. When Ballou reached the steam table, Isaac Reeves said: "Heavy or light?" Since Ballou was hungry, he answered "Heavy", but his answer would not have affected the size of his portion. The mess men knew from Huey that Ballou was on the third tier, and they already had discussed his welcome. They were determined to load his platter with an unmanageable amount of food if they could get away with it. Ballou proved to be more compliant than they had hoped. As Reeves was serving him, he caught sight of Huey Wilson, and his attention was distracted from the food. As a result, without his being aware of it, he received enough potatoes for two hungry men, a bowl of oatmeal filled to the brim and four slices of bread. As Huey, with an impassive face, slapped an over-generous portion of apple butter on his platter, Ballou said a bit loudly, "Five years from now you'll still be right here." Then, grinning and pleased with himself, he turned around to be confronted by Mr Fuhr.

"How long you been in here?"

"I came in this mornin'."

"There's no talking at mealtime. Remember that."

Ballou nodded, and Mr Fuhr, with a small gesture of authority, waved him to his seat.

Conversation was forbidden at mealtime, but words were whispered, phrases trickled from the corners of mouths, heads that did not move and lips that scarcely moved carried on a kind of converse.

Said Quinn to McPeak: "I got a complaint. They forgot the orange juice this mornin'."

McPeak stared at him, grinned a little and murmured, "Do tell."

Johnny Lauter jiggled Quinn's elbow with his own and muttered, referring to the coffee, "This cocoa's real good today."

"Thought it was sassafras tea."

"Can't you tell cocoa from tea?"

"Not when it's jailhouse coffee."

One man murmured to another, "Took too many potatoes – wan' some?"

"OK."

Both glanced over at Mr Fuhr, whose back was turned. Quickly some potatoes passed from one platter to another.

Mr Fuhr's back was turned, but generally speaking he saw more, heard more, knew more than the men realized. He knew the rules also, but there was a bit of elastic in his soul, more so than with many guards. So long as conversation was confined to a whisper, so long as the exchange of food was not too frequent or too flagrant, he did not notice. This morning, however, his attention was being distracted to the second tier, where men under sentence of death were confined. Only three men were being held there at the moment, and they were kept in separate cells, but a conversation had commenced in one of them. The oldest resident of the Death Tier, who was known as Wacky Mike, was an obese, moronic-looking man of forty-five with a tiny snub nose set in a fatty white face. He had been two years in the same cell, with his case pending in the courts, and had developed the sorry ability of holding conversations with himself. These he carried on at considerable length as though there were two, three or even four men in his cell, each of them speaking in a different tone of voice, each expressing a different mood. The men on the range floor could not hear the words of this conversation, but the sharp exclamations of profanity, the sound of argument and silly laughter, amused them mightily. No one knew why a man so obviously loony was not committed to the Federal prison for mental cases, instead of being kept up there to fry. They pitied him, but they also enjoyed him – distractions of his* sort were precious in jail.

One man, however, was not amused. Ballou had come to the meal with great hunger, but by the time he had disposed of only half the food on his platter he knew that he had taken too much. Thinking back, he realized that he had not asked for any bread, let alone four slices, and it was the bread that was killing him. The oatmeal and potatoes were passable, although he had much more of the latter than he could consume with relish, but the bread was impossible – flat-tasting, doughy, the heaviest, most filling bread he ever had eaten. He knew from his cellmate that the rule on food was implacable – a man paid for leftovers by a stretch in the punishment Hole. Under the spur of anxiety he opened his trouser buttons and spooned his food with concentration, although each mouthful was becoming more difficult. Finally, with two pieces of bread and a third of his potatoes still remaining, he knew that he had reached his absolute limit – another bite and he would vomit. He thought of the Hole and stared at his platter, and felt perspiration welling out cold on his forehead. With his eye on Mr Fuhr, he nudged his cellmate, who was sitting beside him. He whispered desperately, "I took too much – what'll I do?"

"In your pocket."

It was the obvious solution, but Ballou had not thought of it, and he cast a grateful glance at the other man. Mr Fuhr was a few tables ahead inspecting the platters of the first-tier men. With haste Ballou snatched a piece of bread and stuffed it into his pocket. The second piece followed, and then, praying for time, he dropped a spoonful of potatoes into his left hand, which he held below the level of the table.

If Mr Fuhr was momentarily unaware of what Ballou was doing, others were not. George Benjamin and Dewey Spaulding, one carrying a large bucket and the other a dipper, were walking along the file of tables offering more coffee. They were exceedingly slow about it, however, because they were watching Ballou with such keen relish. The other mess men, who already were eating, were in a less favourable position to observe what was happening. Jail rules required that they sit at tables removed from those of white inmates, and so they were half a dozen rows behind Ballou. Nevertheless Ben Wellman, who was very tall and who had an aisle seat alongside the wall, had a bird's-eye view of Ballou, who was on the same aisle. "Bread into his pocket," he whispered to Reeves. "Potatoes now." The good word was passed along from man to man, joy accompanying it. Their triumph suddenly waxed bigger. Passing down the inside aisle, George Benjamin, without being asked, neatly filled Ballou's coffee cup. Ballou, who had been concentrating on the disposal of his potatoes, reacted with a cry, but too late... "No more!... Goddamn it, I didn't want any!"

"What's the matter there?" Mr Fuhr asked sharply, swinging around.

"He gave me more coffee, and I didn't want any."

"Did you ask him for it?"

"I certainly didn't."

"Why'd you give it to him?"

Benjamin's answer came with suave politeness. "Why, yes, sir, he sure did ask me. Said 'Fill it up'." He stared at Ballou with an impassive face, but with an unmistakable gleam in his crossed eyes.

Ballou understood then. The four pieces of bread became clear, and the mountain of potatoes became clear, and he exploded with rage. "That's a damn nigger lie!"

"Quiet!" Mr Fuhr snapped. "No more talking! You can leave your coffee, but finish your food."

Ballou felt like screaming with fury. Only a small amount of the potatoes remained, but the thought of eating them was revolting. Sweating, fighting nausea, he filled his mouth and chewed, the potatoes cold now and more greasy than before. Mr Fuhr waited and watched, and it required the application of his full will to swallow. At his table, all around him, the others were finished and also watching. Again Ballou filled his mouth, felt his gorge rise, but swallowed.

Finally he was finished. The platter was clean, and he stared at it with sickly exhaustion and hatred. Only then did Mr Fuhr move off.

At the forward tables, the first-tier men were passing spoons and condiment shakers to the end man on their right. George Benjamin collected the shakers, while Mr Fuhr watched and counted. Benjamin returned with a second wooden box. Mr Fuhr ran his eye over five spoons laid out fan-wise in front of the end man at the first table. He gestured – a tiny, authoritative gesture with forefinger alone. The spoons made a noisy clink as Benjamin swept them into the wooden box. Mess man and officer then stepped to the second table. Mr Fuhr counted five spoons, gestured with his forefinger and the spoons fell. They continued down the line.

In row one Lauter murmured to Quinn, "I've never figured it out... this fussing over spoons. A feller can make a knife out of a lot of things if he wants, don't they know that?"

"Guess they don't wanna make it too easy."

"Let you buy tobacco in canteen, too. What about the glass from a tobacco jar?"

"Stop cuttin' my throat."

Both men fell silent as Officer Fuhr returned to table one. He gestured. Five seats snapped back as* the men stood up. They sidled out and walked in line towards the entrance to their tier. Row by row the first-tier men followed. When they were in their cells and the doors had hammered shut, Mr Fuhr began to dismiss the men of Tier Three.

Walking up the staircase, Ballou's cellmate said jovially, "You got in trouble, hey? I figured you took too much when I saw your platter."

"You don't understand," Ballou cried in a rage. "Those damn coons did a job on me. One of 'em is Wilson, the bastard I had the fight with. They loaded me up on purpose. They wanted me to go to the Hole."

"You don't say!"

"Christ, I'll get that nigger son of a bitch if it's the last thing I ever do. I'll kill him."

"How come you let 'em do it? You got eyes. Didn't you see how much chow they were givin' you?"

"That's the thing: they put it over on me. I was watchin' Wilson, I guess."

His cellmate laughed. "Pretty slick. Anyway, you got off clear."

"The hell I did," Ballou answered, as they stepped into their cell. "I feel like a sick dog."

"Lie down, it'll help you digest."

"Soon as I get rid of this crap." He went to the toilet bowl and began emptying his pocket of the impacted mass* of potatoes and bread.

With a guffaw his cellmate asked, "How come you don't keep it for a midnight snack?"

Ballou retched suddenly, dropped to his knees and began to vomit.

"Oh my Gawd," his cellmate exclaimed, unable to repress his sense of comedy, "he says he's hungry, he eats a good meal and then he throws it all away. People are so wasteful."

Down below, among the mess men, the sense of triumph lingered sweetly. George Benjamin had been congratulated with great heartiness, since he was the architect of the scheme, and the little man was beaming with pleasure. Alfrice Tillman, with exultant spontaneity, had composed a rhyme:

There once was a —— named Ballou,
Who loved potato* stew.
When he came into jail,
We tied spuds to his tail,
And now he's all through
With potato stew. Who?
That —— Ballou!*

Spaulding laughed at the rhyme,* despite his animosity towards Tillman. There was a common cause here that superseded all else.

For Huey Wilson there also had been gratification in the incident – nevertheless, his feelings were mixed, and he knew why. Years before, when he had been called "dirty nigger" for the first time, and when he had begun to ask his first, searching questions about life – boy of four, nose bleeding, one eye swollen from a stoning, heart aching and bewildered, asking "why?" – even then his father had refused to allow the malice of whites to be the only answer. It was a hard, a dreadfully hard world for a child of dark skin to understand. How understand a society where so many deeds gave the lie to so many words; where churches of Jesus Christ, Prince of Brotherhood, were separate for black and white; where so many whites, as poor as Negroes, and themselves oppressed, were such cruel oppressors? Yet never in Huey's home, as in others, had he ever heard the wild cry, "All whites is mean cos they's *born* mean! I'd rather* trust a rattlesnake than a white man – there ain't one I wouldn't like t'see dead. God give us black skins, but He give *them* black hearts."

To this, whether spoken by friends or neighbours or his own children, Huey's father would exclaim sternly, "No, sir. That ain't true! There ain't nobody who's ever been *born* bad, nobody ever. If a black boy grows up bad, it's cos he's been treated bad or teached bad things, or raised up crooked. An' when a white chile grows up to hate us cullid, t'be mean an' cruel to us, it's cos he was teached that way: he don't know no different. But he weren't born mean or cruel – no sir! God don't start *nobody* off with hate in his heart."

Countless nights, as the family sat in the kitchen with his brother reading aloud from the Negro weekly newspaper to which they subscribed, *The Norfolk Journal and Guide*, Huey asked questions and studied over the answers. "Why sure, a man kin hate," his father would say. "A man that don't hate wrong ain't much of a man. All I keep sayin' is this: that when there's nothin' *but* hate in a man's heart, especially a coloured man, when there's no understandin' of human natchur an' no faith in God's goodness, then he's just losted. Cos a man like that kain't have no hope for his own chillen in the future, nor for the world gittin' t'be a better place some day, God helpin'. He's a man who's just pizened with the vinegar of his own hate – he may as well lay hisself down an' die."

Huey had come to believe this – in childhood, through the humane insight of his father's creed – but later, with the aid of teachers, books and his own experience, in more complex fashion. To grasp, as he had over the years, the economics of discrimination, and to know how much cash had been coined from the word "nigger" and from the sweat of ill-paid black labour, was only to add substance to what his father had sensed – that it was not some fixed biological malice within the white man that was the cause of Negro suffering, but a greed for cash profit. And this greed, he finally had come to understand, had been both disguised and defended by a tangled web of racist creed and repressive law, of two-faced morality and hempen justice.* While deep within this web the white heart, part of its time and its place, all too often had become warped and malicious. Even as an adolescent Huey had come to understand some of this. Picking fruit for white farmers whom he knew to be Ku Kluxers, he had seen their kindness towards their own folk or towards their white neighbours. Reflecting over it, he had understood better how backwardness and taught prejudice, and their own grinding struggle for survival, could make them so cruel to the Negro. He despised them for what they were, he feared them – but he also understood them and, in a way, pitied them. As, in fact, he felt impelled to understand Ballou now – if only his feelings would permit. They would not. It was all very well to recall the teachings of his father and tell himself that Ballou had not been born with race prejudice in his heart – any more than the Negro tier man, George Benjamin, had been born an armed robber, or his own grandmother had been born to die of tuberculosis at the age of thirty-nine. Nevertheless, all he really wanted at the moment was to batter Ballou into a pulp. He had no genuine desire to understand him.

As Huey admitted this to himself, his father's image suddenly appeared before him – the thin, stern face, the warm eyes, the ashy dark skin, the tall thin figure. The stern face smiled at him, and Huey felt a warm kindling in his heart, and he whispered inwardly: "Don't worry about me, Pa. I'm sore as hell and scared as hell, but I'll be all right."

* * *

The mess men had finished eating; the steam table, the buckets and platters, were on their way out. It was now twenty minutes past six in the morning. The jail day had begun in routine fashion.

Chapter 4

The Petersons

At this time of the morning the doors of the Federal Courthouse were closed and its corridors were silent. It would be several hours before the old three-storeyed building would be assaulted by a horde of anxious relatives, lawyers, bail bondsmen, functionaries and hangers-on. Nevertheless, in the basement of the building, police officers and bailiffs already were on duty, and other men, behind a locked door, were waiting with mounting anxiety for sentence, for hearing, for trial.

The large detention room, which was known as the "bull pen", was distinguished by its bareness. Along three walls there were wooden benches, and this was the extent of its equipment. A rather dismal room, yet adequate to its purpose. Here several generations of men had sat, as in the way station* of a railway,* each man with his private timetable. Men arrived and men departed, and no token of their passage remained behind. Each new man gazed at the grimy walls and thought, "Here I am, and where do I go from here – and please, God, give me a break!" So it was for Floyd Varney, so it would be for the men who would come here tomorrow and the day after.

Waiting was hard, and so men talked hard and smoked hard – or, like Varney, sat in hard silence. Despite the early hour, some of them already had eaten their dinner – that is to say, the two baloney* sandwiches provided them at the jail. Court would not open until ten o'clock, and there would be no more food until five in the afternoon, but theirs was a hunger born of fear, and it was not to be denied.

Varney was listening to Hal Jude, who was telling a story in a loud voice to the assembled company. Although Jude was a professional pickpocket, he had begun his working life as a distiller of illegal whiskey in the hills of Georgia, and he loved to tell tales – true and false – about his encounters with the Law.

"So there we wuz," he was saying, "makin' for that whiskey still in the dark of the night. I was totin' a two-hundred-pound bag of cornmeal, an' mah pappy had him a two-hundred-pound bag of sugar. We hadn't gone more'n five minutes up that mountin holler when, whammy, a flashlight hits mah pappy right in the face, 'n' another'n lights me up. 'This is the Law!' a feller yells out. 'What y'all doin' with that sugar an' cornmeal?' 'Gonna make sauerkraut,' mah pappy tells him right back. Oh, Lordy, that shoh was a funny 'un, 'Gonna make sauerkraut.' They never did find our whiskey still, though: we had that hid* in an' ol' chicken house."

"You serve any time for that?" one of his audience asked.

"Sho' enough," Jude responded with a rumbling laugh, as though a prison term were equally a part of the jest. "I on'y got three months on account it was mah first time an' I was on'y eighteen year old. But it were mah pappy's fourth time, an' they give him the full five years – he died inside."

"Say – how much money is there in moonshine liquor?" one of the Negro inmates asked with manifest commercial interest.

"It's a whackin' good business," Jude answered with enthusiasm. "You kin make a hunnerd, hunnerd 'n' fifty dollars a week with jus' one small still. The Law ketches some guys, a'course, but on'y one outa five about."

"How come you gave it up, then?" the other asked sceptically.

"Whiskey makin's hard work, man! All night long workin' like an ol' mule in them woods 'n' mountins. I like to take it easy."

Listening to this talk, Varney thought to himself: "But *I'm* not afraid of hard work, *I've* never made money by a racket – what the hell am I doin' in here with guys like them?"

Varney knew, of course, that the question would sound absurd if he asked it aloud. He was here because he had killed a man. Yet for him that was only a superficial answer. He had come to feel that there was some mystery to his life, something big and sinister. He had no belief in God or the Devil – yet there seemed to be malign forces in the universe that again and again had interfered maliciously with his efforts, tossing him about like a cork on a tide. Other men were born to hard circumstances, he wasn't the only one, yet somehow they shaped their lives and made them good in a way he never was able. He had worked like a dog from the time he was ten, but what sort of control had he had over his own fortunes? So very little – always on the outside looking in! Other men held down steady jobs during an economic depression, but he was one of those who got the rough end of the stick – nothing open, buddy. War came, and other men got through it all right, but hard-luck Varney ended in a hospital. How many men were there who went to bed with other men's wives and had themselves a bit of fun, and nothing ever came of it? Not Varney! It was his luck to meet up with a crazy husband and a lying bitch of a wife, and a thick-headed jury that couldn't understand that the killing was an accident. All of his life it had been the same... but why... how... for what reason? It was as though he had been born under an evil star, like some people said. He didn't believe in the power of stars, he didn't believe in anything supernatural – yet there had to be some explanation for all that had befallen him. *Something* had brought him together with Mrs Peterson, some force outside himself had dealt him this crooked hand. And if it wasn't a personal Fate that had been following him from the moment he was born, then what the hell was it?

It was at this point in his thinking that Varney always became confused. In the tragedy that had evolved between him and Mrs Peterson, it was quite true that accident and coincidence had played a part, as they do in all events. Nevertheless, what Varney was as an individual had been much more decisive in bringing him to this courthouse. But this, since he was blindly human, he could not perceive.

Once, in a moment of rare self-disclosure, he had said to Janey Welch, "You know something? Seems to me that all my life I've been searching for something I can't find."

"What?" she had asked.

"That's it, I don't know."

He didn't know, and never would. And if someone had told him that he was an inwardly lonely, distrustful man, and that he lacked confidence in other people and in himself, he would not have understood. He had bought Janey imported champagne for her birthday, but it was not this that could satisfy either of them.

That birthday night had ended badly. Although they had smoothed over their quarrel, Varney had been left in a disgruntled mood, and Janey had developed a headache. The next morning, when he came to work, she was not there. As it turned out, he never saw her again. He set out that evening to call at her home, but he never reached it.

It was Varney's habit after work to stop in for a cocktail at one hotel bar or another. He was not much of a drinking man, and it was not the liquor he wanted. And although he became embarrassed in trying to explain his feelings to Janey, he knew exactly the satisfaction he sought – the sense that at last he belonged in the world of good living. There was no way for him to communicate the profound sense of achievement that burgeoned within him when he stepped into the bar of a fine hotel, taking his seat and ordering a drink on a plane of equality with everyone there. Just to be there was the triumph – to be in the same room with men of substance, with army officers and government officials, and with their women – those glossy, exquisitely dressed women. Nor was there any way for him to explain to Janey why he so relished taking her to such places – or why, pretty as she was, she became more attractive to him when a waiter said: "Yes, sir, right away."

So it was that Varney stepped into a bar early one evening in April and, by accident, met a handsome woman in her late twenties who was destined to shatter his life. Yet, no more than with Varney, was it an accident that Harriet Peterson was alone in a hotel bar. She was an unhappy woman who had, of late, taken to seeking company in such places. Ten years married, with a daughter of six, she was her husband's concubine rather than his wife – possessed, but not loved, used but only superficially valued. Her husband, who was a textile manufacturer, was a handsome, aggressive man, robust and lusty. He also was intensely self-centred, as tempestuous in his angers as an infant, acquisitive and furiously possessive. Anything that belonged to him was precious not because he cherished it intrinsically, but because it was his. And whether his wife was of greater importance to him than his automobile or his fishing tackle, or an excellent piece of real estate, Harriet never knew. She did come to learn that he wanted to possess not only her, but every pliant female who came his way.

Had she been a more independent woman and less afraid of her husband, she would have demanded a divorce. Being what she was, she sought revenge for his adulteries by her own. In the course of time she had advanced from discreet affairs with men of her own set to reckless intimacies with strangers. On this night the man was to be Floyd Varney. Harriet had come to Washington with her husband and child for the Easter vacation. Her child was asleep in their suite with a hotel maid acting as guardian, and her husband, who was seeking a government contract, was out for the night. It was the kind of opportunity she put to use.

It would not have occurred to Varney to initiate advances to a woman like Mrs Peterson. There was a sleek elegance to her appearance that placed her, for him, in the shining world on the other side of the railway tracks. Although he was confident of his own appearance, since he was sporting several months' savings in the form of a new hat, topcoat and tailored suit, he was too lately arrived to a position in life to regard himself as anything but an interloper. Nevertheless, he was at once keenly aware of his attractive neighbour at the crowded bar, and he was not loath to engage in small talk when she gave him the opportunity. She was, he learnt, a divorcee from Philadelphia, in town for a short stay. He, with equal honesty, told her that he was the manager and part owner of a hotel. An hour later they were in a taxicab on the way to his apartment.

If Mrs Peterson had her private reasons for offering herself so casually to a stranger, Varney had a compulsive need to respond. It was much more than male rut for a willing female. Throughout all of his deprived, vagrant youth and his latter years as an enlisted man in the Marine Corps, unattainable women like Mrs Peterson had gazed at him alluringly from society pages and movie screens. Mrs Peterson was the classy dame who belonged to other, more fortunate men; here, for the asking, was the glittering, anointed lay* that always had kindled his curiosity and desire.

They both were satisfied with what they got. Mrs Peterson was not dismayed by his cheaply furnished one-room apartment. She already had guessed that he was not what he represented himself to be, and it lent spice to this particular episode. Varney was strong and greedy in the way he made love to her, and she responded with an abandoned carnality that, for the moment, seemed to her adequate surrogate for the love she really wanted in life.

The experience was deeply satisfying to Varney. He felt more important in his own eyes, more substantial as a personality. When Mrs Peterson was about to leave, he asked when he could see her again. She would not commit herself. Out of a desire to test his power over a woman like this – whose name he did not even know – he told her his own name and the hotel where he worked, and said casually that she could telephone him if she wished.

Two mornings later she called him. It was about ten o'clock, and she asked him to come to a room in the hotel where they had met. Varney, feeling deeply triumphant, suggested an appointment after work. Mrs Peterson replied that she was leaving town – if he wanted to see her it had to be then. He said he would come. He made an excuse of family illness to the hotel management and received permission to leave.

When he arrived, Varney realized at once that Mrs Peterson had lied to him about her marital status. Obviously, no single woman would engage a suite of connecting bedrooms. Mrs Peterson laughed and admitted that she was married. She explained that her husband and daughter had gone to Mount Vernon* for the day, and she wanted Varney now, here and now, and wasn't he glad? Yes, he replied, he was very glad, but couldn't they go to his apartment? She replied by removing her gown. Varney thought to himself that surely he had got mixed up with a crazy, reckless dame, but he didn't leave. This conquest was too satisfying.

In the deepest layer of Varney's being, he believed that life was his enemy, that it always would turn on him and betray him. Life had done this to him so often that by now he expected it. For this reason one part of him was resigned, almost not startled, when he heard a hoarse cry of horror and turned to see a man in the doorway of the connecting room.

It was, of course, an accident that Peterson had returned to the hotel at this moment. On the way to visit the shrine of George Washington his daughter had developed an earache, and he had turned back. Since his wife had pleaded illness as an excuse for not accompanying them, he entered their suite by the child's room and tiptoed to the doorway to see if she were asleep. He went quite out of his senses at the spectacle confronting him.

Despite the fact that he had been sexually profligate for years, Peterson was of the opinion that his marriage was a good one. Of his wife's infidelities he knew nothing. Theirs was one of those unions in which all of the outer forms are observed, everything proper and in order – nothing missing except love. And if Peterson was aware that latterly his wife had taken to having dark moods and fits of weeping, he ascribed it to the mystery of feminine psychology, and was neither perturbed nor concerned. It was of the essence of bitter comedy that this man should go berserk with rage upon discovering that his conjugal property was being trespassed. After a single moment of unendurable anguish, he turned irrational and murderous. He wanted to kill not only Varney, but his wife.

As Varney learnt later, it also was accidental that there was a weapon in the room. Peterson had a partner in business who was a sportsman and a collector of weapons. The day before he had bought his partner a curio, a jewel-studded Gurkha knife* with a curved, heavy blade. He remembered it now, and he leapt across the room to the bureau drawer in which he had placed it.

Peterson was a big man, physically strong, but he was inexperienced in the use of weapons. By the time he had secured the knife and swung around, Varney was out of bed, crouched and ready in the centre of the room. Varney was sick with terror, but he was reacting automatically, with the command of a war veteran trained in hand-to-hand combat. As Peterson rushed at him with the heavy knife held high in his left hand for a downward slash, Varney did not retreat. Instead, with a quick, forward leap, he blocked the other man's swinging arm with his own forearm and, in the same instant, caught him in a wrist lock with his other hand. For a second they were at equilibrium. Then, with a sharp, backward snap, Varney toppled Peterson to the floor, dislocating his shoulder.

Peterson screamed. It was a hoarse, animal bellow of fury and physical agony. Yet, almost as quickly as his body struck the floor, he rolled over and raised to his knees. The knife had been flung backwards out of his hand. He saw it, and saw that he was closer to it than Varney. "Don't touch it," Varney cried. But in the same instant Peterson lunged forward and secured it with his good hand.

It was at this moment that Varney himself – not Fate and not accident – decided his own future. Peterson had the knife, but he was badly handicapped and still on the floor. Varney could have grappled with him and secured the weapon. He did not. Instead, as Peterson struggled to his feet and turned around, Varney struck him. It was a violent, knife-like blow to the Adam's apple, delivered judo-style with the outer edge of his open hand.

Later, in the trial, the prosecutor contended that the blow had been deliberate – calculated with malice to maim or kill. It was less than true. At that moment Varney had no more conscious malice than a boy who, in rage and fright, hurls at a tormentor whatever is at hand, whether it be a piece of bread, a milk bottle or a table knife. Nevertheless, the blow was a mortal one. It fractured Peterson's larynx and caused a haemorrhage into his windpipe. Gasping for air, he collapsed, coughed several times, and was dead of suffocation within a few minutes.

Varney did not know that he had killed; he assumed that the man was stunned. Peterson had fallen face down with one arm blocking a view of his face. Since Varney's only thought was to escape from the room, he did not pause to investigate.

Harriet Peterson had not uttered a cry or moved from the bed from the time her husband appeared. In a blur of stupefaction she watched Varney thrust on his clothes, mutter "He'll be all right" and run from the room. She came to her senses when her six-year-old child, who was standing in the doorway of the connecting room, began to scream to her.

A moment later she was by her husband's side. She turned him over to discover that his face was bluish, dreadful to gaze upon, and that there was a bloody pool soaking into the carpet. She telephoned in hysteria for a doctor.

It was not long after that the police were summoned, but by the time they arrived Mrs Peterson had fabricated a version of the events that was designed to protect her honour before society. In doing this she bore no ill will towards Varney, and had no desire to do him harm. The lies she impulsively told concerned an utter stranger who had used force upon a chaste wife and mother. She merely overlooked the fact that Varney's overcoat and hat were still in her room, and that they bore his initials.

To Varney this was another of the ill-fated accidents that had cursed him from the moment he met Mrs Peterson. But it was no accident at all that a weak, anguished woman, rather than admit infidelity, should invent a dramatic tale of rape.

The story she related was as follows. Her husband and child had left the hotel about ten thirty in the morning for a trip to Mount Vernon. She had remained in her room because of a headache. Half an hour later, feeling somewhat better, she dressed and went out, intending to get some fresh air. In the hotel corridor, however, she became dizzy and apparently fainted. She had no memory of subsequent events until she awakened on her bed. A strange man was there. He explained that he had found her unconscious on the floor of the corridor, had searched her purse for a door key and carried her into the room. Then, before she could say anything, he produced a switch-blade knife from his pocket, pressed the point to her throat and said that he would kill her if she screamed. She fainted again. She stated that she repeatedly returned to consciousness and repeatedly fainted during the time the man was with her. How long it was she could not tell with accuracy. She did know that he used her sexually more than once, and that he threatened her with the knife each time she became lucid and pleaded with him to leave.

In her signed deposition to the police, Mrs Peterson stated also that she was conscious when her husband appeared. She recounted the struggle between the two men more or less as it had occurred. This aspect of her testimony was supported by her child, who made an affecting witness in court as she described the ghastly struggle between her father and a strange, naked man. A high point of the trial, in fact, was the moment when the child, in tears, identified Varney.

Mrs Peterson's lies were impulsive, but they never were disproved. To lend an aura of persuasion, there was her position in good society. Both she and her husband had come from well-to-do Baltimore families, and were considered a devoted couple. In addition, Charles Peterson, as a textile manufacturer, had many friends in the world of commerce. It was sworn to everywhere that he was a jovial, friendly man, free from violent tendencies.

Varney was arrested the following morning. At the haberdashery where he had bought his clothes on a time-payment plan there was a record of his place of employment. He had come to work as usual, even though he knew that he had left his coat and hat in the Peterson suite. Assuming, as he did, that Charles Peterson was only injured, he felt himself in no danger. It seemed likely to him that the Petersons would keep quiet about the affair in order to avoid scandal. When he was arrested on a charge of rape and murder, he went to pieces. He tried at first to deny knowledge of the woman, and this later was used against him as evidence of guilt – as was the additional fact that he had fled the scene. Confronted with the hat and coat, he denied they were his. Asked to explain where he had gone the previous morning when he left work, and what the name of his sick relative was, he had fallen into terror-stricken silence. Finally, he broke down in tears. He admitted that he knew Mrs Peterson and told the detectives what had happened.

Ten days later, Varney was indicted for homicide. Although the charge of rape was not included in the indictment, it nevertheless remained a central issue in his trial. If George Combs, Varney's attorney, had been able to prove that the couple were lovers prior to the fatal incident, it would have been clear that Varney had come to the hotel room with Mrs Peterson's consent. In that case his death struggle with Charles Peterson would have been more clearly a matter of self-defence. However, Combs could not produce concrete evidence on this point. The bartender's memory was too hazy to convince a jury, and the hotel doorman recalled nothing. The taxi driver who had taken the couple to Varney's apartment never could be found.

For lack of any of this critical evidence, Varney's contention of a willing adulteress was not accepted by the jury as a whole. On the other hand, there also were improbable aspects to Mrs Peterson's testimony. Her tale of rape found little support in the fact that none of her garments had been torn, that she herself had suffered no injuries and – most important – that the man had felt sufficiently at ease to remove his own clothing. The defence also pointed out that Varney had reported to work as usual that morning, but had left after a telephone call. Mrs Peterson's hotel had no record of the call, because she, with a thought to her husband, had gone down to the lobby and dialled from a booth. Nevertheless, there was strange coincidence in the fact that Varney had left work and turned up a short time later in the Peterson suite.

Since the members of the jury were of varying opinions on the issue – nine contending adultery, three rape – the indisputable medical testimony of the coroner assumed the greatest importance. The autopsy had established that Peterson's left shoulder had been dislocated before he was killed. This was very damaging to Varney. The prosecution argued that since any man with an injury of that type would be virtually helpless in a physical struggle, further injuries leading to death must have been inflicted by his assailant for reasons other than self-defence. Moreover, it was brought forth that Varney, a former member of the Marine Corps, was well trained in judo fighting. The prosecutor summoned an expert to testify that any man so trained knew that there were a number of extremely vulnerable spots in the human body. One of these was the larynx, or Adam's apple. A severe blow delivered there, particularly with the side of the hand, could kill.

On this point, more than any other, Varney was held culpable. His plea that he had slashed out blindly, with no intention of striking at the throat, was not accepted. The blow itself was unnecessary, the jury decided, and therefore it was not a justifiable homicide.

Yet a decisive question still remained to be settled: whether or not Varney had been the master of his own passions. It was on this issue that Combs strove the hardest in his defence. For it was the jury's duty to decide the legal nature of the homicide. Combs was hoping for a verdict of involuntary manslaughter, while the US Attorney, prosecuting for the government, sought to prove that there had been conscious intent to kill, even if only at the spur of the moment, and that therefore the crime was murder.

Combs, arguing out of deepest conviction, pointed to the law governing homicide. An essential element in the crime of murder, in either the first or second degree, was the factor of malice. What was malice? he asked. It was the *intentional* injury of another without just cause or excuse. Whereas manslaughter was something entirely different. A man who drove an automobile without sufficient care, and thereby killed a pedestrian, was guilty of manslaughter, but never of murder, because the factor of malice was absent. So also it was not murder, but manslaughter, when two men quarrelled, fought in passion, and one was killed. The law rejected the concept of murder in any situation where passions suddenly were aroused to an uncontrollable degree and a slaying was the unpremeditated result. Was this surely not the case with Varney? Even Mrs Peterson had testified that her husband's attack had been sudden and violent, and that he had been armed with a deadly weapon while Varney was barehanded. Which member of the jury in Varney's place, he asked, would not have been terrified out of his senses, and in a state of uncontrollable fear and passion?

Finally, striving to bolster what he knew was the weakest part of Varney's defence, Combs grappled with the coroner's testimony. Peterson's left shoulder had been dislocated, but he then had seized the knife in his right hand. Therefore, was he any the less dangerous to Varney *after* his shoulder was injured than before? Not substantially! Varney still was in mortal danger, and still mortally afraid of an armed man who was trying to kill him. Was it reasonable to assert that a man in that position remained calm, or could act with deliberation and care? Such a man defended himself without thought – he struck out blindly and, unfortunately, sometimes killed. But that was manslaughter, not murder with malice, and it was to embrace such situations that the law had been written as it had.

So Combs had argued, with conviction and eloquence, and Varney had listened with bursting gratitude in his heart. But then had come a deadly rebuttal by the US Attorney. Two things, he reminded the jury, had occurred at the moment in which Peterson fell injured to the floor. The first was that he rose to his knees and looked for the knife. The second was that Varney cried out: "*Don't touch it!*"

What did that warning imply? he asked. Was the man who spoke it in a state of uncontrolled passion? Of course not! Such a man could have shoved Peterson, grappled with him or done any number of things in self-protection. Such a man clearly was in possession of himself and, if he were trained in judo fighting, was quite capable of directing his blows. Indeed Floyd Varney had! That blow to the larynx had taken aim and deliberation: one did not strike there by accident. It had been motivated by malice, by a desire to seriously injure, if not kill. The prosecutor also quoted from the law: "Cooling time intervening, giving the reason an opportunity to resume its throne, a homicide will cease to be manslaughter and become murder."

Varney had shivered and wept inside as he listened to this, wanting to scream out to the heavens that the blow had not been deliberate, that he had been so frightened he couldn't think, that he didn't even recall the cry "Don't touch it!" Finally, unable to support his feelings any more, he had ceased to listen.

It was a tricky case, and the decision to be arrived at was not easy, and the jury had been split for some time. On the first ballot two jurors (accepting the thesis of rape), had held for first-degree murder, five for second, five for manslaughter. Some hours later, the count stood at eight for second degree, four for manslaughter. Finally, after sixteen hours, the panel arrived at a decision dictated less by uniform conviction than by fatigue and confusion. The crime was held to be one of second degree, and Varney was liable for ten years to life.

* * *

At every step of the judicial process, Harriet Peterson had told herself that Varney would escape prison. At first, believing the killing to be an accident, she had sought not to involve him at all. When this failed, she dealt with her guilty conscience by persuading herself that he would be held innocent in spite of her tale of rape. After he was declared guilty, it was far too late for her to admit the truth: by then she had testified under oath and was herself liable for perjury. In addition, she had begun to tell herself that Varney was partially guilty, at least because he had gone too far: there had been no necessity for that final killing blow. Therefore, if he received a short sentence, it would be not altogether unjust, and perhaps she would find some way, anonymously, to send him some money when he was released.

In this manner a woman and a man, strangers in more ways than one, had come together and had been enmeshed by the poverty in their hearts* and in their past lives. Since a dead man could not be indicted for his failings as a husband, Peterson was not to be found in the dock at Varney's side. Nor could an indictment be returned against a Tennessee farmhand who had seduced an illiterate girl of sixteen and then turned his back upon their child. Varney alone was indicted, since his was the hand that had killed, and no witness came forward in his defence from the social jungle into which he had been cast, and in which he had learnt to hunger for all those things denied him – a monogrammed hat and a Cadillac car and a glittering woman.

But now Varney had been convicted of second-degree murder, and he was sweating with fear as he sat in the detention room waiting to be sentenced to prison by a man he did not know, a man who did not know him. As a convicted prisoner will do, he had pondered to excess the convulsive moment, the fatal, irretrievable turning point at which things had gone wrong. Why had he struck Peterson instead of disarming him or pinning him to the floor, or doing one of the many other things possible? Why, by accident, had he struck so true and deadly a blow?

Deep, deep in Varney's heart he sensed the answer, but he never exposed it to himself. Behind this accident were his thirty years of resentment – the anger of a man who has lived badly for those who always have lived fatly and well; anger at the woman for enticing him into her bed out of malice towards her husband, when they could have been safe in his apartment; anger at the husband for returning; anger at both of them (both so elegant and well born and moneyed) for not contenting each other; the stored rancour of his childhood and youth when he had walked shivering through too many towns on winter nights and stared with suffering loneliness at too many lighted windows. All of this was buried in Varney's heart, and he felt it. But it was a type of knowledge that many people sense about themselves, yet never fully comprehend. He told himself only that he was innocent of intention to do wrong, and this was true. And so he sat in the bull pen and asked himself an anguished question: "If God made me, where the hell has He been all my life?"

Only, it was not God who had made either him or Harriet Peterson what they were.

In cell block CB1 all hands were momentarily occupied. The hour after breakfast, said Authority, must be devoted to sanitation. Governments might fall or tornadoes sweep the land, but at seven thirty-five every morning came the first count and inspection.

On the eating range of the west wing the Negro mess mates were scrubbing down the tables and mopping the large expanse of floor. In all cells bunks were being made up army-style, sinks cleaned, walls and steel bars wiped free of dust. The small stores of personal belongings, bought by inmates in canteen, were being arranged in orderly fashion. In addition, a work detail of half a dozen men was cleaning the tier runway under the supervision of Lauter and Quinn. These six, who were volunteers, considered it a privilege to sweep, mop and scour for forty minutes twice a day. By this labour they earned several rewards: an interruption in the monotony of close confinement, the chance to converse with men other than their cellmates and the right to a daily shower bath. When any man on work detail left for other pastures, there always were volunteers for his assignment.

Over the noise of this work there was the steady, wordless murmur that was jailhouse conversation; now and then it was punctuated by coughs, by a hushed burst of laughter or by the intermittent rush of water in toilets. Now also the usual commodity exchange commenced between men in different cells. A man in the corner of one cell could hand an object to an unseen neighbour standing in the corner of the cell adjacent, two hands reaching out into space, touching, exchanging. Jail rules did not forbid this, and so, all day long, a type of commerce and barter went on. A resident of 126, under twenty-year sentence for assault with intent to commit rape, knocked on the steel sheet separating him from 128. Invariably this signal was honoured, and the narcotic addict in 128 walked to the wall, rapped in reply and then directed his words towards the tier runway: "What ya want?"

"Can ya loan me a coupla, three, four cigarettes?"

"What d'ya mean, 'loan'? You've had more'n a packet* from me this week, an' I don't see no smokes comin' back. You think I'm a slot machine?"

"But I told ya, I'm expectin' a money order from my brother. I'll pay ya."

"Yeah, but canteen ain't till Wednesday, an' I'm runnin' short. One is all I can spare."

"OK, thanks." (One was all he had expected.)

In cell 116 a hand rapped on the wall, and in 114 a hand rapped back. 116 asked if anybody had a stamp and an envelope to spare, and 114 answered: "Hell, no, this post office has gone broke." Automatically 116 rapped on the wall of 118.

Since this was a community based on equality of deprivation, men shared with each other, borrowed and loaned as they would not have in the dog-eat-dog freedom of the street. Each of them had experienced the difficulties of his initial commitment, in which he was deprived of all personal property. Until a new man could apply for a canteen book, receive his book and make canteen, he was powerless to buy a toothbrush, a stamp, a cigarette. For this reason any new man with a money receipt was extended credit by other inmates; those who entered without funds depended on charity, and fared less well.

Down the tier line, back and forth, went a miscellany of items precious to men behind bars: a newspaper, some tobacco, a rubber cylinder used to roll cigarettes; a fountain pen, a sheet of paper; a personal note from one friend to another, a joke whispered down the line, a jar of body deodorant. Since this was a Monday morning, cigarettes were getting low, and the quest for smokes was rising to its twice-a-week height. The small jars of body deodorant, owned by some of the men, were beginning to circulate among the more fastidious, because it was two days since the last shower bath, two days before the next. Lauter carried a nail clipper from 110 to 104; 120 borrowed a pencil from 122; 114 exchanged comics with 112. The jailhouse stock exchange was in full swing.

Alfrice Tillman, mopping the floor of the eating range with easy, practised strokes, worked his way up to the steel screen of the tier runway and called in a low voice to Eddie Quinn, "Hey, Barber, how's for a smoke?" Quinn, who was passing out toilet paper, turned around and glanced over Tillman's head as though no one were there. He said: "Anybody speak to me?"

"C'mon, Barber, one of your specials."

"Hand me a laugh."

Tillman, who was very handsome, had the flexible features of a naturally endowed comedian. He puffed out his cheeks as though they were made of rubber, crossed his eyes and wiggled his ears. Laughing, Quinn replied in kind: he pushed his upper denture out of place, rattled it with his tongue – and meanwhile reached into his breast pocket for a tobacco can. His "specials" were cigarettes rolled with a mixture of pipe and cigarette tobacco, the latter coming from the tag end of cigarettes collected daily from other men; the final product was an enormously potent smoke. He slipped one of the neat cylinders through the steel mesh. Tillman said "Thanks, pal" and thrust the cigarette clownishly into the socket of his ear. Then, with a quick glance up forward to check whether the tier guard was watching, he asked: "How's for an airmail stamp, chum?"

"Do I look like the US govinment to you?"

"No, but you sure look like you're some banker or big oil man in the free world."

"Shoh 'nuff," Quinn responded. He slipped into a dialect he considered Negro. "I'se jist so busy an' so damn important, I can't be bothered with trash like you." He gestured with one of the rolls of toilet paper. "Can't y'all see my account books?" He walked off laughing.

Tillman, with a grin, returned to his mopping. His clowning had a purpose. He had come into jail on the Friday just past, and so he had not yet received his canteen book. Although his tier mates had been supplying him with cigarettes to the best of their ability, there was a limit to what a small group of men could do – especially when they knew that his funds were meagre and he could not be expected to pay back. As a result, after two days of tobacco hunger, Tillman had taken to what he called "workin' the ofays" during the clean-up period. This consisted of telling spicy stories, of clowning around and of otherwise earning the nickname of Vaudeville from the men on Tier One. In return for this had come cigarettes and – though he was unaware of it – the growing hostility of his comrades. Tillman considered his tomfoolery an efficient way of extracting loot from white men he despised, but the other Negroes regarded it in a different light. Dewey Spaulding, who was particularly incensed, whispered to Isaac Reeves: "I told you last night. A real, happy ass-licker for Uncle Charlie. I'd like to kick his teeth out."

"Now, take it easy," the older man replied, frowning. "I've been thinkin' since you spoke to me. Canteen comes Wednesday. Seein' I don't smoke myself, I'll keep him supplied with a packet a day. I can afford it."

"But what happens till Wednesday? Maybe you don't want any fight with him because he's your cellmate. But I'll be damned if *I'll* let him carry on like that."

"Now, take it easy," Reeves repeated. "I'll speak to him. He's just a boy."

"He's just a goddamn natural-born Uncle Tom.* It isn't the cigarettes alone. He likes to play the nigger fool for whites. Just look at him now."

Further down the range, Tillman had stopped his mopping and had snagged Quinn's attention again. Holding the lighted end of a cigarette in his mouth, he was making a clever pretence of chewing it. Not only Quinn, but a number of men in the cell row behind, rewarded* him with laughter. Tillman said quickly, "How's for that airmail stamp, big shot?"

Quinn gazed at him with mock disdain. "Look who's talkin'. What do you need with a stamp? You can't write."

"I know I can't," Tillman retorted. "Jus' wanna look at the picture on it."

"So hand me a laugh."

"I jus' did."

"Hand me another."

Tillman glanced up front and quickly returned to his mopping. "If I hand you half a laugh, will you gimme a three-cent stamp?"

"OK."

"Good. It was only a three-cent stamp I wanted in the first place."

Quinn laughed.

"Gimme the stamp, Barber."

"Gimme a laugh first."

"You jus' laughed."

"Only a quarter of a laugh. Say, Vaudeville – what you in here for anyway?"

"You mean the charge on me?"

"Yeah."

"No charge at all."

"Come on – come on."

"I mean it!" Tillman's mopping slowed. "Ain't you heard what happened to me?"

"What?"

"Saddy night, a week ago, I was out after some honey. Had me an address from a friend, said it was the cleanest place he ever was in. Went up to the door – there was a red light on top. Looked at my address – it was the right address." Tillman paused in his mopping, stepped up to the range screen and gestured. "Knocked on the door. No answer. Knocked again." He paused dramatically. "Big door opened. Nice-appearin' white man looked out. Said: 'What you want?' I said: 'Want some tail.' He said: 'OK, haul your tail inside.'" Tillman extended both hands, palms up. "Here I am. Just a case of wrong address. Now the no-good bastids won't let me go."

Laughter rippled out from several cells.

"Cigarette?" Tillman asked, glancing quickly towards the front of the range. "Who's got one for me? Handed you a laugh, didn't I?"

112 responded, and a cigarette passed from Quinn to Tillman; a man in 110 threw another accurately through the range screen. Tillman said "Thank you, gentlemen", thrust a cigarette into the socket of each ear and continued his mopping. Suddenly, with the euphoria of a successful performer, he exclaimed: "You fellers know about this guy? Watch out for him, he's a dangerous customer." Tillman was referring to Huey Wilson, who was drying off a nearby table. Wilson glanced up, but went on with his work.

"Yeah, Lord God, this sure is one dangerous customer," Tillman continued with comic relish. "Got him booked in here for assault with two felonious weapons – not just one... two."

"What'd he do?" a voice called* from one of the cells.

"Beat hell out of a man with his two weapons. One wasn't enough for him – he used two. Sent him to the hospital."

"What kind of weapons?" asked Quinn, waiting for the payoff.

"Show 'em your weapons, big boy," Tillman said.

Face averted, Huey kept silent. He felt humiliation and wild anger at this effort to make a spectacle of him before white men. He didn't know what to say or do.

"C'mon, don't be bashful," Tillman persisted. "They's waitin' to see those deadly weapons you carry."

Huey swiped at the table top, glanced up and then yielded to his feelings. He said with rage: "Why don't you kiss my ass?" Finished with his work, he walked down to the front of the range to turn in his scouring powder and rags as the others were doing.

"You know what his two weapons was?" Tillman explained with an uncomfortable laugh to the white men on Tier One. "His feet. He kicked a man silly, sent him to the hospital. He's got about the biggest-size feet I ever seen. It's writ on his indictment: 'Assault with two deadly weapons'. Sure thing – so help me God... Say, Barber, get me that stamp, will you, General?" He saluted in mock fashion, then strolled down to the front of the range, holding the mop over his shoulder like a rifle, playing for a laugh. Huey Wilson, on his way back to the staircase with the other mess men, passed him by with his eyes on the roof.

"What makes you so damn highfalutin?" Tillman asked bitterly out of the corner of his mouth. Huey ignored him. At the last cell he paused, letting the others go on ahead, and then called in a low tone. McPeak, who had been pacing, came to the bars, took the match he was chewing out of his mouth and said in a worried, morose manner, "I'm writ down for sick call, young feller."

"That's fine. Stay to the back end of the line, will you? They tell me we'll get more time to talk that way."

"OK, sure. How's this work treatin' your ribs?"

"I've been taking it easy – it doesn't bother me. Only hurts when I take a deep breath."

"I don't think you've got anything broken there."

"I hope not. Have you…" Huey paused as Tillman passed by. Tillman glared at him, his good-looking face working with resentment, and Huey returned a contemptuous stare. "Have you heard any more about your clothes?"

"Not a thing."

"I'll ask some of the men on my tier. They might have an idea."

"I'll appreciate that."

"Say… I forgot to tell you before… the exact charges against you are assault—"

"You there!" It was Mr Simmons standing behind the range gate, thirty yards off, pointing his finger. "Upstairs!" His tone was loud, and it was commanding, and it expected to be obeyed. Huey left.

On the fourth tier, as soon as the cell doors had slammed shut, an angry conversation began. Huey had been assigned to the last cell with Eugene Finnerty; next door were Tillman and Isaac Reeves, and on the other side were Spaulding and Wellman. Since they were at the far end of the tier from the officer on duty, Tillman felt free to speak. "Hey you, the new man – Wilson," he called. He was standing at the bars, gripping them. "I wanna talk to you."

It was not only Huey who walked to the front of his cell, but the other men also. All knew what had occurred downstairs.

"What do you want?" Huey asked coldly.

"What's the idea?"

"Of what?"

"Goddamn it, you know what – of makin' a fool outa me in front of those white men!"

Huey had no chance to reply. "Why, how'd he do that?" Spaulding interrupted from the cell on the other side.

"I ast him to show 'em his feet, an' he told me to kiss his ass," Tillman exploded in fury.

"Isn't that what you've been doing to those white men for two days?" Spaulding enquired with savage bite. "If you can be so happy kissing white ass, what's the matter with Wilson's?"

"I don't kiss nobody's ass!" Tillman shouted. "Not white, not black, not green!"

"So you say! Clowning around… playing the fool… Uncle-Tomming the damn white trash on that first tier so they'll give you cigarettes."

"I'm usin' 'em!" Tillman retorted cholerically. "I play up to a white man for anythin' I can git offa him. What's wrong with that? You think I like 'em? I hate every damn one of 'em – but I use 'em!"

"You're not using them: they're using you. They've got a funny nigger boy in you. You're just what they want in a coloured man."

"Goddamn you, shut up!" shouted Tillman. "I'll kick the livin' piss out of you."

"You'll kick who – when?"

"I know your kind!" Tillman continued in a wild rage. "Think you're hot stuff cos you got money – a big-numbers man. Hotshot Spaulding, the big race leader, he's gonna tell everybody else how t'act."

"Shut up, you – you're not a Negro," Spaulding snapped contemptuously. "You're just a white man's patsy, you're a drag on the race."

"Goddamn you, I'll—"

From the far end of the tier came a shout from the guard: "Quiet down there!"

Tillman instantly slipped to the rear of the cell. He sank down on the wall seat with clenched, trembling hands. "That dirty son of a bitch," he cried to his cellmate, Reeves, in an appeal for support. "Where does he get off t'talk to me like that?"

Reeves said nothing. He offered no word of sympathy or comment, and Tillman realized instantly that something was wrong. "What's the matter with you?" he asked bitterly. "You sidin' with them?"

Reeves ran a hand over his woolly grey hair and kept silent. His eyes, which were jet-black and lustrous, were fixed upon Tillman with a look of such compassion that the younger man became uneasy. In the three days of their close confinement he had come to respect Reeves very greatly. Reeves had sons of Tillman's own age who already were established in life – as he himself was not and never expected to be. Reeves was the father he never had had, a family man who lived clean and worked hard and took care of his own. He wanted desperately to have Reeves on his side of this quarrel, which was agitating him profoundly. "You know I ain't got no canteen book. I gotta organize me some smokes somehow, don't I?" he asked defensively.

"Well… the other fellers have been doin' their best to help you out," Reeves reminded him. He, too, didn't like the way Tillman had been behaving, but he knew the jungle life of slum and alley to which Tillman had been born – and in which he still lived – and he felt sympathy for the youth. "Haven't they?" he asked.

"Sure, but it ain't enough! I'm a heavy smoker. An' in this place a feller gets nerves – he needs t'smoke even more. What's wrong anyway with shakin' down that white trash?"

Reeves, searching for the proper words with which to explain, remained silent.

"Damn it, you got something on your mind. Why don't you speak it out?"

"The fellers here are startin' to talk hard on you," Reeves answered slowly. "Say you *like* playin' the funny little nigger boy for those white men downstairs."

"Who says?" Tillman asked fiercely. "Spaulding – that tony* son of a bitch?"

"All of us – me too!"

"Christ," Tillman exclaimed in bewilderment and indignation, "I don't get it. You talk like I was the only one ever played up to the damn pecks* t'get somethin' from 'em. We all does it – we has to! I suppose you never said 'Yes, sir' with a great big smile to some white bastard when you wanted t'say 'Go screw yourself'? Or when Spaulding pays off hush money on his policy station, I suppose he don't glad-hand them white cops?"

Frowning, searching for words, Reeves answered, "What a Negro man *has* to do is one thing. *How* he does it is another. An' what he don't have to do *at all* is still another. We ain't askin' you to spit in the eye of one of the guards in here when he gives you an order. You has to do what he says. We're talkin' about different things."

"How different? Exactly how?" Tillman demanded. "You're callin' me a damn handkerchief head* for gettin' somethin' I need, that's all. But what about you when you're workin' on a job for a white boss? Christ, the first job I ever had was for a tan hustler lived in Goat Alley, three doors from where me an' my ma lived. She usta send me out on the street lookin' up customers for her. I was nine years old, an' I got five cents for a black man, ten for a white. But that's the way the world is for us coloured, ain't it? We gits what we can the way we has to. For that whore it was the only way she could live. For me it was the way t'go to the movies* or buy me a piece of candy. What's the difference now? I need smokes – I'll go nuts in here if I can't smoke."

Patiently, but with quiet stubbornness, Reeves said: "You're arguin' with me sixty a minute, boy, but you ain't stoppin' to think. You ain't nine years old now: you're a man. Suppose them white fellers downstairs say, 'Kneel down an' bump your black head six times if you want a cigarette.' You gonna do that?"

"You know damn well I wouldn't!"

"Why not? You need cigarettes so bad, why you ready t'stop there?"

Tillman was silent, suddenly at a loss for a reply. He stared intently at the older man.

"Look, boy," Reeves went on earnestly, "you need to stand off an' take a look at yourself. You think you're gettin' the best of those white fellers. But how you doin' it? You ain't man to man with 'em, askin' for cigarettes like you would with me. Neither is you jokin' with 'em on an even basis. They're throwin' you cigarettes jus' like they throw peanuts to a monkey in the zoo."

"You're crazy. You're dead wrong!"

"No I ain't! You can jump salty all you want, but they're sittin' downstairs sayin', 'That's how all them coons are, always laughin' an' happy even in jail – ain't got no brains, jus' like a monkey.' You're provin' it to 'em!"

"Screw you!" Tillman said vehemently. "Screw the whole lot of you. I don't know why you're all jumpin' on me, but I ain't buyin' it. I'm askin' for a transfer out of here, that's what I'm doin'."

"That's up to you," Reeves responded earnestly. "But if I was you, I'd do a little thinkin' too. You know *I* ain't got it in for you, Tillman. I like you, boy. But I think you been makin' a mistake."

"Ain't made *no* mistakes," Tillman snapped. "Not one."

"I'd miss you a lot if you was to move out of here,"* Reeves said quietly. He bent down and fumbled beneath his pillow. He found the match box he was looking for and emptied its contents on the blanket. Since no games were provided for transient prisoners, he had blocked

91

out a draught board on the back of a writing tablet, and he used paper slips, marked "R" and "B",* to represent the pieces. "C'mon," he said, "how about a game?"

"Ain't made no mistakes," Tillman repeated. "Not a one."

"A game of draughts'll do us both good."

"Don't feel like it," the youth muttered. "Leave me alone."

The conversation ended as a loudspeaker, high up on the wall of their wing – as in every other building within the jail – suddenly blared out with a strident command. "Now hear this!" a voice shouted from the central control room. "Now hear this! All units make your seven thirty-five count – all units make your count!"

In all buildings and on all tiers, in work rooms and hospital, in laundry, tailor shop and kitchen, the guards began counting the inmate popula- tion. Each officer telephoned his count to the main office – the total was checked, and then the loudspeakers blared again: "Attention all units! The count is clear – the count is clear!"

All was in good order at 7.35 in the morning, and jailhouse routine would proceed as usual.

Next door, Huey Wilson was pretending to take a nap so that he would not be obliged to talk to his cellmate, but he was not asleep. Like any new inmate, he was living uneasily in two worlds. Through his half-opened lids he could see steel bars in front of him, a difficult thing to accept. The bars were implacably there, yet he was teased by a sense of disbelief. He seemed to have been whirled by a tornado into another land, like the child in the classic story book that he always had loved.* Was it really himself in here, in this cubicle of steel and stone? The "real" world was so close at hand, not even as far as an eighteen-year-old could throw a baseball, yet behind these walls a different universe existed. Except, Huey thought suddenly, and not without bitterness, except that in here the same colour line was drawn, and Authority as usual had a white face.

Black and white, white and black, he reflected acidly. It was likely that all new men found it hard to accept the strangeness of being locked up, yet every Negro would know at once that jail was part of the same old Jim Crow world in which he always had lived – merely a danker spot in the familiar jungle. Any white man, for instance, could say that he lived in a city, but to a Negro that same city sheltered predatory animals who might come stalking him, and whole areas into which he could not penetrate. "If I were God," Huey's brother used to say when they were children, "I would change all coloured into white and all white into coloured for one month. Boy, that'd teach 'em – they'd be different to us then."

"Yes," Huey reflected now, they had wished for such miracles in their childhood, and they even had played a secret game together in which they pretended to be white. He could* not think harshly of either of them for their childish game, but the time for wishing miracles was past. He had been lying here the past quarter of an hour playing games with himself – dreaming that he never had walked on that picket line and that he never had been arrested. And, at the same time, dreaming even more ridiculously of the time when he would be an important judge, and a white hoodlum named Ballou would be brought before him, and he would say, "I know this man, a real Ku Kluxer. Lock him up and throw the key away."

Manure and hogwash! The truth was he was scared and bleeding sorry for himself. He was feeling just as abused as he and Jeff used to feel when they were kids and didn't know what made the world go round. Only, he was eighteen now, and it was time he knew what every Negro must know: not to whine because white oppression had singled *him* out in a special way as it had tens of thousands of Negroes before; not to cry because they were threatening *him* with prison, or because *he* might lose his job and be set back in his education. His father never had had schooling beyond four grades *because* he was a Negro; and his uncle had died on a Louisiana chain gang *because* he was a Negro; and his own namesake, his great-grandfather, had been shot down on the streets of New Orleans *because* he was a Negro asking for equal rights for his people – and who was Huey Wilson to dream of miracles, or to waste time wishing himself out of jail? As well wish himself out of his skin!

"A good skin, my own!" Huey thought with fierce resentment. Honest black as one third of the world was black! And shit to them who had exploited his people, abused them, oppressed them for three hundred and fifty years, and still sought to keep them in menial subjection. He would not whine, and they never would make him cry, and before they sent him up for five years, or even five weeks, they'd know that they'd been in a goddamn serious fight!

Huey smiled a little and felt more at ease, and turned over to rest his side. He wondered about McPeak, and wondered what Jeff was doing to help him, and wondered if his parents knew as yet about his arrest. His thoughts* drifted and became disconnected, and then, because he was worn out, he fell asleep.

* * *

A hand shook Huey, and he opened his eyes to see the face of his cellmate, Finnerty.

"Boy, wake up now," Finnerty said. "Rouse yourself quick."

As Huey sat up, the cell door began grinding open, and he saw their tier man, Benjamin, on the runway.

"You got a visit," Benjamin called. "Hop it!"

"Have I got time to wash my face?"

"Hell no, git goin'!"

"Bet it's my brother," Huey exclaimed with sleepy delight as he stepped out on the runway. "Where do I go?"

"Downstairs where we served breakfast. The screw'll have your pass. But it ain't your brother. There's no family visits this early."

Chapter 5

Charles Herrin

Officer Simmons said "Here you are" and handed Huey Wilson a pass stamped "VISIT", on which his name, number, cell block and the exact time were written. A second guard, whom Huey recalled from earlier that morning, was standing by to escort him.

A solid steel door was unlocked, then locked behind them.* There were several flights of stairs and intervening corridors, and finally they arrived at a small vestibule. Here they paused as a door clanged behind them. Facing them, with a glass peephole at eye level, was the door that led to the administrative section of the jail. On their right was still a third door, this one of bars, which gave upon a short, narrow, tunnel-like corridor. The guard, silent until now, pressed a bell button and then gestured towards the corridor on their right. He said with a grin: "That's where you have family visits."

"In there?" Huey asked incredulously.

"Inmates go in there," the guard explained with unmistakable relish, as though the ingenuity of the device appealed to him. "You see those glass portholes in the outside wall? You stand on this side of the wall and your family on the other, and you talk through a telephone. You can look at each other at the same time, see?"

Huey nodded and wondered what shrivelled soul had thought that one up. He asked: "Where am I going now?"

"The Rotunda. This early it must be a lawyer's visit." The guard pressed the bell button again, but at the same moment a pair of eyes appeared at the glass peephole. Keys rattled, the heavy door opened, and Huey's pass was scrutinized. The Rotunda guard said "Over there", and Huey stepped into an immense, high-ceilinged room. At the far end of it, seated at a table, he saw his brother and a middle-aged stranger engaged in earnest conversation. Except for the guard, no one else was in the room.

Huey would not have expected the sheer sight of his brother to affect him so strongly. A lump formed in his throat, and for a moment he had the embarrassing fear that he would burst into tears in spite of himself. It made him realize that deep down he was considerably less composed than he wanted to be. The thought formed – "I'm really a coward" – but he thrust it from his consciousness with anger. He wasn't, and he wouldn't be.

He was halfway to the table before they noticed him, and it made him feel wonderful to see the warm smile and the deeply affectionate look that came to his brother's face as he jumped to his feet.

Jeff Wilson was six years older than Huey, a rangy man who strongly resembled their father in his chiselled features and ashy-dark skin, and in the serious, almost stern expression on his face. There were strong bonds between the two brothers, and Huey, in spite of his need to feel independent, frankly acknowledged Jeff to be his mentor. There was, nevertheless, a touch of envy in the love and respect he bore for his brother. Jeff had been to war and come back an officer, and Jeff already was in his first year of law, and Jeff always had achieved grades in school that Huey never quite could match. It seemed to him that Jeff had proved himself, while the years of his own testing were ahead.

The two brothers shook hands as though months had passed since they last met. Jeff flung an arm around Huey, and his tone expressed deep relief: "I'm sure glad to see you in one piece, kid. I was afraid you got the bejeezus knocked out of you."

"I got banged around, but I'm OK. You don't know how good I feel – seeing you, I mean. They told me it was too early for family visits."

"I'm in on false pretences. Mr Herrin over there said I was his assistant."

"Is he a lawyer? Is he any good? What's his reputation?" Huey whispered quickly.

"He's good, stop worrying. Anyway, he's here to advise us, not to handle your case personally. He teaches law at school – I'm taking a class with him – and he's on the legal panel of the NAACP."*

"That's wonderful. I knew I could count on you."

"Let's go."

Herrin was a slender man in his late fifties, short in stature, bald, chocolate-dark. He had, Huey thought instantly, the look of an old sly bird with his thin-lipped mouth, his bright eyes and his hooked, beak-like nose. It was an expressive, intelligent face, yet somehow a little forbidding.

Jeff said: "Here's the kid brother, professor, still in one piece" – and Herrin, standing up, shook hands with quick formality. He spoke rapidly, almost in staccato fashion, in the flat accents of the Midwest. "So you've been beating up on the white folks, huh?" And then, with a grin, "Is that bad? Sit down, take a load off your feet."

They sat at one end of the large table, and Herrin took a fountain pen and a small notebook from his pocket. He said to Jeff: "You explain I'm only here to advise?"

"Yes, sir." Jeff offered Huey a cigarette, but the latter shook his head.

"I teach and do appeals work, that's all," Herrin said to Huey. "Seeing how your brother is a student of mine and you're aiming for Howard too, I wanted to hear what this was about before recommending a lawyer."

"I surely appreciate your coming down, sir," Huey answered.

Herrin's head bobbed in acknowledgement – exactly like a bird swallowing a worm, Huey thought – and with a sly expression he pointed a slender finger at Huey's chest. "I know the Negro lawyers in this town like I know my own hands. I know who's first-rate and who isn't. I know the ones who're opportunists and won't budge their fat behinds unless a case'll bring 'em money or prestige. You haven't got any money, I hear, and there's no reason to think you'll make headlines. But I'll get somebody solid to defend you unless" – he paused and gazed at Huey with sudden, almost unfriendly, challenge – "as I told your brother, unless you're a jerk who got drunk and screwed himself up. In that case you can defend yourself – I won't waste time on you or ask anybody else."

With discomfort Huey thought to himself that this man sounded as much like a law professor as the men on Tier Four. He mumbled, "I surely didn't." And then, catching the look on his brother's face, he recalled something: a comment Jeff had made to him at the beginning of the school semester about one of his instructors who was addicted to talking slang but was razor-sharp, and the best teacher he had.

Herrin said, "OK, Huey, we'll find out. Now look, I didn't heave myself out of bed so* early without a good reason. The charge against you – felonious assault with deadly weapons – is serious. Now, you haven't been brought before a commissioner for a preliminary hearing yet, have you?"

"No, sir."

"I didn't think so, not on a Saturday-night arrest. That's why I'm here. Now look, here's the set-up: the commissioner who gets your case has the power to dismiss the police charges against you, or to accept them and hold you for indictment by the Grand Jury. We've got the right to bring witnesses into the hearing and to cross-examine the witnesses against you. Clear, so far?"

"Yes, sir."

"If we can demolish the police charges, then it'll be over right there, you'll go free. But get this: the commissioner not only has the power to hold you, he also has the right to raise or lower the charges. You see what that means?"

"I—"

"It means we have a second objective: if you're held, we want you sent up to the Grand Jury on a less serious charge."

"Yes, sir, I get it," Huey responded, and thought to himself, "The old boy knows his business – he's OK."

"Now here's what *I'm* after," Herrin said with obvious relish. "You boys get some coyote of a lawyer and he'll be glad to make a trial out of it. He'll milk you for your family's gold teeth and all you can borrow, and put you in hock for years. No sir, not in any case, I'm advising. I want you to go into that hearing with all the evidence, all the arguments, all the witnesses you can get. You're out to blitz that commissioner. But no lawyer can do a job for you if your hearing's today. That's why I hotfooted down so early. I'm your temporary counsel, correct? I want your permission to delay the hearing if I can arrange it."

"It's all right with me, sir," Huey replied immediately. "Delay it as long as you want."

"Are you sure now? You'll have to sit in jail until the hearing takes place. I don't want any kickbacks."

Jeff said: "Can't he make bail in the mean time?"

"I'll ask, but there's not much chance. The legal process here makes sense – a commissioner doesn't fix bail until after he hears the case. But I'm not talking of your staying in more than two or three days* – just long enough for your lawyer to work up some evidence."

"A little time in here won't kill me," Huey stated airily. "I'm getting an education."

"OK, next item," said Herrin without any pause. "Over the phone yesterday you told Jeff you were attacked by four white fellows you didn't know. But when he went down to the precinct house, the police had a different story."

"What did they say?"

His brother answered: "First of all, that you were wild drunk."

"That's a lie!"

"I was sure it was, it wouldn't be you. Their story goes like this, Huey: you were drunk and looking for trouble. When you passed these white men, you purposely bumped into one of them. He stopped and cursed you out. You knocked him down, and before the others could interfere you kicked him in the face. So then they all jumped you."

"My God, what a stinking parcel of lies," Huey exclaimed with angry laughter.

"I was sure it was, especially when they wouldn't let me talk to you."

Herrin took a tobacco pouch and a huge-bowled pipe from his pocket. He said: "Let's hear your version."

"Listen, Professor," Huey asked, "is it true I can get five years on this charge?"

"Yes, but that's the maximum. You could get less."

The two brothers exchanged glances, and Huey muttered: "Oh boy, that's just great!"

Jeff said: "Take it easy, kid. You're not even indicted yet."

Huey frowned, shook his head and then began. "Saturday night I was going home along Fourteenth Street…"

"What time?"

"About eleven-thirty."

Herrin marked it in his notebook.

"I passed these four white men, but I didn't pay 'em any mind."

"Were they strangers?"

"Yes."

"Did they say anything to you?"

"Nothing. But a couple of minutes later I heard footsteps coming up fast behind me in a way that sounded funny. I turned round,* and there they were, those same four. The minute I turned, they broke into a run. Before I could collect myself, they were all around me. One of them – he's the fellow who's in jail here too, his name is Ballou – said to the others, 'That's him, I'd know that nigger son of a bitch anywhere.'" Huey tensed, body and face tightening, his voice becoming charged with feeling. "I knew I was in for trouble, of course, but they were all around me, and I didn't think I could get away if I ran. There was nobody I could yell to, either – you know how empty Fourteenth Street can get at that time of night* with all the stores closed. So I just tried to play dumb and be polite. I called those bastards 'sir', and said I didn't know any of 'em, and I was sure they were mistaken about me. But then this Ballou louse made it clear. He said: 'You were out at Central High today on that picket line, weren't you?' And when he said that, I kind of remembered seeing him there."

Herrin sat up a little, his head bobbing. "You mean this battle started over the school issue?"

"That's right. There wasn't anything else involved."

Herrin gazed closely at Huey for a moment, his eyes very bright, his big pipe held away from his face. Then he muttered: "This thing has some dimensions, hasn't it?" He began smoking again.

"I kept trying to play dumb and be very polite, and say he was mistaken, but Ballou wasn't buying it. I imagine he'd gotten a good look at me in the afternoon, because I was one of the picket captains. They sure didn't waste time arguing. In the middle of my being so polite, Ballou swung at me. I sidestepped in time, so that he didn't get me in the face, but he hit me on the shoulder and knocked me backwards. Then, before I could do anything, I got jumped from behind." Huey grinned a little and said honestly, but with a touch of embarrassment, "I'm getting shaky inside all over again. Guess I was plenty scared."

Herrin commented, with a softness that Huey found surprising, "No reason to feel ashamed if you were." And then, with sudden, cold anger: "I don't know what's worse – to have to take their beatings or their hypocritical shit. Go on, boy."

"Well," Huey continued more calmly: "Ballou swung at me, and then one of the other fellows grabbed me from behind in a bear hug. He was strong as hell. He pinned my arms and pulled me back off balance. Then, while I was trying to break loose, those three other guys started walloping me."

"Great!" his brother exclaimed. His thin face was set in a hard mould, the lips tight, a muscle working in his cheek.

"To tell the truth, Jeff, they didn't hurt me much. They were so anxious to get their licks in that they were getting in each other's way. But then the guy holding me yelled to them, 'Take turns!' One of 'em, a chunky fellow with a little moustache, pushed the other two away. Then he pulled his fist way back to hit me with everything he had." Huey showed his teeth in a quick grin that was not amusement, but a tension he could not control. "That gave me a chance to move. I was still off balance, see, bent backwards. But as he came in at me, I snapped my legs up with every bit of power I had. Man, I connected! I cracked him with both feet right in the face. He hit the pavement yards back, and he never made a sound: he was out cold."

"Good, good!" Jeff muttered with passion. "I hope you broke his goddamned jaw."

"From what I heard, that's just what I did do."

"A little more than that," Herrin put in. "Last night I called the precinct and the hospital. You sure messed him up, boy. His jaw's broken in two places – some teeth were knocked out and others were cracked, and he has a mild concussion."

"That's even better, that's great!" Jeff exclaimed passionately.

Herrin shook his head. "You don't know what you're talking about – not from the legal point of view." He turned to Huey. "Were you carrying a weapon, or anything that could be miscalled a weapon?"

"Nothing."

"You wouldn't lie to me about it, would you?"

"No!" Huey retorted sharply, resenting the question.

"Take it easy," Herrin said with a smile. He turned to Jeff. "That's the basis for the deadly-weapons charge – his feet."

"I don't understand, Professor."

"The law says that if you use your feet to do serious bodily damage, you can be charged with assault with deadly weapons."

"I'll be damned! I thought they'd have to produce a phoney gun or something."

"One of the inmates told me that this morning," Huey said. "So it's true, then!"

"But listen," Jeff enquired hotly, "in circumstances like that, doesn't a man have the right to defend himself any way he can?"

Herrin's head bobbed, and he waved his pipe. "Yes! But then the legal issue revolves around the question of who was defending himself. Let's hear the rest of the story before we assess it."

"The second after I did that kicking, the fellow holding me let me go – that is, he slammed me down, sort of. I hit the pavement hard, man, I still have a sore tail bone. Then for a minute or two they were all over me, hitting me, kicking me, knocking me down every time I tried to get up." Huey paused, wiped the perspiration from his forehead with the back of his hand and tried to steady himself. Without wanting it so, he was reliving the experience with an intensity that was very painful. "Now comes something to write home about! I heard one of them yell out: 'Pin him down, hold him!' The next thing I knew, two of those guys were on top of me, one across my thighs gripping my legs, the other across my chest. Of course I was fighting like mad, and getting a few licks in myself, but I couldn't shake loose. Then I saw this fellow Ballou standing right over my face with a knife in his hand."

"My God!" Jeff muttered.

Huey gestured, one hand forming a fist. "He had it like this, a pocket knife, and he was waiting for a chance to use it. It was like you wait with a newspaper in your hand for a fly to settle. I don't know whether he meant to get me in the eyes with it, or what. But I hope I never have a moment like that again."

Jeff put his head between both his hands and stared at the table top. Herrin, with his bright eyes fixed upon Huey, was sucking a cold pipe.

Huey laughed oddly. "As Ma would say, 'then Jesus moved it so that a Christian man came along to help me'. I didn't find out till later, of course, that anyone else was there. I guess we must've been fighting three or four minutes on that street without a car* or a person passing by. So who should come round* the corner to rescue me but a white, middle-aged hillbilly from Georgia. His name's McPeak – he's in jail here too."

"Go on," his brother said urgently.

"He told me later that when he first saw us, he was so paralysed he couldn't move. But I guess he moved faster than he thought. He must've charged in like a locomotive, because he knocked Ballou right off the pavement into the street. The next thing I knew, all that weight was off me and I was able to jump up. This McPeak must be hell on wheels in a rough-and-tumble fight. So then we had a wild scramble for another minute or so, we two against the three others – and then, thank God, a patrol car came screaming up, and the cops stopped it."

"A Georgia cracker!"* Jeff murmured softly, with wonder and exultation.

"Jeff, you remember those moonshiners* who used to come into town on Saturday from the Ragged Mountains? He looks and talks like them."

"What do you know about him?" Herrin asked.

"Not much, Professor. They separated us in the precinct, and we're kept on separate tiers in here. We talked a little on Saturday night after we were arrested, and for about two minutes this morning – that's all. I still don't know exactly why he helped me."

"He must've been asked some questions down at the precinct house. What did he say to the desk sergeant?"

"He said he jumped into the fight because he saw three guys against one, and that Ballou fellow waiting to knife me."

"In that case you're in a wonderful position," Herrin exclaimed heartily. "With a man like that testifying at the hearing, you'll—"

"Only, I can't be sure of him," Huey interrupted. "On Saturday night he was wonderful, but what he'll do from now on I don't know."

"Why don't you? He's been arrested too. It's in his own interest to tell the truth."

"No, it isn't to his interest, that's what worries me. He's gotten an offer from the police."

Herrin's head bobbed, and he took the pipe out of his mouth. "McPeak told you that?"

"Yes! Yesterday afternoon a plain-clothes man made him a proposition. It seems that the father of the fellow I injured has some pull with the cops. The name is Davis, I think. Anyway, the detective said they were aiming to send me up for five years."

"Davis?" Herrin asked, writing a note. "What was the proposition?"

"The detective told McPeak that if he went back to Detroit right away – that's his home – they'd dismiss charges against him. They want him to disappear."

"Will he testify to *that?*" Herrin asked eagerly.

"I don't know. When I asked him, all he said was, 'How the hell do I know?' He said he wasn't looking for trouble."

"The detective spoke to him yesterday?"

"In the afternoon."

"And McPeak's in jail with you now?"

"Yes."

"In that case he must've turned the offer down!"

"But then why didn't he tell me straight out that he was ready to stand by me?"

"Yes, why didn't he?" Jeff repeated. "It sounds as though he's undecided about that police offer."

"His manner is different too," Huey continued. "On Saturday night he was real friendly... you know, all there. But this morning he's been different... I don't know... stiff and sort of cold, a kind of wall between us."

"Any chance he jumped into that fight without knowing you were coloured?" Jeff asked.

"Hardly. Anyway, he knew it right after. I didn't feel any prejudice in him on Saturday night, and I still don't."

"Except that he's changed towards you," Jeff argued. "He won't commit himself on his testimony. You know how much prejudice even fairly decent white people have inside."

"Maybe he has some prejudice," Herrin interrupted, "or maybe he's tempted by the police offer, or maybe it's some of both. But the fact remains that this white man *didn't* pass you by on the street and *didn't* take the offer. Not only that, but he told you about it."

"Well... with respect to the police offer, there could be something else on his mind beside me," Huey commented. "He came to Washington for a family wedding. That can be the reason he doesn't want to leave."

"Nevertheless," said Herrin, "this man has been on your side so far. Our job is to keep him there if he's wavering. You can be sure the detective threatened him plenty."

"That's what McPeak told me this morning. Right now the charges on him are assault, disorderly conduct and resisting arrest."

"Simple assault can bring three months," Herrin observed, lighting his pipe. "Add the other charges and they can scare him with six months. Do you know what they're holding Ballou on?"

"Disorderly conduct."

"What?" Jeff exclaimed. "Ballou's the one who wanted to knife you! How open do they think they can be in this damn frame-up?"

"All the way," Huey replied with a sour laugh. "There's no more knife – it grew wings and disappeared." He paused to take a breath, then winced involuntarily. "I—"

"What's the matter?" his brother interrupted.

"I got one kick in the side that was a bad one. It hurts when I breathe deep."

"Have you seen a doctor?"

"They wouldn't get me one at the precinct."

Jeff shook his head and muttered angrily: "You can get a lung puncture if your rib's broken. What bastards!"

"I'm going on sick call later this morning. To tell the truth, I got some bedbug bites yesterday that bother me worse."

Herrin said, "I'll speak to one of the officials on my* way out. They're a little more concerned about public opinion in a place like this than they are in those precinct houses. But if you feel you haven't gotten a decent examination or proper treatment, I want to know it. I'll raise some hell."

"OK, thanks."

"What's this about the knife?"

"When the cops arrested us, McPeak told 'em about it. They searched the street and found it."

"How big was it?"

"A small pocket knife. The blade was about two inches."

"Big enough to blind or kill a man," Jeff commented.

"But not against the law for a man to carry," Herrin pointed out. "Did they turn it in at the precinct?"

"Yes, on Saturday night. But McPeak told me it's disappeared now, the way they want him to disappear."

Herrin reflected for a moment. "There were four of those hoodlums. One's here, one's in the hospital... what about the other two?"

"They were arrested Saturday night, but yesterday they were let go. They walked past my cell on the way out and laughed at me plenty."

Herrin rubbed a hand over his face and muttered, "Uh-huh. They're holding one of 'em on a minor charge so they can appear to be impartial." He suddenly grimaced with anger and contempt. "This is a cute little frame-up, boys. There are three things the damn police have had a lot of experience in: extorting money from hustlers, taking bribes from racketeers and framing our people. Look at the set-up: they have four white men to tell the same story, one of 'em seriously injured, presumably an innocent victim of this burly character here. They also have supporting evidence from the patrol cops – for instance that they never saw a knife, and God knows what other lies they'll go in for. This isn't an easy frame to knock apart."

Jeff asked, "But if McPeak tells the truth, won't that make a tremendous difference?"

"Of course, all the difference in the world. Except that at this moment we can't be sure of him. Why *did* his manner change over the weekend? Why didn't he give a straight answer on how he would testify? He *must* be considering that police offer. He's scared of six months in prison – that's the answer to McPeak."

"Even supposing he runs out on us," Jeff persisted, "will it make sense to the commissioner, or a jury, that a lone Negro would attack four white men?"

"They've thought of that already," Herrin replied. "That's the reason they're charging Huey with being drunk. It's to explain the one against four – he was wild from booze, see? Huey, were you given any sort of test for drunkenness?"

"No, sir, and I can prove I wasn't drunk. Saturday night I had supper at the home of a girl I know. Her folks never serve liquor. They're so church-minded, I doubt they'd even have* liquor in their apartment."

"What's the father's name?"

"Harold Bemish."

"Address?"

"It's on Twelfth Street. I forget the number, but he's in the phone book."

"What's his work?"

"He's Civil Service, in the Department of Commerce. A file clerk, I think."

Herrin gestured with his pipe. "That helps us. He'll be a reputable witness."

"Mrs Bemish is a dental assistant."

"Very good. What did you do from supper time till the fight?"

"We went to a movie, the girl and I. After the movie* I took her home, then started home myself."

"She can testify you didn't drink after supper?"

"Well," Huey cracked with a faint grin, "we did have two chocolate sodas apiece."

Herrin smiled, but Jeff said with mock severity: "Damn it, Huey, you go around being extravagant like that... taking girls to movies...* you'll never have enough money for college."

"Trust me," Huey retorted, "she paid her own way."

Jeff hushed his quick guffaw, but Herrin leant back in his chair and laughed uproariously, in a kind of high cackle. He commented with relish: "In my time I did you one better. I had a girl who used to pay for me."

Jeff asked, in a lowered voice, "What's the guard looking at us for? Can't you laugh in this damn jail?"

"Don't mind him," said Herrin, "he's just a bored time-server. Anyway, Huey, I think we can put up a good case that you weren't drunk. That's something on our side whether or not McPeak testifies."

"Listen," Jeff enquired, "isn't there any way to *force* him to testify? I mean, couldn't you go to the commissioner and demand that McPeak be kept here as a material witness?"

"And what would that accomplish?" Herrin responded. "He's no good to Huey unless he's a *willing* witness. If he's unwilling but we keep him here with a court order, he's likely to testify the way the police want. In that event we'll be worse off."

"I guess so," Jeff muttered.

"I'll have a chance to talk to McPeak this morning," Huey volunteered. "He's agreed to meet me on sick call."

"Good!" Herrin's head bobbed, and he gazed at Huey for a long moment. "I like to talk straight, Huey. Without McPeak on your side, I think you're in a mess of trouble."

Huey nodded glumly. "It's beginning to look that way to me too. If only there were some other witnesses..."

"That's one item we have to find out. What do you know about the patrol car? Did it come by accident or a call?"

"I don't know."

"Well, there are a lot of items to track down. One of the first things is to present this case to the NAACP. I'm on the legal panel there, and I think it's a case they ought to know about."

"Do you think they'll take it up officially?" Huey asked with eagerness. "That'd be wonderful."

"Don't work up expectations – they carry a heavy load. But the fact is... this is more than a question of your defence. McPeak says there's a personal angle – that the father of the hoodlum you sent to the hospital has police connections. But that doesn't change the basic issue. Last week, for instance, I was in New York on the same day that there was a race riot* at a high school there – the Benjamin Franklin. You read about it?"

"No."

"I did," Jeff said.

"Well, it was a dilly! One coloured boy was badly beaten by white students, another was stabbed, thirty or forty were bruised up. Now, I'm sure there may have been some personal grudges involved. But we know that the basic issue was prejudice. And when the police announced that it was no more than 'one of those things' between boys – that was the phrase they used – they knew they were lying, the jerks. I imagine in your case the cops'll maintain it was just an ordinary street fight between a drunken Negro and some whites. But we know there have been* other beatings of Cardoza students, and now comes a frame-up of a Cardoza student with the police participating – and what it amounts to is increased intimidation of the whole Negro community on the school issue. They won't give up easy on any form of segregation, not even on two kids sitting in a classroom. So, as I see it, your case ought to be presented to the NAACP, and to the newspapers, and to the whole community."

Huey said, with an excited laugh: "That's fine with me. I want all the support I can get. This talk of five years in prison makes me nervous."

"I shouldn't wonder," Herrin commented, as he wrote in his notebook. "However, you're not such an easy fellow to frame, Huey. The police case depends upon your fitting a stereotype – but you don't fit it. We can prove that you're working your way through high school by holding down a government job. No hoodlum does that. So it won't be an easy matter for them to picture you as a 'bad nigger'. That's one weak spot in the police case. The other we've taken up already – that no doctor examined you for drunkenness, while you have supporting witnesses to the fact that you weren't drunk."

"Keep talking, Professor," Huey said with a laugh. "You're making me feel a lot better."

Herrin smiled and said, "Your lawyer'll also want to find out about the white men you had the fight with. Who are they… what's *their* reputation… do *they* have any police record? If there's anything unsavoury about them, it could weigh a lot."

"How about canvassing the neighbourhood to find out if there were any witnesses?" Jeff asked.

"Sure. But for that we'll use a white investigator. The NAACP can give us one. We'll also want a doctor's examination of Davis, this man in the hospital. You kicked him when he was standing up, but the other fellows claim he was on the ground. His injuries might prove that he couldn't have been lying down."

"That's a wonderful point," Huey exclaimed with enthusiasm. "That's great!"

"Maybe so, maybe not," Herrin answered cautiously, "but we'll find out. Now, Huey, listen: all these things we've talked about are important. But you know what you're up against in the courts. If the commissioner is prejudiced, he can hold you for the Grand Jury in spite of the evidence – he can set your bail higher than he would for a white man, and so on. You might meet prejudice right down the line – with the US Attorney, the jury, the judge. By far your best defence lies with McPeak. If he stands firm, I don't think you'll even come to trial. Boy, you've got to go to work on him."

"I'll sure try. Have you any suggestions?"

Herrin took the pipe out of his mouth and rubbed the bowl along the side of his nose. "Item one: he may be scared, but if he weren't a decent man, he wouldn't have helped you. So don't approach him as though he's a jerk just because he's not ready to stand up like a hero. You do that and you'll lose him sure."

"Yes, sir. I'll remember that."

"Item two: don't try to bluff him. Don't tell him that if he stands with you, he's just as sure to go free as if he takes the police offer. It isn't true, and he won't believe it."

"Yes, sir. But I certainly want to show him that we stand a good chance to go free at the hearing, don't I?"

"Of course – and the chances are better than good. Item three: it seems to me McPeak must be the kind of man who likes to look at his face in the morning without feeling ashamed. You can make use of that."

"Yes, sir. I see what you mean."

"It means approach him with confidence – above all, for God's sake, without the inner feeling that you can't really trust any white man. That feeling can be a terrible handicap. If there weren't decent whites, we'd be licked, we'd have no future in this country. But we have... Jeff, you got any ideas?"

"I was wondering if McPeak has a lawyer."

"I'm pretty sure he hasn't," Huey told him.

"What do you think, Professor – should Huey offer *his* lawyer to McPeak?"

"Very good. Try it, Huey."

"OK. But..." He hesitated. "I have the impression McPeak's worried about money."

"Tell him not to worry!"

"But—"

"Look, boy, I'll get you a lawyer, a good one. There'll be no fee* for anybody."

Huey said very earnestly, "That's wonderful of you, Mr Herrin, but I think whoever does the work in this case is entitled to be paid. I'd like to take it on as a debt for—"

"You're in debt to me already, both you brothers," Herrin interrupted. "You know how?" He gazed from one to the other with challenge in his bright eyes. "Because I'm here! Because I didn't turn you down! Ten years from now you'll be lawyers. You'll get called on the telephone some Sunday afternoon the way I was. Will you say 'yes' or will you be too busy paying the instalments on that Cadillac convertible to waste time on some poor black boy in trouble?" He stared at them, his thin lips tight, his face almost unfriendly. "Uh-uh, don't say anything," he snapped, as Huey began to speak. "That's a powerful disease, Cadillacitis. It's easy to catch. So deliver me from promises. Just remember how you feel right now when those phone calls start coming in."

The two brothers glanced at each other, and then back at the older man, and were silent. Herrin said, his manner less harsh now, "You know why I like to teach? Because I know that in every class there'll be a few men and women who'll be *real* Negroes – who'll never eat so high on the hog* that they'll forget the children growing up in slum alleys, battered around and pushed around until they end up in jails and prisons, with no one even to speak a word for them. So I'll just wait and see what kind of men you brothers turn out to be. Now, the last item before we break up is this: Huey, what's our strategy if McPeak runs out on you?"

"Why, I don't know, sir."

"You may have to know in a hurry, that's why I bring it up. McPeak runs, the commissioner holds you for the Grand Jury, what do we do?"

"We fight it in court, don't we?"

Herrin's head bobbed, and the sly look came to his face. "I wouldn't advise it. Assuming no new evidence that'll change the picture, my recommendation is to try for a deal. Without McPeak, the trial odds look too tough. We don't want you two or three years* in prison, do we?"

Huey was silent, staring at Herrin, but Jeff asked, "What sort of a deal, Professor?"

"The moment Huey's held for indictment, his lawyer goes to the US Attorney. He asks for a lesser charge – assault with beating. The maximum penalty for that is only six months. In exchange Huey'll plead guilty and get a suspended sentence."

"The hell I will!" Huey exploded. "What give* you that idea?"

"Watch how you talk, will you?" his brother snapped with embarrassment. "Professor Herrin—"

"—can speak for himself," Herrin interrupted. He gazed at the two brothers with amusement, and no anger. "Straight talk is fine with me. You don't like my idea, Huey? You think I'm selling you out?"

Huey stared at the sly, smiling face and, for a moment, couldn't trust himself to speak. He didn't want to antagonize the man, yet he felt betrayed. After what he had experienced on the street corner, the suggestion that he plead guilty was loathsome. "I'm sorry," he said finally, with effort, "I didn't mean to be insulting, Professor Herrin. I know you're trying to help me. But how can I join in my own frame-up? Those white bastards'll lie about me, and you want me to say they're right?"

"All I want is minimum jail time for my client," Herrin responded drily. "What's wrong with that?"

"Pleading guilty, that's what's wrong! Let's go to trial and fight it!"

Herrin laughed indulgently. "Grow up, son. This isn't a football game. You're not being called on to give your best for the dear old team even if you lose. Have you got some idea you'll read good in the newspapers?"

"No!" Huey retorted with controlled anger. "I'm not talking about that. But after what those guys did to me, it's a matter of principle with me to fight it out."

"Jesus Christ, you talk like a moron," Jeff interrupted. "If McPeak runs and you haven't got a chance, are you willing to take three or five years when you could get six months? Where's the principle in that?"

"There's a principle in fighting it, that's all," Huey answered sullenly. "How do you know I won't have a chance? I can prove I wasn't drunk. I can prove..." He fell silent. "I don't want to do it, that's all. It turns my stomach."

His brother chuckled scornfully. "Now I get it. We got a big race leader here. Can't wait till he gets his law degree before he goes on picket lines and—"

"You think I should've stayed home when most of my class was at that demonstration?" Huey asked indignantly.

"Your big job is to put yourself through school. Suppose your government work included Saturday afternoons – would you have cut work to be on that picket line?"

"Let's stop supposing," Herrin put in quietly. "Huey did go on that picket line, and I'll support him there. The trouble that resulted wasn't his fault. But here we are, and what do we do now? Huey, I'll inject a few facts into your hot head. Pay attention: the law defines a felony as any crime punishable by a sentence over one year. No man who's been convicted of a felony gets admitted to the Bar... or very rarely, anyway."

There was a moment of silence while Huey, staring at the older man, absorbed this news.

"It's not a law as such," Herrin continued. "But in practice no Bar association is likely to accredit a man with a criminal record."

"My God!" Huey muttered. "So if I'm convicted on this damn frame-up, I'm finished as a lawyer?"

"Just about."

Huey nodded and turned away from the gaze of the two others. For the second time that morning, he had the fear that he would burst into tears in spite of himself. It was a terrible blow, a much more deadly threat to his life's dream than a prison term. Only his brother knew how vital and close to both of them was their plan of a law practice together.

Jeff put a hand on Huey's arm and said reassuringly, despite his own inner distress, "Take it easy, kid. As I said before, you're not even indicted yet."

Huey nodded, but remained silent, unable to trust himself to speak. Herrin, watching him, maintained an impassive face, but he was thinking hard, trying to form an estimate of this youth. More deeply than Huey realized did the older man bring human understanding to this legal discussion. Herrin remembered his own struggles and the soaring, contradictory ambitions of his youth. He had observed as well the development of a great many Huey Wilsons over the years – Negro boys struggling up from poverty, trying to overcome the extra handicaps of discrimination by driving themselves unrelentingly; going to school and holding down whatever jobs they could get, or dropping out of school to work, and then returning; acquiring an education and a profession by means of a five- or ten-year grind in which they denied themselves normal rest, normal recreation, normal sleep and, frequently, adequate food – yet sustained by visions of a place in the world, of decent living in the years to come, of fame and importance, perhaps. Certainly there was no denying a simple truth: that whenever *any one* of these youngsters won through to a degree in medicine or education or law, *that* in itself constituted a victory by every Negro over the damn colour line. In a land of discrimination one man's birthright was another's attainment, dearly won, warranting celebration.

And yet this victory, this fundamental truth, was not enough for Herrin, and he never would be satisfied with it, not for himself or others. He judged the Huey Wilsons by higher, sterner standards, and he demanded more of them. A young Negro became a lawyer? Splendid. His earnings became adequate for a decent life, even substantial? Excellent. He married? Very good. And what more natural than that he would be attracted by a girl who could dance, swim, play bridge and dress in good taste; who had taken courses in home-making and modern literature in college; who belonged to a sorority that would offer useful social contacts; and who would be an adornment at his fraternity dance as well as a desirable wife? All very natural, even inevitable, in view of the circumstances and roots of his life. But was that all that a Negro lawyer need ask of himself, or his brothers down below should ask of him? An existence of fat, good living was moral enough for a white lawyer, perhaps – no social conscience need flame in him – but for a Negro? In a society that maintained a colour line, what happened to the moral fibre of any coloured man who was satisfied with his own success, who said "My victory stops here, with me"?

This was the swamp in which so many of the Hueys foundered. Herrin had seen them over the years, and he knew! And how was it with *this* Huey? He sensed contradictions, fissures in the young personality. Huey wanted to fight for his rights as a Negro so badly that he felt sold out at the suggestion of any compromise, even with the odds against him. Yet now he was shaking inside at a threat to his law career. Immature, of course – what else at eighteen? But sooner or later these contradictions had to be resolved, and the hand made steady at the driver's wheel. Or else it would be this way and that, essentially directionless, the youthful idealism going flabby. He had seen it before, and he had fought it in himself, and he knew!

Out of the long silence Huey suddenly put a question to Herrin. "That other charge, Professor... assault with beating... that's a misdemeanour?"

"Uh-huh. Maximum sentence is six months. But what we'd ask for is a suspended sentence in exchange for your guilty plea. Seven, eight years from now, when you go before a character committee of the Bar, that suspended sentence can make the difference. Lawyers know how the courts work. A suspended sentence in a case of simple assault will mean to them that there was considerable doubt in your case. So if your record is clean otherwise, I'm quite sure you'll get by."

"You feel positive we can get a deal like that?"

"Confident, not positive, but I wouldn't take anything less. Still, I'll be surprised if we can't work it out. They like to avoid jury trials."

"Yeah," Huey muttered. "Well, sir, I'll certainly think about it."

"You will? How come?" Herrin asked slyly.

"Huh?"

"If it's against your principles to plead guilty, why even consider it?"

Huey looked embarrassed, and said nothing.

"So it wasn't a principle at all, was it?" Herrin continued, needling him. "It was the impulse of a moment – or maybe just hot air?"

"No," Huey muttered. "I'd still like to fight it."

"If you could win, yes. If it* wouldn't get in the way of that Cadillac you want when you're a big-shot lawyer."

"What *is* this, anyway?" Huey asked sullenly. "I seem to be wrong either way. I haven't been talking about wanting Cadillacs. It's on your mind, Professor, not mine."

Herrin laughed softly. "OK, Huey, I won't ride you any more, I'm really your friend. The truth is I like you, and I like your spirit. You're in trouble, but you're not whining about it, and you're ready to fight. That's good. What isn't good is what I smell between the lines. I think you've got some highfalutin idea of how you *ought* to act in this situation – dream stuff. If you do, you'll trip over it. I've seen a lot of boys who were half-baked idealists at twenty – out to save the race, every one of 'em a young Frederick Douglass – and then all grown up into crappy opportunists at thirty. Think about it. I have an idea you don't really know what your principles are as yet. Now we'll drop it. One practical matter: you're seeing McPeak this morning?"

"Yes, sir."

"I'll need a report on that." He reflected for a moment. "Jeff, do you have a class at noon? That's family visiting hour here."

"At* eleven o'clock, but I'll cut it or leave early."

"OK, then. You see Huey and call me at my home at two. I may have a lawyer lined up by then."

Huey said, "Professor, there's a favour we could do for McPeak that might sweeten him a little. He had a suitcase with clothes* when he was arrested. It wasn't sent over here from the precinct this morning, and they never gave him a receipt. He's worried he'll lose his best clothes. Is there anything you can do about it?"

"Not without authorization. If he wants to appoint me his temporary counsel, yes. Or if he wants a white lawyer, we can get him one through the NAACP."

"I'll tell him that."

"Huey," Jeff asked, "what do you want me to do about your job? I called your supervisor this morning and said you were sick. Is that all right?"

"Was there anything in the papers about my arrest?"

"About four lines on a back page yesterday, with your first name spelled wrong. I doubt if anybody* in your department saw it."

"That's good. Well, I've got a week's sick pay coming to me this year, so let it ride like that for now… Do the folks know, Jeff?"

"I telephoned them after I came back from the precinct."

"Yesterday? How? Pop wasn't working, was he?"

"I called Ma at church. I knew she'd be at afternoon service."

"Was she very upset?"

"Well… it was a shock. You know Ma. She never thought a boy of hers would land in jail."

"Was she sore at me?"

."Sure, especially since I couldn't tell her what really happened. But she'll rally round."*

"I don't like to cut your conversation," Herrin interrupted, "but I have to get in touch with the commissioner, whoever he is. And you" – to Jeff – "are supposed to be here as my legal assistant, so you'd* better leave with me."

They stood up, and Huey, gazing at this slender, middle-aged man with his bird-like face and his bright eyes, and thinking of the way he had come down to be of service, of his honest, caustic tongue and the things he had said, suddenly felt immeasurable gratitude, and a sense that he himself was only a child, far, far from being a man who really knew himself. He said, stumbling for words, "Professor Herrin, I don't know how to thank you enough… I mean, I surely appreciate this. I know—"

"Shoot!" Herrin interrupted, giving him a quick handshake. The sly look on his face gave the lie to his words. "I don't care about you: I'm just interested in breaking the colour line in the school system. Five, ten years from now, when we've won this fight on segregation, I'll get a medal from the Phui fraternity* for my good advice in the Wilson case. So long, boy, do your best with McPeak."

Jeff flung an arm around Huey's shoulders and said, "We'll lick 'em, kid. Don't get worried."

"I won't." He stood, scratching the welts around his waist and watching them walk off. At his elbow, startling him, the Rotunda guard said, "Let's go." He turned and started towards the door that would lead him back to his cell, and thought to himself, "Goddamn, it's wonderful not to be alone in the world!" And then, more soberly and with dismay, "He must think I'm a jerk."

Chapter 6

Time Stretch

At eight fifteen in the morning Johnny Lauter, check sheet in hand, was moving from cell to cell on the first tier of the west wing. He was collecting books. Since this was Monday morning, all books had to be returned to the public library; new books, for which the men had written orders the night before from a master list, would be forthcoming by Tuesday afternoon. Eddie Quinn was trailing after Lauter; Quinn was without duties at the moment, and a matter of some urgency was on his mind.

At 112 Lauter collected a biography of Napoleon from Roy Keedy, the elderly optometrist. "How'd you like it?" Lauter asked as the book passed between the bars. Since Lauter enjoyed literary conversation, it was a question he put to most inmates.

"Liked it great! What a man, what a genius!" Keedy replied in a heavily nasal voice. "A book like that inspires you." He sniffed, then sneezed into a wad of toilet paper.

The inmates acquainted with Keedy all agreed that he was a straight guy, pleasant to be with in spite of rather prissy ways. Moreover, they were sorry for him. Without a previous criminal record he had been handed a bad jolt for a man of sixty-one – five to fifteen years. As Keedy explained it, he had been tempted beyond control by the daughter of his landlady, a rosebud of a girl, ripe as a fig, not only willing, but eager – not a cent of money involved. It was the sort of thing that happened all the time, except that most people didn't get caught at it. Nevertheless, the law called it "carnal knowledge of a minor", since the girl was fourteen, and Keedy's days as an optometrist were over.

"So far as I'm concerned," Lauter answered argumentatively, "this Napoleon was a bum! Like the fat-boy, Mussolini. They shoulda hung Napoleon upside down too."

"A bum?" Keedy exclaimed in astonishment. "How can you say a thing like that, feller?" His nose twitched, but he mastered the need to sneeze. "He was perhaps the greatest military genius who ever lived* – he was the emperor—"

"He still was a bum," Lauter interrupted. "You know why?" He levelled a finger. "Cos everything he did was for his own damn glory. He didn't give a damn about people like us. You ever realize the only way them dictators get to be so big is by steppin' on other people's bodies? You ever think of that, huh?"

"All right, but listen, you've got to balance things. What about the Napoleonic code of laws? What about—"

"You wanna argue some more about it, I'll come back later," Lauter interrupted with enthusiasm. "We'll have a debate, huh? Right now get me Jude's book, will you?"

Sneezing violently, Keedy looked around for it.

"Don't tell me he took it to court with him? That'll mess me up."

"Here it is." He slipped a text on public accounting from beneath Jude's pillow. "I don't know why he takes books out. He never reads 'em."

"He's just a lil ol' Georgia hillbilly, that's why, he don't know how to read. I suppose he keeps hopin' for a picture book. Listen, Keedy, don't die of pneumonia before I get back, will you? I wanna have that debate."

"Some cold!" Keedy sniffed cheerfully. "I never get colds, never, but this one caught me the day I came in here, and I can't shake it off. It's too draughty in here, that's the trouble."

"Jail colds are much worse than outside colds," Eddie Quinn put in. "You know why?"

"Why?"

"Cos you're in jail!" Quinn thrust his upper dental plate between his lips and rattled it happily with his tongue. Then, plucking Lauter's sleeve, he asked, "Johnny, you know how far Danbury, Connecticut, is from New Haven?"

"Wouldn't know that, Barber. You thinkin' of takin' a weekend trip?"

"Just askin'," Quinn replied with an air of mystery.

"Uh-huh." Lauter gazed at him for a moment and then moved on. At 110 he collected a detective novel from George Trisler, the former Treasury employee who had accepted a bribe, and a copy of *The Sea-Wolf** from Otha Doty, a coal miner who had taken to stealing automobiles. "How'd you like it?" he asked the latter, since he was not interested in mystery stories.

"Real good, Johnny."

"I told you to take it, didn't I?"

"I didn't get to finish it, though. It's a long one."

"Man, you read slow. If I wasn't tier man, I could read a book like that in a day an' a half."

"Yeah, I read slow," Doty agreed. "Readin' bothers my eyes."

"Man, the almost four years I was in Atlanta I read right through their damn library," Lauter said offhandedly. "Read stories... read philosophy... read about penology... read psychology... ain't nothin' I didn't read." Laughter bubbled in his throat. "I was the best-educated safe-cracker they had."

"You ever read about the Yale University Alcohol Clinic?" Quinn asked suddenly.

"No."

"There's an article in the *Reader's Digest* I borrowed – how they cure up alcoholics there. It's give* me an idea."

"You wanna go to college?" Lauter inquired with his gurgling laugh.

"That's why I ast you about Danbury," Quinn explained with sudden earnestness. "There's a Federal pen there, remember? An' Yale College is in New Haven. Suppose they wasn't far apart?"

For a moment, grinning, Lauter studied the ruined face of his friend; then he asked quietly, "What's on your mind beside dandruff?"

Quinn regarded Lauter with a solemn, questioning expression. "Suppose the Classification Board here wanted to give me a break? They could transfer me to Danbury instead of Lorton, couldn't they?"

"I guess they could arrange it with the Bureau of Prisons if they wanted, sure."

Quinn's eyes began to gleam, a smile of excitement parted his lips. "Last Friday I put in a request slip to see the Board. They'll see me today, maybe tomorra. That's what I'm gonna ast them."

"What good'll that do you?"

"Suppose I'm in Danbury," Quinn explained with mounting enthusiasm, "I get to be one of the prison barbers right away. I do my work A1. Likely some of the officers come to me... they know a good barber when they cross one – the warden himself maybe. Coupla two, three months I do my work, keep my mouth shut. Then I go see the warden. I point to my record, I show him how many times I been put in the clink. Then I say: 'You wanna save taxpayer money? You wanna reuhbilitate somebody? OK, then let me take that Yale cure. I got a three-year sentence, this is my chance to get cured.'"

"I don't quite get it," Lauter protested gently. "How's it gonna work? Suppose Danbury and New Haven are fifty miles away from each other?"

"Maybe one of those Yale doctors comes out to the prison," Quinn argued enthusiastically. "Or maybe they transfer me to the city jail in New Haven. Them's just details – they can arrange them easy enough."

"Sounds like you got something," Lauter agreed slowly.

"You think so?"

"Sounds all right to me," Lauter lied. He knew prison rules and prison boards a good deal better than Quinn. But if this odd notion could make Quinn happy for a few hours, he would not be the one to pull him down from the clouds. "I sure hope you sell it to 'em," he said warmly, and called into 108, "Library books, fellers."

A morose voice replied from the upper bunk, "I gave mine to Hensely in 104."

"Yeah? Well, he better have it, or you'll get another eighteen months."

There was no reply from the upper bunk, and Lauter asked, "Did you read it?"

"Didn't feel like readin' this week."

"Uh-huh," Lauter murmured, and then added, almost tenderly, "Take it easy, Shive, you'll make it."

The other man nodded morosely, and Lauter thought to himself that it beat hell how some guys pushed themselves into jail. Shive, who obviously was as sober and honest as they came, a hard-working plumber on the outside, had threatened to kill the mother of his sweetheart because she was trying to prevent their marriage. Lauter could sympathize with the frustration and anger of a lovesick youth – only, why had he been so dumb as to write the death threat in a letter? Eighteen months for a piece of evidence supplied in his own handwriting.

"Well, how'd you like it, Bell?" he asked the other man in the cell, as a heavy book passed between the bars.

"Shucks," replied the other, "that book didn't do me no good."

"I thought it was funny for a cracker like you to be ordering Leo Tolstoy."

"What d'y' mean?" asked Bell with a puzzled air. He was a homely, bald-pated man of fifty, with the wistful air of one lost in a strange world – as, in fact, he was. A small tobacco farmer from North Carolina, he had journeyed to Washington for an operation at the Veterans' hospital. He had gotten very drunk on the night* of his release, and had been arrested for relieving himself in a public thoroughfare. He now was awaiting sentence for intoxication, for being a public nuisance, for resisting arrest and for spitting in a policeman's face. He was so ashamed of his behaviour that no one on the tier knew why he was there: he refused to talk about it.

"This here book you been readin'," said Lauter, "it's written by Leo Tolstoy, didn't you know that?"

"Didn't hardly notice."

"What're you talkin' about, you didn't notice? You ordered it, didn't you?"

"Man, I didn't want this one," Bell complained. "Said *Resurrection** on that list. I thought it was Bible readin'."

Lauter burst out laughing. "Did you read it?"

"Shucks, the names in that book – I couldn't keep 'em straight. That book didn't do me no good."

Gurgling with laughter, Lauter said, "Here you had a chance to improve yourself, and you let it pass you by. This Tolstoy happens to be a very famous writer, you know that?"

"Well, shucks, I tried it, but it was a story-like. I nevah like to read anythin' less'n I know it's true."

"Me neither," put in Eddie Quinn. "That's why I like the *Reader's Digest*. It's the on'y thing I read. You can depend on every word of* it."

"Why, you two dummies are dumber than I ever thought," Lauter jeered affectionately. "Don't you know you can learn from a story, too? Take *Less Mizerabells* now, by Victor Hugo. That's deep – it makes you think. It's about a Frenchman who was in prison twenty years. He came out, went to work and built up a big business – even became mayor of his town. When I read that in Atlanta, it made me think – it showed what a man could do if he wanted!"

"I don't put no trust in make-believe stories," Bell stated flatly. "I like to do readin' that'll improve me, like the Bible."

"But that's just what I'm talkin' about. You take this Tolstoy – he had a big mind. It don't make no difference if he made the story up – it still can be true to life, can't it?"

"How kin it be true if he made it up out of his own haid?" asked Bell in genuine perplexity.

"Because it can have a deep lesson to it! I can't explain about this particular book, cos I never read it. But last year I took some of his stories out of the public library. There was one there* – about a farmer who wanted more land – it certainly was a corker. It had a moral to it about what happens when a man gets too greedy."

"Greedy – what does that mean?" asked Bell.

"If you eat so much you vomit – that's when you're greedy. This farmer wanted so much land he lost everything. He was too greedy, see?"

"Well, OK," Quinn put in, "but was the story true?"

"Certainly it was true – the idea behind it was true."

"I'm talkin' about the facts: was the facts true?"

"But I already showed you that ain't the reason you read stories, you rummy."

"It's why *I* read," Quinn insisted. "I like to learn, I like facts, that's why I swear by the *Reader's Digest*."

"Who is this Tolstoy, a Frenchman?" asked Bell.

"A Frenchman – Jesus Christ, a Frenchman!" Lauter exclaimed. "Didn't you see the Russian names in that book?"

"I sure thought he was French. I knew a French tobacco farmer oncet was named Leo."

"An' I had a dog once named Carolina, but he wasn't bald like you," Lauter retorted with a guffaw.* He moved on to the next cell.

"Shucks, I'm only bald on my haid," Bell called after him genially. "Ain't bald on my chest or my you-know-where."

"Library books," Lauter called into 106. "Don't keep me waitin', fellers. I'm a busy man, I got big responsibilities."

Mr Kraft, day officer of Tier One, who had taken over from Mr Simmons at eight o'clock, called "Tier man", and Eddie Quinn responded on the double. He asked eagerly "What's the word, Mr Kraft?" – and then, when he had been told, merely nodded. Without disguising his own dismay, he walked down the line of cells to give out the bad news from up front: there would be no Yard on this day. There was no Yard on weekends, and no Yard when it rained, and no Yard on a morning like this when word came down that there were not enough officers to handle Yard. Men cursed and grumbled and asked one another why Yard couldn't come more often than one or two days a week. An hour in the open was like a birthday gift – an hour of sky and sun changed a man's day. Books always killed time, but there would be no books today. The canteen line, the twice-a-week shower and shave, killed time, but neither was scheduled for this day.

In all of the cells of the west wing men settled down to grapple with time.

Time is a thing that has neither flesh nor face, but in jail a man must grapple it* between his hands, he must wage daily war upon it. The invalid, the soldier in battle, the woman in childbirth, know the dreariness of time or the ferocious clasp of time. Yet none of them, nor anyone else, come to know TIME as do those who are behind bars.

A jail cell is a compartment of steel and stone in which two strangers lodge together at the decision of others. Their abode, when it is modern and has been scientifically designed, may be nine and a half feet long, six and a half feet wide. In this space there will be two sleeping bunks, one above the other, a wash bowl and toilet, a wall seat and wall table. In this space the two strangers may be confined together for twenty-one out of every twenty-four hours, sometimes for weeks, sometimes for many months, while they await hearing or trial, sentence or transfer, the length of a judge's vacation or the slow progress of a crowded court calendar.

In a jail cell each man must move in conjunction with the movements of his partner. If one man snores or coughs or cries, the other hears. When one man is bursting with rage, the other must pay attention. The intestinal habits of each become part of the life of the other.

And always both men must grapple with time.

Only a healthy man confined in a cell knows how mocking and obscene time can be – only he can know in his own heartbeat the dull weight of time, can know how arid, punishing and purposeless can be the passage of time. The juices in his body run fast, his appetites are vital, his spirit seeks its own level of expression. But the bars forbid! The bars are at once concrete and symbolic. They stun the flesh and antagonize the mind. They nourish rage that cannot be expressed, heartsickness that has no outlet. The bars are unbelievable: they never are accepted by any inmate, yet always they are there; they are implacable and most terrible.

What do men do in jail when they have nothing to do? What do they do with their time?

Eddie Quinn, fighting time, had retired to his cell in order to lie on his bunk and dream. Eyes half open, occasionally smoking, he would be content to lie in a serene stupor until jail routine decreed otherwise. If he were summoned to duty by the tier guard, Quinn would leap up instantly. Or, if Johnny Lauter came round* for a chat, Quinn would be more than agreeable. But now, being free of duties and alone, he sought the twilight doze of those who have accommodated themselves to prison existence.

He dozed and he dreamt, but he did not think seriously about any subject, for that would have disturbed his serenity. He dreamt that the Classification Board had granted his impossible request, and that he already had been transferred to the city jail in New Haven. With pleasure he dreamt about the brainy doctors of Yale University, who were curing his alcoholism with a combination of psychology and a new miracle drug – but what drug and what method of psychology, he left up to them. The magic waxing bigger, he dreamt about a famous plastic surgeon who said, "Eddie, my boy, your case is a cinch. I'll straighten your crooked eye, I'll take those burn scars offa your face, an' I'll do it all for free. You know why?"

"No, doc, why?"

"Cos you once gave me the cleanest, smoothest shave I ever had in my life. You got the real barber's touch, Eddie, an' I respect a man who's tops at his trade."

Quinn was far from a stupid man, yet not once in the ten years of his excessive drinking had he ever acknowledged to himself that he had ceased to be the man or the skilled, dependable worker that he had been once. Self-delusion is easy when a man has strong need for it, and Quinn's need went deep. He never had been much of a drinker until the night his car turned over on a Pennsylvania turnpike, killing his bride of two months and maiming him. The accident had been the result of his own carelessness, and he had become a man rotted with guilt, and with a sense that the best of his life was over. Nevertheless, his descent from respectable citizen to petty thief had been deceptively gradual. At first his drunks had lasted only a few days, and he had brushed them aside as of no importance. A job lost in one shop was supplanted by another; he always had his skill, his old references. When, for the first time, he was sentenced to a week in jail for disorderly conduct while intoxicated, he emerged a teetotaller – for three months. But then the bouts of drunkenness had come more often, and the intervals of sober employment had become shorter. Earning less but thirsting more, he had taken to petty shoplifting when his funds ran out. Each time he had said to himself, "Well, never again – you're strictly off that, Eddie, m'boy, no more light-fingered stuff for you." And yet the man who never would touch another's property when sober would – and had, when he was gripped by his nightmare thirst for oblivion – steal anything movable in a Woolworth department store, steal the eyeglasses, false teeth and shoes from a dead man in an alley. For when Quinn took to drinking, he became foully drunk; in his alcoholic bouts he would cease working and drink himself penniless; without money, then, he would steal; wild drunk, he would fight; dirty drunk, he would thrust his face into a public toilet to lap water. And yet, observing his drunkenness, it also would be impossible to know how violently ashamed he was, or with what dismay he watched his own wretched, compulsive behaviour; as now, at the age of forty-seven, starting three years in prison for the attempted theft of an eighty-dollar wristwatch, he felt the stupidity of it even more than the burden of time, and sorrowed in the dark shelter of night, and told himself that after this, after this, he never would drink again.

Except that he would! Even now, without being aware of it, he had ceased dreaming about his cure and was enjoying his first drink on his first day of freedom – a long, cold beer with a rye whiskey on the side.

He made a good prisoner, this barber. The guards liked him because he did his work well and never caused any trouble. The inmates liked him because he was gay and friendly, and never whined, and never molested them with the defeat in his heart. And although there was nothing that would happen to Eddie Quinn in these several years of confinement that would prevent a future return to prison, he was an agreeable, obedient inmate. That was all the authorities asked or his society demanded of him.

Out on the eating range, Johnny Lauter was killing time by assembling the books of the entire west wing on two of the tables. Shortly a portable bookcase would be trundled in, he would arrange the books by number on the shelves, and then the bittersweet work of his week would be over. Books always had a double edge for Lauter. Through books he had come to understand a good deal about himself and society, or so he felt, and for this he treasured them. He loved to see books standing side by side, to scan their titles, to mark in his mind the names of any that looked good for future reading. In a passionate, undisciplined way he was hungry for the possible knowledge that any odd book could give him. Yet books also spelled prison to him, because he had not learnt to enjoy them until he had been locked up: books reminded him of the wasted years of his life. For this reason he always was most reflective, and inwardly most melancholy, on Monday mornings.

This Monday was especially bad because he felt himself so close to a court decision. Beneath his laughter at Eddie Quinn's jokes ran a sour current of fear. He did his busy work, he discussed Tolstoy and Victor Hugo with outward zest, but his inner eye could not shake the vision of Johnny Lauter entering a gas chamber.

"I'd feel a little better," he once had said to his wife, "if the cops'd caught up with one of the jobs I *did* do. But to go straight for six years like I have and then get hit with a bum rap – shoot, that's hard to take!"

To all who knew them, the Lauters were a typical American family, citizens without blemish. There was nothing about this sober, industrious car* mechanic to indicate that he had been a juvenile delinquent, a petty thief and an expert safe-cracker, or that he had, at various times, spent twelve years in confinement – in a reformatory, a state prison, a Carolina chain gang and finally, in the Federal penitentiary at Atlanta. There also was nothing about Lauter that could reveal the inner devotion he felt for his wife, who was a simple Georgia farm girl, and who had brought such understanding of human frailty to their marriage that she had purged him of his wolfish bitterness. They had met when he was on conditional release from Atlanta, and without her it would have been impossible for him to sustain the truly heroic effort required of any long-time criminal who is trying not only to change his life, but his way of thought and feeling about society. There were times when he wanted to quit his job, because steady, humdrum work was so much like prison existence, or when he wanted to beat up his employer over a critical word that would have been trivial to another. It was then that her compassion eased and soothed him, and restored his equilibrium. All that was manly and attractive in Lauter grew stronger because he loved this woman and was loved by her. The inner petulance, the distrust, the quick rage of the reformatory boy, gradually drained away. More and more he opened his heart to his wife, and came closer to her. After several years of marriage, life became very good for this ex-criminal.

Then, five years away from prison, his past returned to plague him. An informer for the police, who had known Lauter in Atlanta, stepped by accident into the garage where he worked. They chatted, and the man congratulated Lauter on making the grade in the legitimate world – and then made his report. The next evening two detectives were waiting when Lauter left the garage.

They took him down to headquarters in order to question him about some unsolved jobs in his old trade – safe-cracking. When Lauter protested with passion that he had been living straight for five years, they answered, "Yeah? That's fine." They pointed out, however, that an old-timer like him would be expected to provide himself with a job as a cover.

"Cover?" Lauter cried in indignation. "I'm workin' a forty-eight to a sixty-hour week. I walked into that job three years ago, and now I'm second motor mechanic. I pull a dollar fifteen an hour. I got an apartment. I got a wife an' two kids. I got a savings account. What the hell would I be covering up for?"

All this was great, the detectives told him, but they damn well intended to keep an eye on him. They wanted to know, for instance, if Lauter handled any of the agency money – or if the boss had been finding any shortages of tools or equipment. They knew too much about the character and methods of men with his record not to check up on him. "Keep your nose clean," he was told, "or we'll be shipping your ass back to Atlanta!"

The reflexes of self-preservation, formed in his outlaw years, told Lauter what he ought to do – quietly draw their savings from the bank and then walk out on a Saturday with no more than a couple of suitcases, like any family off for a weekend. They would tell no one, and they would leave no forwarding address.

He discussed this with Amy, his wife, but only half-heartedly. In truth he was anguished by the thought of giving up his good job, of turning his back on their cheery apartment, of leaving behind a household of furniture paid for month by month over two long years. In the end, against inner warnings, he agreed with Amy that they had nothing to fear.

Nevertheless, he took a number of steps in self-protection. Since the wartime job market was still open, he got a Sunday job at a garage* near his home, so that all seven days of his week would be accounted for. In addition, and not without bitterness, he told his story to a friend at the shop, and the latter agreed to telephone him at his home every night between ten thirty and midnight.

For nine months, except for occasional visits to his employer, the police did leave him alone. But then, one Sunday morning, they came to his apartment with a search warrant. There had been a post-office robbery the night before, not five blocks from his home. For three hours, while his wife and children watched in terror, the detectives searched the apartment for evidence, examining furniture, walls, floors, closets, clothes, even the drain pipes in the plumbing system. They found nothing, but they arrested Lauter on suspicion, and took him away.

They pursued their investigation for forty-eight hours more, using the classic methods of their type – that is, Lauter was kept without adequate food or sleep, grilled incessantly and beaten. However, since no confession was forthcoming, and since the police had no evidence at all, they finally let him go.

"We move!" Lauter said to his wife as they wept in each other's arms. "Next Sunday we walk out clean and hop a train. We'll go somewhere ten states away!" This time Amy agreed – but their decision had come too late. Lauter was again under arrest before the end of the week.

A routine enquiry, it seemed, had been sent from Washington to all police departments on the eastern seaboard to ask if Johnny Lauter, safe-cracker, was wanted for anything. The police of Durham, North Carolina, had telephoned immediately to say that they had been searching for Lauter for a month. A tobacco warehouse had been burglarized there, the watchman beaten unconscious and the safe looted of twelve thousand dollars. The watchman, who had been shown a great many photographs of men with burglary records in North Carolina, had identified Lauter as one of the criminals. A writ of extradition would be presented at once.

On the face of it, the charges seemed absurd, and Lauter entered the preliminary hearing with confidence. The city of Durham was two hundred and forty miles away. The witnesses who came on his behalf testified to his seven days of work and to a nightly telephone call during the entire period before and after the robbery. Nevertheless, because of the positive identification by the watchman, the commissioner refused to release him. The writ was referred to a Federal judge, and, because of Lauter's record and the seriousness of the crime, bail was set at twenty thousand dollars. An absurd charge had turned deadly serious.

"Listen, honey," Lauter said to his wife in the ten minutes allowed them before he was taken to jail, "this is a bad one! We'll either win up here or we'll lose down there. I want you to draw every cent we have in savings, go to my boss for the name of a first-class lawyer an' pay him his price. I know those southern courtrooms with their cracker juries. That watchman is a disabled war veteran, a local boy. Who am I? An out-of-town convict with a long record, including chain-gang time. If they get me in that courtroom, I'm finished. An' you may as well know the bad news right now, honey, *I mean* finished." He gazed at her stricken face, and felt like beating his head against the wall, and went on to explain the full measure of what confronted them. There were, he told her, two degrees of burglary in North Carolina. First degree meant criminal entrance into a private home in which people were sleeping, or even into the cellar of a public building where a janitor might be asleep. This was the charge against him. State law permitted only one of two sentences for first-degree burglary: life imprisonment, provided the jury recommended mercy, or death.

Four months had passed since that conversation, with fear mounting in both of them. It developed that the watchman's identification was not to be shaken. Their lawyer had journeyed to Durham in order to show the man a recent photograph of Lauter, rather different from the police photo of ten years before. The watchman had acknowledged the difference, yet insisted that it was the same man. So far as the attorney could tell, neither malice nor deceit were involved. It was a case of mistaken identity, with Lauter's record aiding the error. Nor did the attorney have any greater success in talking to the police. They had a comfortable answer to Lauter's defence: that he could have finished work at six in the evening, driven the two hundred and forty miles to Durham by eleven, entered the warehouse with his partner and cracked the safe by 2 a.m. – the very period during which the burglary occurred – and returned to Washington, ready to begin work, by seven in the morning.

There had been two hearings before a Federal judge, with an assistant Attorney General of North Carolina arguing that the case could best be settled* by submitting it to a jury. Lauter's defence had been the same offered at the preliminary hearing: mistaken identity. As supporting evidence he offered his work record and savings account, the testimony of his two employers and fellow workers, and the dubiously exact timetable he would have had to follow in order to commit the burglary. At the second hearing, however, there had been something else offered in his defence: an unplanned, passionate outburst from Amy, pleading her own knowledge of her husband. She had related incidents from their first year together that he had forgotten; she had dredged from her memory small things that to her – if not to the judge – were the measure of the man she had married. "God in heaven," she had cried wildly to the judge, "don't a man like him ever git the benefit of a doubt? What's he been slaving seven days a week for? Does he have to pay all his life for stealing a bike when he was a kid of twelve?"

Amy had wept, but the judge had not – the judge had been silent. Three weeks had passed since the second hearing, and the judge had kept his silence. He was, their attorney reported, investigating further, and weighing the evidence. Half of July, all of August and September had passed since Lauter's arrest, and now it was October. The children were well, Amy said, but *she* looked more drawn and hollow-eyed at each visit. Their savings had gone for living and to pay the lawyer; the radio had been sold, and their refrigerator taken away by the finance company; but Amy was getting along fine, she said. She was washing and sewing for neighbours, and every week Lauter's boss was giving her seven dollars as an advance on his future wages, and every Saturday she got a food basket from the relief station. There was no need for Lauter to worry about them, she always said. All they needed was for him to come home.

This was the ninth Monday on which Lauter had arranged the library books for CB1. The task being completed and the books on their way out, he returned to the tier runway. He said "How you doin', pal?" to the new man in 130, but he did not pause until he had arrived at 112. Since he had no other tasks at the moment, and since he had no book to read, he needed another way to pass time. A debate with Roy Keedy over the historic role of Napoleon Bonaparte seemed the best idea for the moment. When that well went dry, he would, of course, dig for something else. He was old in the ways of killing time.

In the bull pen of the Federal courthouse Floyd Varney was fighting time with a memory game: he was recalling where he had been and what he had been doing in the month of October in other years. One year ago was easy for him to remember, and he lingered over it because the memory was so pleasant. At this hour he would have been at the hotel, busy with the morning's baking. Corn bread and lemon pie on his ticket, perhaps, with the maître d' fussing around like he always did because he had no confidence in any cook under fifty years – knowing very well, however, that Varney's corn bread had been plenty popular with the customers twice already, or else he wouldn't let a second cook do more than make the mix. Then the luncheon squad of waitresses starting to check, with Janey giving him an elbow in the ribs as though by accident. "Hello, funny face, what you been doing since I last saw you?" (That morning, 7 a.m., as he left her washing the dishes in his room.)

"Earning my pay, beautiful, what d'you think?"

"You mean baking those two-pound lead nuggets you call Parker House rolls?"

"I notice you eat 'em."

"That's cos I love you. A girl'll make any sacrifice for love."

"Yeah-yeah. Say, I got an idea for Sunday."

"Don't you remember? This is my Sunday to work."

"That's right, darn it! I thought we might go on a picnic. We need t'get our days off coordinated."

"We sure do. Why don't you ask Mr Strand? You've got more drag with him than I have."

"I'll speak to him today."

"Swell! Bye now – I gotta set my tables."

"No flirting with the customers."

"Only if they're rich and good-looking like you."

Two years ago, in October 1944, he had been in New York, studying at a school for cooks and bakers. That was good, too, even though he'd had to squeeze every penny in order to get along on his government allotment. But he had had a fine time that year. It was grand to be finished with the war, and to be learning a trade, and to feel that at last the future held promise.

But the October before that had been awful, a nightmare – lying in a cot in the naval hospital at San Diego with a draining hole in his hip and with a case of nerves that wouldn't let him sleep or keep food in his stomach, or hear an aeroplane* pass outside without trembling like a coward.

Abruptly Varney rose from his bench in the bull pen. He began to pace the room with gloomy tension. Obviously this memory game was bad for him – there weren't enough good years to go back to. There were better ways to pass time: he'd list all the states he could remember, for instance, then all the capital cities he could remember, then every recipe he knew for a pie or cake. The last idea was the best one. "Oh Christ, what a morning!" he thought. "What a hell of a morning to live through!" As though he never had done so before, he began to calculate his possibilities. Assuming that he was given ten years, the minimum, he'd be eligible for parole in forty months. However, if parole were denied, he'd still have good time coming to him of ten days a month. That would amount to a hundred and twenty days each year, or four months. On a ten-year sentence that added up to good time of three years and four months. So at worst he'd only have to serve six years and…

"My God, what a morning!" he thought again. He paced the room.

On the fourth tier of CB1, Huey Wilson was killing time by watching the antics of George Benjamin, the tier man. Huey felt depressed, and he was in a mood for low-comedy amusement. Previously he had been recounting to his cellmate the substance of his interview in the Rotunda. Somehow, without the sustaining presence of his brother and Professor Herrin, his situation had begun to seem more and more gloomy. Eugene Finnerty, it turned out, was as sad in spirit as he was in countenance. He had done nothing to bolster Huey's confidence in what he might expect from McPeak. As a result, Huey was having visions both of a prison term and of the abortive end of his law career. It was only an hour past that he had been reminding himself that no Negro was exempt from abuse, and that he had no more reason to feel sorry for himself than for his father* or his uncle, or tens of thousands of others. Yet he *was* sorry for himself, and he did feel abused, and at this moment – even though it made him ashamed – he wished to God that he never had heard of that picket line.

George Benjamin came along to interrupt these thoughts with an exhibition of acrobatics. For all his small size, the tier man was a superb athlete. It was his custom daily to walk the length of the tier runway on his hands, to turn cartwheels and somersaults, and otherwise to keep his muscular body in shape. Today, since a new man was on hand as audience, Benjamin was eager to display himself. Walking on his hands, he suddenly appeared before the door of Huey's cell. Announcing that he was a chimpanzee in a zoo, he began with great relish to hurl insults and obscenities at the ugly humans on the other side of the bars. Meanwhile, with expert skill, he balanced himself on one hand and used the other to scratch, gesture and tear the air. Huey laughed because it was in his mood to do so – in actuality, however, the performance was more ludicrous than genuinely witty. Benjamin, erect, was an odd-looking man at best with his crossed eyes and his ill-assorted features; upside down, with his spectacles hanging away from his stubby nose, with veins bulging in his neck and his mouth distorted from strain, he looked half a monster.

After a few minutes, having exhausted this routine, the tier man snapped to his feet and instantly began climbing the bars of the cell door using feet and hands and swinging his body and head, exactly like a monkey. Arriving at the top, he paused to scratch himself under one armpit, then slid happily down to the reward of Huey's laughter. "Looks easy, don' it?" he asked. "Let's see you climb those bars, boy."

"Uh-uh. Not me."

"You know what it takes? Takes practice – an' this." Benjamin thrust back the half sleeve of his shirt and displayed a bulging, dancing muscle. "C'm'ere, big boy," he said suddenly. He thrust his hand through the bars. "Shake! Let's see who's got the strongest shake. First one to say 'ouch' is the loser."

Huey stepped forward. He was young enough, and strong enough, to find the contest challenging. Nevertheless, out of a sense of sportsmanship, he offered a warning. "My hand is almost twice as large as yours. Gives me an advantage."

"Shake," said Benjamin, grinning.

They gripped hands and applied pressure. After a few moments of contest, Huey's fingers crumpled beneath the vice-like power of the other's grip. "Ouch," he conceded ruefully. "You win." Benjamin, revelling in his strength, continued to squeeze. "You win, let go," said Huey, trying to pull loose.

"Whatsamatter, little Prince of Ethiopia, you weak?" the tier man asked with crude pleasure.

Angry now, and in pain, Huey reached through the bars with his left hand and thrust hard with his thumb into his adversary's neck, pressing against the windpipe. There was an instantaneous, strangled gasp from Benjamin. He let go and jumped back. "Jesus," he cried, more in wonder than anger, "what'd you do there? Felt like you shoved a needle in my neck."

"That's some fighting my brother learnt in the Army," Huey explained, not without satisfaction. "Next time let go, you son of a gun." He stood shaking his hand to restore circulation.

"Man, that's a killer," Benjamin exclaimed in admiration, as he felt his neck exploratively. "I gotta remember that... come in handy some day. Say, how'd you like that shake of mine? Like a steel trap, hunh?"

"Yeah, sure is," Huey conceded. He was too quickly aware of the childish simplicity of the little man to maintain his anger. "You're strong all right."

"Oughta see me lift weights," Benjamin boasted. "I could outlift the heavyweights in the Lewisburg penitentiary. You wanna know why I'm so strong – you wanna know the secret?"

"Secret?"

"Sure! A little man like me don't get so strong jus' by exercise. I got somethin' extra." He waited, peering at Huey with a wise, satisfied look. "What's the biggest strength a man has? It's his man juice, ain't it?"

"His what?"

"Man juice, his jism. It stands to reason it must be, on account it kin make a kid."

"So what?" Huey asked, laughing. "You got more of that than anybody else?"

"I sure have. You know why? Cos I keep mine, I don't waste it on women. It's all stored up inside me. I never been with a woman yit, and I never will be," he added with manifest pride.

"Oh, brother, what a cock-eyed idea," Huey exclaimed with a burst of laughter. "Where'd you ever get that notion?"

"Cock-eyed, eh?" Benjamin smiled with the imperturbability of one who has met the same arguments many times. He pointed to Finnerty, who was sitting on the wall seat, quietly listening to them. "Looky there at that broken-down ol' horse. He's got flat feet, he's got bleedin' piles an' God knows what else. Because of all the screwin'! He's got four kids an' a fifth cormin'. That ruins a man."

"Now, ain't that dumb!" Finnerty exclaimed with mild disgust. "Where'd this world be if men an' womens didn't have chillen?"

"Dumb?" Benjamin echoed. He thrust his face pugnaciously between two of the bars. "You's six feet tall, an' I kin break you in half. Why, it's even made you weak in your mind." He began to chuckle. "Git him t'tell you about the warehouse he burned down," he said to Huey. "The firemens took one look at it and knew it was a put-up job. Any lil ol' boy woulda known it."

Finnerty suddenly burst out laughing and stood up. It was a sad, defeated kind of laughter, and his liver-coloured face was very sorrowful. "I never thought I'd have to spend my time arguin' with the likes of you. Ask him how many times he's been in prison," he said to Huey. "Ask him about them fifteen years he's startin' right now. Oh, he's the smart one aroun' here – oh, yeah!"

"You're damn tootin' I'm the smart one," Benjamin retorted with a grin. "I got fifteen years, sure. But what else I got?" He waved a hand expansively. "Just a cool hunnerd thousand out of that job, that's all. Stashed away where nobody but me kin find it. I'll serve ten years an' then I'll be out. That means ten thousand a year. How many coloured mens make that in a year? Hunh? How many?"

"Oh, man, you tellin' that one agin?" Finnerty muttered, sitting down. "Even believes it!"

"Ten thousand a year," Benjamin continued airily. "That's good pay. I'll only be forty-four when I come out, with a cool hunnerd thousand waitin' for me. Come to think of it, I'm the on'y man on this tier with any sense at all. Yous all a bunch of suckers, got caught for nothin'." Suddenly he was standing on his hands again. "S'long, boys. Ten years from now come see me in my mansion in Paris. I'll buy you a glass of sody water." Laughing, walking on his hands, he disappeared down the runway.

"Is he loony?" Huey asked Finnerty. "He didn't seem like it before breakfast, but he sure talks like a goof now."

"No, he ain't," Finnerty replied in his sad way. "Reckon he's what they call 'stir simple'.* I hear tell he's hardly been free since he wuz a boy, jus' in an' outa prison. He's got some queer ideas, that's all. In most things he kin talk straight. I feel sorry for him."

"My God!" Huey said with a chuckle. "That's some secret he's got."

"You know, I been doin' a lot of studyin' since I been here," Finnerty offered quietly. "It's learnt me a lot. I feel sorry for everybody in here, all good boys. You take Ben Wellman, two doors down. He's a nice boy, never stole nothin', works hard. He works in buildin', I believe, labouring work. You know that's hard work an' it don't pay good. Every Saturday night Ben gits drunk on beer, he told me. Usta be I'd look down hard on a man like that, but I don' no more. I unnerstan' better. Reckon Ben's in jail cos he's human, that's all."

"What'd he do?" asked Huey.

Finnerty was gazing off into space, and it was evident that he was thinking hard as he answered. "His mistake was he got jealous of his wife. Weren't really his wife, but he was livin' with her, cared for her a lot, he told me. He got drunk one night an' beat her up bad for dancin' wild with another man. That weren't right – no man should lift his hand to a woman I say... she got him arrested. But we's all got weakness and bad in us, we's all human, an' human means weak. I'm sorry for the woman, but I'm sorry for Ben. I'm sorry for George Benjamin, his whole life in prison. I'm sorry for me, too."

Finnerty stood up – a tall, ungainly man in his middle forties, with an almost toothless mouth, with lines of worry and sorrow creasing his tired, liver-coloured face. He began to pace the cell in obvious agitation. Huey, lying on the lower bunk, waited in silence. He knew that Finnerty wanted to talk further, and he was both curious and drawn to the man.

Sadly, in a gentle monotone, Finnerty told his story. For fifteen years, he explained, he had worked as a janitor for a white man, who was an importer and wholesaler of rugs. Three months back his employer, Ulrich, had come to him with the news that he was at the point of bankruptcy. He wanted Finnerty's help in setting fire to his warehouse.

"I knew it was wrong, a turrible thing t'do," Finnerty told Huey, "but I let myself git tempted."

Ulrich, it seemed, had promised him a permanent job, a raise in wages and a huge bonus in addition, four thousand dollars in cash. For an unskilled Negro worker, whose labour never had earned him more than fourteen hundred dollars a year, it was a staggering offer. In exchange for the small cheat of a big insurance company, he was being offered, by his standards, lifelong security for himself and his family. He agreed to cooperate.

"Seemed to me like Ulrich had it all thunked out so good," Finnerty said. "There weren't nobody gon t'be hurted, only the insurance company a little, an' *it* could afford a loss. Nobody ever'd know."

The Fire Department, however, had known immediately. Ulrich had taken everything into account except the accumulated experience of technicians. The intensity of the conflagration, the rapidity with which all areas of the building had become involved and the comparatively short duration of the fire all pointed to arson. In putting the automatic sprinkler system out of commission and in using gasoline to start the fire, Ulrich had guaranteed the apprehension of both of them.

"Weren't more'n a week before the polices found out where we'd boughten the gasoline," Finnerty said. "We'd gone into Virginia, buyin' only two cans at a time in different towns, but they tracked it down. Guess those polices is a lot smarter'n we figgered."

Weighing most heavily upon Finnerty, however, was not his bad luck in being caught, but his subsequent behaviour. The police had confronted him with the evidence, threatened him with the maximum penalty of twenty years, and then, like Ulrich, offered him a bribe: a sentence of no more than six years, with a recommendation of parole in one third of that time. He had confessed.

Yet now, as he told Huey, he felt he had done a terrible wrong in confessing. "Oncet I throwed in with Ulrich I were honour-bound t'stick with him, weren't I?" He shook his head and grimaced in a way that revealed his nearly toothless mouth. "Seems so to me. But it's too late now. I'm sure sorry for Ulrich. They give him fifteen years, an' he's got a family too. But that's the kind of mistake a man kin make. I wanted t'do good for my own family, but I only done bad for everybody."

They were silent for a while. Huey, lying on the bunk, was thinking hard. Somehow, without his willing it, his mood had quite changed. He no longer was sorry for himself, and he no longer regretted that he had walked on a picket line before a Jim Crow school. Anger stirred in him – anger at the desperation with which so many people had to live. Here was Finnerty, who blamed himself for yielding to temptation and considered himself weak, and undoubtedly was. But surely it was the man's toothless mouth that told the full story. Huey had seen so many of those gaping mouths in the Negro alleys and streets of his home town. He had seen them also among the white farmhands and whiskey makers of the Virginia hills. Invariably they told the same tale: of poverty and bad diet, of no dental care, of ignorance. Here was Finnerty – black man born at the bottom of society, born with a crown of thorns on his head without knowing it, toiling, toiling for sheer existence – and why shouldn't he have been tempted?

Sighing, Finnerty exclaimed aloud, "I'm feelin' miserable in my heart all the time. How my wife an' chillens're gonna git along, I don' know."

Huey sat up. He leant forward and touched Finnerty's hand, feeling a close, wordless identification with this beaten, sorrowing middle-aged man, so much more sinned against than sinner. He wanted to throw his arms around this stranger and cry out for the world to hear, "Take a look – another poor black man done in!" But Huey was still a youngster, rather afraid of the power of his own feelings in a situation like this, and he merely said hesitantly, "Finnerty, seems to me you blame yourself too much. Seems to me that white man you worked for was mostly to blame."

"Coulda said 'no'," Finnerty replied unhappily. "Can't excuse myself that way. Coulda let him fire me."

"But—"

"You don't unnerstand," Finnerty interrupted. He began to tell his story all over again in order to explain better the depth of his guilt and weakness.

Huey listened, because there was nothing else to do – and in this way both men killed part of a morning's time.

In the cell next door, Isaac Reeves and Alfrice Tillman were passing time with checkers. An unspoken armistice had gone into effect between them. For the moment neither man cared to pursue the question of whether Tillman's conduct with the white men on Tier One had been proper or not. Tillman had made no move to ask for a transfer from this cell block, as he had threatened, and Reeves was acting as though their relations had not changed at all.

Sliding a piece of paper from one square to another of the writing tablet that served as their board, Reeves said, "Got you on the run as usual, sonny boy. King me." Complying, Tillman murmured, "The only usual about it, ol' man, is that it's gettin' warm in here like usual. Gonna be another hot day."

"Ruther be warm than cold. They tell me this place is an ice box in winter, an' full of draughts. King me again."

"Now, what good is that king gonna do you when I got it blocked?"

"I'll get to move it. Don't worry about me, lil boy, worry about yourself. I'm two games ahead of you this morning."

"Stop braggin' an' king me. Say, ol' man, how'd you like t'go fishin' with me right now?"

"You invitin' me?"

"Sure am."

Reeves laughed softly. His black eyes gleamed, and the taut skin on his bony face crinkled all over. "You're like t'break my heart, boy. When my week's work is done an' I've gone to church, there's nothin' I love so good as settin' by the Potomac in the late afternoon eatin' chittlins* an' fishin'.'"

"So why didn't you tell me before this?" Tillman asked. He slipped down from the top bunk, where they both were seated, and banged on the cell wall. After a moment Ben Wellman in 426 called, "What you want?"

"Pass the word down to the Boss Man, will ya?"

"What word?"

"Tell him me an' Reeves wanna go fishin'."

Reeves chuckled, but their neighbour replied in exasperation, "Goddamn it, funny guy, I was takin' a nap."

"I can't help it, this is an emergency. Me an' Reeves need t'go fishin'."

"You an' Reeves can both screw each other."

"Golly, man, Reeves is too old for that, or else we sure would. He's even got grey hair where it don't appeal to me."

Reeves's smile faded. Jokes about sexual perversion, so frequent among men in jail, were repellent to a family man like him. And even though he sensed that much of this talk was the febrile chatter of lonely men starved for woman's love, nevertheless it left him uncomfortable. "C'mon, get back to this checker game," he said to his young cellmate. "Don't run out cos you gonna get beat."

Tillman suddenly stopped grinning, shook his head and lay down on the lower bunk. "I'm tired of checkers, tired of talkin', tired of everythin' about this place," he exploded angrily. "Won't nothin' satisfy me till I'm out on the street again."

After a moment, Reeves responded quietly, "Yeah. It gets to be hard to take sometimes, don't it?" Lithely he swung down from the upper bunk – a slender, grey-haired man with a supple, wiry body. "Personally, I find prayin' a help. The Lord's a friend to a man in trouble."

"The Lord don't listen to me."

"Don't be a jackass, young feller. The Lord listens to everyone."

"Not to me, He don't. An' not to you neither," Tillman retorted sharply. "Why else you in here?"

"Lord didn't put me in here," the older man replied comfortably, "the Law did. Lord didn't tell me to cheat on my income tax: I did that for myself. Didn't enjoy payin' money to a govinment that robs me, takin' my sweat money an' Jim-Crowin' me outa my rights. It ain't the Lord's fault the govinment catched me."

"The Lord sure works in mysterious ways," Tillman retorted. He jumped up in a passion. "Whole millions of coloured folk prayin' to the Lord year after year, but where are they? White's still right, an' we's still niggers! Me – there ain't never been a man could enjoy big-timin' more'n me! If the Lord made me that way, why do He deny me everythin'? I'm a man wants to go places, ride cars, dress flashy, eat good, have women – but what does the Lord give a coloured man like me? Job in a damn elevator in a damn white man's hotel, forty-eight damn hours a week ridin' up and down,

down and up, for what? Not enough pay to buy myself a nice-looking suit of clothes even! Next time I ain't stealin' no damn wallet off'n a drunken white man who gives me ten cents for helpin' him to bed an' thinks that gives him the right t'cuss me out. I'm through with chicken livin', chicken workin'. I'm after the big now… I'm gonna steal big an' live big – or take me a big funeral, no in between!"

"Guess every man has t'work out his own life," Reeves observed quietly. "Only there ain't time to expeeriment much, so you better think hard on it. Only thing I'm sorry for now is I didn't pay their damn income tax. Wasn't worth this to me."

"Man, man, ain't even recreation hour yet," Tillman said forlornly. "How I'm gonna pull this eighteen months' time I got, I sure don't know."

"I'll tell you what I'd do with my life if I was you," Reeves offered quietly, with compassion. "Soon as I got out of prison, I'd land me any kind of job I could, just to keep me goin' a while. But night-time I'd go to a school an' study me a trade, maybe plumbin' or weldin' or carpentry – anythin' at all, jus' so it was a useful skill. That way—"

"Sure," Tillman interrupted in a jeering tone, "I git it. I learn a trade an' then go down to the employment agency." He began to act out the scene with a delicately comic air. "Knock-knock – got any jobs for a good carpenter?" He altered tone and manner to imitate a white man behind a desk.

"'Carpenter? Why, yeah, I got two jobs here. But the first one's for white on'y, an' the second you gotta be a union member.'

"'Why, that's OK, boss, I'm ready t'join the union.'

"'That's fine, boy, on'y they don't take coloured in that union. Tell you what, though, there's a swell job I can git for you if you'll lay ten dollars on the line.'

"'What job is that, boss?'

"'Runnin' an elevator, boy. But you gotta have them ten dollars.'"

The look of comedy departed from Tillman's face. "Damn it, you know that's what'll happen!"

"Sure it happens like that," Reeves replied earnestly. "You ain't talkin' to a cracker, son, I know what us has to face. Only that don't mean a coloured man shouldn't *try* to better himself. Land's sake, there's a million coloured in the trade unions, don't you know that? Workin' machines, some of 'em, doin' skill work. You low-rate yourself, boy. Runnin' an elevator ain't the only thing you can try. You're like too many coloured – you need more git-up-an'-push."

"I don't low-rate myself. I'm just bent over from that white elephant on my back."

"But havin' a real skill could help you, like it's helped me. I never had much schoolin', but my daddy taught me t'be a good stonemason. I got a fine little business now, with my own three boys workin' alongside of me. We're all doin' fine."

"That's just great for you," Tillman said in disgust, "but somebody digs ditches, don't they? Supposin' every coloured man in the US were a carpenter or an electrician or a doctor – you think there'd be jobs for all of us? You think Uncle Charlie's gonna run his own elevators, or his woman's gonna wash her own dishes with her own pretty white hands?"

"Plenty do, but you don't catch my meanin', boy. I ain't sayin' there's no discrimination. Man, I'd maybe be a big operator in this town if there wasn't. Or that they don't try every which way to keep us at the bottom of the ladder. I jus' say each one of us coloured has got to fight every which way he can. There's too many that throw up their hands without tryin'. They say, 'We'll never get to vote, never get anythin' but nigger jobs!' So you ask 'em for a dollar for the NAACP, an' they answer, 'Won't do no good, ruther spend it on whiskey.' Ask 'em what they do, an' they answer, 'Ain't no use for coloured folk to work – never get nothin' out of it – so I play the numbers.'"

"I've been workin since I was fifteen," Tillman retorted. "You ain't talkin' about me."

"I don't know who I'm talkin' to," Reeves answered with sudden gentleness. "I don't know you, boy. I just hate t'hear any young coloured feller speak about goin' in for a life of crime. That ain't the answer to *anythin'*."

"Yeah, I know," Tillman muttered morosely. "I was just talkin' hot 'n' mad. The hell with it – let's play some checkers."

Each in his own way, the inmates of the west wing were fighting time. Some dozed, some dreamt, some talked or played cards. When the oft-repeated narratives of arrest and trial grew stale, men dredged their souls for other topics of conversation. In cell 424 George Benjamin, old time-server, was fashioning empty cigarette packages into an ingenious frame that would hold a photograph of his sister. In 110 Otha Doty, car* thief and former coal miner, drew the figure of a naked woman on the back of a writing tablet, and then sat contemplating it. Time sat down beside him, invisible and unsmiling.

Time, the common enemy, was indifferent to this spectacle of men behind bars, of men steeped in trouble. Naked and innocent they had come into the world, hand and brain endowed by nature for creative achievement, for work and pleasure, love and fatherhood – only to emerge in young manhood with capacities blunted or natures warped – pliable human clay that somehow had lost its birthright. Now these men were charged with or convicted of the crimes of assault, murder and manslaughter; of alcoholism and the use of narcotics; of forgery and armed robbery, of mail fraud and larceny. And though some were innocent, most were guilty as charged – and yet even the latter were fundamentally not guilty of anything at all except the error of having been born to certain parents at a certain time in a certain society. Yet now these men were locked up in little cubicles of steel and stone and, when they emerged, not a few of them would be more warped in personality, more embittered, more rebellious than when they had entered. And so, inevitably, some would commit new crimes and would be caught, and would return again. But meanwhile they were here, and the way of life that had nurtured them, the society that had bred them, could safely ignore them. Because now they were locked up with Time, embraced by the iron arm of Time – safely, safely out of the way for a stretch of time.

At eight forty-five, life momentarily took on a certain liveliness. The morning newspapers, to which a number of the men subscribed, arrived at each tier. Johnny Lauter passed down the line of cells, handing them out to the accompaniment of a singsong patter. "All the news that's fit to print an' a lot of hooey* that ain't." Now the west wing would have reading matter for a little while as the papers passed from cell to cell. A few moments later the loudspeaker came to life, and a voice began calling the names and numbers of those inmates, already convicted, who were due for an interview with the Classification Board. Cell doors clanged, and half a dozen men on Tiers One and Three stepped out briskly. All of them were delighted at this summons, because it meant that very soon they would be transferred either to a penitentiary or to the permanent wing of this jail. In either situation they would have jobs, the privilege of a weekly movie* and an end to the heavy monotony of their present existence.

As for the others – who were awaiting trial, sentence or transfer – there was nothing to do except settle back on their bunks and kill time.

Chapter 7

Conversations

A little before nine o'clock in the morning, an elderly bailiff unlocked the door of the bull pen in the basement of the Federal District Courthouse. He thrust his head inside, gazed around and called, "Which one of you guys is Floyd Varney?"

"Me."

"Your lawyer's here. Come on."

Outside the bull pen* there was a section of desks and tables at which newly arrested men were booked, fingerprinted and otherwise filed away for future identification, and here a number of custodial officials already were on duty. Varney, following the bailiff, passed to the farther end of this basement section, where there was another room, long and narrow, without a door or windows. Its shabby walls had been defaced with a thousand scribblings by men who briefly had paused there; its open toilet was unclean and ill-smelling; and here Varney's lawyer was waiting to confer with him. It was the only visiting room that the Federal courthouse could offer.

George Combs was more or less Varney's age, but his appearance made him look older. He was a tall, lank man, prematurely bald except for a single tenacious lock of reddish hair. His features were rather ill-assorted: heavy cheek bones, a long, sharp nose, a very wide, thin mouth. There was, however, a vigorous masculinity about his appearance that compensated for his homeliness.

The two men shook hands warmly, and Combs asked how Varney had been getting along.

"Pretty good, Mr Combs. What brings you here? I didn't expect to see you before court."

"I have some things to discuss with you."

"Any news on my sentence?" Varney asked nervously.

"Nothing definite. I'll tell you about it. Let's get comfortable."

They sat down on opposite sides of the cigarette-scarred wooden table that occupied the centre of the room, both men leaning forward a little so that their talk would not be overheard.

A relationship had grown up between these two that was personal, important to both of them, and therefore rather different from the usual relationship between client and attorney. Varney not only liked Combs, but had come almost to revere the man. The basis for this attachment, and for his profound gratitude, lay partially in the fact that Combs sincerely believed in his innocence – even more important, however, was the fact that Varney was without family, friends or beloved, and he had found in Combs a bulwark in an otherwise hostile world.

For Combs there also was a very personal aspect to their relationship. He practised commercial law, and a case like Varney's, which involved murder, adultery and sordid newspaper columns, was not attractive to him. He had come to represent Varney by default, not choice. The latter, with no place else to turn, had appealed to the manager of his hotel for help in securing counsel. The manager had referred the matter to a legal firm of his acquaintance, and Combs had been assigned to make a recommendation.

It was Varney's good fortune that Combs was a humane man. After several interviews it had become clear to Combs that no established attorney in the criminal field would be likely to accept the case. Varney offered an undesirable combination – little money and a very difficult defence. Yet Combs had come to believe strongly that Varney was innocent of purposeful wrongdoing. Even more important, he felt that Varney, as a man, had been receiving the dirty end of life's stick from the time he was born. Rather than hand such a man over to what might be the indifferent efforts of a court-appointed attorney, Combs had offered his own services.

The case had cost him time, money and prestige. He had set his passion to serving an innocent man, but all he had succeeded in doing was in giving the false impression to his colleagues at the Bar that he was willing to defend a guilty man for money. Privately, he now felt that he had been quixotic in taking the case in the first place, and mistaken in continuing with it after Varney had rejected his considered advice to plead guilty. It had come to a most unhappy conclusion for both of them, but nevertheless Combs was committed to seeing it through. And indeed there was nothing he still would not do on Varney's behalf if he could.

"Floyd," he began, "is there anything important in your past life that you haven't told me about?"

"I don't think so."

"I don't want any surprises in court this morning, pal. When I make my plea to the judge, I want it to be accurate. I don't want him to point to your probation report and tell me I'm lying."

"I wouldn't do a thing like that to you," Varney replied with feeling. "Look, Mr Combs, you've been doin' your level best for me, don't I know it? It ain't been a business proposition with you either. So the least I can do is play straight with you, and I sure have."

"OK, good! You see, I've changed my mind since I last spoke to you. I've decided to go into your personal history when I speak to the judge."

"How come?"

"I'll tell you why in a minute. There's something else first." Combs interrupted to light a cigarette from a fresh package. He glanced towards the open doorway, then slid the packet* across the table to Varney. "Can you use 'em?" Varney slipped the packet into his pocket and murmured his thanks.

"I saw Pollard on Friday," Combs said, referring to the assistant US Attorney who had prosecuted the case. "I asked him if he'd join me in recommending the minimum sentence."

"And?"

"He won't do it, Floyd. I'm sorry."

"Goddamn that cold fish!"

"I didn't think he would. Remember I told you that?"

"So what's he gonna do, stand on the same fifteen years he offered before trial?"

"He's moved away from that."

There was a moment's pause while Varney stared at Combs. Then he said quickly, "He's askin' for more?"

"Floyd, you know the judge doesn't have to pay any attention to Pollard's recommendation, don't you?"

"Sure, I know it," Varney answered with impatience. "But what *is* he gonna recommend? Let's hear it."

Combs hesitated. Then he replied softly, "Ten to thirty."

Varney's mouth sagged open, and a stricken look came to his face. He didn't speak. After a moment Combs said, "Naturally, it won't change what I ask. I'm shooting for the minimum, which can get you out in about three years."*

Varney exploded with rage. "I don't get it! What kind of a ratty son of a bitch *is* this Pollard? Before we went to trial he offered me a flat fifteen years and a recommendation for parole. That would've gotten me out in five. Now he changes it to ten to thirty, so that even if I get parole I gotta serve ten. Is that fair? Does it make sense?"

Combs remained silent. Varney, who knew what the other man must be thinking, said defensively, "Well, maybe I should've taken that original offer. I'm not blamin' you – you told me to cop the plea. I just never dreamt that woman'd lie against me the way she did. But what I'm gettin' at now is this: how can Pollard ask for a sentence that doubles his original offer? What kind of a man does it make *him* out to be?"

Combs smiled wryly. "Are you asking me if he has a conscience? I don't know – but I know he made no commitments. You pleaded not guilty, he won the case, that's a ribbon for him. It's no skin off his nose now if you get five years or twenty-five."

"That's not what I mean," Varney replied intensely. "Look here – let's say a man commits a crime who's a real menace to society: he's got to be put away. What difference does it make if he *pleads* guilty or if a jury *finds* him guilty? He's the same menace either way, ain't he? He oughta get the same prison term either way!"

"That's right."

"OK – then take me. Let's say I deserve a prison term. But if the US Attorney could offer me fifteen years if I *pleaded* guilty, how the hell can he stand by and see me get ten to thirty because a *jury* found me guilty?"

"It happens every day."

"But where's the justice in it?" Varney retorted angrily, his voice rising. "I—"

"Take it easy, Floyd."

"Excuse me… I mean, a man has the right to defend himself. Is he supposed to get an extra penalty for pleading not guilty?"

"He's not supposed to, but usually he does."

"All along I been figuring the worst I could get is fifteen," Varney said miserably, "with parole in one third of the* time. Now you tell me I might get more."

"Haven't you known it all along, Floyd? Second-degree murder runs from ten years to life."

"Well, sure, but I never figured I'd get any more than that fifteen years. Where's the justice in it, Mr Combs?"

Combs smiled drily. "There isn't any – who said there was? Listen, Floyd – you're a funny guy, damn it. You've had about the hardest life of any man I ever met. You've been kicked from pillar to post, you've had your nose rubbed in the dirt, but you're full of the damnedest illusions. You talk about justice like a schoolkid, as though everybody involved in the courts is a pure soul who wants to see justice done. For all I know

Pollard is a nice guy, good to his wife and children, and all that. But that doesn't mean he has any personal interest in your welfare. What's the use of kidding yourself?"

"Well, sure," Varney replied defensively, "I've been around, I'm not dumb. Only I thought you might have a real talking point with him – I mean, because of his original offer to me."

"That's why I went to see him. But that's all it was, a talking point. He didn't have to listen, and he didn't."

"Oh, Jesus!" Varney murmured. He sat with tight lips, his handsome face pallid, his blue eyes showing his fright.

Combs said gently, "Floyd, I hope to God you'll get the minimum. But I'd be a bad friend if I didn't prepare you. The way our courts operate, men get bargain offers to plead guilty. It has nothing to do with justice. It certainly has nothing to do with the amount of time a man should get for his rehabilitation – granted our penitentiaries rehabilitate men, which is another joke. It is purely a matter of the prosecutor chalking up a record of convictions, and of the courts saving trial time and money. That's why you got your fifteen-year offer."

"Oh, Jesus!" Varney murmured again. Then he asked weakly, "You suppose the judge knows about it?"

"I doubt it."

"Is there any way you could tell him?"

"It wouldn't make any difference. No pre-trial offer like that is binding on a judge. He'll make up his own mind."

"How about the six months I've been in jail since I was arrested? Don't that count?"

"That's up to the judge too, it's a matter of his personal discretion. The law doesn't recognize jail time put in before sentence. I'll point it out, of course, but that doesn't mean he has to pay attention to it."

"So that's the way it shapes, huh?" Varney asked bitterly. "I'm supposed to start thinkin' of ten years minimum before there's any chance of parole, or serving twenty years if the Parole Board don't like me. No, sir – that's no proposition for me. I'd sooner cut my throat."

"Well, now, take it easy, pal. I'm not expecting a sentence like that. You're a man without a criminal past. You've got a fine war record. If I didn't feel pretty confident that you'd get the minimum sentence, I wouldn't tell you so. It's what I'd give you if I were the judge."

"Yeah, but you believe I should've been freed on justifiable homicide," Varney responded dully. "There's no reason to think he does."

"No, but there's no reason to start thinking in terms of your serving twenty years." Combs reached over and tapped the back of Varney's hand with his fingers. "You've had a lot of guts all your life, Floyd. Don't lose your nerve now."

"Well I ain't, I ain't," Varney replied fretfully. "What about the question of my appeal? You said you were gonna make up your mind about that."

Combs glanced at his wristwatch and lit a fresh cigarette from the stump of an old. "Floyd, I'm sorry, but I honestly don't think an appeal will get us anywhere."

"It's a chance, ain't it?"

"No. I've studied the record back and forth. You got a bad jury decision, but you got a fair trial. The judge didn't make any rulings that are a basis for a reversal."

"But all along," Varney said piteously, "you kept telling me this judge was a punk."

"He is. If it had been a constitutional case, he probably would've pulled boners,* I know his record. But yours was straight criminal. His charge to the jury was sound, his rulings were fair. I just don't see any basis for successfully arguing a reversal."

"I bet if I had a thousand bucks to lay on the line, you'd appeal!" Varney burst out vehemently. Then, instantly contrite, he stammered, "Jesus, I apologize, Mr Combs. That was a lousy thing to say, I didn't mean it. I trust you."

With an angry flush staining his thin cheeks, Combs replied, "You were thinking it, so it's just as well you said it. Now I'll tell *you* something. If you had a thousand bucks, I'd take it, because I'm entitled to it. Since we're speaking frankly, I'll tell you something else. The only fee I got from you was three hundred and seventy dollars, and I paid out more than that for expenses. You think it didn't cost money to canvass all those taxi drivers or buy the court record, or—"

"Mr Combs, I could kick myself," Varney interrupted miserably. "I didn't mean it. I'm way off my beam this morning, I'm scared stiff, Mr Combs. I'm just so damn scared they'll give me the works."

Combs was silent for a moment. Then he said more temperately, "Floyd, an appeal wouldn't cost anything. The big expenses are behind us. You could sign a pauper's oath and the government would pay for the printing bill. All it would require from me is the time to write a brief and to argue it before the court. That isn't much. Don't you know I'd be willing to do that if I thought we could get a reversal?"

"Oh sure, I know you would," Varney said earnestly, meaning it with his whole heart. "Look – I'm with you all the way! You say no appeal, that's OK with me. All I'm sorry for is I can't pay you now what you deserve. But I promise you, when I get out, no matter how long it takes me—"

"Forget it."

"But I want you to know—"

"Listen," said Combs, looking at his watch, "I'll have to leave in a few minutes, and I've got one more thing to talk about."

"OK."

"You may be surprised in court this morning. I think Mrs Peterson may be there."

Varney gaped at him.

"I got a call from a reporter last night," Combs explained. "He saw her in the lobby of the Shoreham Hotel. She wouldn't talk to him, but I have a feeling she came up from Baltimore to see you sentenced."

"That's sure rubbing it in!" Varney muttered angrily. "I'd like to kick her friggin' teeth down her throat."

"That's why I wanted to prepare you. I don't want you to lose your head and say something."

"I won't. But what kind of a dame is she, anyway? She didn't give a damn for her husband. Why does she want to see me sentenced? What satisfaction does she get out of that?"

"I don't think it's so hard to understand. The time I went to see her about you, it was very clear the kind of a woman she was – scared and weak. She didn't want to hurt you, she only wanted to protect her good name – so she put a knife in your back."

"OK, but what's her damn idea in comin' to see me sentenced – just to get her picture in the papers again?"

"I doubt it. My guess is she has a half-ass conscience. She's guilty about sending you up, and she's scared stiff the world won't believe she's an outraged wife and mother, so on both counts she can't stay away when her husband's murderer is sent up."

"Listen," Varney muttered, "you don't think... you don't suppose..." His voice trailed off.

"What?"

"...her conscience is really bothering her? That she's thinkin' of tellin' the truth?"

"And go to prison herself on perjury?" Combs asked. "Don't be silly. It's a half-ass conscience she's got, not a whole one."

"Christ, yes, I oughta know that," Varney muttered. "You stay six months in one of them damn cells an' all sorts of wild ideas come into your head. I can't tell you how many times I've dreamt about her doin' that."

"Yeah," Combs said softly. "Now listen – last time we talked I told you I wanted to emphasize the respectable side of your life in my plea. But especially if Mrs Peterson is in the courtroom, I want to do a switch. Nothing I say will ever make you as respectable as Mrs Peterson in the eyes of the judge. So I want to start back and tell where you came from, and how you got here, and leave nothing out."

"You mean about my ma too?"

"Everything! I want to throw the whole miserable story into his face. It's one of the reasons *I* decided to defend you – maybe it'll have some effect on *him*."

"I wish you could leave out about my ma."

"Floyd, I wanted to use it in my jury summation, but you said no. Now, for Pete's sake, man, your ma's dead and buried. You've got nothing to be ashamed of: you didn't choose her. Your life's a credit to you, and I want to use it for what it's worth."

"Well… if you say so."

Combs stood up. "Good. I'll run now. I want to make some notes for my plea. See you in court."

"Mr Combs – one of the men in jail, who's had a lot of experience, was sayin' we oughta make a pitch to the judge on the grounds I was drunk."

"Oh, sure, that would be great," Combs replied with a chuckle. "That's what Mrs Peterson said in claiming rape, didn't she – that you'd been drinking? Didn't we deny it?"

"Jeez, I forgot."

"You listen to those jailhouse lawyers and you'll end up a lifer."

"Yeah, I was dumb on that one." Varney hesitated, then made the earnest, heartfelt little speech he had prepared in advance. "Mr Combs, whatever the sentence is, I want you to know that you're the best Joe* I ever met in my life. Nobody else in my whole life ever went out of his way for me like you have. I still don't know why you did it."

Combs shrugged. He answered seriously, with candour. "You came my way, and I guess you hooked into my conscience, Floyd. I suppose nobody likes to see injustice done, even though most of us don't feel the call to do much about it. There must be a lot of guys like you who need defending, but after today I'll just go back to making a living for my family. I'm only sorry as hell it didn't turn out better for you. You don't belong in prison."

"You did your level best, Mr Combs. Nobody could have done better."

Combs extended his hand. "Good luck, pal."

They shook hands warmly and walked out of the room. As one bailiff opened the barred door to the upstairs world for Combs, another unlocked the bull pen for Varney. Combs stood in the elevator, thinking sombrely, "How the devil can prison be the right answer for a man like Varney?"

At nine fifteen in the morning the loudspeakers in cell block B1 erupted with a strident announcement: "Now hear this!" the voice in the control room said. "Now hear this: all men signed up for sick call... all men signed up for sick call... get your pass from your tier officer!"

In cell 430 Eugene Finnerty rose from the wall seat where he had been sitting, head cupped in his hands, gazing out into space. "Wilson," he called, and jiggled Huey's foot. "Sick line."

"Huh?"

"Sick line."

Huey heaved himself up from the bunk with a sheepish look. The last thing he could remember was Finnerty talking to him about his case. He said, with a touch of embarrassment, "Guess I fell asleep on you."

"Uh-huh."

"I'm sorry. The last two nights I didn't get much rest. I'm wide awake till I lay down for a while, but then I—"

"Didn't bother me none," Finnerty interrupted. "I unnerstand you's tired. You remember what I advised you about goin' to the back end of the sick line?"

"Yes, I do."

"I sure hopes you make out good with that white man, Huey."

"Thanks. I appreciate the ideas you gave me."

They waited at the bars, listening to the harsh, grinding clangour that was rising in the west wing as more and more cell doors were opened. Finnerty said, rather paternally, "You better git some medicine for them bites, boy. You was scratchin' hard in your sleep. You'll git 'em infected."

Their cell door jarred, then ground open. As they stepped out on the runway, Finnerty said, "I'm gon leave you soon as we gits downstairs. I works to the head of the line if I kin, see, cos of my condition. If I gits into the hospital early enough, they lets me sit in a tub of hot water. That does me good, better'n any medicine they got."

Halfway down the runway they were met by Benjamin, who was carrying their passes from the tier guard. Benjamin said, "You gon see that white man now, Wilson?"

"Uh-huh."

"Watch him close, buddy."

"Sure."

"The best way is if'n you kin get* him t'sign somethin'. That way he kaint back out."

"Uh-huh."

"Say, Finnerty," Benjamin continued with a sudden change of manner, "you go'n' down t'have your rear end tickled again, hunh? You watch out for that doc, now, I heerd* stories about him."

Finnerty grimaced in silent disgust, but Benjamin doubled over with a whoop of laughter. "Got your number, ain't I, ol' man?"

Suddenly now, as they strode back towards the stairway, all of the other men of the mess crew were standing at the front of their cells. Spaulding called out to Huey, "You going down to see McPeak?" Huey nodded, and the other called heartily, "Good luck, hope you make out fine."

"Thanks."

"Good luck kid – good luck, Wilson," others called. Even Alfrice Tillman nodded as Huey passed, although he couldn't quite manage to say anything. Their quarrel was too recent, and it still burned.

"I got real friends in here," Huey thought with pride as they clattered down the iron steps. No matter what the differences in these men, or the disputes, jeering and acrimony amongst them, they remained a solid group where the frame-up of another Negro was concerned. It was, he thought, a lesson worth the price of a few days in jail, and one he had needed.

Huey and Finnerty were the last men of the west wing to arrive at the assembly point on the first floor. Half a dozen others, all whites, were waiting before the steel-mesh gate, conversing in low tones. Standing a little apart from them, sombre-faced, a matchstick between his teeth, was McPeak. He winked as Huey came up to him and said, amiably enough, "Thought you weren't gon t'show."

"Had to come down from heaven," Huey whispered slyly, with a grin. "They like us in the second balcony, even in jail."

"Shoot," McPeak replied seriously, taking the matchstick from his mouth, "I don't go for that stuff. I'm agin this discriminashun.* Live an' let live is how I say."

Huey gazed at him in silence while a good warmth kindled inside him. At this moment, dressed as McPeak was in blue jeans, with a black stubble of beard from two days of not shaving, he looked so much like one of the illiterate moonshiners from the hills around Charlottesville that his sentiment took on added force. Huey had a flashing memory of another stocky, bearded man who had said to him, not too many years ago, "Hey, you nigrah boy, c'm'ere. I'm looking for a nigrah grocery store called Carter's.* Give y'all a dime if y'take me there."

Not "boy", but "nigrah boy". Not man to child, but white man to that black-skinned thing who surely would dance or grin or run an errand as demanded. Huey had known Carter's, and had known also that it was one of the outlets for illegal liquor in the coloured slum called Scottsville. And although the dime had looked good to his ten-year-old eyes, he had replied quietly "Never heard of it" – without adding "Mister" – and walked off.

But it was not this way McPeak was regarding him, and not the way he would regard McPeak. With a surge of gratitude he whispered, "*You* certainly let *me* live. Without you I would've been dead or blind, maybe. I owe you more than I can say."

"Shoot," McPeak replied soberly, as the gate opened and they passed through, "somebody had t'do somethin'. You was in deep water." He laughed a little. "Lucky for both of us them polices came along. I don't have the wind for a long fight."

In the outside corridor they were joined by five men from the east wing of the cell block. Lagging behind, they got on the end of the line. Huey whispered, "I have some good news for you."

"Like what?"

"I've seen a lawyer already."

McPeak pursed his lips and nodded with interest. Then he said, "You was startin' t'tell me before what the charges agin me was."

"OK, men," an officer called out. "Single file, no smoking, no talking. Start down."

The line of fourteen men clumped down two short flights of stairs and then halted before a door. The officer moved forward, unlocked the door and motioned them ahead into a narrow basement corridor. The door clanged shut behind them, and they marched in single file for almost a hundred yards. There, after another door was unlocked, a hospital guard took over and the Rotunda officer departed.

They were admitted to a large windowless ante-room with benches on both sides. Other men, from other sections of the jail, were already there.

"Sit down!" the burly hospital guard said to them. "You can talk if you keep it quiet, but there's no smokin' in here or in the hospital. When the door opens, the first four men on that side go in. The others move up. Next time the first four on this side. If I catch anyone smokin', I'll write him up."

Having delivered himself of these instructions, the guard unlocked the door leading to the hospital, passed through and slammed the door behind him. Instantly a hum of general talk began, and three or four* of the men took cigarettes from their pockets. They lit up with the special satisfaction that comes from defiance, but they kept their cigarettes hidden behind cupped hands. It was one thing for the guard to smell smoke when he returned, but it was quite another to be able to pick out the offenders.

Huey and McPeak had found seats at the end of their bench; there were a dozen men ahead of them. "This is swell," Huey whispered. "We'll have time."

McPeak nodded and asked immediately, "What's them charges on me?"

"Assault, disorderly conduct, resisting arrest."

A flush spread over McPeak's lumpy face, and he spat the match he was chewing to the floor. "Those goddamn polices! I hate polices – Jumpin' Jesus, how I hate 'em. Your lawyer tell you how long I could git on those?"

"Six months… but it could be much less, of course."

"Ain't that fine," McPeak muttered. "That's all I need in my life!" He turned away and sat staring at the floor, his tightly pressed lips working with anger.

"Listen," Huey began eagerly, "I…" He paused as the hospital door opened and an inmate orderly called out, "OK, let's start sick call!" The first four men on the opposite bench, one of them being Eugene Finnerty, jumped up and went out. The door slammed. "…I had a long talk with a lawyer this morning. He says if you and I stick together our chances are great. He's sure we can win at the preliminary hearing. We'll go free without a trial."

McPeak's small blue eyes were very attentive, but his lumpy face maintained an impassive expression. He asked bluntly, "Why's he so sure?"

With enthusiasm Huey began to summarize the morning's discussion. The police charges against both of them, he pointed out, were dependent upon two lies: the first that he had been drunk, the second that he was the sort of character who would pick a street fight with four white men. Granted that the police were cooperating with the other men and that the knife had disappeared, if McPeak testified to what he had seen, the frame-up would surely crack wide open – because Huey had respectable witnesses to testify that he had spent the evening without drinking.

Furthermore, his school record and his record as a Federal employee would destroy the second lie – that he was some good-for-nothing bum inclined to street fighting. "Of course," he added frankly, "if you were a Negro, we wouldn't be in such a strong position, but you're not. You can prove that you're from out of town, and that you didn't know either me or the other fellows before you saw us on Saturday night. So there's every reason for the commissioner to believe you're telling the truth about what you saw. Add that to my evidence, and we're free!"

"Uh-huh, mebbe so," McPeak responded cautiously. "On'y it'll still be the word of them four agin us two – with the polices sayin' they didn't see no knife. The commissioner might believe us, or he might hold us for trial anyway."

"I doubt it, Mr McPeak. Just look at the cock-eyed story those other fellows have to sell. It won't stand up against what we say, and against the witnesses I can bring."

McPeak was silent.

"Besides," Huey continued eagerly, "my lawyer's going to track down the record of every one of those fellows. Supposing their reputations aren't so good, eh, or one of 'em's been arrested before? That'll be still more evidence on our side. I imagine we'll get some help from the NAACP on that. Professor Herrin—"

"What's that?"

"What?"

"That NA-something?"

"An organization – the National Association for the Advancement of Coloured People. It's pretty important – a lot of white people support it too."

"Uh-huh. Reckon I've heerd of it in Detroit." McPeak took a fresh match from his shirt pocket and thrust it into the side of his mouth.

"It's in the bag for us, don't you see? If we stick together, we'll get off together. On the other hand" – Huey hesitated and then stared fixedly at the older man – "without your testimony it's certainly a different situation. My lawyer thinks I'll be in real trouble then."

"Yeah," McPeak commented softly, "four white men in a Dixie* court-room agin one coloured feller. Them ain't good odds."

The hospital door opened, and the first group of men, minus Finnerty, passed to the end of the opposite bench, one of them muttering, "You could be dyin' in here, and all they'd give you is an aspirin." The first four on their side of the room went out, and Huey and McPeak moved up.

"So what do you say?" Huey asked. "It looks good for us, don't it?" He stared anxiously at McPeak, but the reply he hoped for was not forthcoming. McPeak chewed his match, cleared his throat a little and said nothing. After a bit he folded his muscular, hairy forearms over his thick chest and fixed his gaze on the opposite side of the room, as though something of interest were occurring there. Since nothing was, Huey felt dismay and exasperation. What did it require, he wondered, to get this man to commit himself one way or another? Sooner or later he'd have to – didn't he realize that? McPeak was acting with him like a man playing poker. He was open and friendly until the game began, but then he clammed up and held his cards close to his vest. And what were the stakes – the police offer? Of course! The only possible conclusion about McPeak was that the son of a bitch was getting ready to run. Run and be safe – and never mind about a Negro getting sent up for five years. Or would "nigger" be closer to the way he was thinking?

Anger swelled within Huey. He felt like taking hold of the man and shaking him. Why couldn't he see... Abruptly Huey's thoughts took a different turn, and his anger towards McPeak was supplanted by dismay with himself. This, he realized, was exactly what Herrin had warned him against – getting angry because McPeak might be looking for an easy way out. Was it this hillbilly who was acting strangely or himself?

He began to feel ashamed, and very stupid. How quick he was to forget that McPeak had saved his life! And to forget also that only an hour ago he himself had been regretting that he ever got involved in a picket line! Why couldn't he allow McPeak to have the same worries about prison and the same regrets – especially when the man had a way out? Suppose their positions were reversed – would he be so brave that he wouldn't be tempted to run?

"You have to persuade the man, damn it," Huey told himself. "You need to appeal to everything that's decent and honourable in him. If you just get angry, you'll lose out with him for sure. What kind of a jackass are you?"

"Look, Mr McPeak, is there anything you feel worried about?" Huey asked in a controlled tone.

"Huh, plenty!" McPeak muttered, chewing his match.

"I mean about how we stand on our case?"

McPeak half-turned. "This lawyer feller you got, who is he? How do we know he's guessin' this right?"

"Look," Huey replied eagerly, "he's not just any old lawyer, he's a *professor* of Law. He teaches at a university."

"How come he's *your* lawyer, then?" McPeak enquired bluntly. "You some rich man's boy?"

Huey laughed a little. "Hell no. How it came about is that my brother, Jeff, is studying to be a lawyer, and Professor Herrin is one of his teachers. When I got arrested, my brother called him up for advice."

"I see," McPeak murmured reflectively. "Well, that's real good, ain't it, a big man like that bein' on your side?"

"On your side too, Mr McPeak, if you want him."

"Shoot, young feller, don't 'Mister' me. Tom's the name."

"OK, mine's Huey. There's something I have to explain, though, about Professor Herrin. He came down to advise me, but he can't be the actual lawyer in the case. Because of his teaching, see?"

McPeak nodded, but looked dubious.

"He's going to get us somebody real good. And like I said, he'll be your lawyer too, if you want him. Or if you want a white lawyer, Professor Herrin can get you one."

"I ain't got no money for lawyers," McPeak announced bluntly. "Y'all may as well know that right now. I'd ruther—"

"Wait, I forgot to tell you," Huey interrupted eagerly. "God, I'm dumb today! Lawyers won't cost either of us a penny. No charge at all!"

"For the hearin', y'mean?"

"All the way down the line!"

"Even if there's a trial?"

"That's right."

"How come?"

"Because of what I tried to tell you on Saturday night about the reason for the fight. You remember?"

"I remember, but you better study it out for me a little more," McPeak responded carefully.

The hospital door opened. The first four men from their bench filed back into the ante-room, while four others rose from the bench opposite. The returning men sat down behind Huey, and he moved closer to McPeak so that their conversation would not be overheard.

"Look, Tom, it's like Professor Herrin said this morning – the real cause of that fight is the kind of schools this city has for us Negroes, and what happens when we ask for something better. None of those white fellows knew me personally, but Ballou told 'em I'd been at the demonstration to get that high school opened up to coloured students. They wanted to beat me up for getting out of line, see? I'm a coloured boy who wasn't staying 'in his place'."

"Yeah, reckon I unnerstand," McPeak replied softly. He was gazing at Huey squarely again.

"Only you came along and stopped them," Huey continued. "So now, with the help of the police, they're trying to frame both of us."

"Uh-huh."

"They figure if they can make it hot for a coloured fellow like me, that'll scare a lot of others, shut 'em up. I'm not the only Negro student who's been roughed up in these past months. But I guess this is the first time they're trying to send one of us to prison."

"Yeah, I know that game good," McPeak said abruptly, with conviction. "An' I sure don't like it."

"What do you mean?"

"I'm talkin' about that ol' lynch game," McPeak replied, as though surprised at the question. "Pushin' fellows aroun'! My experience weren't a colour matter, like with you. But amounten' to the same thing. Jesus Christ, I hate t'git pushed!"

"What experience was it?" Huey enquired eagerly, feeling that at last he was getting a handle on the man.

"Back in Detroit in the Thirties, when we was tryin' t'git us a union. Shoot, they'd fire guys for even talkin' union, 'n' blacklist 'em from work everywhere in the whole industry. They beat up a lot – they even killed some. It's the same ol' lynch game, ain't it? You knock one guy down so a hunnerd'll be scairt."

"Now," Huey thought with satisfaction, "I know something. There's my talking point." The hospital door opened and an exchange of men occurred.

"They're sure runnin' those fellers through fast," McPeak commented with a laugh. "I hope they's all in good health."

"Yeah," Huey muttered. He was beginning to feel the pressure of time. "What auto company you work for, Tom?"

"Usta be Bohn Aluminum,* now it's Ford. I'm a spot welder," he added with a touch of pride.

"I understand there are a good many coloured working there."

"Quite a few."

Knowing the answer, Huey asked, "Are they in the union?"

"I should say so." McPeak's response had unmistakable warmth. "We wouldn't even have no union if you coloured wasn't with us."

"I'm sure glad to hear you say that!" Huey hesitated a moment, then observed, "Guess you know not every Georgia-born white man feels the same way you do."

McPeak burst out laughing. His lumpy face lit up with good humour, and his small blue eyes began to gleam. "We crackers ain't so dumb: we kin learn. Ain't sayin' I always felt the same way about you fellers. I shore didn't." Still mirthful, he added: "Took me workin' my lil ol' balls off for five dollars a day... an' them ol' foremen shovin' a hot poker up my rear end to work faster... that teached me all right, teached me good."

"Guess it did," Huey responded with a smile. He was thinking hard. All of this was fine, and it began to explain McPeak, but how was it to be applied to the question at hand?

"You know who taught me the mostest about gittin' together with your folks?" McPeak volunteered. He spoke with the zest of a man who has come upon one of his favourite topics. "A coloured fellow named Eddie Johnson – we called him 'Balance Wheel'. That was when I was at Bohn Aluminum an' we had us a sit-down strike. Plenty of time t'chew the fat day after day, man, we practically had us a schoolhouse in there. This Eddie sure was smart. He showed us in dollars an' cents how the companies was playin' the white agin the coloured t'keep us both down. Both of us havin' worser conditions an' worser pay, y'see, cos we wouldn't git together for our own advantage."

"Yeah," Huey commented softly, "that's right." He watched with wonder the animation in the man's face.

"By God," McPeak continued, with sparkling eyes, "so long as I live I'll never forgit one thing Eddie Johnson said to us oncet. He said that when a labourin' man wants to better himself, there's two keys t'open the door of his betterment. One of 'em's a white key, he said, an' the othern's black. Without'n both of them keys workin' at oncet, he said, you kaint open that door." McPeak, without being aware of it, put his hand on Huey's knee in an expression of closeness and enthusiasm. "Young feller, that there is *bottom* truth. I found that out."

Very aware of the hand on his knee, Huey said, thinking hard, "So now you're a strong union man, eh?"

"The day I ain't I'm gon have my ol' head examined," McPeak replied heartily. "That ol' union give me some pay a man kin eat on. It give me workin' conditions that don't altogether kill a man. Give me seniority. Give me vacation with—"

"Look," Huey interrupted, unable to contain himself any longer, "we're the two keys in this situation, aren't we, Tom? A white key and a black key. If we work together, we can open this jail door for both of us."*

With a rapidity that left Huey stunned and heartsick, McPeak's face changed. The animation vanished, the little blue eyes went cold, the impassive poker look returned. "Mebbe so," he replied, and busied himself in searching for a fresh match to chew.

The hospital door opened, and an exchange of men passed in and out. Huey and McPeak moved up on their bench, with four men still ahead of them.

Searching his mind for arguments, wondering how he could persuade McPeak to cast away his fears and commit himself to testifying – and beginning to feel acutely worried about time – Huey said, "Look, Tom, I forgot to tell you something else. My lawyer wants to be so positive we'll go free at the hearing that he's delaying it a few days. He wants us to hit that commissioner with all the evidence, all the witnesses we have. That way—"

"Days? How many days?" McPeak interrupted sharply.

"Two or three."

"Oh, that's great!" McPeak snapped with indignation and rancour. "You fix up the hearin' to suit yourself, but never mind about me. I got one week's vacation, an' you arrange I kin spend it in jail. The hell I will!"

Stunned, realizing instantly that he *had* arranged this with Herrin without thinking about McPeak – indeed, without even the idea of consulting him – Huey said falteringly, "Tom, I'm awfully sorry, but we can—"

"My niece's weddin' is Saddy," McPeak interrupted with intense anger. "I got t'be back in Detroit for work on Monday. Ain't seen my sister or her family for six year. Ain't seen my brother in eighteen year. Why, he's comin' all the way up from Dade County, Georgia... ain't never travelled so fur in his whole life. I—"

"Listen—"

"—had me seven days in all with my kinfolk, an' two days is gone already, me sittin' in a gawddamn jail. Now you tell me—"

"Tom, listen, please," Huey burst in desperately, knowing that he was losing the man, "I can fix it, I can change it!"

"How kin you? You said—"

"But I'm seein' my brother again at twelve o'clock. I'll explain about you. He'll get the lawyer to fix up the hearing for today or tomorrow."

McPeak paused, breathing hard. "You sure you kin do it?" he asked suspiciously.

"I know I can!"

"How come?"

"Because ordinarily the hearing would've been today or tomorrow anyway. All the lawyer has to do is say he doesn't want a delay."

"An' what about *that*?" McPeak asked. He turned around briefly as the door of the hospital opened and the men on the opposite bench exchanged.

"Your lawyer had a lot of good reasons for delayin' the hearin', didn't he? What happens now – we go in cold an' they hold us for trial, huh?"

"No – we can win just the same!" Huey replied firmly, hoping it was true, and knowing there was nothing else he could say. "Sure, Professor Herrin had the idea of looking through the whole neighbourhood to find out if there were any other witnesses to the fight, and things like that. But we can have the main evidence any time we want – like *my* witnesses. There's the family I spent the evening with, my job supervisor from the printing office, someone from my school. That's all we need to win – aside from you!"

"Hm!" McPeak said, his anger subsiding, "Mebbe."

"I'll tell my brother to change the hearing – right?"

"Uh-huh."

"Now, about your testimony," Huey continued. "It may be the lawyer'll want to see you before the hearing. Is that OK with you?"

McPeak glanced up at the ceiling, fiddled with the matchstick in his mouth, then observed, "I got something botherin' me. What happens to us if we git held for trial? Your* lawyer advise you about that?"

"Christ, is there no way to get this damn cracker off that dime he's standing on?" Huey thought with anguish. A bit wearily he replied, "In that case, we'll go free on bail. You'll be able to see your family tomorrow."

"Who's gon t'put up the money for that?" McPeak asked in a testy, almost childish tone. "I got my bus ticket, a few dollars, an' that's all. I didn't figure on no expenses here. I sure kaint git in touch with my wife less'n a couple days. An' I tell you right now, I ain't gon to my sister for money. I don't want her side of the family knowin' nothin' about this. I'd never live it down."

"Why wouldn't he live it down?" Huey wondered. Was it because he had landed in jail or because he had helped out a coloured man? "Look, Tom," he said soothingly, "bail for you won't cost much. I asked the men on my tier about it. On minor charges like yours—"

"Six months ain't so minor," McPeak interrupted.

"That's the maximum. It could be thirty days or probation. You don't have a police record, do you?"

"No."

"So the bail might be two hundred dollars, say. A bondsman puts it up, that's his business, and we pay him ten per cent, twenty dollars. I'd be more than glad to put it up for you, Tom. I've got it."

"Wouldn't want you to do it," McPeak muttered, but it was obvious that he was relieved.

"I'd be glad to. It's little enough after what you did for me."

"Have to come back from Detroit for a trial," McPeak muttered heavily. "This sure is a big mess."

"Tom," Huey pleaded, "you're way ahead of the situation. I'm figuring we'll both be clear by tomorrow morning. We won't even be thinking of bail or a trial."

"Mebbe. But I ain't gon count on it. I don't trust them polices."

The hospital door opened, a shift of men went in and out, and now Huey and McPeak were at the head of their line. Huey began to feel a frenzy rising within him. Only four men on the opposite bench were ahead of them. At most he had a few minutes more.

"Tom," he said urgently, "I've got a good idea. How about you have a talk with Professor Herrin, or the other lawyer he's getting for us? I can arrange it. That way you can size up the situation for yourself."

"Got it sized up pretty good already," McPeak answered in a spiritless way. And then, slyly, gazing at Huey out of the corner of his eye, "You'll make out all right, I reckon. Nawthin' t'worry about, not with a good lawyer like you'll have."

Huey grunted involuntarily, with a feeling in his abdomen of actual physical pain, as though he had been struck. It was not the lack of conviction in McPeak's tone that hit him so hard, but the sudden guile after all the evasions. McPeak wouldn't commit himself – he wouldn't even agree to talk with a lawyer. What did it mean, then, for him to pretend suddenly that everything would be all right for Huey? It meant he himself had decided to run!

There was silence between them now. McPeak was chewing his match and watching flies on the ceiling. Huey was tasting the gall of his defeat. He knew where he was now without mistake: alone. He'd go into that hearing alone, with four white men and the police against him, with prison and his law career in the balance. McPeak was letting him down hard, but why not? He had performed one act of courage, why should he do another? It was too clear what the man would be risking if he didn't take the police offer. And for what? To help out a strange Negro. For a Georgia cracker he was decent enough, but no damn hero – and why should he be?

Out of his disappointment, his sense of personal failure, his understanding, Huey suddenly spoke out what he had been afraid to say all along. He had not wanted a head-on collision with McPeak. Nor had he wanted to press the man in a way that would turn ugly. But now, whatever came of it, he had an inner need to speak with complete honesty. "Tom," he said, "Tom!" And waited until McPeak turned to face him. "Listen to me a minute. I'm always going to thank you in my mind for what you did for me. And I'm sorry as hell it got you into this trouble. I know you turned down that offer from the police, or else you'd be out of jail already. But I think you're considering it now. I don't blame you, Tom. Believe me I don't. But you're not the kind of man to make deals with the police. If you do that, you'll be ashamed of yourself for the rest of your life."

McPeak flared. His eyes blazed, his lumpy face flushed with rancour. "I'm in here, ain't I? What do I got t'be ashamed about? What call you got to be tellin' me off? If not for me—"

"Then why don't you say straight out what you intend doing?" Huey demanded, with a burst of passion he couldn't restrain. "Why all the hide-and-go-seek? Tell me right now!"

"Shit!" McPeak snapped. He half-rose from the bench in his anger. "Don't push me. Every damn son of a bitch pushin' me aroun' since I got off that damn bus. I got things on my mind, an' I don't like t'be pushed, you hear?"

Huey heard, and was aware that others were listening too. There was more to say, and he wanted to plead with McPeak not to misunderstand, but the hospital door opened and the inmate orderly was standing there. The orderly beckoned to the men at the head of the opposite bench, and then turned to McPeak. "You two guys are the last on this line, aintcha?"

McPeak nodded.

"OK, let's go."

"I had to leave him sore at me," Huey thought with sick misery. "I'm just a natural-born fool."

Chapter 8

Floyd Varney, sitting alone in the bull pen, was enjoying a false tranquillity. In the half-hour that had passed since the departure of his attorney, his mood had undergone a number of changes. The news given him by Combs – that Mrs Peterson might appear in court to see him sentenced – had left him so furious that, for a time, he could think of nothing else. It was not enough, he had kept telling himself bitterly, that she had convicted him with perjured testimony: now it was important to her to be in on the kill. Fine manners and elegant clothes and a perfumed body – but when it came down to bedrock she had as much human decency as a pig in a wallow. And he who was blameless, who merely had defended himself from her crazy husband, would stand there in handcuffs while a judge sentenced him.

Varney's rage had turned then from Mrs Peterson to Pollard, the US Attorney. Here, he had told himself, was an even worse betrayal. He understood why Mrs Peterson had lied, but he never would understand why a representative of the Department of Justice wanted to punish a man for pleading not guilty.

Pacing the bull pen, oblivious of the other men, Varney had succeeded for a while in taking a sickly relish from his own anger and from the image of himself as a man betrayed. But then, because he was impotent to do anything about either Mrs Peterson or the prosecutor, his anger had begun to drain away. Fear came then – the unnerving, chilling fear that had been lying in wait all the while. Pollard intended to recommend ten to thirty years. And the judge... what would the judge do?

Varney's pacing had ceased at this point. He had sat down in a corner of the room, alone and very still, an unlit cigarette between his lips. Feverishly he had begun to tell himself that he knew the judge was decent – he could tell by his face that he was a man of heart and understanding.

He told himself this, but in the next moment grew cold with fear again as he thought that no judge ever knew what prison time meant. Where was the judge who had spent even a week in one of the prisons to which he sent other men for ten or twenty years?

Thinking along in this way, so frightened and lonely that his spirit could not bear it, Varney sought refuge in magic. His mind fled back to a crowded courtroom where the issue of his guilt or innocence still was undecided. "Ladies and Gentlemen," Combs was saying to the jury, "when you hear the facts in this case, I think you will agree with me that this unfortunate slaying was an act of self-defence, and that Floyd Varney deserves to go free."

In this way, by dreaming nonsense, Varney achieved a false calm for these last, terrible moments before court opened. But then, suddenly, the door of the bull pen was unlocked and a bailiff thrust his head inside. He called out loudly, so that even Varney heard him, "Any you guys wanna use the toilet before you go to court, line up."

Varney rose, feeling as though something had just died within him. His heart began to pound, and a cold sweat bubbled out on his forehead. He held out his wrists for the handcuffs.

At this hour of the morning the Negro inmates of the west wing were enjoying their recreation period on Tier Five. This tier, which contained no cells, was barren of all equipment except for a wall bench, a water fountain and two unsheltered toilets. Here a man could walk a full thirty yards in one direction before he needed to turn, and he could talk to someone other than his cellmate – and, if it pleased him, he could stare at the opaque skylight and imagine what the heavens were like, what the day was like. All men looked forward to recreation because it meant freedom from cell confinement for an hour or sometimes longer. Nevertheless, when the period was over, most inmates were ready to depart, because a man could pace a thirty-yard stretch only so long, a man could stare at a skylight only so long, and then he wanted a change, even the return to his cell.

Since Huey Wilson and Eugene Finnerty had not yet come back from sick call, the group on hand consisted of only five men, who were strolling abreast, taking their exercise and carrying on a discussion in common. Today, as on most days, the talk had to do with the question of race progress. Dewey Spaulding already had observed with bitter amusement that it made no difference how a conversation began among Negroes, or whether it was in jail or outside: sooner or later it turned into the same channel like a stream of water returning to its bed. This morning it had begun with an amiable dispute between Spaulding and his cellmate, Ben Wellman, the issue being the number of fights Joe Louis had had since becoming heavyweight champion of the world.* Recreation coming along, the two men had continued their argument up the stairs, thereby involving the others. A man might be a stonemason like Reeves, or in a shady racket like Spaulding, but the proud and brilliant career of Joe Louis was no less precious to one than to the other. As a result, by a coordinated listing of names and dates, common agreement was quickly achieved. To the chagrin of the original disputants, both were found to be less accurate in their estimates than the little time-server, George Benjamin. This caused Benjamin to crow with vanity and to remind everyone that he knew more boxing and baseball records than any other man in jail. The boast, although true, was obnoxious to Wellman for a particular reason. Wellman never spoke of it, but he had dreamt once of following in the steps of Joe Louis, only to find out through successive disasters that he had small talent for professional fighting. However, since he felt himself one of the boxing fraternity, it was a source of annoyance that Benjamin, not he, should have won the debate. Moreover, he didn't like Benjamin. Not too long ago he had been relieved of his week's wages by an armed robber, another Negro, and robbery was Benjamin's profession. It was not hard for Wellman to feel that out on the street Benjamin would be as willing to prey upon him as upon anyone else. Accordingly, he gave vent to an acid comment. He pointed out that since Benjamin spent most of his time in prison, he had nothing more important to stuff into his empty head than baseball and boxing records. This slur, coming from most other men, would have provoked an offer to fight. However, since Wellman was six feet three, with the physique of an oak tree, Benjamin contented himself by retorting that a man in his position, who had a hundred thousand dollars stashed away, certainly had more important things on his mind than any ass-dragging ditch-digger like Wellman. To this Wellman responded, with the contempt of a working man for a stir-brained windbag, that he'd rather have his thirty-two dollars a week than the hundred thousand pieces of toilet paper Benjamin was dreaming about. The exchange of insults might have continued indefinitely had not Isaac Reeves, who always acted the role of peacemaker, turned the conversation in another direction. "How'd Jackie Robinson* do last week, anybody know?" he asked loudly.

"Still leading the International League," Tillman answered immediately, with enthusiasm. "Man, what a ball player! How those Brooklyn Dodgers* could use *him*!"

"They ain't never gon call him up," Benjamin predicted with assurance. "The big Leagues always have* been lily white, and they always will be."

"Why'd they hire Robinson out of the Negro League, then?" Spaulding asked. "They didn't have to do it. We'll break into the big Leagues before five years, you'll see."

"Won't never see it," Benjamin replied, as he suddenly did a back somersault and then resumed his position on the line. "Uncle Charlie ain't lettin' none of us in on the glory or the cash."

"Man, you got your eyes turned right back to slavery," Spaulding told him. "This country's changing, but you don't know it. You been in prison so—"

"Whites still on top, ain't they?" Benjamin interrupted as he did another somersault. Landing badly, he almost jarred his eyeglasses off his stubby nose, but he caught them and continued imperturbably, "Maybe you's a big-numbers man, with nice clothes an' a flashy car, but walk yourself into Harvey's restaurant an' they'll say, 'Back to U Street,* black crow, you kaint eat here.'"

"God, how can anybody talk to a man so ignorant?" Spaulding asked the others. "Have I said there's no more colour line? I just said we're breaking through more and more, and we'll do it in baseball too."

"You're damn right, we will," Tillman agreed with enthusiasm. "I…" He stopped abruptly as he saw the look on Spaulding's face and realized that he had no business agreeing with Spaulding about anything. It was only two hours gone that Spaulding had called him "a white man's patsy" and "a drag on the race". They were due for a showdown on that, and both of them knew it.

"There's something on my mind about all this," Reeves said reflectively as their line reversed at one end of the range and started its saunter towards the other. "I think there's something we always lose sight of. We've got our eye on all our big Negroes like Louis, Robinson and so on. Now, I ain't sayin' they ain't doin' a lot to advance the race: they sure are. But there's somethin' us smaller fellows could be doin' that's even bigger, only we don't do it."

"What's that?" Spaulding asked with interest.

"We could be buyin' coloured, buildin' up coloured business," Reeves answered with enthusiasm. "Suppose Ford were a Negro, or DuPont?* Wouldn't the whole race be respected more?"

"Suppose a rabbit had wings?" Benjamin asked with mirth. "Then it wouldn't bump its ass on the ground every time it jumped. On'y it does, an' Rockfeller* weren't born black in Pig Alley, like me."

"Ain't no *noo* idea to buy coloured," Wellman put in. "But Sears Roebuck* is still the cheapest place when I needs a pair of jeans."

"Buying coloured's an old idea, sure," Reeves responded with enthusiasm. "But there's something new now. It's the number of coloured who've moved into cities in the last twenty years – millions altogether,* livin' close. Suppose we all organized ourselves to buy coloured in everything? In a coupla years we could have our own chain groceries, our own Sears, our own big businessmen. If we did that, don't you think we'd be respected more? An' if—"

"If, if, if," Wellman interrupted. He broke from the line and sat down heavily on the wall bench. "I'm so tired of 'if', 'tomorrow', 'next year'. I want some jubilee in my life right now. If I had my 'if', I'd be back in Japan. On'y time I felt like a whole man in my life."

"Japan?" Tillman cried with interest. He walked up to Wellman. "When were you there?"

"In at the surrender.* Stayed there five months, came home this January."

"Where?"

"Osaka."

"Goddamn. I was in Okinawa the same time. Got there in October last year an' came home April this."

"You have yourself a big time there, like I did?"

"Hell no, that Okinawa's no place for nothin'. I couldn't wait t'git out of that Jim Crow army, anyway."

"Jim Crow army or not, it were good for me in Osaka," Wellman said with naked longing. "In my free time I were really free. I met a swell Jap girl – I would've married her if the army'd let me stay there. Her folks didn't care about colour. I could've done good for myself in Japan. Ain't nothin' here for me now but 'if', 'tomorrow' 'n' 'heaven'."

"Yeah," Tillman agreed, "we sure fought the wrong war, didn't we?" He sat down by Wellman's side. "We's right back where we was, shovelling manure for Uncle Charlie."

The walking had stopped now, and there was moody silence for a moment. Then, as Huey and Finnerty, just back from sick call, appeared on the tier landing, Spaulding called out eagerly, "Hey, Wilson, you got any broken ribs?"

Huey shook his head. "The doc said I was only bruised. He taped me up."

"Did he X-ray you?" asked Benjamin, as Huey joined the group around the bench.

"He looked at me through a fluoroscope."*

"Without no X-ray he kaint tell crap about whether you got broken ribs or not," Benjamin said with authority. "I know, I worked in a hospital once."

"Cleanin' toilets," Tillman observed. He whooped with laughter and slapped Benjamin on the rear end. "Professor Backhouse, what do you charge for a visit?"

"Oh, dry up, you two," Wellman said with contempt. "We got things to talk about. Wilson, how'd you make out with that white man?"

"No good. He's taking that police offer."

"Did he tell you that straight out?" Spaulding asked in surprise.

"No, but he wouldn't agree to testify for me. It amounts to the same thing."

"How do you like that!" Wellman exclaimed with keen disappointment. "First he helps you, then he leaves you to take the rap by yourself. No guts."

"Like I said this mornin'," Benjamin put in, "you kaint trust no white man till he's dead."

"Benjamin, don't you ever read a newspaper?" Spaulding asked sourly. "You ever hear of the Scottsboro Boys?"*

"Course I did."

"Who the hell helped save them from the electric chair? A couple of white lawyers! Don't you know that?"

"I didn't say whites never do *anything* good for us," Benjamin retorted defensively. "Just said I wouldn't trust 'em. Them lawyers got plenty of cash out of it, don't forgit."

"Oh, beans!" Spaulding snapped. He turned back to Huey. "Guess it'll be rough on you now, Wilson."

"Guess so." The reply was casual, ostensibly careless, but Huey was not hiding his feelings from these men. Disappointment and anxiety were too clear in the sombre expression of his face and in the heaviness of his tone. Moreover, he was acutely unhappy over the fact that he and McPeak had parted in anger. He hated to think that the next time he came downstairs McPeak might be gone, carrying with him the belief that all a white man got from a Negro in return for saving his life were hard words. He had hoped to see McPeak after sick call, but the latter had been sent back to the cell block with an earlier group. And just now, crossing the first-floor range to the staircase, he had hoped to give him a friendly wave of his hand – only to find that McPeak was lying on his bunk, apparently asleep. It had turned out very badly between them, and Huey felt miserable about it. He was sure that his brother or Professor Herrin would have done much better.

"I'm sorry, Wilson," Isaac Reeves said softly. He gave Huey's arm a quick squeeze. "Don't you give up, though. You go in there an' fight 'em hard."

"Don't worry about that." Huey took a small bottle of calomine lotion, which he had been given in the hospital, from his hip pocket. He removed his shirt and began applying the lotion to the ugly welts around his middle. Big Wellman asked, "That adhesive tape itch you?"

"No."

"My skin can't stand it at all. Drives me crazy."

"I don't mind," Huey replied. Above the waist his torso was swathed with broad bands of the white tape. "Lets me breathe much easier."

Tillman suddenly clapped both hands together. "I got an idea. How about we load McPeak up with chow at dinner time like we did that other guy?"

"Nothing doing!" Huey told him sharply.

"Why not?"

"Look," Huey said more patiently, "you got this man all wrong." He began to explain how disastrous the arrest had been for McPeak, and the difficulties that a trial would cause him. "I can't blame him too much for wanting out."

"On'y you're left holdin' the bag," Finnerty said in his soft, apologetic manner. "That don't seem right when he could git you off jus' by speakin' the truth."

"Well, sure, if he had more guts he would," Huey replied, as he put on his shirt again. "But I won't forget what he did for me, I'm damn grateful to him."

The low mood in the group, which had been dispelled by the appearance of Huey, returned now, and a gloomy silence settled down. Men took seats on the bench, side by side, and began to smoke. Benjamin tried a series of cartwheels for diversion, but then, losing his zest for activity, lay down flat on the floor and stared at the skylight. Presently Isaac Reeves began to speak.

"I'm the oldest man here," he said earnestly. "I can tell you things *is* gettin' better. Forty years ago a coloured man couldn't hardly raise his head in this country. Couldn't vote hardly anywhere, the Ku Klux Klan holdin' parades in the streets, lynchings every—"

"You ever hear about Isaac Woodward?"* Big Wellman interrupted with sudden intensity.

"Naturally I did."

"Well I *knew* him," Wellman continued, his huge body seeming to swell larger with anger. "He was in basic training with me, a good boy. So in February *this* year – not forty years ago, goddamn it – the army give him his discharge. Three hours later, he gits arrested for talkin' salty to a bus driver in Batesburg, South Carolina. Fifteen minutes after that, the chief of police has him in jail. An' when he come out, how was he, ol' man, hunh?"

"Blind, I know," Reeves answered with soft unhappiness.

Wellman held both brown fists in front of him, staring at them. "Isaac Woodward, blind for the rest of his life, his pore eyes gouged out by a cop's billy.* Oh, Jesus Christ. An' you talk about things gittin' better!"

"Sure," Reeves said unhappily, "an' Willie McGee waitin' for the electric chair right now in Mississippi,* an' seven poor boys framed up for rape in Martinsville, Virginia,* an' some neighbours of mine beat up this summer by white police for nothin', just nothin' – but I still say its gettin' better. I've seen a lot of change. Negroes comin' up in all walks of life where they never were before, gettin' respected. Seen the CIO* take us in on an equal basis where we never could join a union.* Seen white an' coloured walk on the same picket line. We're makin' real progress – don't turn your eyes from it."

"That's right," Tillman offered with cynical amusement, "it's jus' like with me. Each week that furnished room I live in gits better on account I'm killin' off the bedbug population two hunnerd a week. I on'y got two million four hunnerd thousand t'go."

"That's why I stay in prison," Benjamin cracked as he rolled over on his side and grimaced like a clown. "Runnin' water, flush toilets, bed to yourself – man, I know *how* to live! I live better'n most coloured folks."

"Never mind," Reeves persisted. "The day's soon comin' when we'll be free an' equal. That's what I keep my eye on."

"I sure believe that too, Mr Reeves," Huey put in quietly.

"Only it won't come unless we stick together," Spaulding added with a sidewise glance at Alfrice Tillman. "The more damn handkerchief heads we got, the more drag on the whole race."

"Meanin' anybody aroun' here?" Tillman snapped belligerently.

"Meanin' whoever the shoe fits."

There was angry silence for a moment, with Tillman not quite knowing how to handle the oblique challenge. Then Finnerty said, out of the sadness of his own thoughts, "Sometimes I don't have much faith. We shook loose those slavery chains in Civil War time,* but they put new ones right back on us."

"A long road," Reeves agreed quietly, "but I'm readin' the signs."

"I always thought I'd like t'be a school teacher, on account I like chillen," Finnerty went on, speaking out of his personal mood of sadness. "Never even got through fifth grade – had t'go to work. Now I'm in jail. Didn't git nowhere in my life – nowhere."

"Hell, ol' man," Benjamin cracked, "you got somewhere: you're a great big arsonist. Got your picture in the papers 'n' everythin'."

"It ain't no jokin' matter," Finnerty replied softly, in gentle reproof. "My life is worth somethin', cos I'm a human being. Your life is worth somethin'. We hadn't any of us to be spendin' time in jail. Weren't born for that. Weren't born to be discriminated against. God didn't writ any of it down that way."

There was silence for a moment, and then Reeves said forcefully, "I sure never do see all this cryin' we do. Sittin' around, talkin' the blues. There's only one thing Negroes oughta talk about: not how bad discrimination is, but how do you fight it, how do you lick it? Right now we ought to be talkin' how we can help young Wilson here."

"How the hell can *we* help him?" asked Wellman.

"I just thought of something *I* can do," Reeves answered. "My wife's comin' to visit me tomorrow. I'm gonna tell her to see the president of my Lodge in the Elks. I want my Lodge brothers to go to work on his case."

"I'll appreciate that, Mr Reeves," Huey said gratefully. "Any support like that'll be fine."

"Now *I've* got an idea," Spaulding volunteered. "Wilson, I expect to go free any day now. The only reason I'm in here is cos my boss is having a fight with the police. They want more loot, and he won't pay it, so they picked me up. But in two, three days they'll make a new agreement and I'll be outside. So I'm pledging you right now twenty dollars for your trial expenses, and I guarantee to raise some more from the boys I know."

"Oh man, you got it made now!" Tillman exclaimed sarcastically. "If Spaulding 'n' them big-shot policy boys git behind you, you're in, nothin' more t'worry about."

Spaulding stood up slowly and slowly walked in front of Tillman. The latter jumped up.

"What do you mean by that?"

"Mean what I say!" Tillman stepped sideways from the bench, moving out so that he would be free to manoeuvre if it came to a fight. "You're a big shot, aintcha? You must have a lot of *big* influence."

"Tillman," the older man commented with quiet venom, "I know just the kind of foxy little crap artist you are. If I told you I'd give you a job running numbers for my station, you'd be yessing me all around the place. You'd suck up to me like you've been sucking up to those whites downstairs. You're not a man, you're a f—— leech."*

173

Shaking with indignation, his fists clenched, Tillman cried, "Some day I'm gonna meet you out on the street. I'm gonna beat you so bad your own mother won't know you."

Big Wellman was suddenly there by Spaulding's side. "Listen here, boy," he said sternly, "I don't like how you've been carrying on with that white trash neither. Now, we ain't gon talk *no* more about it. You're just gon stop it, y'hear? An' if you don't stop it, I'm gon lay for you on the stairway an' throw you head first down a whole flight. An' there'll be six witnesses t'say you slipped."

"Hold on now, no need to fight," Reeves cried in distress, as he hovered around the three. "We can handle this a better way."

"It's done been handled!" Wellman replied sternly, as he walked back to his seat.

"I'm gittin' a transfer!" Tillman announced loudly. He moved off, with his fists still clenched, and began to walk the range by himself.

Big Wellman said, "Wilson, is there any way we all could help you with McPeak? Git him t'change his mind?"

"I don't know how. You got any ideas?"

"Kaint think of any. But a couple of us might try an' talk to him on sick call tomorrow."

"If he's here. But I imagine he'll leave today sometime."

"I kaint give you even fifty cents for your expense fund," Wellman said seriously, "on account I'm completely non-financial now. But if there's any other way I kin help you, I'd like to."

"I sure appreciate the way you men are trying to back me up," Huey said warmly. "It makes a fellow feel good." And then, to Spaulding, "Thank you a lot."

"Let's hear a little more about your talk with McPeak. Maybe it'll give us some ideas."

"OK. The truth is I didn't do very good with him," Huey answered with regret. They settled down and he began to talk.

Four tiers below, the subject of their conversation was lying on his bunk in a state of moral paralysis. For the second time in his adult life McPeak was faced by a major conflict between his self-interest and his code of ethics. He was suffering from a violent headache – which he attributed to jailhouse food and constipation – and from enervation and lassitude. The two aspirin tablets he had received in the hospital had not relieved his headache, which had begun to assail him during his conversation with

Huey Wilson, and now was more intense. He had tried to fall asleep when he returned to his cell, but to his dismay he could not sleep – something odd for a man who generally was able to nap anywhere, at any time. This in turn was making him worry about whether or not he was having an attack of high blood pressure.

All of his life McPeak had been strong and well – or, as he was prone to remark, if not all his life, then certainly since his service in the navy in World War I. Before that, he had been afflicted with what the residents of Dade County, Georgia, called "tooth misery". He had begun having his decayed teeth extracted after his fifteenth year – this being the only type of dentistry acceptable to the citizens of his mountain community – and he had completed the job in the navy. He never was a man to let hardship stand in the way of his own benefit, and so, when he learnt that the navy would supply him with artificial plates without cost, he persuaded the dental technician on his destroyer to extract the remainder of his healthy teeth. Since that time he had been free of physical ills, and it had come as a stunning surprise the year before to learn that his blood pressure was higher than it should be for his age. A routine examination, offered by the medical service of his trade-union local, had disclosed the condition. Even though the physician had been quite reassuring, telling him that the rise in pressure was not yet serious, that it could be controlled and that his heart still was sound, McPeak had become oppressed with anxiety. No man survived in the car industry unless he was able to maintain the production pace. Indeed, so intense was McPeak's new concern with his health that, advised to reduce his weight, he had taken to dieting with such vigour that the doctor had ordered him to slow up. Right now he could not recall whether there was such a thing as an attack of high blood pressure, but he could not help fearing that his violent headache had a more serious cause than constipation.

Nevertheless, whatever his uncertainty about his physical condition, McPeak was very clear about the moral problem he faced. Ever since his conversation with Detective Stoner the afternoon before, he had been trying to think his way through to a decision – but with no result other than an increasing* paralysis of will. Self-interest urged that he accept the police offer and run. Yet, his sense of justice and his conscience, together with a chronic stubbornness of character, had made it impossible so far for him to come to that decision. For one thing, he hated the pushing-around he was getting. He had travelled from Detroit to Washington for a family wedding, and it made his gorge rise to be told by the police either to leave town or to face charges. Of even stronger force, however, was the fact that in mind and heart McPeak believed in the principle of trade-union solidarity – and therefore he despised any sort of scab. Even though this was not a trade-union matter, his conscience kept insisting that if he deserted Huey Wilson at this point, leaving him to face the frame-up alone, it would be exactly like scabbing on his fellow workers in a strike.

This he acknowledged to himself – while all the time* yearning to run. What he was seeking was a way to desert without feeling ashamed of himself, but it was not easy for him. Indeed Huey Wilson had stabbed deep in telling him that he wasn't the sort of man to make a deal with the police, and that he would be ashamed of it for the rest of his life. McPeak had reacted with an angry outburst that was not honest indignation over an insulting suggestion, but a mask for his embarrassment and his inner turmoil. For what Wilson did not know was that McPeak was being held under arrest – not because he had turned down the police offer, but because he had not yet accepted it. He had told Detective* Stoner that he would think it over, and sometime during the course of this day he was expecting to see Stoner again.

Now, as he lay restlessly on his bunk, arguing with himself first one way then another, yet all the while trying to make up his mind to run, McPeak regretted his meeting with Huey on sick call. He had come away with personal feeling for the youth, liking him as an individual. It made desertion more difficult, a more intimate betrayal.

McPeak was not a man given to philosophic speculation, yet there was an irony in his present dilemma that he could not help perceive – namely, that a decade ago he would have avoided this trouble altogether. The beating-up of a lone Negro by four* white men would have put little strain upon his human sympathies or his sense of fair play, and he would have passed it by as none of his business. But years of life and work in Detroit had changed him in not a few respects. In the pursuit of narrow self-interest he had learnt new ways of thinking: now, as he clearly perceived, those new ways were in conflict with his self-interest. "Usta be, when I looked at a coloured man, I jist saw his colour," he had said once to the friend he called "Balance Wheel". "But I've changed now: I see a man."

It had been a difficult change for McPeak to make, and it had not occurred all at once, or easily. Like most men he generally decided his behaviour in life by the slide rule of self-interest. For this reason he had been more than four years at work in Detroit before he perceived that either he had to alter his traditional attitude towards Negroes or else turn his back on what he desperately wanted to succeed – the rising trade-union movement in the automobile industry. He was working then in the core room at Bohn Aluminum, a factory that made parts for General Motors.* It was hard, dirty work at best, but with millions unemployed in those depression years the management required man-killing effort in return for a subsistence wage. "There's five hungry Joes waitin' outside for your job," the foreman used to say. "You got any complaints, quit! You can't make the production schedule, you're fired!" ("Leave town or face charges," Detective Stoner had said, and it was the same damn pushing-around McPeak always had hated.)

The complaints were mountain-high in those years, and they built the union. McPeak never had belonged to a union on any of his previous jobs – his ideas about the labour movement were hazy – but he signed a card the moment it was offered to him. What he did not know at first, since the small, secret group to which he was assigned consisted of white men only, was that Negroes also were being recruited. When he discovered it, he was appalled. With vigour and indignation he protested this policy to the organizer of the group, and his sentiments were supported by a number of others. Some weeks of intense controversy followed, during which McPeak began to perceive – yet would not admit – that no union could succeed in the car* industry if it did not include all of the workers. No matter what his arguments, he always was confronted with the same question: "How the hell we gonna lick the car companies if we don't have unity?"

He had no answer, but he could not ignore the question. Unity was not an abstract word to McPeak. After four years in the core room, he knew how helpless any individual was to slow down the killing work pace, or to raise his wage even a penny an hour. He wanted unity – but with white men, not coloured. When it was pointed out to him that Negroes were a significant percentage of the two thousand workers in their plant, and that if they weren't accepted in the union they'd surely be scabs in a strike, McPeak had no answer. All he could say was that it went against his grain. Or again, when he was asked why he wouldn't organize with the same men he had been working with for four years, he would reply that he had no choice over the hiring policies of the company, but that didn't mean he had to eat with the niggers at lunch (which he didn't) or consider them his equals (which he didn't). "Brother McPeak," he was told in reply, "you better get off that Confederate dime you're standing on – it's got no money value any more. The company's tryin' to keep us split in ten different ways cos the one thing they don't want is us gettin' unified. An' one sure way to split us wide open is your way – coloured against white. So you better make up your mind whether you're for the company policy or the union policy, cos you can't be for both."

Not even after he found himself deserted by most of his supporters in the group could McPeak make up his mind one way or the other. He had no solution to the problem of unity, but he was a stubborn man, slow to change, reluctant to give up the social code he had believed in since childhood. At that time, however, there had been his wife to talk to, as there was not now, and she had been vigorous in assailing what she called "his backward, Georgia ways". Katy was her name, and she cherished this man of hers, but there was nothing subservient in her love for him. She knew from her own childhood in a mining town of Illinois how desperately a working man needed a union, and she had had her own experience in Bohn Aluminum before their marriage and her pregnancy. "Great God Almighty," she would snap at him in exasperation, "you come home so dog-tired you hardly can eat your supper – you're so beat up these days I hardly see you except you're asleep – but when it comes down to rock bottom, you only wanna talk union, not do anything about it."

"Sure I do – I joined up, didn't I?" he would reply. "But—"

"But what?"

"You know what!"

"I sure do. You're more worried about sittin' down in the same room with a coloured man than you are about the size of your paycheck. That's a fine how-do-you-do! That Georgia brain of yours is sure missin' a cylinder. Now I'll tell you somethin', Mr Man. You married me an' you didn't waste no time gettin' me pregnant. How about you start worryin' about this kid of yours I'm carryin'? I want it to have enough t'eat so it'll grow up strong. I don't want no Georgia pellagra* in *my* family."

"OK, OK, I'm still in the union, ain't I?" he would reply. "Stop naggin', stop hollerin', leave off."

McPeak's head was in the union, but his heart was riven, and finally he stopped trying to think his way through to a solution. He still carried a union card in his pocket, but he ceased going to meetings and he made no effort to recruit others. There came a day then, in the winter of 1936, in which the situation at his plant exploded. As it happened, McPeak's was the first among the car* factories to go on strike.*

Lying on his bunk in a jail cell, his heart torn once again, McPeak realized that he had forgotten nothing of those events, that no effort on his part could erase the memories, the conversations, the faces – and, worse, that they had become part of him and were now stalking him along with the face of Huey Wilson and the conversation with Detective Stoner. What he had been once, he no longer was, and the first of his turning points was as vivid to him now as it had been then.

It had come about in the following manner: one of the leaders of the Bohn Aluminum union, by the name of Freddie, had been identified to the company management by an informer. When he came to work the next morning, he was stopped at the gate, his work badge was taken from him and he was fired. An hour later, by vaulting a fence, he made his way into the plant. The word spread immediately from shop to shop: "Freddie got the bounce." It was clear to everyone at once that if Freddie were not reinstated, the union at Bohn Aluminum had little future. In a number of the shops, one of them being the core room, the most active union members shut down the power and began a sit-down demonstration in protest. The cry went up, "No Freddie, no work!" The foremen were screaming and cursing, running up and down the rows of seated men, threatening that all would be fired. And then, when a few of the men in the shop made it clear that they were ready to return to work, the further cry went up, "Now we know who the stool pigeons* are! Union men, show your buttons!"

It was only at this point that McPeak, pinning his button on his shirt and yelling with excitement "No Freddie, no work!" saw that by his side there was a Negro with his button already displayed. Since Freddie was a white man, this was McPeak's first lesson in the adhesive power of common interest. One of his arguments in the months past had been that no coloured man ever was dependable, and that the union would find itself deserted by its Negro members in a crisis. The crisis had come, the lines were forming, and McPeak's transformation had begun.

In the weeks that followed he felt himself, as he was to say later, turned upside down and inside out. The strike, which had begun with more spontaneity than plan, turned into a siege. What had started as a demand for the reinstatement of one man became a life-and-death struggle for the job of every striker, for wages and working conditions and for the right to organize. The company refused to budge, and the strikers stayed inside, in possession of the plant. Within a short time, there were similar strikes throughout the industry.

It was a hard time, and a desperately anxious time. About three hundred men and women were inside the plant, both Negro and white, while hundreds marched on a twenty-four-hour picket line outside. More quickly than McPeak could realize, he began to feel the Negro workers as indispensable allies in this struggle for his personal welfare. As a group they were as solidly for the union as the whites, he could see that. When the strikers bedded down for the night, their conduct was no different from his own. Men and women separated themselves, there was no drinking, there was none of the funny business he would have feared. He began then to know Negroes by their first names, to see them as individuals, to perceive that their humanity and their yearnings were no different from his own. He began to learn also, and this was very hard, that there were some among the Negroes who were smarter than he was, who knew more about trade unionism and had better ideas in a crisis. There were so many crises and so many feverish meetings that he finally admitted to himself that if there was one man in the entire plant whose judgement he always would trust, it was a shrewd, calm Negro who had earned for himself the nickname of "Balance Wheel".

There came a day then, it was the nineteenth day of the sit-down, in which he saw something he never would forget: the public exposure of a company informer, a Negro, by another Negro. That afternoon, with a willing heart, McPeak did something that would have been utterly impossible for him a few weeks earlier. The sit-downers had planned a demonstration of their morale – it was to be a parade around the large area of junkyard behind the factory itself. The line of sit-downers, singing and whooping, paraded through all of the shops in the plant and then out into the back area that was a slush of mud and dirty snow. While they marched along one side of the steel-mesh fence that enclosed the property, a cheering picket line kept pace outside. At the head of the parade were a number of men with improvised musical instruments. One was beating a hammer on an empty oil can. Another carried an aluminium automobile part, shaped like a harp, which he strummed with a nail. Third in line were two men who each carried a large metal pipe. They were blowing alternately into their pipes, one of them saying "boop" and the other "bump", both using different tones in harmony. One of these men was a Negro from the core room, and the other was McPeak.

Nine years later, on a street corner in the city of Washington, McPeak had done something that many another man, however decent, would have been afraid to do. Yet, when he had run to the aid of a lone Negro being assaulted by four* white men, it was not from conscious decision. There had not been time for reflection, and the act had been wholly spontaneous. Impelling it, however, had been the past ten years of his life: the bitter struggle for the union; the lessons he had learnt from a man called "Balance Wheel"; the bone-deep sense of unity that had grown within him. And all of this he understood the moment the fight was over.

Yet now, in this jail cell, he wished that he never had seen Huey Wilson. He didn't regret his interference in the fight. In truth he was proud of that. But he wanted it to have ended there. It seemed to him as though he had done enough. It was easy for a young man who had no responsibilities to say, "Let's battle it out, we're sure to win." Wilson could afford to lose. He could go to prison for five years and still come out a kid, with his whole life ahead of him. He wasn't forty-eight, with a seniority rating on his job to protect. He didn't have a wife and two young kids, or instalments to meet on a refrigerator, or rent to pay on a house. Talk was easy when you were strong and healthy and only eighteen years old. But after six months in jail Tom McPeak would be up shit creek, and his family with him.

Lying on his bunk, fretting, torn, his head aching and his brain in a whirl, McPeak tried and tried to think his way through to a solution. It seemed as though whichever* way he turned, it was bad for him. He despised Ballou, and he hated to see Ballou get away with this frame-up. A boy like Wilson was the stuff that Balance Wheel was made of, the best. How on earth could he run out on Wilson and leave a dirty mouth like Ballou to tell his lies at the hearing? He knew the kind Ballou was, he had seen his type operating in the union, snot-nosed* and prejudiced, unwilling to learn, always ready to break up unity over the colour issue. A kid like Wilson was worth a thousand of Ballou.

So long as McPeak's thoughts ran in this vein it seemed impossible that he could do anything except stand by Huey Wilson and face the music. Yet, the moment he tried to make up his mind in a decisive fashion, one part of him rebelled. "What for?" came the question. "Haven't you done enough for that coloured boy? Look what you're lettin' yourself in for."

McPeak knew all too well what the consequences might be: he had studied them over a dozen times since his conversation with Detective Stoner. It was all very well for Wilson to speak of them both as the white and black keys to the situation – throwing back his own words at him, McPeak hadn't missed that – but this was a police frame-up, not a trade-union struggle. Wilson could argue all he wanted that the case would be dismissed at the hearing, but he knew better. This one was headed for a court, and no mistake about that. So what then? If they kept him in Washington to wait for the trial, it might cost him his job and his four years' seniority. He had deliberately given up his eight years at Bohn Aluminum to grab a better job at Ford's during the war, but a man without any seniority at all was lost when lay-offs came. Four years was little enough – why was he called on to risk it?

Or suppose they let him out on bail? Then he'd have to come back for the trial – more expense, more time lost from the job, more pay days down the drain with the budget slim enough at home as it was. And who the hell could guarantee, in a lousy frame-up like this, that they both might not be convicted? That was all he needed, a nice little six months. He'd come out broke: no job, the family in debt, with his blood pressure worse, no doubt. Why on earth should he take chances like that for someone he never had met before?*

So McPeak argued with himself, but the arguments came to a dead stop whenever he said to himself, "The hell with it, I'm leavin'." He couldn't leave, he didn't want to stay. Yet in five minutes or several hours he'd be taken out of his cell to see Detective Stoner. What would he say?

McPeak groaned aloud. He wished that his wife were with him so that he could talk it over with her and she would give him a push one way or the other. He wished that the detective never had made the offer, so that he would be helpless to do anything but the right thing. He wished that he could get good and drunk and wake up back in Detroit. Most of all he wished for a miracle to happen by which he would be relieved of any need to make a decision – for the charges against both of them to be dismissed, or for Detective Stoner to say to him, "OK, bud, I'll make a deal with you. Keep your mouth shut and you won't have to leave town. We'll lower the charge against Wilson to simple assault and give him probation."

Only they wouldn't! The decision was still his to make, and he knew it.

What he had been once, he no longer was – yet, what he was now somehow was not equal to this situation. He lay there suffering, arguing with himself, and wishing.

Chapter 9

The Judge

Judge Stokey's court was already in session when Floyd Varney arrived in the custody of a bailiff. They entered the courtroom through a door at the rear, Varney's handcuffs were removed, and he was directed to a row of benches near the judicial dais. Here, in guarded isolation, half a dozen other men sat with hollow nervousness waiting to plead or to be sentenced.

Now that the appalling moment had arrived, Varney found to his surprise and pleasure that he was quite in control of himself. The wild pounding of his heart had ceased, and he felt unexpectedly serene. He was very glad of it! Whatever the sentence would be, the one thing he didn't want was to act the weakling, or to give the newspapers any more hot copy. He had had a bellyful of their dirty stories* about the alleged rape. In the Sunday supplements the word "alleged" always was in small print, but the drawings left no room for doubt: Mrs Peterson on the bed, while a brute held a knife to her throat; Mrs Peterson being stripped naked by clawing hands, while the small print asked, "Did it happen this way?"; the husband in the doorway, struck dumb with horror; the fatal blow, with the killer's face like that of a wild beast, slavering with the joy of murder. In his more reasoning moments Varney sometimes wondered why the jury had let him off with second degree when he already had been convicted and executed by the damn newspapers. Whatever the sentence was, he'd give them no more copy this morning.

His eyes sought out the judge. For some moments he scrutinized this man who would sentence him, watching him in whispered conference with a clerk. In the course of his trial Varney never had known how to regard Judge Stokey, because the latter's face always was so impassive, washed clean of emotion, as befits the judicial countenance. Yet now, studying the man's sharp-featured, freckled visage, it seemed to him that it was not unkind. A bit fox-like, perhaps, yet not cruel or overly stern. George Combs regarded Stokey with disdain, and had called him a "punk", and Varney bore this in mind. Yet the important thing, he told himself now, was that the man *had* to be smart, with good legal training, or he wouldn't be sitting where he was. No one like that would be taken in by newspaper stories. Stokey had heard the evidence; more than likely he even disagreed with the jury's verdict. It was a sure thing he'd settle for the minimum.

Feeling increased optimism, Varney glanced next towards the attorney's bench in front of the spectators' railing. Other men with briefcases were there, but not Combs, and he felt a quick twinge of distress. He relaxed a moment later when he spied Combs in conversation with Pollard, the US Attorney. They were standing close together near the empty jury box, Combs wearing a wide grin and the prosecutor chuckling. Varney's confidence waxed bigger as he watched them. This, he told himself, was a deal in the making – Pollard would join in a request for the minimum sentence, maybe a recommendation of parole as well. Oh, that Combs, he thought fondly, a prince of a man, a man with a heart big enough to make up for all the heels* in the world.

In this way, with the eagerness of all frightened men, Varney misinterpreted the formal cordiality existing among most members of the legal profession, and found passing satisfaction in a notion that had no basis in reality. No agreement had been reached, and the US Attorney still intended to ask for the longer sentence.

Up front, the judge had finished his conference. The clerk rapped once with his gavel, and Pollard moved away from Combs to take his seat at a forward table. Combs sat down on the attorney's bench, took a pad from his briefcase and immediately began to scribble a note. Varney watched him, waiting for him to look up, but he did not.

A case was called. The man beside Varney, an elderly, obese Negro, rose from his seat with a grunt. He was directed by a bailiff to a spot in front of the judicial dais. There he was joined by his court-appointed attorney, a white man who looked like a crook to Varney. A low-voiced conference began about a change of trial date, and Varney once again celebrated the fact that he had George Combs as his lawyer. He told himself that when he was free he would pay Combs ten per cent of his wages for years and years, until he had been paid handsomely – it was no less than he deserved.

With intense curiosity Varney turned now to see if Mrs Peterson was among the spectators. His glance swept the rear of the room, but he didn't find her. He began to examine the rear section row by row. The benches were crowded, as they usually were on calendar mornings, by relatives and friends of those scheduled for appearance and by those who were free on bail and had been summoned to be present. In that gallery of strained faces Varney saw first not Mrs Peterson, but – to his astonishment – Janey Welch, his former sweetheart.

Janey's eyes met his as soon as he spied her, and an expression of such deep compassion came over her face that he knew she had come in sympathy and forgiveness. He turned to pulp inside. Janey had not attended his trial, nor had she responded to a message he had sent her through Combs. Varney had not blamed her for this, and had wished only that there were some way in which he could ease the wound she had received – at the very least, to let her know that he had been sincere and faithful in their relationship until the episode with Mrs Peterson.

He felt now that perhaps she understood this – or why else should she have come? He ached to speak to her, to embrace her, to thank her. Gazing now at her sweet face, seeing her russet hair neatly braided as always, the clear, honest eyes and the warmth, the indescribable warmth of her look, he felt such sadness, such loss, such anguish over what he had done as he never had felt about anything before. Not when he was arrested, not when the jury pronounced him guilty, not even in the dreariest hours of his imprisonment, had he comprehended so deeply the crime he had committed upon himself. His heart cried out wildly, "Why was I so blind? It was Janey I needed all along, not the running around. Why didn't I know it before?"

He turned away from Janey's look and Janey's face, and wiped his eyes roughly with his hand, and felt lost and shattered beyond repair. "Janey, Janey," his heart cried, and it was the bleakest moment of his life.

The court clerk banged his gavel loudly and called a new case, US versus Harold McCauley. A lawyer walked forward, but no one else, and the clerk called again, "Harold McCauley?"

"Comin'," a man answered loudly from the last bench, and Varney, turning to the sound, saw Mrs Peterson.

She was staring at him, and their glances locked. For one moment, although he couldn't understand it, Varney felt pity for her. He saw her drawn, pallid face, he saw the strain and the anguish, and her guilt – and he felt the same pity for her that he would have felt for any sick, tormented creature. But then, abruptly, Mrs Peterson turned her glance away. Her features became stony, her head tilted back in frightened hauteur, and Varney's mood changed to bitter rage. She became for him not a weak woman, but a traitorous slut who could have saved him by a few truthful words and instead had damned him – and now had come back to see him damned. It was insufferable!

He stared at the floor, unable to gaze upon either of these women, the one he had cast aside, or the other who had cast him aside. He felt numb.

Meanwhile, the court calendar was advancing. A woman said loudly "Not guilty", and trial was ordered for October twenty-seventh. The next case was called – there was a shuffle in the courtroom, and the clerk said, "Edward Porchet, how do you plead?" The gavel banged, the docket advanced.

When the pleadings were finished, the judge began to sentence men already convicted – and Varney's mood changed at once. His senses quickened. For the moment he forgot Janey and he forgot Mrs Peterson. Fear returned. He began to tremble.

The reporters in the courtroom also became attentive. There was more newspaper representation than usual on a calendar day because Floyd Varney was up for sentencing, and because word had passed in advance that Mrs Peterson might be in the courtroom. Indeed, Mrs Peterson had appeared shortly before ten o'clock, smartly attired, even though in widow's weeds, with a half-veil enhancing the charm of her pallid face. She already had been interviewed, though not very satisfactorily, since she refused to acknowledge in so many words that she was there in vindictiveness. Yet, since her presence in the courtroom had no other significance, the reporters already had a partial story worth the front page of their newspapers, and they hoped for more later on.

There was an air about Judge Stokey this morning that began to command attention. Usually he disposed of his sentences in as rapid a manner as possible, as though the obligation were distasteful. This morning, however, two things were evident to the court attendants and to those of the reporters who were regulars: that Judge Stokey was in a mood for speechifying, and that Judge Stokey was of a mind to give whopping sentences.

The first case called was that of Robert Goins, a man from Varney's cell block. He had been found guilty of technical violation of the Mann Act,* but the court clerk expected a suspended sentence because of the odd circumstances surrounding the case. Goins, a West Virginia carpenter aged forty-seven, freely acknowledged that he had brought with him across the District of Columbia boundary line, for what the law called "intent of fornication", a woman of thirty-four to whom he then was formally engaged, whom he wished to marry and who had grown big with child during the months of his custody and trial. The man had no criminal record; he was a deacon in his mountain church, and the woman herself testified that his intentions from the first had been amorously conjugal rather than those of a pimp or a dealer in prostitutes. Nevertheless, they had been apprehended together in a room in a motor court by two detectives of the Vice Squad. Goins was brought to trial, held guilty according to the letter of a law* that had been designed for quite another purpose – and Judge Stokey now sentenced him to a year and a day in a Federal penitentiary. Yet, not without a serious utterance to go along with it: that the moral standards of a community were its first line of defence against social decay, and that if the senior members of society were not punished for flouting the law, how then would young people ever learn to behave? For this reason, he said, he was denying the attorney's plea for suspended sentence. He would, however, be willing to recommend parole, provided the man's conduct in prison gave warrant for his doing so.

The reporters scribbled a note, a pregnant woman in the rear of the court burst into sobs, and a second culprit was summoned before the bench. This one, aged nineteen, had pleaded guilty to the forgery of a twenty-dollar unemployment cheque rifled from a mailbox in his slum tenement. His lawyer, begging the court's indulgence and receiving it, pleaded the youth of the offender, the illness of his mother as motivation, the trifling sum, the established evidence that the money had been used to pay a doctor. He asked for a suspended sentence and probation. The judge, clearing his throat, observed drily that the twenty dollars had belonged to a family no less badly off than was the boy's. The embezzlement of mail matter, he added, was a serious crime meriting up to five years, and forgery had been involved as well. He next pointed out that the government had seen fit to prosecute not for those more serious crimes, but merely for petty larceny. Judge Stokey thereupon pronounced the maximum sentence, twelve months, and Lee Huntington, unemployed Negro youth, was led away.

There were whisperings on the lawyer's bench and among the reporters. No one knew why Judge Stokey was off on a rampage, but it was apparent that he was. It was made even more apparent by the case that followed – that of the burglary of a clothing store by two first offenders. The goods pilfered had been worth three hundred dollars; the two young men, both in their early twenties, had committed minor indiscretions of a mischievous sort as juveniles, but had no criminal record. The court clerk expected a sentence of one to three years. Instead, Judge Stokey, pointing out that planned crimes against property were even less excusable than crimes of passion, sentenced them both to four years with a recommendation that they be denied parole.

Varney did not realize the significance of what was occurring. He was waiting for the sound of his own name, and the time given other men did not particularly concern him. George Combs, however, was profoundly disturbed. He knew that the sentences were unusually heavy, and he was afraid that this boded ill for Varney. Yet there was nothing he could do, no way now to delay sentence until another day. He pondered the judge's manner, weighed his comments to the court and re-examined the plea he himself intended to make. It seemed clear that Stokey was addressing the newspapers this morning. Was it in preparation for a light sentence in the Varney case or a heavy one, or was there some other reason? There was no time for Combs to investigate and no way for him to guess. He decided, however, that since publicity seemed to be walking hand in hand with Justice on this day, he himself would speak to the press as well as to the court. And while he didn't give a damn about the nature of the press stories, he was willing to play that gambit if it would have any effect upon Judge Stokey.

US versus* Varney was the last case to be called. Many of the spectators had departed by now, since the cases in which they were interested already had been handled. But the reporters remained, Janey Welch and Mrs Peterson remained, and a significant quiet fell upon the courtroom.

Standing before the judicial dais with George Combs at his side, Varney had a moment of such sweeping terror that he was afraid of what he might do in the next moment – weep like a child or bellow out his innocence, or collapse to his knees and gibber. He did none of these things, merely stood very stiffly, a handsome young man more than usually pale, fighting with himself to recover the poise and confidence he had enjoyed earlier. He answered to his name with a slight stammer and felt embarrassed that he had spoken so loudly, although in fact he had not spoken loudly at all. He heard Combs ask His Honour for the privilege of making a plea before sentence, and he heard His Honour assent. The court clerk motioned for him to return to his seat, but Varney did not understand until Combs whispered to him. He obeyed then like an overfatigued soldier in combat, his brain spinning with confusion, his forehead and temples burning. He sat with his lips parted, breathing rapidly, his hot eyes fixed upon Combs.

Combs, tall and very straight, stood behind the table with his briefcase and several sheets of handwritten notes before him. He began to speak quietly, yet loudly enough to be sure that the row of reporters, at their desk behind the spectators' railing, could hear him – and that the judge himself would be aware that the reporters were hearing him. His tactic was clear in his mind: to present the ugly facts of Varney's life with such force and sharp challenge that even the press might take note, and the judge himself be impelled to sentence leniently.

"Your Honour, I wish to put into the scales of justice the total life of my client. Floyd Varney—"

At this early point the judge interrupted. "I hope counsel will bear in mind that, in his summation to the jury, counsel touched upon his client's war record and other such facts. Since I am well acquainted with the record, it is not necessary to repeat it."

"Of course, Your Honour. However, certain relevant information was not given to the jury because, at that time, my client requested that it be withheld."

"Counsel is not attempting to advance new trial evidence at this point?"

"No, Your Honour, merely such facts as I feel you surely would wish to weigh in determining sentence."

"Very well, go on."

With slow emphasis Combs said, "Floyd Varney is the illegitimate son of a prostitute! He never knew his father – perhaps that is just as well. He was born to a life not only of rural slum poverty, but of the worst moral degradation possible in our society – and that can be pretty bad. His mother continued to be a prostitute during his childhood, and, as he grew older, she used him as an errand boy in her trade. Until the age of ten Varney never saw the inside of a church or a school. What he knew about life and morality he learnt in the two-room shack of a whore on the outskirts of Chattanooga, Tennessee."

Combs paused for an instant, and then his voice began to take on fire as his genuine feeling for Varney took command of him. "Your Honour knows that no child ever chooses the circumstances of his birth. Varney's early environment, over which he had no control, was strongly calculated to lead him into crime. Yet search this man's life and you will find that never before this moment has he even been charged with a crime. It is no accident that this is so: Varney *willed* it so! On his tenth birthday, with seven miserable dollars saved from tips earned as a messenger boy for his wretched mother and her patrons, Varney ran away from home. He became a vagrant – but a vagrant with a moral purpose in his life: to be different from his mother, whom he had seen steal from men while they slept, to be free of a mother who kissed him in drunkenness and beat him in sobriety – and to go to school like other children. All this I know because Floyd Varney has told it to me, and because I believe him. But if it should be thought that I have been taken in by my client or by my own sentiment, then I offer the confirmed facts of his life in evidence."

Combs paused for an instant to consult his notes. The courtroom remained very quiet, except for the pencils of the reporters. Judge Stokey was leaning forward with a thoughtful frown on his face, his small bright eyes shifting from defence counsel to the reporters and back again. Varney, sitting alone on the prisoners' bench, was listening with morbid fascination. It was his own life Combs was relating – and yet, somehow, his life from a new and astonishing perspective. All of it was true and familiar, but he never had thought of it in quite this way.

"How does a boy of ten manage alone in our world?" Combs asked harshly. "He manages badly! He does farm chores from dawn to dark for a day's food and a night's sleep in a barn. He fishes in a river and sleeps under a bush. When winter comes, he goes to the police in Knoxville and is put in an orphanage. I have the orphanage records at hand, Your Honour. The boy, Floyd Varney, stayed there until spring and then left. He left because he had felt a strap too often before at the hands of his mother. He left with a bloody welt on his cheek from the buckle of a monitor's belt. Was the beating justified – had he violated discipline? Perhaps – if beating a boy of eleven with a belt ever is justified. Varney left – yet not to become a juvenile delinquent. He left with a spelling book, a reader and a will for honest work – a boy of eleven with a moral purpose. He picked fruit. He was a grocery boy. He was a stable boy. He was a pin boy in a bowling alley. He never held any job too long because he was afraid of the police, afraid he would be returned to an orphanage. He was a Western Union messenger in New Orleans. He was a fisherman's helper out of Gulfport, Mississippi. And sometimes, when he was hungry, he begged. But he never stole, Your Honour! And I have written evidence for at least half of the jobs I mention."

Combs paused, his wide mouth pressed tight, his sharp chin jutting forward in challenge. Despite the passion in his voice and his own emotional involvement with Varney's fate, one corner of his brain remained distant and objective, estimating his performance. Was he being too verbose... was he making an impression on the judge... what about the reporters? He wished he could turn and face them. With the quick decision, right or wrong, required of public speakers, he resisted an impulse towards quickening his narrative. "The hell with him," he thought, concerning the judge. "Let him interrupt if he wants to. It's my job to shoot the works."

"These are merely bare facts, Your Honour. But I know you will appreciate the loneliness, the misery, the confusion of those early years. This boy was robbed of the birthright that should belong to everyone in an advanced society, which…" – Combs caught himself; he had been about to add with bitterness "which our society is not" – instead he gestured and left the thought unfinished. "He always was outside looking in, knowing how cold the world can be. And if it were to be asked what sustained him, then I myself would answer in the following way: that beyond his courage and his innate decency, he must have believed in the American dream – that he, like everyone else, had a future in our society. Or else, many times, he would have abandoned hope."

In the rear of the courtroom Janey Welch was crying soundlessly, a handkerchief pressed to her mouth, tears blurring her vision. Mrs Peterson, without the relief of tears, sat with a waxen pallor on her face. This was a narrative dreadful for her to hear, and, although she did not dare, she wanted to run from the room. She had not expected this, and the guilt she already felt towards Varney was being stoked by Combs into a fire. This was the price she was paying for her good name in society, and she would pay it now for the rest of her life.

Rather quickly, upon an impulse that reversed his decision of only a few minutes before, Combs only broadly sketched in Varney's years from fourteen to eighteen. He pointed out that those were the years of the great economic depression when sixteen million others were unemployed. No wonder then that Varney had no steady work – that he bummed the land, sometimes begged, sometimes slept overnight in a county jail. (This he mentioned in order to explain any jail notations in the probation report.) "I tell you this," he added vigorously. "There were winter nights when Varney was glad to be in jail as a vagrant – and what man with a heart can condemn him for that?"

At this point, with care, with discreet selection of his words, Combs began to build up the psychological portrait best inclined to explain the killing of Charles Peterson. "Your Honour – in describing Varney's background I don't wish to assert that he emerged from those awful years as a paragon of virtue. I think I know my client. I say in all honesty that I believe his nature was somewhat warped by his experiences. I think he was made envious of others and, perhaps, overgreedy for pleasure. But that, surely, was inevitable. For too many years a town to Varney was only a place where others lived in comfortable homes – a home was only a window, with him on the outside looking in." Combs extracted a letter from his briefcase.

"I ask Your Honour to consider something else. At the age of eighteen Varney had a WPA job* in Cincinnati, Ohio, his first steady employment in years. Three nights a week he attended elementary school. Two nights a week he received instruction in boxing at a YMCA.* I have here a letter from his boxing instructor, Mr Mullins. He pays Varney a compliment. He says that if Varney had turned professional, he might have gone far. Why? Because in addition to boxing skill he had the fighter's instinct."

Combs paused briefly to let this phrase be absorbed. "When a man of the boxing fraternity speaks of the fighter's instinct, Your Honour, he does not mean an anti-social instinct. He is trying to convey a particular quality within a fighter that results in aggressiveness, in stubborn determination, in a sustained drive to defeat his opponent. The greatest fighters have had this instinct. Ask a psychiatrist and I think we will learn why they have it – as Varney had it. Because somewhere within them is a fund of hostility that seeks outlet. I am being very honest here, Your Honour – I am not trying to paint with false colours. I freely state that I think Varney had this inner hostility. He was not born with it: it was nurtured in him by eighteen years of a life he didn't want and didn't choose. It was nurtured in him further when war came. Varney volunteered for the Marines, surely an honourable act. But inevitably the fighter's instinct was further developed in him. He was made a boxing instructor, he was taught judo defence and, in turn, taught boxing and judo to other young men in order to develop their fighting instinct. This is what his country wanted of him."

Now, in final passion, Combs began to plead for a degree of insight from the judge that the jury had been unable to give. "When Varney was discharged from the Marines, with a Purple Heart* for a wound received in battle, did he return to society as an anti-social element? Did he take a gun and rob? Did he pick fights in bars? Was he arrested for assaulting women? No! There are no charges against him, no record of arrests. He entered a GI school* to learn a trade – that of a cook and a baker. What was his school record? Excellent. What was his employment record? Excellent also. Your Honour – I know that I cannot dispute the jury decision before this court, although with my mind and heart I cry out that a wrong verdict was rendered. I merely beg Your Honour to consider that if Charles Peterson did not die accidentally, as I believe he did, in the course of a wild struggle in which he had a knife and Floyd Varney only his bare hands and his fear – then something else beside Varney was in that room compelling him to a final blow. That, Your Honour, was Varney's life, Varney's childhood, Varney's training in the Marines – the sense of self-defence and fighting aggressiveness our society nourished in him, demanded for his survival, rewarded. But Varney himself is not a killer. Varney is not a criminal. Varney is not a rapist. Varney does not belong in the company of jailbirds. Put his dead mother and his unknown father in jail. Jail the economic stresses that kept him unemployed. Jail whatever sent him to war. Varney has been in a kind of jail all his life. What has the American dream been for him? He has earned the right to consideration. Only you can give it to him, Your Honour. I ask you for it, for the understanding due an unplanned act of passion. Varney has suffered six months' imprisonment already. I ask that you declare this to be time served, and that you give him the minimum penalty of ten years. I urge further your personal recommendation of parole at the end of one third of his sentence. I am asking for your human understanding, for your mercy and for justice."

Combs sat down, inwardly shaken, glad for the first time in six months that he had accepted this ugly case, feeling vindicated in his own eyes. The cold, remote corner of his mind, still sitting in judgement, told him that he had done well, that he had pressed the judge hard. He felt confident of a reasonable sentence; he felt the contentment that only those know who give of themselves without desire for reward.

For several moments the judge sat in silence. Then he asked quietly, "Has the US Attorney any recommendation?"

Varney leant forward, sweat bursting out on his forehead. Pollard arose, walked forward and said strongly, "I have, Your Honour." He was a short, nattily dressed man of about Varney's age, and he spoke with the easy confidence of one who has a jury verdict behind him. "Counsel for the prisoner undoubtedly is a humane man, but I'm inclined to think his humanity is misdirected. He forgets that a man died at the hand of his client, and a jury of citizens declared it to be a wilful killing with malice. For this reason they rejected the concept of manslaughter – that is to say, a killing out of uncontrollable passion – and found it to be murder in the second degree. The government recommends a sentence of ten to thirty years." He returned to his seat.

The judge said nothing for quite a long time. There was a faint frown on his usually impassive face. Then the frown cleared and he announced quietly, "I'm ready to impose sentence."

A bailiff motioned to Varney. Agitated and fearful as he was, Varney still had thought for Combs, seeking to convey by his glance and tremulous smile that he was grateful, everlastingly grateful. He took the position designated before the judicial dais. He fixed his hot, beseeching eyes on the sharp-featured stranger who was about to decide his life. He thought, "If there's a God in heaven – give me a break." He waited in that agony of agonies, a state of utter helplessness.

Like many occupants of the Bench, Judge Stokey was unfitted for his job. This was not because he was a stupid or a vicious man, since he was neither. In ordinary day-to-day contact he was decent and reasonably tolerant. Nevertheless, the position of a judge is one of extraordinary responsibility; the power to send men to prison is an awesome one that, by any profound standards, properly calls for deep human wisdom, for social insight and for unusual objectivity. Of these qualities Judge Stokey possessed no greater measure than was to be expected from one who had achieved his position by virtue of a conventional history: from Harvard law school to the Washington firm of his uncle; next, to a position on the legal staff of the Department of Justice; following that, an appointment as an assistant Federal attorney; and finally, after ten years of being a prosecutor, of associating with the right people in the right circles and of supporting the political party in power, he had received an appointment to the Federal Bench. As a result, it could not be said that his lively intelligence had a more profound grasp of the problems of crime and penology than that of many another citizen. Indeed, somewhat less, since he had had ten years of conditioning in the mentality of a prosecutor.

For all of these reasons, although he had taken serious note of Combs's remarks, he had not been moved. In the course of the trial he had made up his own mind about Varney. No matter what the man's childhood, he was not inclined to feel much sympathy for him. As he saw it, a hotel cook had seduced the wife and then taken the life of a respectable member of society. These were the facts, no matter what else surrounded them, and they offended Judge Stokey in the deepest sense. It was as though he himself were to return from court on this very afternoon, find his wife in the arms of his chauffeur and be murdered for his intrusion. There were no excuses for that, no matter what the role of the woman. Varney never should have trifled in the first place.

Nevertheless, Judge Stokey was quite aware that Combs had pleaded Varney's case in a way that might be affecting to other people, including – as he thought of them – the callow and irresponsible members of the press. Therefore he felt it advisable to explain his own attitude in an adequate manner.

"I have listened to defence counsel most carefully," he began. "Counsel is sincere, eloquent and, I believe, in most respects accurate. I accept what he had* to say – that the boy, Floyd Varney, had a miserable childhood through no fault of his own. I believe one can admire Varney for the struggle he has put up to be a law-abiding citizen. But I point out to defence counsel, and to the public at large, that when men come before our courts they come not for their virtues, but for their transgressions. Defence counsel does not claim that Varney, because of his early life, did not know the difference between right and wrong. To the contrary, defence counsel stresses his client's morality. A jury weighed that morality and found it wanting. A jury held Varney guilty of murder in the second degree, and it is my duty to level sentence."

The judge paused, drank half a glass of water and resumed talking in a calm, firm tone. "There is latitude in the sentence I may impose. I am asked to weigh the prisoner's early life and his fine war record, and I do. But there are other facts I also must weigh. A decent man struck dead in the prime of life. A wife and mother subjected perhaps to rape or, if not, to widowhood. An innocent child for ever scarred by a frightful experience and left fatherless. If Varney was not a rapist, then at least he entered into adulterous relations with a married woman. Confronted then by her husband, he killed. Defence counsel pleads with me that Varney's early life developed in him a fighter's instinct. Perhaps so. But if this fighter's instinct – or ought we to call it a killer's instinct? – was the product of his early life, then who can say he will not kill again? The prosecutor reminds us that the jury found he killed not in self-defence, but unnecessarily, wantonly and with malice. I find nothing to the contrary in the evidence. It was exactly that – unnecessary, wanton and malicious."

Judge Stokey leant forward, and his voice became severe. "Justice should be tempered with mercy, not corrupted by sentimentality. I cannot blink my eyes at murder. Varney murdered. A jury of his peers rendered the verdict. It is against my conscience to be found wanting before that jury or before the needs of society."

Stokey paused slightly. Upon sudden impulse he lowered somewhat the sentence he had been prepared to give for the past two days. "Floyd Varney, I hereby sentence you to a Federal penitentiary for a term of from twenty-five years to life."

An involuntary howl, as of a dog struck brutally without warning, burst from Varney. There was such anguish in his cry that for an instant the judge appeared dazed. His eyes shifted over the courtroom to the reporters, to his clerk, as though seeking support. Had he made a mistake? his eyes asked. Then, abruptly, he pulled his black robe around his figure and gestured for Varney to be removed.

Varney stood with his head drooping forward limply, his eyes half closed. A bailiff took hold of his arm with strong fingers and led him away. Judge Stokey whispered to the court clerk, who banged his gavel and called, "All rise." The judge left his bench. The clerk said "Court dismissed" and then observed to a bailiff by his side, "The poor jerk would have been better off with straight life. That way he would've been eligible for parole in fifteen years; now he's gotta wait twenty-five."

"That's payin' a lot for a roll in the hay," the bailiff responded.

Mrs Peterson, surrounded by reporters, was called upon for a statement. With Varney's howl echoing in her ears, with the painful knowledge that she would see him and hear him in every night's sleep from now on, she said in a faltering tone to the reporters, "Justice has been done."

Chapter 10

Monday's Beans

In the west wing of cell block B1, the inmates were preparing for their midday meal. On the first tier some were standing at the door of their cells, while others were washing. Talk was lively, because most men felt a sense of accomplishment that came from nothing more than their having passed through the ordeal of an aimless morning. At the same time a number of real pleasures were now in the offing: that of leaving their cells, of eating a meal and of coming closer to the hour when they would be allowed upstairs for recreation. So, anticipating some relaxation from the heavy grip of Time, they chattered with zest, wisecracked and indulged in physical horseplay. A typical jailhouse joke, concocted by Eddie Quinn, travelled the range: "Hear about the new man just came in? Got caught rapin' a virgin seventy-five years old, but on'y got three months. You know why? The judge said it weren't more than petty larceny." Men laughed and passed it along to the cell next door.

Presently the mess men, who had been serving dinner in the east wing, were admitted to the range. Spaulding and Reeves came in pushing the gleaming steam table, while others carried the platters of tin cups and bread and the two large milk cans containing cold tea, which was the usual dinner beverage. There were the familiar calls from the men on Tier One: "Hey, what's to eat, what's the bad news?"

"Gran'ma's musical fruit," George Benjamin answered, thereby telling them the main course was beans.

"Oh brother, them again? What else?"

"Boiled 'taters, what else?"

"Any cake?"

"No cake. Pickled beets."

"That cook sure must love pickled beets."

"That cook ain't no cook," replied Benjamin, strolling on.

Alfrice Tillman, carrying the mailbox, was walking alongside the steel-mesh screen of the tier runway. Although none of the white men observed it, Tillman was an object of close attention on the part of his own tier mates. He himself was quite aware of this, and, although he would not have admitted it, he was about to conduct a strategic retreat. While he still refused to accept the criticism that had been levelled at him – namely, that he had been playing the handkerchief head for these white men – in actual fact he had been shaken by the unanimity of the opinion against him. In addition he was definitely worried by Wellman's threat to throw him down a flight of stairs. It was something Big Wellman could – and he feared would – do. Nevertheless, Tillman was too proud to change his behaviour all at once. The solution he had worked out was a compromise: he would carry on talk with the white men as usual, but he would not ask for cigarettes or accept any. In that way, while saving face, he hoped to give no grounds for further criticism.

Eddie Quinn, seeing him approach the screen, rushed up to him as usual with an opening gag: "Hey, Vaudeville, I got a question for you. What would you ruther do – what infants do in infancy or what adults do in adultery?"

"Oh my, don't ask," Tillman answered with a chuckle.

"Not so bad, eh?" Quinn asked, clicking his dentures. He kept pace on the runway as Tillman traversed the range. "You got one for me?"

"Why'd the moron tiptoe past the medicine cabinet?"

"Cos he didn't wanna wake up the sleepin' pills. C'mon, you can do better than that."

"What's the sure remedy to cure bad eyes?"

"What?"

"Eatin' carrots. You know how I know?"

"How?"

"Cos nobody ever saw a rabbit wearin' eyeglasses."

Quinn uttered a mock groan. "Vaudeville, you've lost three cylinders since this mornin'. Here – smoke one of my specials an' get funnier."

"Got some work t'do," Tillman muttered. He quickly set the mailbox down by the range door, leaving Quinn standing nonplussed, a cigarette* in his hand, and walked off towards the steam table. There, on sudden impulse, he said aloud to the other mess men, who had been watching him, "Anybody got a smoke for me?"

There was a moment of silence. Slowly, Big Wellman took a packet* from his pocket, removed one cigarette and tossed it over.

"Thanks. Got a match?"

"You can't smoke now," Wellman told him, "you know that."

"Forgot," Tillman replied with satisfaction. He put the cigarette in his shirt pocket and, with a grin, took his place behind the steam table.

Huey Wilson, standing next to Isaac Reeves, said urgently, "Is it OK now?"

"Guess so. Just keep your eye peeled for the mess officer. When he comes in, get back here."

Huey nodded and strode over to the tier screen in front of the last cell. This was his first opportunity to speak to McPeak since their quarrel on sick call, and he had been enormously relieved to discover that McPeak still was in his cell. It gave him the opportunity he wanted for an apology and – though his hope was faint – it meant that the man still might be reached.

McPeak was lying on the lower bunk, his face turned to the wall. Huey called to him in a low voice. McPeak, who had heard, did not stir. At the approach of mealtime he had guessed that Huey might come along like this, and he had made up his mind to feign sleep. There was nothing he wanted to say to Huey at this point, and nothing he cared to hear. So far as he was concerned, they were talked out, and he wanted no more pushing from anybody.

After a careful glance towards the guard at the front end of the tier, Huey called more loudly, "Hey, Tom – Mr McPeak!"

In 128 a wizened-faced shoe clerk, who was awaiting transfer to the hospital prison for narcotics, called out to Huey with curiosity, "Whatsamatter with him in there?... I tried to talk to him before, too... is he deaf or dead?"

"He's asleep."

"Well, he better wake up now, or he'll miss his beans," the other replied, walking to the cell wall. He began to pound energetically on the steel sheet. "Hey, 130, time t'eat."

McPeak groaned and decided the game was lost. He rolled over, sat up and went through the motions of emerging from sleep.

"Hey, Tom."

McPeak gazed beyond the bars of his cell for the first time, nodded casually and thrust a fresh match between his teeth. Then he came forward, saying non-committally, but in a not-unfriendly tone, "How you doin', young feller?"

"OK. I want to tell you something." Although Huey was aware that both men in 128 were at their door listening, he decided to speak without reserve. "Tom, I'm awfully sorry I made you sore at me. I realize you have to make up your own mind – and that it isn't easy for you. I just want you to know that whatever you do, I'll always be grateful to you for how you helped me."

There was nothing spontaneous about this little speech, because Huey had rehearsed its content a dozen times. Yet, when he came to speak it, it was with intense sincerity, and with all of the gratitude he genuinely felt. McPeak flushed crimson. He had expected recriminations or further pleading, not this sort of sympathy and understanding. He started to reply, became confused, then mumbled irrelevantly, "I got the headache awful bad." His eyes shifted away from Huey, back again, and then he said, "There's somethin' I forgot – will you tell that feller on the mess line, the one who give out the bread this mornin', that I appreciate his warnin' me? I mean…" He stopped.

"Yeah, I know about it," Huey said.

They stared at each other. All of this was fine and amiable, but no amount of small talk could cover the strain between them. They both felt it, and both fell silent, and then Huey, observing the mess officer enter the range, said, "Bye now, got work to do." He walked away, glad that he had had the opportunity to speak his piece, yet far from happy. McPeak was clearly lost to him, and it was not easy to accept the consequences. He understood McPeak, but deep down he could not help feeling contempt and anger towards him as well.

McPeak, chewing his match hard as Huey walked away from him, knew what the youth must be feeling, because he felt the same way about himself, and thought "Jesus Christ, why'd I ever git mixed up in this?", and wished that he never had come to Washington in the first place.

Next door, Jay Spencer, the narcotic addict, exchanged glances with his young cellmate, who had been convicted of stealing stamps from the post office in which he worked. The older man said with intense curiosity, "What d'y' suppose that was all about, Ernie?"

"Wouldn't know – but what I'm trying t'figure is how a white man gets so thick with a coon in the first place. You could see they were thick, couldn't you?"

"I'll tell you," Spencer observed with a reflective air, "I've noticed somethin' real interesting about people: you take two fellers who need each other bad and they soon find out colour don't mean much. Like if I needed a shot bad an' I had my needle but no stuff; then along comes a coloured fellow with the stuff but no needle. I tell you we'd share equal an' we'd love each other. I'd say to hell with his colour an' mine too. It's just pigment, that's all – just pigment."

"Not to me," the other replied sternly. "I got my self-respect. I'd never get thick with a dinge for any reason. Man, they're low."

"The hell you wouldn't," the older man stated with a laugh. "Why, just the other day you were tellin' me what hot pants you used to get for a brown chick worked in your post office. If she hadn't turned you down, you would've gotten thick with her right quick, wouldn't you?"

"Not the way I mean it. I mean friendly, equals."

"For Godsake – if you go lay in bed with a woman, ain't you bein' friendly an' equals?"

"Hell no. I can lay a girl without her bein' my equal. A whore ain't my equal: I just pay her."

"But if she's brown or black an' you still *want* to lay her, then her colour don't matter to you, does it?"

"Not that way, no – but you'd never see me sit down in a restaurant with her."

"You mean you'd lay with her in bed, but you wouldn't sit at a table with her?"

"I sure wouldn't."

"Oh, brother," the narcotic addict exclaimed with a guffaw, "I may be a hophead,* but the birds never sung to me crazy as that."

The cell doors opened, and the dinner line formed. The men moved forward, taking their portions of bread and beans – light, medium or heavy – the boiled potatoes, the pickled beets garnished with onions and the cold, weak tea. When it was Eddie Quinn's turn at the steam table, he whispered quickly to Tillman, "Ain't no beans in heaven, I hear," and Tillman whispered back, "You an' me ain't goin' t'heaven – we'll git beans." When it was McPeak's turn, he was glad that Huey was not on the serving crew, since fewer men were needed than at breakfast, and he took the occasion to nod in friendly fashion to Finnerty. The other nodded back and, with a slight smile, offered him a single piece of bread, but McPeak refused even that.

The men sat down in rows of five at the steel tables, wondering what it would be like to taste a piece of steak or chicken, some fresh eggs or fruit – but ate what they had, spooning the food hungrily.

When the line from Tier Three reached the steam table, the mess men went on the lookout for Art Ballou. They already had discussed what their behaviour with him should be at this meal, but if Ballou expected a new attempt to overload his platter, he was mistaken. Isaac Reeves, who was dishing the beans, said with bland face, "Light or heavy?" When Ballou replied "Light", meanwhile staring at Reeves with a contemptuous expression that said "You just try loading me up", he received as minuscule a portion as Reeves could defend before the mess officer. With comprehension and anger Ballou snapped, "I said 'light', not nothin'. Gimme some more." Reeves obliged with celerity, but this time it was all the ladle could hold. "That's too much, take some off," Ballou ordered, his voice rising with exasperation and his milky skin flushing a bright red. "Don't think I don't know what you're doin'."

"What's the matter here?" the mess officer asked sharply.

"The matter is—"

"Keep your voice down, I can hear you."

"—he either gives me too little or too much. He won't give me what I want: he's tryin' to do a job on me like they did this mornin'."

"Mr Fuhr," Isaac Reeves said sadly, in his best churchgoing manner, "I think this poor young man is a little touched in the head. First he asks me light, then he comes back for more, an' when I—"

"That's a damn—"

"Quiet, both of you!" Mr Fuhr ordered. "Let's get a move on here. How much of those beans you want?"

"About half only."

"Take half off!"

Reeves complied, smiling sweetly, and Mr Fuhr kept step with Ballou as he moved along the steam table. There were no more incidents.

All was in good order in the west wing at eleven fifteen of this Monday morning, and the inmates at dinner even had a bit of entertainment from the Death Tier for the second time that day. On this occasion it was not Wacky Mike, but a Negro by the name of Roberts, who had been let out of his cell for a turn at exercise. Not many years back Roberts had been a well-known middleweight boxer, and his trial for the murder of his niece, with the sordid details of incest that surrounded it, had received considerable space in the local newspapers. It was rumoured among the men that Roberts was due for execution within a few days, because his last appeal already had been turned down by the Supreme Court. Notwithstanding this, the man used his daily exercise period as though he were preparing for a new career in the ring. Stripped to the waist, he shadow-boxed on the runway for all of the half hour allotted him. He was a delight to watch. His body was superb, with tawny skin tight over a supple, athletic frame; his movements were precise, deft, yet explosive with power. He bobbed, weaved and ducked; he retreated, went on the attack and worked his way through an endless repertory of blows and manoeuvres. And perhaps the element in his performance that most fascinated the men below was his indifference to their presence. Roberts was not showing off for them, because he performed in the same way when they were in their cells. This they knew because occasionally he was given a second exercise period at night, and then they could see his dancing shadow on the wall of the cell block. And whether the men realized it or not, what Roberts conveyed to them was a sense of irrepressible life, of the tenacity of the life force even in the face of its imminent end. To men facing the dreariness of months or years of prison it was a wonder, and it kindled their own spirits. The eating range was very quiet, and there were fewer whispers than usual. Nevertheless, at eleven twenty,* as Officer Fuhr reported it later, a breach of discipline shattered the decorum of the meal.

It was the custom of the administration to allow second helpings of some foods. Since Tillman and Huey Wilson had not been needed in the serving of the meal, by arrangement with the other mess men it fell to their lot to handle the second round. Carrying trays, they walked down the outer aisle of the file of tables, pausing at request. Then, circling the tables, they proceeded up the inner aisle along the wall. Art Ballou, absorbed in watching Roberts on the second tier, did not hear the low call "Beans – beans" as Huey Wilson walked past him. Wilson was two tables beyond Ballou when the latter, who still was hungry, came to life. "Hey, boy, beans here," Ballou called after him. Huey turned around with measured slowness to find the source of the call. Ballou beckoned to him and said again, with a cold little grin, "Here, boy."

Huey stared at him for a moment, feeling his flesh grow hot. Then his mind warned quickly, "White man's jail!" He turned his back and walked away.

Instantly Ballou's arm shot up in the air in the customary signal to an officer. After a moment Mr Fuhr noticed. Since Ballou was seated on the far aisle, Mr Fuhr spoke to him across a line of four other men. "What is it?"

Ballou answered in a loud voice, with feeling and indignation, "I want some beans, but that damn coon passed me by! He damn well heard me too!"

The range floor became very quiet. At the rear tables the other mess men had heard, and they stopped eating. They sat very stiffly, with their eyes riveted on Mr Fuhr.

For a moment the officer gazed at Ballou in silence, and then, without comment, walked to the steam table. Tillman and Wilson were both there, standing quietly, their faces and bodies under severe control. Mr Fuhr asked, "Did one of you pass up a man who wanted beans?"

"I did!" Huey answered hotly, in a voice as loud as Ballou's. "He called me 'boy'. I don't pay attention to anyone calls me that. I'm not a boy, I'm a man – and I'm sure not *his* 'boy'."

There was a moment of pause. Then Mr Fuhr said quietly and non-committally, "Take the beets around." He turned to Alfrice Tillman. "There's a man down that aisle wants some beans."

Tillman picked up the heavy pot with a burst of nervousness. As a lift* operator in a white man's hotel he had been called "boy" so many times that it almost had ceased to be the insult to him that it was to other Negroes – never liked, but shrugged off and accepted. Yet in here, where all were equally behind bars, it somehow was different, and right now it was profoundly different because* the issue had been raised. He knew that if Ballou called him "boy", he would do exactly as Wilson had done. This he had to do, and indeed a part of him yearned for the opportunity to do it. Yet, at the same time, a corner of his heart resented Wilson and the situation he had created. They were in jail, and Wilson's way asked for trouble. White men had a lot of mean words, but words broke no bones, and coloured had been living with them a long time. Why was it necessary to raise a storm in jail over one little word?

He walked down the aisle.

Ballou said "Very light", but made no other comment. Tillman served him and retreated to the steam table with a feeling of exhaustion. All eyes shifted to Huey Wilson, who was walking down the outer aisle with a bowl of beets. Men held up a finger and murmured "Light" or "Medium", but no one said anything else. Coming down Ballou's aisle, Huey felt himself growing hot again. He had the feeling that there was more to come, and that Ballou was the sort who would try something else. Ballou did. Just as Huey reached his table he shifted his body and thrust both of his legs* into the narrow aisle, blocking it. Holding out his platter, he said loudly, "Beets here, boy. Very light."

An ashen pallor came to Huey's face, and he began to tremble. The desire to beat that grinning face was almost overpowering. Nevertheless, all he did was to mutter, "Get your damn feet out of the way."

"You there!" Mr Fuhr's voice cracked out sharply as he pointed at Ballou. "Sit around straight! And you" – pointing to Huey – "give him some beets and let's get this meal over with."

"I told you before," Huey answered in a hot voice, "I'm not his 'boy'. I won't serve anybody calls me that."

"I know you're not," the guard retorted impatiently, "but you've got a job to do in here, so do it!" And then, as Huey turned his back* and started for the steam table, he snapped, "Stand still!" The issue suddenly had changed. It no longer was a feud between two inmates, but a question of obedience to the authority of a guard. "I gave you an order to serve that man. You do it, or I'll write you up for discipline."

Huey stood still for a moment, staring at Mr Fuhr with blazing eyes. Then he stepped back to Ballou. In a strangled tone he asked, "How you want it?"

There was a happy grin on Ballou's face. He replied "Very light", and then, in a whisper that only Huey could hear, "you f—— nigger."*

The large serving bowl was still a third full of the pickled beets and onions. With a convulsive gesture Huey flung all of it into Ballou's face.

For a second Ballou sat still, stunned, not even hearing the laughter that burst forth all around him. He was a ludicrous figure with beet juice and slices of beet and onion all over his hair, face and clothes. Then he bolted up, fists swinging. Huey, automatically holding on to the bowl, had no means of defending himself except by the bowl itself. Holding it in front of him as a shield, he retreated up the aisle. Ballou struck at him in a choleric frenzy, his fists hitting the bowl, hitting Huey's arms and his shoulders as he sought to reach his face. Mr Fuhr, in the mean time, had been racing around the file of tables to the inner aisle. He reached Ballou from behind, gripped his shoulders with both hands and swung him around with sinewy power. "That'll be all!" he said with dangerous severity. "Take your seat. Quick!"

Ballou sat down. The other men, silent and tense during the short fight, began again to hoot at his appearance.

"Be quiet!" Mr Fuhr called sharply. The laughter shut off, but hands were clapped over mouths and bodies quivered.

"What's your name and number?" Mr Fuhr snapped at Ballou, as he whipped out a notebook.

The youth told him in a sullen voice.

"Go to your cell."

Ballou obeyed. He walked with a defiant swagger, knowing that every man on the eating range would be watching him.

"Quiet!" Mr Fuhr ordered as laughter rose again. He waited until Ballou appeared on the third tier and then strode to the steam table. "Name and number?"

Huey told him.

"Go to your cell."

Huey walked to the staircase with an ashen, impassive face.

After that, routine took over. On the second tier the condemned man returned to his shadow-boxing. Mr Fuhr counted the five spoons at each table, and George Benjamin swept them into their wooden box. The men filed out in quiet order. Shortly thereafter the loudspeaker came to life, announcing that it was time for the eleven-thirty-five count. The officers entered all tiers, checked the occupants of each cell and reported back that the inmate population was intact, and all was as usual.

Yet all was not as usual in the west wing of CB1. The mess men were scrubbing down the eating range in silence, and with a vigour and a haste* that were noticeable. Theirs was a desire, unspoken but held in common, to get upstairs and see Huey Wilson. As well, all of them were on edge. Something nasty had happened between a white man and a Negro, and their inner tension had not subsided. When Eddie Quinn called out jovially to Alfrice Tillman, who was mopping the floor, "Hey, Vaudeville, how do you like your beets – with onions or down your neck?", he did not get the laugh he expected, even though his advance was obviously friendly. There was no response at all. Quinn waited, then popped his upper denture and rattled it vigorously, but the other man still did not laugh. "Hey, Vaudeville, what little bug bit you?" Quinn asked with genuine lack of understanding.

"My name's Tillman!" It was said with quiet sullenness.

"How the hell do I know your name's Tillman?" Quinn asked amiably. "You never told me, did you?"

If this withdrawn attitude among the Negro inmates was unusual, the busy talk among the whites was equally so, since there was a uniform topic of discussion, the fight, and uniformity was rare in jailhouse conversation. To some of the men, like Eddie Quinn, the incident at dinner had no significance beyond its comedy, which they had found delicious. Without moralizing about it one way or another, they were delighted with what Huey Wilson had done, because it had resulted in a laugh. They continued to chuckle over it, played it out in pantomime and stored it away for future recital. There were others, however, of equal number, who had passed from laughter to resentment. These felt indignation over Wilson's behaviour. Whatever they were themselves, and whatever their status in society, they held one principle in common: that all Negroes were inferior to all whites, and that Wilson was too damn big for his breeches.* "Back in Carolina where I come from," their sentiments* ran, "he'd answer quick when he was called 'boy'... in my part of the woods we'd learn him – we'd cut him down to size fast, man, fast..."

There were still others, comprising the smallest group, who took Wilson's side. Otha Doty, coal miner serving time for stealing an automobile, said with strong feelings* to his cellmate, "That coloured feller was in the right. I was born and brung up in West Virginia, but I worked in the mine with a coloured feller who was a damn good friend of mine. He was true blue, that feller. No one had the right to call him 'boy' – he sure was a man."

To which his cellmate, a former Treasury agent, could only reply, since he was physically afraid of Doty, "Everyone's entitled to his own opinion." But he added to himself: "Will you listen to that nigger lover?"

So the men talked, chewing the matter over from all angles, arguing, laughing and killing time.

On Tom McPeak, however, the incident had had a very painful effect. The more he saw of Huey Wilson, the more he liked him personally, and the more he despised Ballou. While he was too unfamiliar with jail procedure to know the sort of discipline that would be meted out, it was clear that Huey was due for punishment. McPeak found the prospect unaccountably distressing. There had been a moment, as Huey walked to the staircase, in which he had yearned to cry out, "I'm with you, kid, all the way down the line." He had wanted to, but he had not. And now, in his cell, he was pacing up and down with extreme restlessness despite the fierce pounding in his head. To no purpose whatsoever* he was carrying on imaginary, chaotic conversations with Wilson, with his wife, with the old friend called "Balance Wheel". Suddenly, however, he stationed himself at the bars of his cell. The mess men had finished their work and were turning in their equipment to the guard. With his restlessness increasing, McPeak waited for them to return. The first to pass his cell were Ben Wellman and Dewey Spaulding. "Hey," McPeak called to them in a low voice, "ssst!" The two paused.

"Do me a favour, will you?" McPeak asked urgently. "Tell Wilson I'm sorry he got in trouble, but I'm sure proud of the way he handled that son of a bitch."

The two men stared at him. Then Big Wellman said in a hard tone, "You a friend of* Wilson?"

"I sure am."

"Then don't just talk about it – do what you should!"

Both gazed at McPeak for another moment, their faces neither friendly nor unfriendly, but serious, hard and challenging. Then they walked to the staircase.

McPeak sat down on his bunk, rested his throbbing head in his hands and tried his best not to think any more and not to feel what he was feeling.

Three tiers above, Huey Wilson was trying hard to avoid the conclusion that he had acted with more passion than wisdom. It was fine to recall the elation he had felt at the moment of hurling the beets into Ballou's face; it was fine also to tell himself that he had given every white man in the wing a lesson for the future. But now the high moment had passed, and there was no use saying that he didn't care if he was punished. He did care – he was intensely anxious about what was to come. And worse, there was no way he could suppress the gnawing sense that he had fallen into a white man's trap in a white man's jail.

As soon as he heard the footsteps of his tier mates, Huey rushed to the door of his cell. There was nothing he intended to say – not yet, anyway – but he was burning to know what they would say to him.

Passing him, George Benjamin cried, "Wilson, if I live t'be a hunnerd, I'll never see nothin' sweeter'n that. You were great, feller, great." And Alfrice Tillman said with equal enthusiasm, "Boy, you sure showed that white trash where t'git off. Thought I'd die laughin'." But the other men expressed no such sentiments, and the hot, pleasant pride within Huey began to water down. The others waved or nodded to him as they passed to their own cells, but their faces were troubled. It was not disapproval he caught from them, but a sombre reserve.

A moment after the clangour of the cell doors had ended, Huey turned to speak to Finnerty, but he was interrupted by a soft rapping on their cell wall. Isaac Reeves, standing in the near corner of 428, called, "Wilson. Wanna talk to you."

"I'm here."

"Gosh darn it, son, I hope you don't take it wrong what I'm gonna say. You're a fine young feller, but you gotta learn to control yourself better. You need to think before you act. Was it worth goin' to the Hole?"

"I don't know," Huey replied defensively. "Don't know what the Hole is."

"You're gonna get punishment for throwin' them beets, don't you know that?"

"Yeah, but one thing led to another, so I couldn't help myself. You think I should've served that son of a bitch, him callin' me 'boy'?"

"No," Reeves's voice came back, "I certainly don't. You did absolutely right there. But—"

"So then that damn guard boxed me in, didn't he? Maybe you didn't hear him. Told me if I didn't serve Ballou, I'd get written up anyway. I either had to crawl or do what I did."

"No!" Reeves replied firmly. "That's where you stopped thinkin'. You coulda told the guard you just wouldn't serve Ballou. Then if he brought you up for discipline, you'd have a case to argue. But you can't argue you had the right to throw a mess of beets over a man."

"Never mind, Wilson," came Tillman's voice, "I'm glad as hell you did it. A man's got to break loose sometime. You showed that white trash what we're made of."

"No," Huey said unhappily, "you're wrong, and I was wrong. It was a mistake. You're right, Mr Reeves, I should've stood where I was and not budged." He suddenly laughed in an extremely boyish manner. "But it sure felt good. God, I felt like a million dollars. I felt grand for a coupla minutes."

There was sadness in Reeves's voice as he answered, "Yeah, I know. A man builds up steam like a boiler, and then he just has to let it go. But I've learnt two things in my life, sonny. The first is we coloured has got to fight for our rights all the time, in every which way, just like you did over him callin' you names. But the second is we gotta stay alive while we're doin' it, an' not get hurt more'n we need to. I ain't sayin' knuckle down or do the Uncle Tom. I'm just sayin' fight smart, an' don't get lynched if you can help it."

With a sharp pang Huey recalled the morning's argument with Professor Herrin. Then it had been the question of pleading guilty, if necessary, in order to avoid a longer prison term that would serve no purpose. Now Reeves was saying more or less same thing. Twice in one morning, it seemed, his judgement had lacked good sense – too much heat and too little reflection.

Huey turned to his cellmate. "So all of you think I'm going to the Hole, eh?" His manner was careless and quite false to what he felt.

"That's what Benjamin says," Finnerty replied softly, "an' he's the most experienced here."

"I don't know what the Hole is."

"It's some cells down below. They put you in by yourself."

"Hell, is that all?" Huey exclaimed with relief. "That won't worry me."

"You're in the dark," Finnerty continued softly. "No lights at all. Can't talk to nobody. Nothin' t'sit on but the floor. Nothin' t'eat 'cept a little bread an' water."

"Oh!" Huey exclaimed. And then, with a nervous little laugh, "No beer? So how long do they keep you there?"

"Benjamin figures you'll get a week, maybe more."

"Christ! I'm a growing boy, I'll starve to death."

"You'll sure git mighty hongry an' lonesome, boy. I'm sorry."

"Yeah, so am I," Huey muttered. "Guess if I'd known that, I would've controlled myself better. Aw, the hell with it. They won't make me cry. I can take it!"

They were quiet for a moment, and then Finnerty rapped on the wall of 428.

"I'm here," came Reeves's voice. "Been listenin'."

"Huey here didn't have no dinner, remember?" Finnerty told him. "I don't have no canteen things, but I bet Spaulding has: he bought a lot on Friday. Maybe he'd like to give Huey somethin'?"

"That's a good idea," came Reeves's voice. "I'll pass it along. I've got some peanuts left myself."

"Thanks," Huey said to his cellmate. "I'm hungry all right – I'll eat all I can get. Listen, I'm expecting a visit from my brother, and it's important I see him. What happens now?"

"I don't know. Better ask Reeves."

Huey repeated the question to Reeves, and the older man said he didn't know either. The query went down the line to Benjamin in 424. A few minutes later, using his privilege as tier man, Benjamin himself appeared on the runway in front of Huey's cell. He was carrying two candy bars, a package of mints and a stick of chewing gum. It was evident, from the expression on his face, that he relished this call upon his knowledge. "Excuse me for delayin' you," he said with an air that was very special, "but I was movin' my bowels. What's that you wanna know?"

Huey told him.

"It all depends," Benjamin answered authoritatively, as he passed the candy through the bars. "When a man goes to the Hole, he loses all privileges – no visits, no nothin'. But if your brother's comin' t'day, he oughta be here soon. Visitin' hour comes right soon – twelve, twelve thirty. More'n likely they won't call you for discipline till later, so you'll git to see him all right."

Next door Reeves passed two bags of peanuts to Benjamin, who handed them to Huey and continued talking. "The Hole ain't so bad: it's all how you take it. Now, with me it's just a chance t'catch up on my sleep." He waited for Huey to ask the inevitable question.

"How many times you been in?"

"Six," Benjamin replied proudly. "Once for three weeks straight. Didn't faze me at all.* Not eatin's good for a man: cleans his system out."

It was quite true that Benjamin had been in the Hole, but only once, and for no more than two days. It had been a terrible experience for him, because he suffered from mild claustrophobia. In all of his subsequent years in prison he never again had transgressed in any serious way.

Eating the peanuts, Huey asked another question. "I was going to tell my brother to arrange my hearing for today or tomorrow. What happens now?"

"You kin tell him," Benjamin responded with assurance. "When the jail gits a court order, they gotta obey it. They'll take you out for the hearin', then put you back in."

"But suppose the commissioner gives me bail?"

Benjamin rubbed his face. "Guess I don't know the answer to that one," he replied with honesty. "Could be they'd hafta let you go, or could be the jail boss'll call up the commissioner an' git him to stay bail till you's done your Hole time."

"Maybe you won't have to go to the Hole at all," Reeves put in from next door. "You do your best to explain, Wilson. Don't lay down, but don't be sassy."

"I don't feel sassy at all," Huey muttered. "I feel like a damn fool for screwing myself up. But that Ballou sure can get under my skin."

"I wish I knowed what goes on in the brain of a feller like that," Finnerty said. "He hates us so much he's willin' t'git in trouble himself. I sure wonder why."

No one answered him, and he continued reflectively, "It's always seemed to me that whites are more like lil chillen than we is. They do such non-sensible things."

There was no comment from the others. The mood of the fourth tier was low. Conversation died away.

In the basement of the Federal District Courthouse George Combs was waiting to see Floyd Varney. Combs was very unhappy and very angry, and he dreaded the interview. What did an attorney say to a client who has been sentenced perhaps to life, at least to twenty-five years? There had been no lecture on this in law school, there was no guidance to be found in the body of social etiquette. Did one say, "I'm sorry?" Or, "It won't be too bad, you'll get used to it"? Could one offer the comfort of saying, "After all, you'll be eligible for parole when you're fifty-five?"

Combs was not a naive man, and therefore he could understand the manner in which money or power could corrode a human spirit, insulating it both from understanding and generosity. Certainly he could understand this in a man like Judge Stokey. What he could not comprehend, however, was the man's own moral code by which he could, on one Monday, give a year and a day to a noted gangster who had pleaded guilty of pandering and, on another Monday, sentence Floyd Varney as he had.

The bailiff appeared, then Varney, and Combs felt like weeping. He had noticed Varney's pallor earlier, but the man's face now had the waxen look of a chronic invalid. Varney's eyes wore a dull glaze;* his shoulders were sagging, and he looked years older.

"Floyd," Combs burst out, "what can I say? I feel as though I'd been run over by a truck. I can't even think."

Gazing at him with dull eyes, Varney said quietly, "That's all right, Mr Combs. It wasn't your fault."

"Listen," Combs said fiercely, "I'm not stopping on your case. I said I wasn't going to appeal, but now I will. I'll find some grounds. I'm also going to move for a reduction of sentence. Floyd, if there's any damn thing I can do, even if it's only a one out of a thousand chance, I'll do it."

"That's fine, Mr Combs," Varney said hopelessly, believing in none of it. "You sure made a good pitch for me this mornin'. I appreciated it."

"I just can't understand it," Combs cried helplessly. "I can't imagine what got into the bastard."

"He sure handed it to me, didn't he?" Varney asked dully.

Suddenly there was silence between them, because there was nothing to say, absolutely nothing.

"I'll find some basis for an appeal," Combs burst out. "I'll take the court record to every lawyer I know. I'll get ideas from everybody."

Again there was silence.

"I'll go and see* the US Attorney. I'm sure he was as shocked as I was. Maybe he'll join me in asking for a reduction of sentence."

Silence.

"Christ," Combs thought, "let me get out of here."

"I can't pull that time," Varney murmured suddenly. "It's too much."

Combs, not quite sure he understood, muttered, "You keep up your hope, Floyd. If Pollard joins me, I know we can knock some time off your minimum."

"No you won't," Varney answered hopelessly. "That judge knew what he was doin'. He won't change it."

"He was talking for the newspapers. But a week from now, when we get him in his chambers, I'm sure we can persuade him to come around. Besides, there's always the appeal. We're not through yet, Floyd. You've got to keep up your hope."

With a direct simplicity that made Combs feel like a hypocrite, Varney asked, "What for? You told me yourself we didn't have a good appeal. Why should I kid myself?"

"I'll try everything I can, Floyd. I promise you!"

Varney nodded. They both fell silent. Then Varney held out his hand. "Thanks for everything."

Combs squeezed the limp, dry hand and muttered, "Keep up your hope – don't give in."

"That's too much time for me," Varney muttered in a kind of abstracted reply. Body sagging, he walked slowly away towards the door of the bull pen.

Chapter 11

The Porthole View

By the noon hour it had become uncomfortably hot in the west wing. The October sun at meridian was an unseen, malicious enemy; its rays, baking the roof of the cell block, turned the cavern below into a humid oven. Men lay shirtless on their bunks with wet handkerchiefs on their foreheads. Conversation in most cells had died down, or was muted and dull. When an occasional door ground open or hammered shut, or when water roared in a toilet vent, the sounds beat and echoed with oppressive force through the heavy atmosphere.

Notwithstanding the heat, tier man Eddie Quinn was moving from cell to cell in order to collect cigarette butts. Since Quinn had no canteen funds, a considerable degree of effort was involved in keeping himself in tobacco. However, unlike other men who entered the jail penniless, Quinn had a resource to fall back upon: his skill as a barber. Since the jail offered no regular barber facilities for transient prisoners, the administration appreciated the presence of an inmate capable of cutting hair. Quinn was supplied with comb and scissors in any recreation hour he chose to go to work. While it was strictly forbidden for him to put a price upon his labours, he could not be prevented from discussing the pleasure of tobacco with his customers. As a result, any inmate with a canteen fund usually expressed appreciation for his haircut by the voluntary gift of a package of cigarette papers or an occasional small tin of pipe tobacco. Quinn, in turn, mixed this tobacco with the shredded ends of other men's cigarettes, and by this means kept himself in smoking comfort – forty cigarettes a day, hand-blended and hand-rolled. Now, as in every noon hour, he was canvassing the tier for what he called "the loot". With his shirt pocket already half full of crumpled cigarette ends, he paused at 118, which was a steady source of supply. He thrust his upper denture between his lips, rattled it vigorously, popped it back into place and enquired, "Any nice gentlemens here with some nice ol' butts for free?"

"Ain't no gentlemen in here, just convicts," a young man, Paul Costello, replied with a laugh, His gaiety was forced. He was a professional card player under indictment for receiving stolen property – a charge he swore was false, but which had him worried. He offered Quinn a heavily laden wooden ashtray, saying humorously, "I had to land in jail to take up smokin'. Shows you what the wrong environment does."

Quinn emptied the tray into the breast pocket of his shirt and replied, "Thank you, my good man, this is appreciated. You wanna try one of my hand-made, sanitary-sealed Perfecto Perfectos?" Costello said he would, and Earl McCutcheon, his cellmate, took one also. "We goin' out to the Yard this afternoon?" McCutcheon asked in slurred tones. He was a worn-out bartender who had turned beggar, and was under his fourth arrest for posing as blind.

"Uh-uh, didn't you get the word? No Yard today."

"Las' time was Wednesday. Five days without Yard, it's terrible for your health." McCutcheon's speech was a bit hard to understand because his only teeth were two in his lower jaw. "They ain't treatin' us right. We oughta send in a complaint to the Department of Justice."

Chuckling, Quinn said, "Beats hell how we get pushed around in here, don't it?"

"It's a lot better than an army stockade,* I'll say that," Costello put in.

"Hey – I thought you never served time before," Quinn jeered. "Told me this was your first arrest, didn't you?"

Costello began laughing. "That army thing didn't count – it was a crazy snafu. I was in this camp that was just gettin' started, see, it was before Pearl Harbor.* One day a delegation came out from the local town to inspect things – the mayor an' his wife, an' a lot of other ladies. Well, some of us cooks were out in front of the cook tent preparin' hamburgers. It was a hot day, an' we had our shirts off. Now, the way we were flattenin' out those hamburgers, see, was to slap 'em on the back of the guy next to us. So those women saw us, an' one of them said, 'Oh my, what an unsanitary way to prepare food that men have to eat!' So before I could think what I was doin', I answered right back, 'That's all right, lady – you oughta see how we prepare doughnuts!' Well, I never had a better laugh in my life, but I lost a stripe an' got a month in the stockade."

"Man, that's rich," said Quinn laughing.

"Women, women," exclaimed McCutcheon.

A call from the guard interrupted their pleasant conversation.

"Tier man – on the run!"

Responding, Quinn was joined on the runway by Johnny Lauter, who had been dozing in his cell.

Quinn said, "Yes sir, Mr Kraft? Need any legal advice?"

The guard permitted himself a faint unofficial smile as he unlocked the runway door. "Lauter, you got a visit. Out this way."

"A visit?" Lauter exclaimed. His sallow face turned very pale.

"*That's* what the phone says – let's go," the guard replied impatiently. And then, as Lauter passed through and the door was locked again, the guard said to Quinn, "You cuttin' hair today, Barber?"

"No sir. I seen at dinner that a buddy of mine just hauled in on Tier Three. I wanna meet him on recreation."

Mr Kraft nodded and commented, a bit slyly, "You don't need smokes today, huh?"

"That's it," Quinn replied amiably. "I'm doin' lovely in here, just lovely."

The news that he had a visit had thrust Johnny Lauter into a panic. Although his wife came twice a week for the half-hour allowed families, Monday never was one of her days, since she did sewing for a neighbour. His visitor, therefore, would have to be his attorney, and that meant only one thing: that the judge had ruled on his extradition. In a few minutes from now he would know whether he was free – or on his way to what he believed would be a lynch trial and the gas chamber.

Not too many years ago Lauter would have met a moment like this with a bravado air and with his feelings under iron control. "What the hell," he would have said, "I can take it either way" – and, in a sense, it would have been true. But his years of marriage had made him too human for that. Now he wanted desperately to live, wanted his wife, wanted the years ahead with his children. He was shaking inside with an anxiety that was almost insupportable.

When he reached the vestibule of the Rotunda and presented his pass, he said in a hoarse voice to the guard, "Lawyer's visit?" The guard consulted his list and replied to Lauter's bewilderment. "No – family." He unlocked the barred door that led to the familiar visiting corridor.

Relieved, yet with a sudden new worry – that something had happened to one of his children – Lauter half-ran down the overheated narrow corridor. Since only two other inmates were visiting, he was obliged to peer through one porthole glass after another in order to find his wife. At the last one he saw her. For an instant he was too distraught to remember the telephone. He broke into speech as though they were face to face rather than separated by a concrete wall and inch-thick glass. But then he saw his wife's lips moving and snatched his telephone off the wall hook.

"Amy, what's the matter?" he burst out, interrupting whatever she was saying. "Are the kids OK? Wha—" He stopped. It was nothing she had said that made him pause, but something in her face – a glow, a radiance that conveyed so much he couldn't comprehend it. Then he heard her – and it was the cry he had imagined in ten thousand lonely moments:

"We've won, Johnny! You won't be sent back! Darling, sweetheart, it's all over!" Abruptly she was crying with relief, yet laughing with heart's joy at the same time, and Lauter stood with his knees sagging, trying to take it in, to be sure of it.

"How do you know?" he asked hoarsely. "Are you positive? Who told you?"

"Your lawyer. He called me this mornin'. It's all over, Johnny. You're goin' free!"

"Did he get it from the judge himself?"

"Yes! The judge said he was satisfied to give you the benefit of the doubt. He's signed your release already."

"So why don't they let me go?"

"It has to come by mail. The judge is sick: he's at his home in Virginia."

"Oh Christ, how many days will that take?"

"The letter'll get here this afternoon or tomorrow mornin', Mr Pepper said. It was sent special delivery."

"When was it mailed?"

"Early this mornin'."

"How does Pepper know all this?"

"He called the judge long distance to ask how he was and to find out if he'd reached a decision. They've always been sort of friendly, you remember him tellin' us that?"

"There's no mistake? It can't go wrong?"

"Oh darling, stop worryin'," she cried reproachfully. "It's all over, you're gonna get out. Why ain't you happy?"

It was not so much her words or the full acceptance of their victory at last that made Lauter begin to weep, but the glory of her face. She was not a pretty woman, this wife of his, and he never had been so moonstruck as to think that she was. Yet he had learnt in his marriage how beautiful a woman can be when love kindles her features. The tenderness of her look, the rapture and joy in her eyes, told him again what the months of separation almost had stolen from him: that she needed and wanted him no less than he needed and wanted her. He began to weep with such intensity that his body shook, and he could not speak and could not see her. He was weeping with happiness over their marriage; and he was weeping with exquisite relief at this passage out of the Valley of Death;* and he was weeping with exultation at the thought of returning to life – to a day's good work; to the sweetness of his children's greeting* at evening; to reunion with a wife who was bound to him by ten thousand thousand moments: of their meeting and courtship and cleaving together; of their love and its seed; of the night when their first-born had had convulsions, yet had lived to grow healthy and strong; and of all, of all, all!

But there was bitterness also in Lauter's tears, because his thoughts had leapt ahead. This was victory at a price, and the price they would need to pay was flight. They would have to do now what they should have done the moment the city police learnt about him: move elsewhere. Another town, another hard start, and the hope that this time the damn police wouldn't find out.

"Darling," his wife was saying, "we're both crying so hard you'd think it was bad news. What's the matter with us?"

"It's good all right, it's good." He wiped his eyes with his bare arm and began to grin at her. "Mrs Lauter, you never looked so sweet to me as you do right now, you know that? But it ain't fair. A man oughta be able to kiss his wife at a time like this."

"Honey," she said, "I did you a kind of dirty trick. Mr Pepper called me over two hours ago, an' he was gonna call the jail to have them tell you, but I wouldn't let him. I just had to come here an' tell you myself."

"A dirty trick,"* he replied tenderly. "Jesus, how I love that judge! Imagine, a judge with a heart, and it happens to me."

"I love that Mr Pepper too. He fought so hard for you, Johnny."

"Yeah, I know, I know."

"Darling, I called your boss. He was glad as he could be. He said come back to work whenever you're ready. Your job's right there."

"Yeah, he's another square Joe," Lauter said with feeling. "He's sure been on the level.* Most guys in that position* would've washed their hands of me. Listen, Amy, we gotta move."

"I knew you'd feel that way," she replied sadly. "But I sure hate to have you lose that good job. It ain't wartime no more – jobs ain't so open."

"I know, but we gotta move."

"Where'll we go, Johnny? When?"

"Not right away. I been figuring." He laughed a little. "In here there's nothin' to do beside figure the angles. The Washington cops'll lay off me for a little while now. I'll work for three, four months, say, pay the boss off an' build up a little stake. We'll have to pinch pennies to do it, honey, but I can count on you, can't I?"

"Sure, Johnny."

"Then I'll hit for some other city – we got time to decide where. Once I get a job, you an' the kids'll come."

"You don't think the cops might lay off you altogether, do you? I mean here?"

"We can't take that chance, honey. Do you wanna take a chance on them bein' good fellers? I sure don't. Ain't it better to go where I ain't known?"

"Yes! Sure," she said firmly. "I'm with you, Johnny. Sometimes I get my mind on how nice it's been here, our nice apartment an' everythin' – but that's foolish. I'm with you, Johnny dear, we'll make out fine wherever we go."

"Thanks," he said huskily. "An' I know you'll make a nice home wherever we go."

"Gee, I wish I could kiss you, Johnny."

"I wish I could kiss you too, Amy."

"I wish I knew if it was this afternoon or tomorrow you were comin' home."

"Just our luck it won't be till tomorrow. But we can take *that*, can't we?"

"Yeah, we sure can."

"Do the kids know?"

"Sure, what do you think?"

"What did they say?"

"Well, you know, Billy's too young to understand altogether, but I think he knows you're comin' home. But Janet – you should've seen her. For a whole hour she went around the house huggin' her teddy bear and singin'. You know what she was singin'? 'Nice Daddy's all well. Nice Daddy's comin' home. I'm gonna give nice Daddy a big kiss.' She just kept singin' that over and over."

"They really like me, don't they?" Lauter said in a choked voice.

"What do you mean, silly, we all *love* you."

"That's somethin' of a test of a man – if his kids like him," Lauter went on. "It shows he ain't so bad." He began to weep again, but there was no bitterness in his tears now, and his wife, on the other side of the concrete wall, wept for his happiness.

* * *

It was twelve thirty now. All portholes were occupied in the visiting corridor, and there was a confused rise and fall of a dozen voices talking at once. Since the day was hot and the ventilation less than adequate, the atmosphere in the narrow corridor had become stifling.

At porthole number three Huey Wilson was concluding a hasty report to his brother of the conference he had had with Tom McPeak. Wiping his face and neck with a handkerchief, he finished off by saying, "So that's how it looks to me. He's made up his mind to run."

"I see!" Jeff's voice was low and disgruntled. "That's hell!"

"Now listen carefully," Huey continued. "Do you think there's any chance of arranging the hearing for today?"

"What? How come?" His brother responded with surprise. "We talked it all out this morning, didn't we? Herrin postponed the hearing until Wednesday. You agreed to it."

"Sure, but I've got a new idea, Jeff. Look – McPeak's a decent guy, and he isn't happy about running out on me. He's ashamed of himself – I know it. So my idea is this: if we can get him into a hearing right *now*, this afternoon, and have Professor Herrin go to work on him with some real sharp questions, he'll break down and tell the truth."

"But don't you remember what Herrin said? He said McPeak'll do you harm unless he's a willing witness. If he's unwilling—"

"I remember," Huey interrupted, "but I think we've got to take that chance. By tomorrow he'll be gone for sure. Then where'll I be?"

"Where'll you be if he doesn't tell the truth? Or suppose he leaves in the next two hours? Then you'll be stuck with the hearing but your lawyer won't have had a chance to prepare any other evidence."

"I realize that, Jeff, but I'm figuring it this way: without McPeak testifying for me I don't have a ghost of a chance of getting clear at that hearing. They'll hold me for trial sure."

Jefferson frowned, then muttered, "I suppose so."

"OK – so what's the difference what other evidence we present?"

The reply came slowly. "I guess you're right, kid." And then, with sudden decision, "You want me to call Herrin about it right now? I don't know if I can reach him, or if it'll be possible to arrange a hearing for this afternoon, but I'll explain your idea."

"Wait a second, he needs to know a few other things." Huey plugged his right ear with a finger because the man beside him was talking loudly. "In the first place we made a bad mistake in delaying the hearing without asking McPeak what *he* felt about it. We included him in our plan without even consulting him, you see? Boy, did he hit the ceiling when I told him! He has one week of vacation to spend in a family reunion, and we privately arrange for him to spend most of it in jail."

"My God, of course," Jefferson exclaimed with regret, "that was a terrible boner!"

"So that's another reason to try and get that hearing today."

"All right. What else, kid?"

Huey hesitated, mopped his forehead and then said with keen embarrassment, "You better tell Professor Herrin I got into some trouble since I saw you."

"How come?"

"That white fellow I had the fight with, Ballou, he's kept it going in here."

"Did he jump you again?"

"Not like that. But at breakfast he started calling me names – I can't give you all the details now –and just a while ago at dinner it got worse. I got pushed into a corner and I lost my temper."

"What did you do – slug him?" Jefferson asked with dismay.

"No, but I threw a mess of beets in his damned face. Now I'm up for punishment."

"Jesus Christ! Why didn't you realize—"

"Lay off, Jeff, will you?" Huey interrupted. "I made a mistake, I know it, I could kick myself for it, but this isn't the time to lecture me."

"So what's the punishment?"

"From what I hear, they'll put me in the Hole for a couple of days, maybe a week."

"What's that?"

"It's a punishment cell where they put you alone and feed you bread and water. You're in the dark."

"You can't even read?"

"You can't do anything, not even talk."

"My God, what kind of a damned, medieval—"

"Look, Jeff, I can take it. If others can, I can. The reason I'm telling you about it now is that a man in the Hole loses all privileges. So if they do put me in and you come for a visit, you'll know why you can't see me."

Jefferson asked, in a voice heavy with anxiety, "They won't beat you up or anything like that, will they?"

"No. They do in some of the State pens, I hear, but not in Federal any more. I guess the Hole's bad enough. Now listen, I don't know if Professor Herrin has had any experience with a problem like this, but the word I get in here is that he can demand that they let me out of the Hole to go to my hearing."

"Oh, man, nice and complicated! And what about bail if you're in there?"

"I don't know. Ask Herrin to find out, will you? You want to call him now?"

"OK."

"But tell the guard out there your visit isn't over. I don't want to be sent back."

"Don't worry about that," Jeff answered with assurance. "There's someone else to see you."

"Who?"

His brother smiled at him. "You'll find out."

Huey watched his receding back and wondered with excitement if the visitor could be Ann Beemish, the schoolmate he had taken to a movie on Saturday night. She was a girl he really liked, and if it was she who had come... Huey's speculation broke off. Inmates were only allowed family visits – he had been told that already – so it couldn't be Ann.

With astonishment, with a warm shock, he saw the face of his father appear at the porthole. He went weak with small-boy gratitude. Without being aware of it, he was reacting in the same way as he had at many other moments of his life when he had needed his father in one way or another, small or large, and his father had been there, reliable, unreservedly on his side.

For a few moments they did not speak. Wilson senior was fumbling for the telephone while trying to see his son's face. Since the light of the Rotunda was much brighter than that of the corridor, his vision needed to adjust. Then he smiled and said, with an effort at lightness, "There you are, Huey. What a queer way to hafta talk to somebody."

"Pa, it's sure good to see you! When did you come up?"

"Took the bus las' night. Got here a coupla hours ago."

"I'm awful sorry about getting into trouble like this, Pa. But I couldn't—"

"Jeff done tol' me all about it," his father interrupted. "It weren't your fault, that's clear. So you jus' rest as easy in your mind as you kin."

It was said firmly, and Huey knew it was meant with utter sincerity, yet . the tension in his father's face made his heart ache. He had been aware that this would be a body blow to his parents, but it was easier to think about it in the abstract. He knew how hard his father and mother had slaved to make the family a good home, and to raise children who would achieve something in life! "Git an education," his father had said countless times. "Git t'be somebody. You all got it in you, an' we'll help you." From earliest times Huey had known that the admonition expressed more than the usual longing of any parents who loved their children. It was the deep, special yearning of Negro parents who knew what obstacles their children would face from ghetto life and job discrimination, and who therefore urged them to have extra zeal, to expend special effort, to be unflagging. Yet now, without warning, the white fist had struck – and what would their years of yearning weigh in a white man's court?

"Pa," Huey said with sorrow and love, "I hope you don't feel too bad. I think I'll get out of this all right."

"I hope so!" A stern look came to his father's face, and his eyes turned hard. "I want you to know somethin', sonny. Your brother thinks 'twere a mistake for you t'go on that school picket line. He says you oughta pay attention to nothin' but your studies. Now I—"

"Gosh, Pa," Huey interrupted with quick defensiveness, "it landed me in a lot of trouble, I know, but most of my class was on that picket line and—"

"Now wait, hear me out," his father interrupted in turn. "I don't agree with Jeff. I think he's dead wrong!"

"You do?" It was asked with deep astonishment. That his parents never would turn their backs on him, no matter what he did, Huey knew in mind and heart too well to doubt it. Yet he had assumed that they, like his brother, would be very critical of his straying from the straight path of work and study. "After all," he could imagine his mother saying, "it's what you do in school that's gonna git you t'be a lawyer, not traipsin' out to dances or picket lines."

With the same sternness his father said: "Look here, Huey, I wouldn't ever like to hear of one of my boys hangin' back when other coloured folk were standin' up for their rights. You start livin' like that an' you'll end up with no backbone at all. When all those other boys* were goin' out on that picket line, you sure belonged there too."

"Gee, Pa, I'm glad to hear you say that," Huey told him with feeling. "Jeff kind of upset me, but I couldn't see it his way."

"I want you to be a lawyer too, if you kin. But more'n that, I want you to be a man, a real Negro man. I don't want you ever to forget whose name we give you."

"No, sure, I know what you mean, Pa. I'm awful glad you came up. It makes it a lot easier for me now."

"Shoot," his father said, smiling a little despite the worry crease between his brows, "don't look for trouble – that's what I've always tol' you, but stan' up to it if it comes. It's come to you now, sonny, like it's always come to a lot of cullid. I expect you to stan' up to it the way you should."

There was a moment of silence between them, and then Wilson senior said: "Why d'you keep wipin' your face, Huey? Is it hot in there?"

"Hot as the devil, Pa, hot as working a cornfield in August. What's Ma saying?"

His father thought about this for an instant, and then asked bluntly: "What's on your mind?"

"You know Ma. Even when I was a kid she'd get awful upset if I got into a fight with a peck. She wouldn't care whose fault it was, just didn't want me fighting with 'em."

"Son, what's the matter with you?" his father answered, almost with annoyance. "Your ma didn't want you kids bein' no-'count,* sure, or gittin' into trouble with the police like the gangs in Cox's Row,* but you're grown up now an' she wouldn't want you bein' a han'kerchief head, neither. A thing like this come along, she's gonna cry about it, sure. She done cry an' holler for an hour after Jeff called her. But then she went out to raise bail money for you from everybody she know in the church."

"She did?" For the second time Huey was utterly astonished.

"She surely did. I come up here this mornin' with three hunnerd dollars. It was your ma raised more'n half of it jus' in one evenin'."

"Gosh, Pa," Huey said emotionally, "I guess I got about the best folks in the world."

His father laughed almost gaily, his thin, lined face crinkling all over. "The trouble with you is you's only eighteen year ol'. You needs t'be a lil older 'fore you appreciates what real good folks you got."

"I know, Pa."

"Shoot," his father said more seriously, but tenderly, "I'm only funnin' you a little. We's no better'n a lot of other folks with their kids. We do our best, that's all. An' you're good kids, you're worth it."

"When you going back home, Pa?"

"I dunno. Gon wait'n see what happens. I hear you got good lawyer advice, but I aim to stick my nose in things a little."

"What about your job?"

"That'll keep, I won't lose it. Your ma's comin' up too."

"When?"

"Soon as we fin' out how much bail they'll put on you, an' that we've got enough." He smiled slyly. "She's the best one for gittin' loan money, y'know, on account she's a pillar of the First Baptist Church, an' I sure ain't."

Father and son burst into laughter. In twenty-seven years of a good marriage there had been one area in which mother and father never had got* together. Wilson senior maintained that Sunday was made for a tired working man to sleep, drink beer and fool around in his vegetable garden. Whatever other folks wanted to do – specifically his wife – they were free to do it, provided they let him alone.

"Pa," Huey said, "I'm sure glad you came up here, but it'll run into money. Hotel rooms—"

"I'm way ahead of you," his father interrupted. "While you're in jail, I aim to sleep in your bed in your room. Jeff's done arranged it already."

"That's a swell idea. Who thought of that?"

With a chuckle his father responded: "Me. I kin smell how to save a penny fast as any man."

"But look, Pa, about bail – Mother's being great, but I know it must be hard on her to go around telling everyone I'm in jail, and begging loans. There's another way to handle bail—"

"Sure, I know that too, from way back," his father interrupted. "On'y a bondsman costs you ten per cent. Suppose they put two thousan' on you? We lose two hunnerd."

"I wouldn't want *you* to lose it. I've got savings."

"No, sir, that's college money. We won't touch that, not a penny," his father replied severely.

"But—"

"Looky here, boy, if you'd stole somethin', we'd be ashamed you're in jail. But we ain't ashamed over this, we's mad. Jeff's writin' down to your ma about it t'day. Won't hurt other folks in Charlottesville t'know about it an' git mad, too. Could be their boys instead of you. Let 'em chip in. Anyhow, you ain't runnin' from your bail – they'll git it back."

Huey burst out laughing without quite knowing why. "You got everything all wrapped up, haven't you, Pa?" he asked affectionately. "Guess there's nothing for me to do but lay back easy and get fat."

His father turned around for a moment and then said quickly, "Jeff wants t'talk to you. But I got one thing more t'tell you after." He stepped aside, and Jeff's face appeared at the porthole.

"I'm sorry, Huey, I called Herrin at his home, I called the college, I called the NAACP. He wasn't at any of those places, and I couldn't track him down."

"Jesus Christ, that's terrible! Listen, keep trying him, will you?"

"I'll surely reach him by two. That's when he said he'd be home."

"Do you think at that hour there'll still be a chance of arranging a hearing for today?"

"I don't know, kid. I'm not enough of a lawyer to know those things."

"Jeff, listen... don't tell Pa about the fight this morning – I mean, that they might send me to the Hole."

A bit sarcastically Jeff replied: "You think he's too young to know the facts of life – or is it just that you're ashamed of yourself? What happens if he wants to visit?"

"OK," Huey responded with a sigh, "go ahead and tell him. Listen, one more thing – one of the men in here had an idea, I don't know whether it's good or not – that when I go to my hearing there ought to be a protest demonstration by some of the kids from my school. What do you think about it?"

"I don't know. Sounds a bit extreme to me, not too legal. But I'll pass it on to Herrin. You want to talk to Pa again? I think our time's about up."

"Yeah, I do."

"Kid, good luck. You know what I mean."

"Yeah. Thanks."

"Stiff upper lip and all that. If you get too bored, recite poetry to yourself or something."

"Sure, don't worry about me. And thanks for all you're doing, Jeff."

"Shucks, kid." He gave Huey a quick grin, and then his father's face returned.

"Huey, boy – one thing Jeff tol' me has me worried. If things go bad at the hearin', an' that white man don't stan' up for you, I want you to think mighty careful. No use t'buttin' your head agin a stone wall. You don't want t'risk no five years, sonny, not if you don't hafta. That'd be crazy."

"Yeah, Pa, guess I've come around to that myself. But let's wait and see what happens, huh?"

"OK. Our time's up." His father paused, and then, for one instant, his control went to pieces. His lips quivered, his dark eyes became filmed with tears, and he couldn't speak. Then he seemed to snap himself up taller, and his expression became firm again. "You're a good boy, Huey. An' you're no weaklin', that's sure. Whatever happens from this, I know we's gon t'be proud of the way you do in your life."

Then he was gone, and Huey leant his forehead against the wall of the corridor and tried to feel all that his young heart was telling him – of what it meant to be loved by family without qualification, without reserve, just loved. Then he heard the voice of the guard calling to him from the vestibule. "Number-three porthole – you're through, ain't you?"

He straightened up and walked out.

"I'm short! I'm so short you can't hardly see me," Johnny Lauter cried with exultation as the tier guard admitted him to the range.

"Pipe down," the guard said tolerantly. "What are you talking about?"

"Won my case, goddamn it! The judge just ruled. I'm goin' free this afternoon or tomorrow."

"You don't say," the guard responded with mild interest. "Good for you."

Eyes shining, so excited that his whole body was shaking, Lauter ran inside the first cell, 102, where Eddie Quinn was taking a nap. Lauter woke him up with a punch on the arm and burst out with his news. Quinn's face lit up, and he gave an abandoned whoop of pleasure, so loud that the guard called: "You two pipe down in there – what's the matter with you?" Instantly Quinn ran to the door, thrust his head out and said: "Sorry, Mr Kraft. We'll watch it." He leapt back to Lauter, pumped his hand, slapped him on the back and demanded details. Then, presently, the two of them walked down the line, giving out the news to all of the others. There was no one who was not glad to hear it, because any man behind bars likes to see another go free – and yet there were few who didn't feel inner sadness and envy, including so good a friend as Eddie Quinn. Quinn thought: "Two years an' four months before I'll be short like this. Oh brother!" Yet, trailing at Lauter's heels, he said aloud: "Guess your kids are gonna be glad, hey, Johnny? Must be great to be goin' out to a family."

"Great?" Lauter responded happily. "That's an awful small word."

It was not too often that a man got good news like this, and a buzz of talk followed them down the range. Men chatted and men sighed, and the afternoon felt both lighter and heavier. But presently routine took over again.

Mr Kraft called "Tier man!" – and then, when Quinn had responded, he said: "Recreation! Roust 'em out. Police cells before going up."

Quinn nodded and walked down the runway with his mouth funnelled between both hands. "Recreation! Clean up your cells! Neat up your beds. All out who's goin' up. No haircuts today." He poked his head into 108 and said to Carolina Bell, "Cover your pillow with your blanket. You can get writ up for that."

"That so? Thanks for tellin' me."

"Hey, Barber, any haircuts t'day?" a man called from 110.

CHAPTER 11

"Didn't you just hear me say no?"

"Whatsamatter, your union call a strike?"

"Got a date t'go swimmin'."

All of the cell doors on the tier opened simultaneously with a great clanging percussion of steel upon steel.

"All out who's goin'!" Johnny Lauter called happily. "Them who stays gets locked up again!"

The men began to form into line.

On the Death Tier Wacky Mike yelled out shrilly: "Screw everybody! Burn up the whole world. Blow her up."

"Not before I get one drink," Quinn called in reply. Men on the first tier guffawed.

"Burn her up," the shrill voice called.

The line began to move.

Chapter 12

The Wisdom of the Street and the Field

At one fifteen of this October afternoon, the recreation tier was a hot box. While some of the more energetic men slowly walked the floor for exercise and a few played cards, most men merely sat and smoked.

All talked, however. The recreation period not only meant release from cell confinement, but from cellmate as well. Here, where the white inmates of both Tier One and Tier Three could mingle freely, a man found the opportunity to tell his private tale to a new face or to suck nourishment from a group. Men reflected upon one another's experiences, argued matters of jurisprudence, exchanged stories that were true, exaggerated or false. In a familiar jailhouse roundelay, with passion or wistfulness, ignorance or cynicism, they spoke the wisdom of the street and the field as they had come to know it.

Sometimes, when a man needed to unburden himself to a friend he could trust, the talk was hushed and private. Thus, Eddie Quinn to his old pal and drinking companion, Browney Carrera, who had been hauled in on a minor charge: "I'm on the skids, Browney; I've lost control of the wheel."

Carrera: "Forget it, pal. You're only temporary down in the dumps."

Quinn: "No I'm not. I've woke up to myself, Browney. A three-year sentence is a big jolt."

Carrera: "It's a rough one all right."

Quinn: "You an' me are different, see? How many times you been locked up altogether – two?"

Carrera: "This is the third."

Quinn: "That's what I mean. Once in a long while you pull a disorderly conduct. It don't count. You got control of your boozin', you don't go pickin' up things in department stores when you're drunk like I do. I didn't usta be this way, Browney, but that's how I am now – what's the use of lyin' to myself? I just gotta get a cure."

Carrera: "But listen, Eddie – what'll you do if the Classification Board don't transfer you to Danbury like you're gonna ask them?"

Quinn: "I'm countin' they will! They got everythin' to gain by it – wonderful publicity for the Federal prison system. What the hell, they're supposed to reuhbilitate us, ain't they?"

In this manner two old friends might talk, sitting close together, speaking in whispers. More often, however, there would be nothing private about a conversation, and it would be much closer to philosophic discourse.

Talking work:

Cabel Duff: "I started workin' in the soft-coal mines of Ohio when I was twelve. I loved coal minin'. Woulda been there yet, only I got the miner's asthma, had to quit when I turned forty."

Otha Doty: "You make me laugh. I quit minin' the day my buddy got kilt by a slate fall, an' brother, I ain't nevah goin' back to it. What the hell – there's no percentage in the average man workin' at an honest job. You work your guts out for forty years an' end up in the poorhouse."

Duff: "I'd rather end up in a poorhouse than here."

George Newberry: "You can say that again! I've never been in jail before, and I never will again."

Doty: "What you guys in for?"

Newberry, with a sheepish grin: "I'm a housepainter. I got laid off, so I started collectin' my unemployment insurance. Then I got a chance for two weeks' work for a neighbour; he was remodellin' his house, but I kept collectin' my insurance. I don't know how the devil they caught up with me. Some stool pigeon on my street, I guess."

Duff, with a loud guffaw: "Shake hands, buddy, I'm in for the same exact damn thing. I'm a plasterer."

Newberry: "You don't say! Ain't that one hell of a law? It's *our* insurance, we paid it in, but they give me three months' jail time for collectin' it."

Doty: "That's what I've been sayin', ain't I? It don't pay for the average man to work honest. You don't see any bankers in here, do you? You think they don't steal plenty?"

Talking tattoos:

Paul Costello: "I seen a woman in Hawaii, every damn inch of her had a tattoo on her."

Jay Spencer: "I know a hophead has a snake curled clear around his back an' belly."

Herbert Fife: "Maybe you won't believe it, but I seen a feller in Leavenworth had a bulldog tattooed on the head of his pecker."

Waxing enthusiastic, the men roll up their sleeves, unbutton their shirts and display their tattoos.

Talking freedom:

Hal Lovelace, ten years for felonious assault with intent to commit robbery: "Johnny, what you gonna eat your first night out?"

Lauter: "Any damn thing my wife cooks for me. Whatever it is, it'll be wonderful."

Lovelace: "I got my first meal all planned, but it ain't what you'd think – no steak or anythin' like that. It's gonna be oysters an' orange juice – all I can hold, nothin' else."

Albert Dodson, fifteen years for counterfeiting: "Ain't it a funny thing how a man can have years of stir time ahead of him but keep dreamin' of his first meal out? The human mind is a funny thing."

Lovelace: "I'll say. What makes a man go on the illegit anyway? We know we're gonna get caught sooner or later."

Dodson: "I didn't. I thought I had it figured out so they'd never catch up with me. Cleared six thousand in three weeks – boy, I was sittin' pretty."

Lauter, with a gay laugh: "Money! Like I've always said – the trouble with most convicts is they were born poor."

Talking farm as they walk a concrete floor:

Carolina Bell: "I kin see you don't know mules."

Lorenzo Witt: "I know 'em good enough never to have one."

Bell: "A mule's so much smarter than a horse – there's no comparison."
Witt: "Could be."

Bell: "A mule can work harder, takes less to feed."

Witt: "I won't argue it."

Bell: "A mule won't drink too much water when he's hot – a horse will. A mule will never eat more than is good for him – a horse will."

Witt: "Won't argue that neither."

Bell: "If a mule steps into barbed wire, he'll just lift his foot up an' out, do it clean. But a horse will pull an' pull an' cut hisself to pieces."

Witt: "Yep, I seen it myself."

Bell: "Then what in hell are you arguin' favour of horses for?"

Witt: "What else will a mule do? A damn mule will wait a year for the one time you ain't lookin', then he'll kick out an' kill you. Give me horses."

Talking economics:

Tom McPeak, trying to forget his troubles: "You ever realize there kaint be rich people without a lot more who's poor?"

George Trisler, former employee of the US Treasury: "How do you figure that? Everybody's got the same chance to get rich."

McPeak: "No, they ain't. Suppose a man owns* a hat factory. How does he make his profit?"

Trisler: "From what he sells."

McPeak: "Right. But if'n it costs him two dollars t'make a hat, he has t'sell it for two fifty or three, don't he?"

Trisler: "Sure. He makes his profit from the consumer."

McPeak: "Right. But who's the consumer? Mostly just workin' people, ain't they?"

Trisler: "Sure."

McPeak: "Who pays 'em?"

Trisler: "The people they work for."

McPeak: "Like the owner of that hat factory, right?"

Trisler: "So what?"

McPeak: "So that owner paid his workers less for makin' hats than he got for sellin' 'em, didn't he? An' every other factory owner does the same, don't they?"

Trisler: "Sure. That's how they make their profit."

McPeak, in triumph: "You just proved my case. For there to be rich people, everybody else has to get much less. That's how come there's so many poor. If you don't have poor, you couldn't have profits."

Trisler: "That's crazy. It's all screwed up."

McPeak. "Where's it screwed up?"

Trisler: "I don't know, but it's got to be."

Talking politics:

Earl Holcomb: "I look for a new war in two years."

Larry Trent: "What the hell you talkin' about, Pop? We just finished a war, I just got out of the army."

Holcomb: "You heard Churchill a coupla months ago, didn't you? We gotta lick Russia."

Trent: "Maybe *he's* gotta lick 'em, but not me. Boy, if that one comes, I'm takin' to the hills. I was in Germany, I seen their tanks – they're murder."

Holcomb: "We got the atom bomb, an' they ain't. We'll lick 'em in two weeks."

Trent: "You lick 'em, Pop. I'll be watchin' from the hills."

* * *

So the men talked, casually or with relish, or with essential boredom. Yet, when they were deeply serious, their conversation always ran to jails and penitentiaries, to police and judges, to trial and sentence. In this area strangers found sudden kinship, and all felt in common a keen artificial brotherhood founded on steel bars and confinement.

Johnny Lauter: "Justice? There sure ain't no equal justice. For housebreaking in this city a man gets ten years. In North Carolina he gets the gas chamber. Is that justice?"

Hal Lovelace, with genial envy: "What are you beefin' about, Johnny? You're on your way out."

Lauter: "So I'm one guy got a square deal. How many times does it go the other way?"

Otha Doty: "So help me God, fellers, there was a coloured boy in Nashville workhouse with me who stole a carton of cigarettes an' the judge give him forty years. Drop me dead if it's a lie."

Lauter: "A sentence like that don't surprise me. There's many a judge has a finance share in a road gang."

Larry McCormack:* "Where's the justice in one man makin' bail, the other man can't make it? It's a cold-cash justice: if you got the money, you buy out."

Ernie Nichols: "How *about* that, hey? It took 'em three months to put me on trial for a charge that got me a three-month sentence. So now I'll serve six – the first three is only dead time. Christ, they tell you the court calendar is crowded, or your judge is on vacation – but meanwhile you're in jail, ain't you?"

Lauter, with sudden passion: "You're talkin'. I been four months here on twenty-thousand bail I couldn't meet. Now they say it was all a mistake."

Larry Trent: "If anybody here really wants to know about justice, take a look at me. Five months ago I come out of the army. I rest up for a month, then I start lookin' for work. I hear there's a lot of buildin' goin' on in DC,* so I head this way – I'm an iron worker. First night here I pass a garage* an' hear shots. I hit the pavement an' see three guys run out. They jump into a car, but I get the licence number an' a good look at 'em. I go down the street an' call the cops. It turns out later those guys are members of a big gang – they call 'em the 'False-Nose Gang'. The cops arrest 'em, but those guys got a big lawyer an' plenty of bail money. They're out on bail in one day. But the cops tell me they need me as a *material witness*: they wanna get this gang, they don't want me skippin' town or gettin' shot.

So I get ten-thousand bail slapped on me, an' I been two months in here waitin' for somebody else's trial."

Hal Lovelace, with venom: "Serves you right, you sucker: why didn't you keep your damn nose out of it? Anybody helps a cop deserves what he gets."

So they talked, whiling away the recreation hour, killing a little part of the long day.

Tom McPeak, wandering from group to group, listened, talked when the opportunity offered and worried. Without his being aware of it, he was coming to a decision. The hours he had spent behind bars, and now these conversations on the recreation tier, were slowly but inexorably turning him away from Huey Wilson. He just didn't want to risk imprisonment – that was the whole of it. The sheer possibility of its coming to pass was making him shrivel inside. He had his conscience and his sense of solidarity and his sense of shame, but they were withering away in this cage of steel and wire and stone. His thoughts now were running in one direction only: that he had done enough. It had not been his fight in the first place. It was not as though it were a union struggle, where he'd stick to the end no matter what happened. This was a matter of race prejudice – it was as old as the United States itself, and it wouldn't be solved in a day. There was no call for Tom McPeak to go to jail over it.

Yet, even while thinking this way, McPeak still was worried and unhappy over Huey Wilson. Somehow everything had been made worse for him by the dinner fight, and by the fact that Huey was due for punishment. He had tried to put it out of his mind by talking to other men, but he wasn't being very successful. Wandering the tier, he listened for a few moments to the hot talk about justice, and then took an opportunity to ask Johnny Lauter a question.

"Say, feller, what're they gonna do with those two guys who had the fight at dinner?"

"Shove 'em in the Hole."

"What's that?"

Lauter explained what the Hole was, and McPeak, frowning, exclaimed: "That sounds rough."

"Ain't no picnic," Lauter agreed.

"Rough, hell," snorted Otha Doty. "Maybe none of you knows what 'rough' is. I'd ruther pull one week in a Federal Hole than one day on that damn Nashville chain gang. No man who ain't put in chain-gang time knows what 'rough' is."

"Amen!" said Lauter quietly. "I've done both."

"Chain gang?" McPeak asked naively. "They usta have 'em in Georgia when I was a boy, but I thought they was all done away with."

"*What?*" Doty asked. "*What?*"

There occurred then one of those explosive changes only possible among men like these. Whereas jailhouse conversation usually was conducted with an even temper, Doty suddenly began to speak with incredible intensity, and with his drawn, iron-hard body quivering with fury.

"Where you been livin' recently – on Mars, buddy?" Violently he pulled up one trouser leg and pressed his sock down against his half shoe. There was a wide strip of discoloured skin around his ankle bone. "You think I was borned like this? That's from leg irons – I worn* them nineteen months. They put 'em on with rivets the first day, an' they never came off till the last day of my State sentence, three weeks ago. I worked with 'em, ate with 'em, slept with 'em – with a three-foot step chain between both legs."

"Holy Jesus," McPeak exclaimed. "That's in Nashville?"

"The city workhouse!" Doty replied with fury. "You live in a barracks next to the jail. They feed you beans mornin' an' night, seven days a week. They sleep you in rows an' tie every last man to a bull chain all night long. They put a stinkin' slop bucket by your bed – if you wanna use it, you gotta get permission. All day Sunday you sit on a box by the side of that slop bucket – you ain't allowed to lie on your cot or play cards or do nothin'. The other six days of the week you work!"

"An' man, he means *work*!" Johnny Lauter put in fiercely, spitting the words. Lauter's mouth was tight; there was a blaze in his eyes, and he no longer was the man who had gone straight, or whose family was waiting for him to come home in the next few hours. Right now he was Lauter, the time-server, with his memories and his wounds.

"I'll say *work*!" Doty cried. "They trucked us to a rock quarry outside the city every daylight – didn't take us back till dark. Twelve hours we worked in summer, ten hours in winter!"

"Swingin' a sixteen-pound hammer," Lauter said in a voice thin with pain. "'Go git it!' the guard says to you. 'I wanna see that number on your back an' that number on your ass, an' I don't wanna see your friggin' face all day long!'"

"It's non-human the way they make you work – it's just non-human!" Doty cried, his body quivering from the magnitude of his indignation. He was a man of thirty, dark-haired and dark-eyed, his features good but ferociously gaunt, the weathered skin taut over the bones of his face.

"I went into that workhouse weighin' a hunnerd an' eighty-nine – when the doctor weighed me here I was a hunnerd an' twenty-four. I seen two men drop dead in that quarry. I seen men faint in the sun – they throw water on 'em, tell 'em t'go git it or they'll string 'em up. There ain't one of you who'd treat a dog the way we was treated!"

When Doty first had commenced this recital, there were only five others around him. By now, however, there was a gathering of half the men on the tier. Most merely listened – some, however, who had suffered similar imprisonment, began to speak out in a bitter chorale. Of a sudden these men were like the actors, chorus and audience of a classic Greek play, all of them united by a common passion, all pondering the grim tragedy of fate and retribution.

"You know what I think of when I wake up every morning?" Doty asked the assemblage. "I think to myself, 'There's some poor guy doin' his first day on the Nashville gang – God help him, God pity him... if there's a God in heaven, let him look down!'" In the mouth of another man this sentiment would have sounded maudlin, but Doty's sincerity was unmistakable. "My first day in the quarry a guard says to me, 'Hey, boy, you ain't usin' that shovel right.' Man, after three hours I was tired – I'd been livin' soft for two years – I just had to slow that shovel now an' then. 'You do it like this,' the guard tells me. He starts shovelling gravel on that truck so fast only a damn machine could keep it up twelve hours. So I go back to work. I do as fast as I can till I'm ready to drop. I got blood blisters on both hands the size of blueberries. An hour later he comes up to me again. 'Reckon I gotta show you oncet more,' he says to me real soft like. He takes the shovel out of my hands and then whams me across the face with it – knocks me cold. That's how they break a man in on that chain gang. Look there, you can see the scar."

A deep bass voice in the assemblage cried out: "Brother, he's talkin' true! I did ninety days on a Georgia gang. I seen things go on in that swamp that God Himself would turn His face from."

Another voice said: "But there's some that's better. I did road time in Virginia. You lived rotten an' ate rotten, but they didn't chain you or beat you up."

"Sure," cried Johnny Lauter, "there's all different kinds of camps even in the same state. But we're talkin' the rough ones, an' we know what we're talkin' about."

"Brother, we sure do," the bass voice said again. "Hittin' men with their pistol butts, with their shotgun butts, with them lead-loaded hickory sticks they carry. All t'make you work faster'n any human bein' *can* work, with the superintendent gettin' a money cut of the business. God help all them poor Joes down there right now."

"An' suppose you're sick, you can't work?" cried Doty. "In Nashville they take you back to the barracks, chain you to a post an' make you stand in one spot for twelve hours. You ever try standin' in one spot that long?"

"Is that all they did to you in Nashville?" Lauter asked fiercely. "I pulled nineteen months on a chain gang in North Carolina. You talk back to a guard in that camp or break a tool, or do any damn thing you're not supposed to – includin' bein' sick – an' they let you have it. I've seen them shave a man's head, strip him naked an' cover him with molasses. Then they strung him up by his arms from a tree limb for the flies to go at him, kept him there seventy-two hours. I seen 'em spreadeagle men on the ground an' whip 'em with a bull whip till they was almost dead. I seen a coloured fellow whipped so hard on the first crack that his skin broke an' the blood spurted up high as my shoulder. I heard men scream till I—"

Suddenly Lauter was silent, and then the other men became silent. Mr Jonas, a youngish, good-looking officer, was standing on the outside of the group, holding a bundle of letters. He had been listening for several moments without being noticed. Now, as all faces turned towards him, he said quietly, with a humorous note in his voice: "You heard the man! Guess it's lucky you're all in Federal – me too. Now we'll have mail call."

"What's so good about Federal?" a voice asked somewhere in the crowd, and there was laughter.

"Roy Keedy," Mr Jonas said, paying no attention to the remark, "Paul Moses... Earl Holcomb..."

Quietly the men waited for their names. The passion play had ended. Yet it was not forgotten, and it would be played out again. Tomorrow it might be the crude horrors of county jails, and the next week it might be the Pittsburgh workhouse. Always there would be men* with ulcerated hearts who would cry out: "I seen things in that place that God Himself would turn His face from."

Tom McPeak, standing alone, was churning inside with only one emotion: he wanted to be out. He no longer was afraid of the visit of Detective Stoner – now he wanted it to come.

As any man will, when he has been sentenced to a long prison term, Floyd Varney was pondering escape. He was sitting in a corner of the bull pen of the Federal courthouse, a dead cigarette between his lips, his face pallid, his brain working feverishly.

Ideas raced through his head, plans came and were rejected. Too many doors, too many walls, too many bars, too many guards! Each time he tried to fashion a plan, the practical difficulties loomed up as insuperable, and at that point his thoughts would slide off into fantasy. With wild hunger he would dream of a miracle in which all obstacles faded, all doors were left open, all cell walls dissolved. But only for a moment! He would return then to reality, to defeat, to his absolute helplessness. He would return to the monstrous, incredible fact that he, Floyd Varney, would have to remain in prison for a minimum of twenty-five years.

He sat alone, separate from the other men in this basement room, locked in a universe of his own. Yet, each time the door was opened by a bailiff, he roused instantly to pay brief attention – as though, through this link with the outer world, some magical reprieve might be forthcoming from the judge, from his attorney, from God. When the door opened upon a man from his own tier, Hal Jude, Varney had the usual spurt of irrational hope, followed by despair. However, since he knew Jude and since he needed to speak frankly to someone, he waited to catch his eye.

Most men returned from court with sombre faces, but Jude was grinning and exultant. Although he had received a sentence of two years, he announced jubilantly to all present that he had beaten the rap again. His satisfaction was genuine. Unlike most of the men there, Jude was a criminal by preference, a man who pursued his trade with no regrets, no sense of wrongdoing, no secret desire to be an honest citizen. When Jude had money, he spent it lavishly and childishly; when he was broke, he picked pockets – and this he would continue to do so long as his fingers were nimble. For this reason prison time to him was a kind of regrettable occupational hazard, but it was not an unforeseen disaster. At the age of fifty, he had a record of twenty-three arrests in fifteen states, but he had served only five years' cell time. Since, on this occasion, he had been caught on a crowded bus in the act of stealing the wallet of an FBI agent, he had expected a longer sentence. Two years was a gift from Heaven: he would be free in approximately nineteen months – it was to be scratched off as a rest cure.

Strutting around the room, Jude gave free vent to his exultation. Since the judge who had sentenced him was a woman, it was inevitable that he would express himself in fitting terms. "That jedge sure went for me, there's no other reason. She got soft for me, just couldn't bear t'give me time. It sure pays t'be borned good-lookin' like me – haw, haw!"

Whatever the reason for the judge's sentence, Jude was entitled to his own interpretation. It was true, however, that he was a handsome man, with the rugged, honest features of a successful business executive. One could not judge from his appearance that he was illiterate, or that he had no more sense of social morality than a child, or that he came of a family of sharecroppers* in which the father had died of syphilitic paresis,* two sisters were tubercular and his elder brother was in prison for distilling illegal whiskey. Strutting the room, he crowed in glee: "Look at me, you guys. I was borned lucky. Take a feel of me."

Coming upon Varney, Jude slapped his knee in an excess of good spirits. "Hey, boy – you hear about me? I pulled a deuce. Touch me, kid, I was borned lucky. You got your sentence yet?"

Varney nodded.

"What'd you pull?"

The answer came in a mumble.

"What was that?"

Varney repeated it more loudly, and the grin slipped from Jude's face. He was a coarse, egocentric man, but he felt instantly that awed respect for Varney that even a brute will feel for a dying man. He said nothing. If Varney had answered ten or even fifteen years, Jude might have exclaimed: "Well now, boy, that's rough – guess you'll have to settle down an' git married now." There were many such things that inmates said with perverse, hardbitten humour to a man who received a bad one. But there was nothing at all to say to twenty-five years – no jests to be made, and no comfort to be offered.

In silence he sat down beside Varney. Slowly he rolled a cigarette, licked the edge of the paper, sealed it. He was thinking what all men, even the most sympathetic, would think at this moment: "I'm sure glad it ain't me!" He inhaled deeply, then murmured: "That's rough, kid." Varney did not reply. Suddenly, however, he turned, leant close to Jude and whispered: "You've done time before, haven't you, Georgia?"

"Yea, boy."

"Federal?"

"On'y State."

"Where'll they send me with a hitch like this – Alcatraz?"

"Could be. But they have long-timers in all the big pens – Atlanta, Terra Haute…"*

In an intense whisper Varney asked: "You think a guy could walk out of one of those places?"

Jude pursed his lips. "From what I heerd, there's mighty few evah make it. They shoot 'em down."

"I've got nothin' to lose."

"It'd take a lot of figurin'."

"I got nothin' but time."

"The thing is this, kid – them big pens are tight security, real tight. You'll be a long-timer, and they got things rigged so that long-timers are kept on short rope. They're watchin' you day 'n' night."

"But some men have broken out of 'em, haven't they?" Varney asked fiercely.

"Sure. On'y they usually git 'em befoah they travels far. From what I heerd the hard part is this – a man not only has t'figure how t'break out, but he's gotta figure what he does afterwards* too. A man needs somebody on the *outside* workin' with him. You got some close folks you kin depend on, folks willin' to take chances for you? Remember, it's up to five years' prison time for *them* if they gits caught."

Varney shook his head.

"You're up agin a mighty tough deal, then, kid. Suppose you work two, three years gittin' t'know the place an' figuring a plan? Then suppose you make it ovah the wall without gittin' shot? Where are you then? You're wearin' prison clothes. You got no money. You got nothin' to eat. You got only your own legs for gitaway. They count you every thirty minutes in those big pens, so you don't got much leeway time. They call out the police and the state troopers and set up road blocks. They put it on the radio. They ask every damn farmer in the county to patrol his property with a shotgun. Kid, it's a tough one to beat."

Varney nodded. A dull hopelessness came into his eyes. He turned from Jude to gaze off into space. There was no more talk between them. Then, after a bit, Jude rose and walked off.

Varney sat in abysmal loneliness, even his fantasies stricken now; sat hearing the judge's voice pronounce twenty-five years to life; sat thinking of endless prison days, endless prison time; of prison meals, stone floors and stone walls; of cell days and cell nights; of the gnawing, hopeless hunger for woman's love; of the miserable crawl of life, the leaden weight of life when every tomorrow is the same as today – and knew in his heart that he would rather be dead. And so now he began to think about that – about how a man in prison could kill himself, and so escape.

In the middle of the recreation period, conversation ceased as the loud-speaker in the west wing suddenly shouted an order:

"Now hear this, now hear this. The following two men report to their tier officers: Huey Wilson – 64464... Huey Wilson – 64464... Arthur

Ballou – 64462... Arthur Ballou – 64462. These two men are wanted in the Rotunda immediately!"

In the moment of after-hush on the recreation tier, Eddie Quinn sang out: "There they go – elevator stops at the Hole."

Another voice, from the card-playing group that was seated on the floor, called out with feeling: "I hope that sassy nigger gets a month!"

"How come? He didn't start the fight, he don't deserve no punishment at all!" This was McPeak, speaking with equal feeling. He had been watching the poker game for some minutes past.

"What the hell you talkin' about?" the other asked with surprise and rancour. He was from the third tier, a man in his late twenties by the name of Foley. "Ain't you got eyes in your head? Didn't you see what happened?" He stared at McPeak with the air of one examining an idiot.

"Sure I saw it. I heard what Ballou said that started it too."

"Like what?"

"He called that coloured feller all sorts of names, didn't he?"

"Didn't call him nothin' but what he is. A coon's a coon, ain't he?"

McPeak hesitated. He knew already that this discussion would be fruitless. Nevertheless, he was involved and he was irritated, and his need to defend Huey Wilson at this point was somehow made more urgent by his private decision to quit the case. He said slowly, with acid in his voice: "I never could tell the kind of man somebody is by the colour of his skin. There's lots of white folks I wouldn't have in my house."

"An' lots of niggers you would, eh?" one of the other players put in slyly.

"Could be! I take a man like I find him," McPeak retorted.

"I'll be goddamned!" Foley exploded. "So what would you do if a nigger threw a mess of beets in your face – say thank you an' lick his ass?"

"Maybe he would," the sly voice put in. "Maybe he's that kind of a guy."

There was a ripple of laughter from the card players and from several of the other spectators.

McPeak spat the match he was chewing to the floor. "Very funny," he snapped with contempt.

Foley raised his voice, and there was an aggressive, belligerent note in it. "You ain't answered my question. What would you do?"

Foley's voice was loud, and a quality in it sent a message along the tier. Conversations were interrupted, and men began to gravitate towards the poker players.

Again McPeak hesitated, reason and anger in conflict. If there had been any way to break off the conversation without appearing to back down, he would have done so. He knew that it was stupid to talk to men like this. Theirs was a type of ingrown anti-Negro prejudice that life itself could sometimes change, as it had with him, but a single conversation never could. Nevertheless, others were around now, a question had been put to him, and he couldn't leave it unanswered.

"Looky here," he said, "this fightin' between Wilson an' Ballou didn't start in here. Saddy night Ballou an' three other white fellers jumped Wilson on a street corner an' liked to kill him. You wanna know what kind of a low-down snake this Ballou is, I'll tell you. He had a knife out ready to blind that Wilson boy when—"

"That ain't how I heard it!" Foley interrupted. "I'm in the cell next door to Ballou, an' I heard it straight."

"Whatever you heard from Ballou was straight goddamn lies," McPeak told him loudly. "I was on that street corner an' I saw it."

"Well! So now we're gettin' the lay of the land," Foley answered sarcastically. "You an' that nigger boy are pals – no wonder you're stickin' up for him."

"Pals ain't the word for it," the sly voice put in. "I told you before – the old boy likes black meat."

"You shut your dirty mouth," McPeak exploded in a rage. "I don't take that shit from no one."

"You'll take it from me," Foley said with a sudden bull roar. He jumped to his feet. He was over six feet, a man of enormous girth, barrel-bodied, weighing close to two hundred and fifty pounds. "You'll take anythin' I give you and like it." He was only two yards away from McPeak, and he stepped closer, his bull head thrust forward, his face swollen and red.

"Ain't no screw around," the sly voice called encouragingly. "Let him have it, Joe."

"Break it up, for Chrissakes," Johnny Lauter cried suddenly. "You guys wanna fight so bad you willin' to get extra sentence time?"

"Mind your own business, buddy," someone else called. "Ain't no screw up here, let 'em fight. Go ahead, Foley, smear the bastard."

Foley made no move. For a good many reasons, most of them having nothing to do with McPeak, he was aching to hammer somebody with his fists. Since it couldn't be the parole officer, who had just sent him back to prison for violation of his conditional release, McPeak was a fine substitute. Nevertheless, Foley had been in prison before, and he knew how to operate in a situation like this. Either there had to be no witnesses at all to a fight – or else, in a crowd like this, you needed to be smart and make the other man strike the first blow. Choosing his words with care in order to achieve this end, Foley said loudly: "There's only one thing lower than a nigger – an' that's a nigger lover like you who calls himself a white man."

In the next instant Otha Doty was standing between Foley and McPeak. He was as tall as Foley, considerably less heavy, but a formidable adversary. He cried out with intense passion: "I come from West Virginia, an' I had a damn good friend who was coloured. I worked five years in the mines right next to that feller. I cried like a baby when he died. You wanna fight about it, don't pick somebody twenny years older'n you are. Try me on for size, you son of a bitch."

"Screw comin' up the stairs," Eddie Quinn sang out. "Break it up fast."

It was not true, and Quinn's reason for lying was not pacific. He would have enjoyed a good fight as well as the next man. This particular quarrel, however, showed signs of developing into a free-for-all with half a dozen men involved. Nothing like that could escape the notice of the guards, and the result would be unpleasant – both tiers might lose recreation and Yard for some time. That was too much of a penalty – the entertainment wasn't worth it.

The lie was effective. Within a few seconds the crowd had dispersed, the poker circle was restored, and the tier looked normal. By the time it was realized that no officer had appeared, the antagonists were separated and no one was inclined to lay down a new challenge.

Tom McPeak, who had cooled off a little, sought out Otha Doty and said: "Thanks, pal. I ain't such an easy mark as that bull bastard thinks I am, but it's just as good I didn't git into no fight with him. I got the high blood pressure – it ain't good for me to git so mad or fight."

"Chee-rist!" Doty exclaimed. "That kinda talk just makes me boil. I know it's just cos guys like that are dumb – they been brung up t'look down on coloured folks and they don't know no better – but it makes me boil anyway. Why, that feller I knew, he was a square Joe – I didn't care what his skin colour was. You work side by side with somebody an' you git to know what he's like. That feller was true blue."

"You say he died?"

"Kilt in a slate fall. Must've been two tons fell down on him – I never want t'see anythin' like that agin'. It ain't so bad t'die, I reckon, if it happens clean. But he didn't die right away: it on'y got him from the waist down. Chee-rist, it was awful, chum. Me workin' like crazy with my crowbar to try an' lift that rock offa him, an' him screamin' an' tellin' me to git out before more came down an' got me."

With a sensation of pain mounting in his stomach, although he didn't know why, McPeak asked: "You git him loose?"

Doty shook his head. "Couldn't. He died after about five minutes. I never went back to that damn coal mine." He sighed and spat on the floor.

"Lucky it didn't git you too. Guess you were mighty scared."

"No," Doty replied, "wasn't scared then or afterwards. Just had my mind on helpin' my buddy."

"Yeah," McPeak said dully, feeling the pain in his stomach. "Guess that's how it is."

"A man don't think about hisself at a time like that," Doty said. "That's been my expeerience. You just think of doin' what you kin."

"Yeah," McPeak agreed. He moved away.

Lieutenant Snider, a man with many years in the prison service, was thoroughly cynical about the inmates who came before him for punishment. Merely by a first glance at Art Ballou, for instance, he was sure that he knew the anatomy of the hard-boiled punk with whom he was dealing. Ballou was due for punishment, and the lieutenant intended to administer it, yet he was ready to assert in advance that it wouldn't teach him anything at all.

The lieutenant was not particularly thoughtful about matters of penology, yet one problem always baffled him: the fact that punishment had so little effect upon most criminals. When he first had entered the prison system, the treatment of inmates had been much harsher than it was now. Guards had carried clubs; discipline had been tighter and the food worse; there had been less recreation. The reforms of 1930 had come along, and, while they had made life easier for both inmates and guards, so far as the lieutenant could see they had achieved nothing else. The incidence of crime and the percentage of men who returned to prison continued as high. It was a slicker method of administration, but that was all. Punishment was still at the heart of it, even though Authority wore a glove on its hand – and punishment still did no good. Year after year men were released from abominable State prisons to turn up later in Federal – or from less harsh* Federal prisons to end up on a chain gang. Clearly the nation's penal system did not meet the problem of crime, but what the solution might be the lieutenant did not know. Nor did he care very much. He was fifty-three years old, and what he cared about was the pension that would be coming to him a few years hence. Therefore his rule on the job was to make no mistakes, to follow regulations and to be unconcerned about their effect. In truth, fruitless as these regulations were, the lieutenant knew no way in which they could be improved.

"Ballou," he said, "Mr Fuhr has given me a report of what happened at dinner. Fighting's against regulations. You got anything to say for yourself?"

Ballou, who was standing in front of the lieutenant's desk with Officer Fuhr by his side, kept silent for a moment while his gaze shifted from lieutenant to guard and back again. He was afraid of going to the Hole, although he would not have acknowledged it to anyone, and he was eager to minimize his punishment if he could.

"Lieutenant, sir," he began very politely, following the advice given him by his cellmate, "I certainly do got something to say for myself, yes sir. This nigger I had the fight with – he was arrested for fightin' with me Saturday night. You happen to know that, sir?"

"No, but what's it got to do with your breaking regulations?"

"Well, I'm only here on suspicion of disorderly conduct, that's all. But that nigger has three charges on him! One of 'em is felonious assault with deadly weapons."

"Look here," said the lieutenant, "I'm not a judge and I'm not trying your case. My business has to do with what happened today at dinner, that's all."

"But they're connected," Ballou explained in an aggrieved tone. "That's what I'm tryin' to tell you, sir."

"How are they connected?"

Eagerly Ballou launched into a recital of the manner in which Wilson and the other mess men had overloaded his breakfast platter, and had deliberately passed him up on seconds at dinner – all of this in order to make him break discipline. He admitted that finally they had succeeded. He was sorry about that, but he was only human. What was a man to do, he asked, when a nigger threw a mess of beets in his face?

"Hm, yes," the lieutenant said. "But you would've been a lot smarter if you'd just sat in your seat. I'm not excusing Wilson – he's up for discipline, too – but you can't claim self-defence or physical danger. The rule says no fighting, and you broke it. I've got no basis to let you off without punishment."

"Jesus Christ," Ballou burst out, losing his control in the instant, "all I can see is that you're takin' the side of that nigger."

Lieutenant Snider flushed. He was a plump, florid man, with close-cropped white hair, and his forehead turned beet-red against the white hairline. He had been feeling already there was* something fishy about the obsequious politeness of this youth. These tough punks had all sorts of ways of behaving when they were up for discipline. "I'm giving you two days in the Hole for fighting," he announced in an even tone, "and one day more for disrespect to an officer."

Shaking with indignation, Ballou cried out, "If you think that'll teach me to kiss nigger ass, you're mistaken."

"We'll make it four days," the lieutenant snapped. "I advise you to button up your lip before you get more time."

Ballou's eyes blazed, but he kept still.

"All right, Mr Fuhr," the lieutenant said, "take him down." He watched them leave. The moment the door to his office shut and he was alone, his anger vanished. It was impossible for him to deal with a snotty cur* like Ballou without becoming angry – yet Ballou already had merged with all of the other Ballous, and anger was pointless. He began to write up the necessary report.

Down two flights of iron staircase from the Rotunda there was a basement corridor where a guard was sitting by a steel-barred door, his hands clasped over his heavy paunch, his eyes closed. At the sound of footsteps he stood up immediately, thoroughly awake, his jaws beginning to grind on a cud of tobacco. He was a man close to sixty-five who looked like a caricature of a brutal prison guard – very tall, very heavy, with sagging jowls and a seamed hound-dog face, with small eyes and a loose mouth. In point of fact he was an agreeable man with an inward fund of compassion for all inmates. He was so old in prison service, having begun as a youth in various State prisons, that sometimes he felt like an inmate himself. His name was Croy, and off-duty the other officers called him "Pop".

Mr Fuhr extended a slip of paper that bore Ballou's name and number. He commented dispassionately: "A customer, Mr Croy. Four days."

With a rattle of keys Mr Croy opened the door. He said, "In here, Mister." Ballou entered the corridor with a swagger, and Mr Croy followed, locking the door behind them. Mr Fuhr remained waiting outside.

Mr Croy's job was a dull one, and, as a man, he loved conversation. For this reason he instantly began a monologue designed to edify Ballou and to relieve the monotony of his eight-hour job. "Now let's see, Mister, here we have seven cells, all of 'em the same, only one in use, so I guess we'll give you number seven, that's a lucky number." Mr Croy's voice was very deep, with a slight wheeze to it, and he sighed and rumbled his words in a low monotone. "Now, you get fed three times a day down here, just the same as always. Course you only get two pieces of bread for each meal, but a strong young feller like you can get along fine on that." Mr Croy unlocked the door to number seven, which was of solid steel with a sliding panel slot at eye level. The light from the corridor illumined a cell of less than normal size that was bare of equipment except for a washbasin and toilet in one corner. Mr Croy nodded his head, and Ballou strode inside.

"Got any cigarettes on you, Mister? I want 'em if you have."

Ballou gave him a rumpled pack containing only a few cigarettes.

"How about matches?"

Ballou grinned in surly fashion and produced a box of matches.

"Turn your pockets inside out – just to make sure."

As Ballou obeyed, Mr Croy said amiably, his bass voice rumbling: "We bring a mattress in here every night for you to sleep on. Once a day a doctor comes to look you over. Most men come out fine – nothing for you to worry about. Now, you ain't got any more smokes on you, have you?"

"You can see my pockets, can'tcha?"

"Sure. Now strip!"

"What for?"

"Strip, Mister."

Angrily Ballou unbuttoned his shirt. He removed it with a quick, yet uneasy and awkward motion, and stood holding it.

"I'll take it, Mister."

"Do I gotta stay in here naked?"

"Hell no, you're in Federal, not some crummy State pen. But it's my job to collect all cigarettes. Hand 'em over."

With intense disappointment Ballou handed over his shirt and the two packages of cigarettes he was concealing, one in each hand. Since dinner hour, when he knew he was headed for a stretch in the Hole, he had been carrying the two packages beneath his shirt, in the loose fold of material above his belt line.

Mr Croy dropped the cigarettes into a pocket, shook out the shirt, then draped it neatly over his arm. "Now let's see if there's any rabbits in your pants, Mister."

Sheepishly Ballou removed his trousers. Just below each knee there was a handkerchief bound in kerchief style, the knot in front, the swathe in back.

"Housemaid's knee, no doubt," Mr Croy said amiably. "Let's have 'em."

Held snugly behind each knee were a third and fourth* package of cigarettes donated by generous men on his tier. Mr Croy took them, shook out the handkerchief and said: "There wouldn't be no matches in your shoes, would there?"

Ballou took off his shoes. Beneath the arch of each foot there was a somewhat crumpled box of matches. He handed them over. Mr Croy pounded the shoes on the floor, then tossed Ballou's clothes back to him. He said with a laugh: "Whatever you've got hidden up your rear end you can smoke."

"Ha-ha!" Ballou muttered in a fury of disappointment. He began to dress.

"Yes, indeedy,"* Mr Croy said amiably, as he removed the laces from Ballou's shoes, "this is a Federal Hole, not State, and a man can be thankful for that. You got a clean cell with an air vent. Why, I've seen some had six inches of water in 'em, or with mice running around, or so small a man couldn't stand up or lie down. In here you even get to keep your clothes. You got a toilet instead of a piece of newspaper. You got all the water you can drink, instead of just a measly little cupful three times a day. You're just plain lucky you're in Federal." He dropped Ballou's shoes on the floor. "No yellin', singin', whistlin', or you'll get more time down here, Mister. No knockin' on the walls, no nothin'. Bye now."

Mr Croy stepped out, slammed the heavy door and locked it. He marched at an even pace to the entrance, opened the door there, locked it and said to Mr Fuhr: "Now, there's a boy who'll spend prison time in his life." He began taking package after package of cigarettes from his pockets. "I never use these myself."

"I don't smoke either, Pop," said Mr Fuhr, "but I'll pass 'em around. I'll be back in a few minutes with someone else."

They nodded to each other – Mr Fuhr walked away briskly, and Mr Croy sat down. He spat a brown slosh of tobacco juice into a tin can on the floor, closed his eyes and slipped at once into the twilight state in which he passed time.

In his quick glance at Huey Wilson's folder, Lieutenant Snider had observed a number of unusual items. Wilson was a high-school senior with no record of previous arrests. Moreover, as evidence of good character, he was working in government service while attending school at night. Obviously, he was no hoodlum. Nevertheless, the charge against him was felonious assault with deadly weapons, quite serious, and in his very first day in jail he had become involved in a fight. The facts were contradictory enough to tease Lieutenant Snider's interest.

As soon as Wilson entered his office, the lieutenant felt that he understood. He had dealt with a good many Negro inmates in his time, and it was his belief that most of them suffered from an inability to adjust to what was, after all, a white man's country. In the lieutenant's opinion it was not altogether their fault, yet it was a social problem that could not be solved by letting them labour under illusions. Merely from a first glance at Wilson's face – seeing the tight, proud, unyielding expression – the lieutenant was prepared to guess why a youth like this had been in two fights with white men within a few days. So many of them were too damn touchy for their own good. A disparaging remark that could have been let pass, or even a fancied insult, and this was the result – an otherwise law-abiding coloured boy in jail.

"Wilson," he said, in a not-unfriendly tone, "the officer here reports that you threw some beets in a man's face at dinner. You know you can't act that way in jail. It calls for punishment. Have you got anything to say for yourself?"

"Yes, sir, I have." Huey paused for a moment, cleared his throat and tried to control his nervousness. "I made a mistake when I did that, and I'm sorry about it. But that fellow Ballou was part of a gang that almost killed me in a fight on Saturday night and—"

"I know you were in a fight," the lieutenant interrupted, "but what happened outside is none of my business. Stick to what's gone on since you came in here."

"That fellow's been picking on me in here too. I'm on the mess crew, and he's been calling me names I won't take from anyone."

"Like what?"

"He wanted some seconds at dinner and he called me 'boy'."

"Is that why you threw the beets in his face?" the lieutenant asked with a frown.

"Not for that, but I wouldn't serve him. I'm not a boy, I'm a man. I'm a coloured man and I'm proud of what I am, and I won't allow anyone to treat me as an inferior."

The lieutenant rubbed his face, then asked, "So why'd you throw the beets?"

"One thing led to another. First he called me 'boy'. Then, when I wouldn't serve him, he called me a 'coon'. When I came around a second time, he called me a 'boy' again and put his feet in the aisle so I couldn't get past. Then this officer" – referring to Mr Fuhr – "ordered me to serve him. Nothing would've happened if he hadn't given me that order." Huey saw the quick look of resentment that came to Mr Fuhr's face, but he was too indignant to care. "When I started to obey the order,

Ballou called me a 'f—— nigger'.* I wouldn't take that on the outside from anyone. Am I supposed to take it in jail? Is that what the rules say about coloured men?"

The lieutenant sighed, knowing already that his guess about the youth had been accurate. He said patiently: "Wilson, you're an intelligent young fellow. You can realize that inside a jail there'll be all sorts of men, all sorts of words passed. But it's one thing to take it out in talk, and another to start a fight. You started a fight. That's one of the most serious things a man can do in jail."

Feeling it might be wiser to keep his mouth shut, but unwilling to do so, Huey said: "This officer ordered me to serve Ballou. Why didn't he order Ballou to stop his name-calling? Isn't that just as much his responsibility?"

"Oh, for Christ's sake," the lieutenant exclaimed impatiently, "you're in jail, Wilson. I didn't put you in here – Mr Fuhr didn't put you in here: you brought your own self here by getting into a fight. Then—"

"But—"

"Don't interrupt me. Then you start a fight in here because you were insulted. Do you intend to go through life fighting over every word? If you do, this won't be the last time you land in jail. Four days in the Hole, Mr Fuhr."

The guard jerked his head, and Huey, holding his features under tight control, started out of the office.

"Listen, Wilson," the lieutenant said more quietly, "I see by your record that you're trying to get somewhere in the world. But more than one man has botched up his life by being too touchy and too quick to fly into a temper. Think it over. Maybe you'll learn something useful out of this."

Huey did not turn around and did not reply. After a moment Mr Fuhr waved him out.

Writing his report, the lieutenant wondered whether four days was too much punishment, but then decided it was not. This was a boy who needed to learn the facts of life... not that the Hole would do him any good.

Guard and inmate walked down the two flights of stairs in silence. Mr Fuhr's face was flushed, and he obviously was very angry, but Huey didn't give a damn. He felt so indignant over the patronizing white man's crap that the lieutenant had been trying to hand him that he could think of nothing else.

When they reached the basement corridor, Mr Croy spat into the tin can, stood up and slipped the large keyring from his belt. Mr Fuhr said with quiet venom: "Four days, Pop, but I would've given him a month. This is a real troublemaker – he's got a mouth as big as his black ass."

Huey stood very still. He knew instantly that there was danger in the guard's manner.

"You don't say," Mr Croy responded with curiosity. "What did he do?" He unlocked the steel door and waved Huey inside.

"He don't like how I run my job," Mr Fuhr explained acidly. He followed them into the corridor.

"You comin' in?" Mr Croy asked in surprise.

"I'd like to see the door close on this boy." Mr Fuhr explained. "He's just such a big, smart, know-it-all nigger, I want to see his face when the door closes."

Mr Croy stopped at cell number four, unlocked the heavy door and waved Huey inside. Stepping warily, his eyes on Mr Fuhr, Huey obeyed. All sorts of thoughts and frightening notions were racing through his mind, but one idea dominated: that this guard wanted an excuse to beat him up, and that he was trying to provoke him into making a wrong move.

"You got any cigarettes on you?" Mr Croy asked.

Huey shook his head.

"We'll see. Strip. Throw your clothes out here. Shoes too."

"I've got this," Huey said in a tight voice. He held out the bottle of calomine lotion. "They gave it to me in the hospital this morning."

"What's it for?"

"I got some bedbug bites at the precinct house. It's calomine lotion."

Mr Croy uncorked the bottle, smelled it, rubbed some on his hand. Then he nodded and returned it. "You can keep it." He took Huey's shirt.

"Yes, sir," Mr Fuhr said venomously, "this black son of a bitch is full of complaints about how this jail is run. Complained to the lieutenant about the way I do my job."

"You don't say," responded Mr Croy, as he examined the shirt.

"This is one coon who could use a little working-over," Mr Fuhr said insinuatingly, in a lowered voice. "He needs to learn some manners."

Mr Croy paused in his work. He gazed intently at the slender, angry-eyed officer by his side. Then he said in his rumbling monotone: "Take it easy, feller."

"I'm taking it easy, how about you?" the other enquired in the same insinuating manner.

"Down here's my responsibility," Mr Croy replied firmly. "I ain't breakin' no rules."

"Didn't ask you to."

Mr Croy said nothing. He began examining Huey's trousers. A moment later, with a slight grimace of anger, Mr Fuhr picked up Huey's shoes and began removing the laces. Then he launched into talk again. "Isn't he an ugly son of a bitch, though? They ain't come very far from the apes, have they? Give him a tail and you sure couldn't tell him from a monkey."

"Take it easy, will ya?" Mr Croy said with impatience. He tossed shirt and trousers back to Huey. "Get dressed. Now pay attention: the rule in here is silence. No talkin', whistlin' or singin'. No knockin' on the walls. You'll get two pieces of bread three times a day, and a mattress at night to sleep on. Let him have his shoes, Mr Fuhr."

"Sure." Mr Fuhr was holding both shoes with the fingers of his right hand, his arm held across his own body. Without warning, using all of his strength, he flung them at Huey. One shoe struck him on* the hip and the other hit him in the groin. The latter was a punishing blow. Huey gasped violently and then stood rigid, unable for the moment to breathe, while the pain spread its fire to his belly and chest.

"Goddamn you!" Mr Croy cried explosively. "What the hell you do that for?"

"Keep your voice down," Mr Fuhr retorted in a whisper. "It was an accident. They slipped out of my hand."

"Crap!"

"You going to report me, Mr Croy?"

"If it comes to anything, I'm protecting my record," Croy replied in a threatening voice.

"It won't come to anything."

"You think he won't beef?"

"One nigger has no beef when two guards say otherwise."

Mr Croy stared at him in anger, then turned to Huey, who was beginning to breathe more normally. With a decisive gesture Mr Croy slammed the door shut and locked it.

"Get out of here," he said to Mr Fuhr.

"Sure," the other replied, smiling. "Take it easy, Pop, huh?"

Within the pitch-dark cell Huey stood where he was. The pain was passing slowly.

Chapter 13

The Afternoon Drag

At half-past two in the afternoon the recreation period for the white inmates came to an end. Fifty-odd men clattered down the iron staircase, leaving behind the invisible debris of their conversation (about which no one ever was troubled) and a litter of cigarette butts; one man with a push broom remained to take care of the latter.

On the first tier, with a familiar, metallic clamour, all cell doors opened in unison. Except for half a dozen men on work detail, all of the other inmates stepped quickly into their burrows. The heavy doors slid back, locking with a stupendous crash as though a vast iron shutter had been slammed down over the range. For a brief interval harsh, percussive echoes hurtled back from the wall* and roof, slashing through the cottony heat of the wing. A few moments later the soughing rustle of men's voices began to be heard along with the varied other sounds normal to a cell block: water running into sinks; a hacking tobacco cough from the third tier; the thud of a fist on a steel wall, signifying that the commodity exchange had reopened. By two fifty-five the tier runway and staircase had been swept and scrubbed down, and the guard was checking the equipment to be sure that no one had hidden a mop handle in his cell. By three ten the men of the work detail had enjoyed their showers and were back in their cells. Shortly afterwards the loudspeaker came on with a programme of popular music, and the inmates of the west wing settled down to the afternoon drag.

The shank of the afternoon was always* heavy time, but it was especially dull on a Monday without books. The music on the loudspeaker was as much irritant as diversion, because the acoustics of the building made a raucous hash of most sounds. Men lay on their bunks in bored somnolence, dozing, dreaming, wishing, feeling exhausted from nothing and from everything. As a result, there was an inevitable stir of interest when a number of men who had left for court early that morning appeared at the range gate and were admitted by the guard.

There were seven in all, Jude and Varney from the first tier, five from Tier Three. As they traversed the eating range on their way to the rear of the wing, faces appeared behind cell doors and voices called in low tones, "Hey... how'd you come out... how much time you get?" It was not curiosity alone that prompted this concern. A kind of solidarity was at work here, the peculiar brotherhood that unites men behind bars – not by ties of affection or aspiration, as with those who struggle for a common cause, but by bonds of loneliness, self-pity and common resentment. For this reason, when a man from Tier Three replied to a stranger on Tier One "Just a little ol' six years, that's all", the latter called "Tough luck, boy", and for the moment felt genuine sympathy.

As the five men from the upper tiers disappeared on the staircase, attention centred on Varney and Jude, who now were walking back on the tier runway towards their cells. Jude's face was beaming with triumph. On the bus ride from the District Courthouse he had been sensitive enough to restrain his glee, because he was handcuffed to Varney. Once inside the cell block, however, with the eyes of other inmates upon him, he could think of nothing but himself. He walked with a strutting posture that said "Look at me, look at me"; he held up two fingers to indicate his sentence; he left little droppings of triumph at every cell door he passed. "Pulled only a deuce when I could've gotten ten... Buddy, you should have seen the way that female jedge went for me... It pays t'be borned handsome, fellers... Jus' a lil ol' rest cure an' I'll be back on the street..."

Varney was silent. Of the seven men he was the only one who had failed to respond to the calls from the first tier.

Other men had returned from court with sentences equally as long as Varney's, but, unlike him, most returned with a rage that sustained them, or with the hope that they would achieve a reversal in a higher court, or a cut in sentence, or a pardon... a reprieve of some sort. Varney had neither hope nor rage to lean upon. He felt no rage, because he really felt no deep surprise over his sentence. Only for a moment had his conscious mind been shocked. In the innermost recess of his heart, to a degree that he himself was not aware, he always had been prepared for rejection and defeat. And now that defeat had come with such smashing finality, there was no resistance in his spirit, only a pained acceptance. For him this prison sentence was merely the completion of a lifelong pattern: of desertion by his father even before he was born, and of neglect and abuse by his mother; of the farmers who had exploited and cheated him, of the orphanage guardian who beat him and of years of hardship and loneliness. It was a part of all this that disaster should come to him at the very time in his life when he had achieved a plane of decent living, and in the manner it had! For a comfortable woman had lied about him to a comfortable jury, and a comfortable judge, between breakfast and lunch, had sentenced him to twenty-five years to life. Only one thing was left to Varney now, and he wanted it: to win a small, bitter cheat over the world that always had been so unfriendly to him; to refuse this judge, this woman, this nameless everybody, the satisfaction of his imprisonment. In the course of the past few hours he had entered a private world of his own. He was removed now from other men; he had passed beyond the point where either the sympathy or the encouragement of another human being could have any effective meaning for him. In his world there was only a bitterness that could not be borne, a hopelessness that was suffocating, and a single, compulsive need: of ending his anguish by self-destruction.

Johnny Lauter, who was standing on the tier runway with Eddie Quinn, had known immediately that his cellmate had received a heavy sentence. In Varney's sagging posture, in the dullness of his eyes and the waxen pallor of his features, there was a communication of despair that anyone could read. Quinn whispered: "Uh-uh – pulled a bad one." Lauter nodded, and they waited in silence as Varney entered the tier runway and approached them.

"Hello, Floyd," Lauter said sombrely, "how'd you make out?"

There was no response from Varney, merely an abstracted glance, as though Lauter were a stranger. He entered the cell they shared together, crossed immediately to the sink and thirstily drank some water. Then he stood very still, gazing at the tin cup in his hand. Lauter and Quinn exchanged glances and followed him inside. Lauter sat down on the lower bunk, while Quinn remained standing by the doorway. Quinn said softly: "Did you get a bad one, pal?"

Still holding the tin cup, Varney sank down on the wall seat and peered at Quinn with a frown, as though seeing him for the first time. He asked with annoyance "What?" and then said, "Yeah, a bad one."

"What was it?"

There was a pause. An unhealthy flush stained Varney's waxen face. "Twenty-five to life," he said, and suddenly clapped both hands over his face.

His dry sobs were terrible to hear. They were not loud or uncontrolled, but there was something about them that made the other men want to bolt from the cell. His weeping was more than sad, more than despairing: it was like the sobbing death cry of an animal.

Yet it passed quickly, almost as though too little life force were left to sustain such grief. After a few moments he straightened up in his seat, rubbed a coat sleeve over his eyes and reached into his pocket for a cigarette. But then, with the cigarette between his lips, he forgot to light it. He sat staring at the floor.

Quinn said, with a heartiness he did not feel: "Don't you worry, pal. I've seen plenty of these long sentences cut down before this. Ain't that right, Johnny?"

"Absolutely."

"You listenin', pal? A judge wants his name in the papers, so he hands out a big one. Ten days later he holds a private little session with your lawyer an' cuts it in half."

Varney remained silent. There was no way of knowing whether he was paying attention or not. Nevertheless Lauter said eagerly: "You take Marty Breen, who was in Atlanta with me. The army gave him sixty years for desertion an' rape. He served two years and they cut it to thirty. Before I left they cut it again to a flat fifteen. He'll probably be coming out any day now."

"Remember, you can appeal this, too," Quinn added.

Varney made no response. It was like talking to dead flesh. Nevertheless Quinn tried once more. "Your lawyer's gonna ask for a cut in sentence, ain't he?"

Slowly, frowning, Varney raised his eyes. "What?"

"I said – your lawyer's gonna try for a cut in sentence, ain't he?"

"Yeah, sure," Varney replied without interest.

The jazz music coming over the loudspeaker was suddenly interrupted. The voice of Authority came on: "All officers – make your three-thirty-five count, all officers make your count." The music came back on again.*

Quinn, glad of the excuse to leave, muttered: "Gotta get back for the count – see you later," and departed at once. Varney said nothing. A few moments later, however, as the guard passed their cell and looked inside, Varney seemed to become more alert. He said to Lauter "Afternoon count, huh?", stood up immediately and began to take off his clothes. The unlit cigarette was still between his lips. Quickly, with an air of purpose that Lauter could not understand, Varney stripped to his shorts. His jail blues were beneath his pillow, where he had placed them, neatly folded, that morning. The suit of clothes he had worn to court he now discarded without interest, throwing trousers and jacket in a heap on his bunk. Dressed, he began to survey the cell as though he were viewing it for the first time. When his glance fell upon the tin cup on the wall table, he picked it up, stared at it with close absorption as he had earlier and then set it down again. Once more he scrutinized the cell. Suddenly, he snatched his toothbrush off the cardboard shelf above the sink. Frowning, intent, he stared at it. He tested its tensile strength between his fingers. Utterly absorbed, ignoring Lauter's presence, he knelt down and began rubbing the end of the handle on the concrete floor. After a dozen strokes he inspected it. The handle was made of plastic, and the friction of the rubbing already had left a mark.

Lauter called out to him sharply, "What's on your mind, Floyd?"

Quickly, as though startled, Varney turned round.* He stared at his cellmate. There was a hot feverishness in his eyes that had not been there a little while before. He said with animosity: "Nothin'." Then he sat down on the wall seat with his back to the front of the cell. He began to rub the end of the toothbrush on the floor, turning it from side to side after each several strokes.

Lauter stood up and walked closer. He asked sternly: "What're you makin' a shiv for?" There was no reply from Varney. He blew dust off the handle end and continued his work.

"Floyd!"

Silence.

Lauter touched Varney's shoulder, then suddenly shook him. Varney turned round* with an angry frown.

"What are you makin' a shiv for?"

For the first time since he had entered the cell, Varney made direct contact. He asked softly: "Let me alone, Johnny, huh?"

"Tell me."

"Let me alone, for Chrissakes."

"I want an answer."

"It's none of your business."

Touching his arm, Lauter said: "Look, Floyd—"

Angrily Varney shook off the hand. "You don't let me alone, goddamn it, I'm gonna go wild, you hear me? Get away from me now."

Lauter did not move. He said quietly: "I got my rulin' today. They ain't gonna extradite me. I'm goin' free this afternoon or tomorrow, probably tomorrow."

A puzzled look came over Varney's face, as though he had heard something that was tantalizing, yet not altogether comprehensible. He sat still, obviously trying to focus his thoughts. Then his eyes widened. "Goin' free?"

"Yeah."

It seemed to Lauter as though the other man were shrivelling physically before his eyes, becoming smaller in his seat. After a moment Varney whispered "That's fine, Johnny", and there was such envy and aching sorrow in his tone as to make Lauter quiver. It took another time-server to understand – and God, yes, he understood. If it had been possible, he would have kept this news a secret from Varney until his release. But there was too much at stake here, and Varney had to understand it.

"Listen, pal," he said bluntly, "what happens to me if you kill yourself? I'm gonna be charged with murder. You don't wanna do that to me."

Varney stared at him with feverish eyes, but said nothing.

"You ain't got the right to spoil things for me," Lauter continued, in the same blunt manner. But then, more gently: "For your own sake, too, you oughta think it over a little. Right now you're punchy. You can't think straight."

"I'm thinking straight," Varney answered hoarsely. "I know what I'm doin'."

"Aw listen, pal," Lauter said persuasively, "a man can always kill himself. What's your hurry? Suppose next week the judge cuts your sentence?"

Varney shook his head. "He won't."

"How do you know till your lawyer tries?"

"My lawyer asked for the minimum," Varney answered dully. "The US Attorney asked for ten to thirty. It was the judge raised it over both of 'em. He ain't gonna cut it – he knew what he was doin'."

"But a man oughtn't to give up till he knows for sure. You still got an appeal too. You're givin' up too easy, Floyd."

Varney said nothing.

"An' listen, kid," Lauter continued eagerly, "it ain't so bad in them big pens as you think. You can't judge by a lousy jailhouse like this. You get a job an' it makes the day go. There's plenty of recreation – movies* once a week, a ball game on Sunday, checkers, ping-pong. You make good buddies with one or two guys. You..." Lauter stopped. He could see that he had lost ground. Varney's eyes had gone dull, and his face was slack and grey with despair. It had been exactly the wrong thing to say. "Well, anyway," he burst out passionately, "you got no right to get *me* into trouble! That's no way for one man to do to another. You hear me?"

Varney replied slowly, dully: "You won't get in trouble, Johnny. I'll wait till night."

"For Chrissake, how does that protect me?"

Varney hesitated. "You can say you were asleep."

"Great! Why's that gonna stop 'em from hangin' a murder rap on me? Floyd, you're so punchy you can't think. Your brain ain't workin' at all. We'll be locked up in this cell together an' they find you dead. I got a long record. Don't you know what they can do with that?"

"I'll write a note," Varney said stubbornly. "I'll put you in the clear."

"Shit!" Lauter snapped. "Don't tell me to gamble my life on a note. Even if I get cleared of it, I'll be held here for weeks while they investigate an' work me over. No, sir, I ain't buyin' it. I'm goin' home to my family tomorrow, an' nothin's stoppin' me!" His mouth worked for a moment, and then he said roughly: "You wanna knock yourself off, that's your own business, but be a man about it. Wait till I'm out of here – I'll be gone tomorrow for sure."

Varney looked at him and then down at the toothbrush.

"Gimme it," Lauter said. He held out his hand.

With a convulsive movement Varney jerked the toothbrush out of Lauter's reach.

"You goddamn lunatic," Lauter exploded, "all I gotta do is walk out of here an' tell the screw what you're up to, don't you know that? You make me, I'll do it!"

Wretchedly, brokenly, Varney whispered: "No, Johnny, you're my pal, you wouldn't stool on me."

"Stool? Where'd you learn that word?" Lauter asked savagely. "I'm supposed to stand by an' let you hang a murder rap on me? Why, you double-crossing punk, if you don't stop workin' on that shiv, you'll see what I'll do."

"I don't want to double-cross you," Varney said with a whimper. "I don't want to get you into trouble." He began to sob again in the same dreadful, hopeless manner as before. "I can't take it, Johnny. I don't wanna see tomorrow. Maybe tomorrow I won't have the guts for it."

"I'm sorry, Floyd," Lauter said sternly, "but I'm lookin' out for myself. There's no way I can help you, but you *gotta* help me. I'm goin' free, an' I won't let you stop me."

"I won't stop you," Varney said. "I'll find a way to put you in the clear."

"How?"

"I don't know yet. Maybe you'll go out before tonight."

"It don't look like it."

"I won't do it if you're not in the clear, Johnny. I mean that! I swear it!"

261

"Then why don't you stop workin' on that shiv till I'm gone?"

"No," Varney replied in a frightened manner. "No! I'm wrappin' it up tonight – tonight. I never want to see tomorrow. But you'll be in the clear. I'll find a way." Suddenly, as though some inner fury had exploded within him, he swung round* on the wall seat with his back to the front of the cell. With fierce intensity he began to rub the end of the toothbrush handle on the floor.

"You hadn't oughta be thinkin' of it for your own self either," Lauter said morosely. "A man shouldn't give up so easy."

Varney did not reply. There was a long silence.

"I'm goin' out of here," Lauter announced abruptly. "Between now an' supper I'm stayin' out, givin' myself an alibi. Before we get locked up for the night, you're gonna give me that shiv or I'll damn well call the screw. I ain't takin' no chances on a double-cross. You hear me?"

Varney kept silent. Lauter walked out.

The two young men who had fought at dinner and who were being punished by confinement in the Hole were several cells removed from each other. As it happened, each of them was profoundly disturbed for reasons that, to some degree, were similar. These two, who were of the same age, were very different in personality, in the moral standards they accepted and in their intellectual development. Each thought of himself as an individual possessing initiative and free will, and this most certainly was true. Yet it* was equally true that both young men, who had issued from American loins upon the American earth, were in compulsive rebellion against the accepted order of their society.

It was the experience of the jail administration that no prediction could be made of the manner in which any individual would endure the solitude and darkness of the Hole, or the deprivation of food. The reactions of both Ballou and Wilson were more or less uniform in the first hour of their confinement. They found it unnerving to be alone in an impenetrable darkness, not to be able to see or to hear anything. In a curious way their minds comprehended the situation, while their senses could not. Their eyes carried on an unceasing struggle to see, and their ears kept straining for sounds. Yet, however unnatural the environment, both men began to relax to it after a time. It was only then that the real ordeal of existence in the Hole confronted them. While it was some hours before they would begin to have the ache of hunger, boredom and loneliness already were beginning to torment them.

CHAPTER 13

Ballou's first effort in self-defence was to try to* sleep. He lay down on the concrete floor, pillowed his head on his arms and shut his eyes. He was quite tired, because his sleep in the two nights past had been inadequate – yet, to his surprise, sleep eluded him. He changed his position, but the floor remained just as uncomfortable, and his mind was not at ease. He was, he realized, nervous and agitated, but he did not know why. Presently he sat up, rested his chin on his cupped hands and cursed softly. He was bored, very bored. How in hell, he wondered, did other men pass time in the Hole?

Suddenly he felt thirsty. He stood up and groped with outstretched hands towards the rear of the cell. He found the washbasin, put his mouth to the faucet and sucked from the flow. The sound of running water gave him unexpected pleasure, and he forced the tap down several times. He decided that he had discovered a form of entertainment. The rule of the Hole was silence, but he had found a way of making noise with impunity. "I got a right to take a drink of water, don't I?" he would reply if the guard came running.

Smiling in the darkness, Ballou kept the heel of his hand pressed down on the water tap while he waited for footsteps on the range outside. After a few minutes, not hearing any, he flushed the toilet half a dozen times in succession. Again he ran water in the sink and again he flushed the toilet.

Suddenly he was bored and vexed. He wanted to yell out at the top of his lungs "Screw you, you damn screw" and to pound on the door. It required effort to do neither.

He decided to take a walk. He pressed the fingers of one hand to the wall as a guide and, in this manner, moved round* the invisible cell. Half a dozen times he navigated the total area, which was small, and then he was bored with that entertainment also.

He sat down with his back to the wall and with his legs sprawled out. He knew suddenly what he wanted above everything else: a cigarette. His lips and throat were hungry for the feel and hot spice of a smoke. In a muffled tone he began to swear at the guard who had taken away his butts. But then, after only a few moments, he fell silent. He sat still, with his hands and teeth clenched. He was beginning to feel more and more agitated.

"Christ!" he suddenly muttered aloud. "What do other guys do in here?" He couldn't talk, he couldn't whistle, he couldn't sing, he couldn't smoke, read or play solitaire; he certainly couldn't sleep all the time. What else was there?

The obvious answer came to him: a man had to occupy himself by thinking. The sensible thing for him to do was to think of all the good times he ever had had, of funny jokes and cheerful things. That would be the way to make time pass comfortably.

Having instructed himself in this manner, Ballou at once began to think not of good times or cheerful things, but of an aspect of his life that was disagreeable and wounding: his relationship with his parents. Instantly he felt anger, resentment and contempt.

What a four-flusher* his father was, he thought – what a cheap liar! Bragging about the important guy he once was in the fight game, almost had a crack at the heavyweight championship. The old man's tin horn had sounded sweet when Ballou was only ten years old or twelve – until the day he'd gone to the library and looked up some back newspaper files and found out that the great muscle man was never any more than a four-round* preliminary slob, a punching bag with a glass jaw. What a blowhard! Always talking about how the boss down at the barrel plant thought so high of him that he was gonna make him foreman... Oh, sure! Only, he never got off the labour gang, and he never came home at night except he looked like a nigger from the muck on those second-hand oil drums, and it took him five years to get a raise of five cents an hour. But oh, brother, the way he could blab about raising his kids up right! He'd go down to Jerry's Family Saloon on a Saturday night, swill beer by the gallon and brag how he worked so hard to support his family. Only, he never forked up the money to buy his kid a pair of roller skates or a halfway decent ball glove, and it took a major operation to squeeze an ice-cream cone out of him. What a slob!

Ballou grimaced in the darkness, feeling contemptuous and superior. The memory of a recent conversation with his father caused him to chuckle harshly. He had returned to his home for the first time in ten days to be confronted with the news that his mother was in bed with pneumonia and his father had a lay-off from work. "Jeez, Art, I'm sure glad you turned up," his father had said. "Things is tough around here. I'm collectin' unemployment insurance, but that sure ain't enough with the doctor askin' three dollars every visit, an' medicines expensive as hell. Can you help me out, Art?"

It had been as sweet a moment as Ballou could remember. Here he was, eighteen years old, and his great big slob of a father was down on his knees to him, asking for help. He could have replied: "Tell you what, Pa – I'll pay for the doctor if you'll use your beer money for the medicine" – and that would have been sweet. But even sweeter had been the expression on his father's face when he had taken two fifty-dollar bills out of his wallet and handed them over without a word.

Thinking of it, Ballou chuckled out loud again. His father's face had taken on the look of a beef steer hit on the head by a mallet. In two weeks of work, forty-eight hours a week, the old slob never earned that much take-home pay. The big muscle man might be able to lift ten thousand oil drums a week, but when it came to the brains to get close to money, he was strictly missing.

"Jesus Christ, Art, how do you come by dough like this?" his father had cried out.

"I told you I got a job sellin' jewellery, didn't I?" he had replied. "I'm doin' pretty good."

"I'll say!" his father had exclaimed in wonder. "But it's strictly on the level, ain't it, Art? I mean – there's nothin' illegit about it, is there?"

How tempted he had been at that moment to tell the old man that it was illegitimate as hell, that it wasn't jewellery, but marijuana – and then see what he'd do! The old slob boasted so damn much about how he wasn't rich but he'd always led an honest life that it would have been a hot one to tell him the truth. "So maybe you wanna give me back the money, huh?" he would have asked – and what a pickle the old man would've been in then. But the joke wasn't worth the risk, and he had kept* his mouth shut. Then, as he had expected, the old slob had begun to cosy up to him. "Say, Art, what's the name of this company you're workin' for?... Listen, Art, how come you ain't home more? This is your home, you know."

Home! Three stinking rooms in a fire-trap tenement, with cockroaches in the sink and the smell of dead bugs coming out of the walls, with the toilet in the hall and three people waiting in line every time you had to go – and the old slob called it a "home"!

"I can't, Pa. My job keeps me travellin'," he had answered.

"But you come into Washington sometime, don't you?"

"Sure, but I got a pal who has an apartment. I stay with him."

"But we miss you, Art. Don't you miss seein' us? Your ma was sayin' to me only this mornin', 'I wish we could see Art.' A young feller has to go his own way in the world, I know that, but you oughtn't to forget us like you been doin' these past months. After all, we raised you up good as we could, Art, we took care of you – seems to me you oughta show us a little gratitude."

That was the biggest laugh of all! Nothing but nagging, complaints and lickings from the time he could remember, and he was supposed to show gratitude! "Art, why ain't you washed the windows yet? You promised if I gave you an ice cream you'd wash 'em right away. What kind of a little cheat are you? You want me to tell your pa? You know what *he'll* do."

"Pa, Art wouldn't go to the store for me today. I called to him in the hallway, but he ran down like he didn't hear me."

"Is that so?" Bang! Wallop! "Maybe that'll make your hearin' better, huh? What kind of a son are you?"

"Pa – the truant officer was here today. Art ain't been to school all week."

"What? So that's the kind of a little sneak you are, hey? Takin' your books in the mornin' an' comin' back sweet as pie in the afternoon – by God, I'll knock the sneakiness out of you if it's the last thing I ever do!"

Sitting in the darkness of this isolation cell, Ballou shivered with the same frustration and anguish and rage that those beatings always had made him feel. How many times he had sworn that the day would come when he'd give his old man a licking that would send him to the hospital. That time hadn't come yet – the old man was still in his forties and strong as an ox – but it would, it would. And in the mean time he'd play the old slob like a fish on a line. He'd hooked him good with that hundred dollars, but real good. There'd be no more money like that. Maybe once a month he'd show up at home to let the old man work his big ass off for a touch – and then he'd say: "Sorry, Pa, I'm payin' for that new car of mine an' it's keepin' me broke, but here's a dollar if that'll help." Christ, it was going to be sweet – he'd play that game until the old bastard was twisted into a pretzel.

Ballou spat on the floor. He felt angry and irritated. He had started out to think of funny things and good times, and he had ended wanting to smash somebody in the face. The worst of it all, the one thing he never could forgive his father for was the way he was so satisfied with himself. Satisfied to live in that lousy dump, satisfied to work year after year in that lousy job, satisfied to come home every night so covered with oil he looked like a nigger. How many times the kids on the block had sidled up to him grinning all over, and cracked wise about it... "No crap, Art, your whole family's part coon, ain't it?" But when he had repeated it to his father, all he ever got was a laugh. The old man never had been ashamed: he was too much of a slob to be ashamed of anything.

Again Ballou spat on the floor. Then, with irritation, he told himself that there were better things to put his mind on. He got to his feet, put one hand on the wall and began again to circle the cell.

He started to think of a girl he had taken up to Joe Davis's apartment on the Friday afternoon just past. In his mind's eye he recalled how she had looked on the bed as he had been undressing her. The memory excited him. The little chick had been so high with marijuana that she hadn't even known what he was doing, and when she'd come out of it and seen the blood on the sheet, she'd cried for an hour. But she hadn't said "no" when he'd gone after her again, and she'd even paid for the reefers beforehand. It was a sweet, sweet racket he'd gotten into – he was cosy, cosy... he could tell the world what living *was*!

Ballou stopped walking. A paralysing thought had come to him very suddenly. He began to tremble under the weight of it. He was the one who had recognized the nigger, Wilson, on the street Saturday night. He was the one who had suggested they give him the works. But now Joe Davis was in the hospital with a broken jaw – *and suppose Joe blamed him for what had happened?*

Slowly Ballou lowered himself to the floor on legs that seemed to have turned to rubber. He was so frightened that he could not think. Mind and heart were overwhelmed by a vision of disaster. He needed Joe Davis like a vine needed a tree, but Joe didn't need him. The hundred and fifty dollars a week he had been pulling down for the past four months depended on Joe. It was Joe who had the police connections they needed. It was Joe who had the tie-up with the wholesaler. It was Joe's apartment they used to push the stuff. The whole operation depended on Joe – and what would happen now if Joe kicked him out of it?... Where would he be then?

He'd be in the gutter – he'd be nothing! He'd be an eighteen-year-old kid with no place to go. There was no use fooling himself that *he* could start a set-up just as good. He hadn't realized before this how damn tight Joe had kept the strings in his own hands. The key to their whole success was the detective in the narcotics bureau that Joe paid off. That was what prevented raids, or would give them a tip-off if a raid was coming. There was no way to be safe in a racket like this, especially when you were pushing the stuff with high-school kids, without* good police connections. So whose bar and grill was it that the headquarters police had been going to for twenty years? The one belonging to old man Davis. And it was Joe Davis who had worked up the marijuana angle without his old man even knowing about it.

That was the trap in his sweet little racket: it was all in the hands of Joe Davis. Joe had the connections and the money to operate with. And if Joe turned on him, he'd be finished. From being on top of the world he'd be nowhere. He didn't want to be a fool like Tom Feeny, who had pulled off a couple of stick-ups, walked around like a big shot for three months and then ended up in Leavenworth with a fifteen-year sentence. And he damn well didn't want to live like Freddy Pyle, another slob like his father, doing pick-and-shovel work for seventy-five cents an hour. As far as Art Ballou was concerned, that was as bad as being in prison – it was just a life of back-breaking nigger slavery. Christ, only once in a lifetime did a fellow make a wonderful connection like he had with Joe Davis… easy work, money comin' in, all the girls he wanted…

Ballou sat very still, huddled against the wall, his knees drawn up against his chest, his head sagging down. He felt lonely and frightened and full of meanness, as he had so many times in his childhood when his mother had locked him in her dark bedroom closet in order to punish him. Savagely he told himself that if Joe Davis double-crossed him it wouldn't end there – hell no! After all he'd done to build up the business, he wouldn't take it lying down. Joe might be paying off to the city cops, but he wasn't paying off to the federals. A little phone call to the federals and Joe Davis would be on his way to Atlanta.

This thought, that he was not helpless to retaliate if he got a dirty deal, was very heartening. It made him feel much stronger in the situation. Dwelling on it with relish, he realized something else: that the sheer threat of what he could do might make his partner think things over. Joe could be as sore as he liked over what had happened, but he wasn't dumb. He'd get the point – he'd either have to play along with Art Ballou or give up his nice little racket altogether.

No, Christ no, Ballou thought suddenly, he was way off the beam – this damn Hole was making him lose his senses. The worst move he could make was to threaten Joe Davis. Joe was smart – smarter than he was, he was willing to admit it. If he could think of a double-cross, so could Joe. All Joe needed to do was to pretend that he was taking it lying down. A couple of days* later there would be a raid when he was handling the apartment alone, and that would be it. It would be Art Ballou who would be going to a pen, not Joe Davis.

Feeling tense and distraught, Ballou got to his feet. With one hand pressed to the wall, he began to circle the cell. His need for a cigarette was tormenting. If only, he thought, he could get out of this place and see Joe in the hospital! For all he knew, this was all in his own imagination. Up till now he and Joe had worked together like two pieces of silk. They not only were business partners, they were friends. Wasn't it Joe who had been saying all along that he couldn't work the high-school angle without Art? In the first place Joe was the daytime manager of his father's grill. In the second place no man of twenty-five could push marijuana around a high school. Joe could sell in other ways, but this high-school outlet was the best one he had at the moment. It was Art Ballou who had gone back to his old high school and drummed up the trade. And gotten into other neighbourhoods too! Why, a week didn't pass without Joe saying what a good job he'd been doing. And wasn't it true that Joe was as scared of Central High turning into a nigger school as he was? They'd talked it over, and Joe had sent him out to get as many kids as he could to that demonstration. Once the coons took over Central High, they'd lose that good outlet to nigger pushers – Joe knew that as well as he did.

So what was he worrying about so much? What was all this damn imagining for? He'd gotten into a sweat over nothing at all. Joe was a good sport – ten to one he wouldn't hold this against a buddy. Laid up in a hospital, he needed a partner even more now than before. It was only the other day he was talking about how the two of them were going to build bigger and bigger. There wasn't nearly the money in marijuana that there was in heroin, and Joe had ideas about that. There was good money in call girls too, and Joe had been including him in *all* of his plans. "I'm the boss and you're my manager, Art," Joe had said only last week. "You stick with me and you'll end up on top, kid – right on top." So what was there to worry about? What was all the sweating for?

Several cells away, a toilet flushed, and the noise broke into Ballou's thoughts. Instantly he began to think of Wilson. He told himself that he hated all niggers on general principle, but with this Wilson fellow it had become personal now. He wished to hell he hadn't been so scared to use his knife like he should have. He had been waiting for the chance to carve his initials on that coon face, but what he should have done was cut his damn eyeballs out.

Ballou sat down suddenly. The darkness and the silence had become very oppressive to him again. He had the nasty, helpless feeling of being back in that damn bedroom closet his mother always shoved him into. "That'll teach you to lie to me. Now you just stay in there till your pa comes home, and then we'll see what *he'll* do." Christ, he thought, he would have had a better time of it if he had been brought up in an orphanage.

"Never mind, kid, you're livin' sweet now," he suddenly muttered aloud. The image of the girl he had had on Friday came back to him. He stretched out on the floor and began to think about her. He told himself happily that there were going to be a lot of chicks like that in his life, a lot. There was a sweet life ahead for Art Ballou. He was on the beam. He'd ride that beam – and to hell with the suckers and the slobs.

Tired now, he drifted off to sleep.

Huey Wilson was three cells removed from Ballou. It was more than an hour since the two guards had left him, but Huey's rage was only just subsiding. The physical pain of being struck in the groin had passed after the first several minutes, but the painful fury in his heart had not. It had seemed to Huey as though he would burst from the violent feelings he could not express. At one moment, seeking relief, he had knelt down and beaten his fists on the concrete floor. It had seemed to him that never, never had he felt such anger at the domineering insolence of the white world. And yet, as he knew, it was not true: it was only his mood of the moment, because a thousand times before he had felt anger or heartsickness or indignation equal to this – and what Negro had not? This was the very manner in which Negroes lived in the United States: enduring, always enduring, striking out for their freedom at every opportunity, but so often forced to live with angry hearts and clenched teeth, having no way in a given moment except to endure in silence.

For a while then, out of the intensity of his feelings, Huey had forgotten everything that had been good and joyous in his past years and had remembered only the indignities, the insults, the pain of white domination. An image had come to him, clear and devastating, of a day in which he had gone shopping with his mother. He had been four, or perhaps five, not too young for instruction in the etiquette of Jim Crow – and he had received it. There had been a railing down the centre of the store, with whites buying on one side and Negroes on the other. Although he had been in this store before, Huey had wondered at the railing for the first time, and had asked his mother. "Hush," she had replied, "I'll tell you later." Ah, the keen sorrow of that day for them both! On the other side of the railing it was not difficult for a woman to buy a hat or a dress, because she could try different sizes and styles until she found the right one. But on their side it was forbidden to try on anything without buying it. So, when his mother had paid over the hard-saved sum, and when they were out on the street where she could try on what never could be exchanged, the pretty new hat for Easter was found to be too small. She had burst into tears openly, there on the street, sobbing with frustration and outrage and helplessness. Huey had cried along with her, not understanding fully, but beginning to learn about life in his distress at seeing big Mother, strong Mother, crying like a child for all to see. And such were the daily, small lynchings to be endured.

Huey's mind had turned then to the wretched Negro slums of Charlottesville – Cox's Row, that ran off his own street, Happy Hollow, the Gas House District, and the worst of them all, Old Scottsville Road. Unpaved areas, without sewage, without lights in the streets or water in the homes! Ill-built, tumbledown shacks owned by white real-estate sharks, who charged the high rents made possible by segregation. Poverty, dirt and malnutrition nurturing disease, vice and crime – the ugly fruits of oppression.

And how quickly a Negro boy learnt that this job was for coloured, but that was not! How quickly he was taught that this park, this section of the street car, this part of the movie house,* this church of God were not for him! And how quickly he learnt also the penalty for transgression! He had recalled the* hot summer day when he and his brother had walked into the country to pick blueberries. Their mother had promised them a pie for their labour, and they knew that their father had a great fondness for berry pie, and they had felt big with a sense of their share in family life. Then, in a stretch of woods, they had come upon a man, the remains of a young Negro man. His skull was smashed, and one hand had been hacked off. His genitalia had been amputated and stuffed into his mouth. And the letters KKK had been cut into his chest with a knife. In that, and in other ways, were young Negro boys taught the meaning of white supremacy. As by a pair of shoes in the hands of a prison guard! '

But now, in the passing of this hour, Huey had felt his rage through to the end, only to find that it was neither here nor there. What was here was darkness, silence, aloneness – and the gnawing worry over what would happen to him.

From the time that the heavy steel door had closed upon him, he had been too tense with feeling to sit or lie down. At first, by pacing off the length of his cell, he had learnt that five steps would take him from wall to wall. He had begun to walk then, automatically counting his steps while thinking of other things, only to find suddenly that he had struck a wall with his foot, and very nearly with his face as well. By orientating himself with his hands, he had perceived that in the darkness he had not been walking in a straight line, and that he had run into a side wall. Thereafter, like Ballou, he had circled the cell, one hand on the wall for guidance, reversing his direction when his arm became tired.

Now he was tired all over, the anger replaced by a feeling of nervous exhaustion. He sat down with his back against a wall, but his sore tail bone made the position uncomfortable. He stretched out at full length on his stomach, resting his face on one arm, and found that he was as weary as though he just had finished a day's farm work. He told himself that it would do him good to sleep for a while, but his eyes remained open, staring at the darkness.

He realized what it was he wanted to know: the exact time.

How long had he been in the Hole? He didn't know – it seemed like hours, six or seven, yet he knew it couldn't be long at all. His sense of time had deserted him. In normal life he always could guess what the hour was with reasonable accuracy, but right now he didn't know whether it was two o'clock or five. And yet it was important for him to know! If it was two o'clock, there still was the possibility that he would be called out for a hearing, but if it was evening already...

Restlessly he got to his feet and began again to circle the cell. It had been only this morning, after seeing his brother and Professor Herrin, that he had thought to himself that it was wonderful not to be alone in the world. But now he felt utterly alone, intolerably alone and lonely. Even worse, it was his own fault that he was in the Hole. Throughout the day he had been making an utter fool of himself! Talking like a jackass in front of a big man like Herrin, a professor of Law – the man must have thought he was dealing with a jerk! Somehow his feelings always got the better of him, making him say things or do things that later seemed completely stupid. With McPeak running out on him and the odds so heavy against him, it was absolutely right for Herrin to suggest a deal if they could arrange one. But he hadn't stopped to think about that – he had shot off his big mouth about how he wanted to fight this on principle.

And what a fine mess of things he had made with McPeak! Jeff would have handled a man like that – he could have drawn out the best in him. Now McPeak was out of jail, or would be leaving – and where was he? In a black hole, because he had lost his temper in a white man's jail! From morning to night he'd been acting like a child. It took a man with sense in his head and balance in his character to climb over the barriers of discrimination. His father always had told him that, and he had known it from reading about Negroes who had accomplished things. But if you were too weak or too headstrong, you didn't end up big or successful: you ended up in one sort of a hole or another, like Huey Wilson.

He lay down on the floor again. His heart suddenly felt so heavy and so full of woe that he wanted to weep. He would be held, convicted and sent up, he knew it now. Herrin could say what he wanted about arranging a deal for a misdemeanour, but if the police could keep it a felony, they would. And so Huey Wilson would become a number in prison for up to five years, and when he came out he'd be up cripple creek – college gone, law career gone, dreams gone.

Oh, those dreams! he thought bitterly. Piled up one on the other like summer clouds! He'd been dreaming those big fool dreams since the time Jeff first had started his scrapbook. How many hours they'd spent over those newspaper photographs, Jeff telling him who everybody was, both of them dreaming!

"Who's this old man, Huey?"

"George Washington Carver."*

"Who's he?"

"A big scientist, one of the biggest in the country on farming."

"And who's this?"

"I forget."

"Carter Woodson* – he's a teacher and a history writer. Mr Elkins says he's a great scholar."

"What's a scholar?"

"A scholar is…"

So for hours upon hours, memorizing the names, the faces, the achievements of Dr Du Bois and Paul Robeson, of Marian Anderson and Roland Hayes, of Walter White and Charles Houston,* of band leaders and blues singers and theatrical stars – of all who had climbed over the barriers to fame, to success, to achievement for their people.

And oh, the private dreams of glory, not even shared with his brother… The recurrent image before sleep – Huey Wilson outlining the theory of an important case to other attorneys of the NAACP, and Huey Wilson arguing before the Supreme Court, eloquent, on fire with knowledge and determination like Thurgood Marshall,* fighting for the rights of his people before the eyes of the whole nation.

And the tender dreams – of buying a fine big house for his parents, modern and wonderfully equipped, and giving them all the money they needed to furnish it, and giving his mother a thousand dollars more so she could visit the brother and sister she had not seen for so many years.

And the intimate, flattering dreams – of meeting the great figures he had admired so long, of being well dressed and accepted by them as an

273

equal because he, too, was important in the world. He would be doing great things, and everybody at the fraternity dance would know it, and the lovely girl in his arms would know it also, and she would be smiling at him with glowing eyes…

Only three days ago these dreams had seemed possible. His life had been so smooth – no trouble, everything in its place. Now he and his dreams were in a jail, a Hole, a courtroom, a prison!

Of a sudden the struggle of living felt too formidable for Huey's eighteen years. "Get ahead, get ahead," his family always had preached. But despite all his efforts, this was where he had arrived: at disaster!

Tears came, and he muffled his sobs with a hand over his mouth. He felt wounded beyond repair.

What was it that gave a man conscience, McPeak was asking of himself – that could make a simple decision so hard to arrive at, and that, once it was made, could fill his mind with images of pointing fingers and contemptuous faces? At recreation he had decided, but the decision was like ground glass in his belly. One memory was especially tormenting. It had been evoked by Otha Doty with his tale of a Negro buddy killed in a mine accident, and of how Doty had fought to save him. A lesson in human brotherhood – McPeak understood that – and it stung. The labour movement had a slogan in which he deeply believed: an injury to one is an injury to all – but he never had thought that it would turn into a bed of nails for him to lie upon.

During the great sit-down strike McPeak had seen many acts of brother-hood, but one especially had been unforgettable, and he could not thrust it out of his mind now. Four weeks after the beginning of the strike he had received permission to leave the plant because of the birth of his first child. He had, however, continued to put in regular picket duty outside the plant. One frozen winter morning the headquarters of the union had sent out an emergency call for manpower. At one of the plants, Briggs Meldrum,* an attempt was being made to break the picket lines by police force and to run* in scabs. Reinforcements were needed.

By the time the contingent of men arrived from Bohn Aluminum, the wide street in front of the factory was almost obscured by the smoke of tear-gas bombs. Police, scabs, strikers were in wild combat, with posses-sion of several* factory gates as prize. Even now, almost ten years later, McPeak could remember the terrible confusion of the scene – the sight of bleeding faces, of coughing men with eyes streaming… the wild cries and commands... the knots of men in physical struggle... and the sense of excitement and fear that had exploded within him. At a direction from a picket captain his contingent had rushed forward to defend a weak point. They were met by a barrage of tear-gas bombs from the police. A man at McPeak's side was struck on the forehead by one of the canisters. He staggered back with a cry and then sank to one knee in a daze. McPeak, observing some of the others, seized the bomb at the cost of a burnt hand and hurled it back. With his eyes streaming, and cursing wildly, he hurled back a second. But then came a charge of mounted police, and, in their area, the union men broke ranks and ran to* safety.

It was only then that he saw the man who had been at his side, and whom he had forgotten. Isolated, still dazed, his vision affected by the tear gas, the man stood helpless, a target for the police. A glancing blow on his back from the club of a rider sent him staggering against the flank of another's horse. The horse wheeled and knocked him to his knees. McPeak, like a hundred others who were in a position to see what was happening, stood paralysed with horror. In his mind's eye now he still could see the young striker on his knees, the uncovered blond head and the arc of the policeman's club rising high for a blow. It never fell. Out of the whirl and smoke and confusion a man appeared, leaping at the rider with reckless passion. He caught the policeman's arm from behind and ripped the man himself out of his saddle. He ducked away as the horse reared, and then, seeing his chance, leapt to the picket on the ground. In one explosive movement* he bent, swung the young man over his shoulder like a bag of flour and ran for safety. Two of the mounted police pursued him, but he wheeled and turned, and avoided their clubs until, with a rush, a mass of the pickets ran forward to his aid and the policemen retreated.

McPeak understood then, as he understood now, the full significance of the act. It had gone beyond the union creed that an injury to one was an injury to all. It had been human brotherhood on the highest plane, and it had made him feel better as a man, because he had witnessed it. With pride in himself he had remembered it on Saturday night, glad that unthinkingly, upon decent impulse alone, he had done something of the same sort. Yet it had been impulse, and now the impulse was gone. And what was it, he wondered, that separated a man's heart from his head like this? His heart still wanted to stand by Huey Wilson, but in his mind he already was out of this jail, clear of it all, ready to keep his mouth shut if they'd only leave him alone.

Wearily, with cynicism, he reflected that all men had some things on their conscience they were ashamed about, and there was no reason why he should be an exception. He wished Huey Wilson the very best, but as they said down home, every fox looks out for its own cubs. He'd had as much of this mental strain as a man with high blood pressure could afford. The doctors said a little alcohol once a day was good for high* blood pressure, and he'd tell the world he'd use more than a little of that medicine if he got out tonight. Five minutes after Detective Stoner let him go, he'd be having his first beer in a saloon. He'd drink his way right down to his sister's house, and to hell with explanations – he'd be stewed, that's all, and they could lump it.

Chapter 14

The Cocktail Hour

In the west wing of CB1 the inmates were emerging from several hours of apathy to a state of greater liveliness. The heat in the cell block was diminishing, and the mess men already had passed through to serve supper in the east wing. Men were washing up, and conversation was on the rise. Mr Kraft, tier guard for the eight hours past, had arrived at his three-room apartment and was exchanging the news of the day with his pregnant wife. Mr Jonas, who had replaced him, was brooding over the high cost of living, wondering whether the security of Federal employment was compensation for the low wage of a prison guard. It was four twenty in the afternoon, and jail life was moving on an even keel.

For Johnny Lauter, however, nothing was as usual, and he felt nervous enough to jump out of his skin. Seeking moral support, he had taken Eddie Quinn aside and told him that Varney intended to commit suicide. It presented an ugly problem, because the fundamental law of prison life was that no inmate ever informed upon another. Yet, as Quinn agreed, it was equally fundamental that no inmate caused trouble for another. Varney had the right to kill himself, but he had no right to place Lauter in jeopardy of a murder charge. In the light of this, the two friends arrived at a plan of action. Until supper time Lauter would stay outside of his cell and keep himself in view of other inmates. The moment for decision would come as soon as supper was over, when everyone was locked up for the night. They would ask Varney to hand his shiv over to Quinn for safe keeping until morning. If he refused, they would report him to Mr Jonas at once. A man in prison always could kill himself. There would be no essential harm done to Varney.

Although this plan seemed sound enough to protect Lauter from actual danger, he remained intensely nervous and sick at heart. He had the sense that he was sleepwalking through a nightmare rather than living in a world of reality. He liked Floyd Varney a great deal, and there was something fantastically unnatural in a situation where the other man was methodically preparing for suicide and he knew it. Indeed, it was the more incredible because one part of his mind could not forget, even for a moment, that by tomorrow morning he would be home with his family. To feel free, as he already did, to feel all of the goodness of life waiting for him outside – and yet to be in here and to have a cellmate preparing to die – was utterly unnerving. He felt intensely grateful to Quinn for the latter's understanding and moral support.

The two men were standing together in front of 112, making conversation with the occupants. Quite deliberately Quinn was trying to divert Lauter by a flow of bright chatter. Having run through a series of jokes, both fresh and stale, he was embarking upon something else. "Georgia Boy," he said to Hal Jude, "seein' as you pulled on'y a deuce today where any honest judge would've given you life, an' seein' how Johnny here is leavin' us, the drinks are on the house. What'll you have?"

"A gallon of beer, some rat cheese an' sour pickles," Jude responded immediately.

"Beer before supper?" Quinn enquired with raised eyebrows. "Are you a gentleman or just a low-down pickpocket?"

"Now, what's wrong with beer befoah supper?" Jude asked with a grin. "I like it fine."

"Rustle my bustle, it ain't etiquette – it's lower class. This is a high-class joint I'm runnin'. Don't you know gentlemen drink cocktails before supper? Where were you brung up?"

"OK, Barber, then I'll do like my pappy whenever he entertained sassiety – make mine white mule* with a little sody water."

"T-t-t-t-t!" Quinn protested gently. "White mule's illegal. We get caught drinkin' it, we'll all be sent up."

"Brother, we've done been sent," said Roy Keedy with a laugh. He sneezed violently.

Quinn peered at Keedy. "Who *is* this creature, Georgia – you ever seen him before?"

"Don't pay him no mind – just a convict."

"You mean a law-breaker in *my* saloon? What'd he do?"

"Got caught rapin' a duck in the park."

"It wasn't a duck, it wasn't in the park and it wasn't rape," Keedy commented cheerfully, "but it sure wasn't worth jail."

"Double Martini comin' up for Perfessor* Keedy," Quinn announced. He began an elaborate pantomime. "Twelve jiggers Gordon gin... half jigger dry Vermouth... shake with ice... strain into cold cuspidor... onion or olive, Perfessor?"

"Olive, please. Onions give me gas."

"Here you are, sir, hope it ain't too sweet. The usual for you, Mrs Lauter – Rum Daiquiri?"

"Only if you* join me, Mrs Quinn," Lauter responded, with as much lightness as he could.

"Indeed I will, indeed. Let's see now… one jigger Grenadine… one ounce lime juice… twenty jiggers light Bacardi… Give the Grenadine to Mrs Lauter, throw the lime juice in the sink an' Mrs Quinn'll drink what's left."

The men laughed. Quinn said gaily: "You know somethin'? Most hard drinkers settle down to straight whiskey, but I never did. I like cocktails, highballs, pure alcohol with orange juice, rum an' Coke, rum without Coke, brandy, wine, beer" – he flapped his tongue rapidly against his upper lip – "lup lup lup lup… stop talking like that, Mrs Quinn, you're drivin' Mr Quinn crazy."

"An' you're the one who wanted a cure," Lauter jeered affectionately.

"Wanted? I *am* cured. Offer me a drink."

"You know when you'll be on the wagon, Eddie? Not before you're in a box an' they're drivin' you to the cemetery."

"Oh, Chee-rist," Quinn laughed, "I can see it: they're just about to lower me into the grave. Standin' there is my ol' pal, Browney Carrera. He's cryin' so hard he can't bear it. So what does he do? He uncorks a bottle."

"An' what happens when he uncorks the bottle?" Lauter added. "You're stiff as a board, you got rigor mortis, but you sit right up an' open your mouth."

Quinn coughed with laughter. "It could happen."

"Say, fellows, I just thought of something," Roy Keedy put in seriously. "What happens to a man when he dies in prison?"

"What do y'mean what happens?" asked Jude.

"What do they do with the body? I'm sixty-one, I got to think about that."

"What do you think happens? They bury him."

"Sure, but where?"

"In the prison graveyard," Quinn put in quickly, "where do you think?"

"What?" Keedy asked with concern. "You mean to say if I die in prison and my brother comes to claim me, they won't give my body up? I'd want a decent burial at least, I'd want to be in my family plot where my folks are."

"It ain't allowed," Quinn told him seriously. "You gotta serve your time first. They put you in the graveyard an' make you serve your time. After that, your people can come an' get you."

"Why, the sons of guns!" Keedy exclaimed indignantly. He jumped up from his bunk and began to pace the cell in wrath. "If that isn't the meanest thing I ever heard of. It's criminal."

"There's somethin' even worse than that," Quinn told him gravely. "There was a case down in Lorton where a man died the same day he got parole. They let his wife come an' get him all right – but for the next six months she had to take him around to the parole officer once a week."

Jude exploded with laughter, though clapping a hand over his mouth to muffle the sound, and Keedy blushed for his own gullibility. "Here, have another cocktail," Quinn said happily.

Lauter alone was not amused. His thoughts had gone to Varney, and there was no relish for him in the jest. For all he knew, Varney might be dead right now. With effort, and with sour dismay in his heart, he said: "Another drink, Mrs Quinn, I feel like gettin' stewed tonight."

Varney was not dead, and he was finding that he was not as ready for the act of suicide as he had supposed. Since the moment that he had decided to kill himself, he had been clinging to the hope of an easy death by bleeding. In adolescence he had witnessed such a death, the result of a work accident. He always had remembered the fuzzy calm of the dying man, the quick stupor and lack of pain. This is what he had been planning for himself – one slash across an artery, and then a painless sinking into oblivion. But now it seemed impossible for him to achieve it with the weapon he had forged, and his flesh was recoiling from the alternatives that confronted him. In some forty minutes of steady work he had transformed his toothbrush into a lethal tool, but it was far from being a knife blade. He had worn down half an inch of the handle end into a kind of dagger tip that was triangular in shape. Although the point of the dagger was sharp, its sides were blunt. It was clear to him that it would take many hours of careful work to turn one side of the toothbrush into an actual cutting edge – and certainly it could not be accomplished by the time lights went out.

He did not want to wait for another day – yet he recoiled at what this dagger would require. He had tested it on his hand, and he knew that the point would not pierce his skin without substantial pressure. With this weapon there were only limited possibilities, and these were either impractical or beyond his will-power. To stab for his heart seemed certain of failure. The toothbrush, made of plastic, was neither rigid nor strong, and it was of a thickness that surely would cause it to hit bone and break.

To drive it into his eye, seeking the brain, was too horrible – he knew that he never could force himself to do it. He could find a pulse in his neck and try to plunge the dagger there – that would cause mortal bleeding if he struck hard enough, and *if* he was successful in piercing the artery. Yet it was all too likely that he would miss – he had tested this also by examining a surface vein in the hollow of his elbow. Again and again he had pressed the dagger point against the vein, and each time it had rolled to one side or another, away from the pressure, like a resistant rubber tube. He wanted things to be certain, not left to luck. What he needed was a tool that would cut. By itself alone, the toothbrush wouldn't do.

Hunched over the wall table, the toothbrush in his hands, Varney asked himself if he really did want to die or if it was only a passing mood. He asked this question of himself, and then, for a moment, his brain stopped functioning. Ever since court, his mind had been acting in this manner: feverishly alive for a while, giving him the sense that his thoughts were live coals in his skull – and then suddenly becoming torpid.

He sat still, staring at the toothbrush, yet hardly seeing it. The afternoon music hour had ended, and the routine noises of the cell block came to his ears – the murmur of idle talk, the sound of water running into a basin. Suddenly a door ground open on the third tier, and a shudder ran through him. God in heaven, the answer came, he did want to die! He had only to think of his sentence, of the endless, hopeless days and nights that lay before him, to know that he preferred death to that kind of existence. It would be twenty-five years before he'd even be eligible for parole. How could a man live like that – without any joy, without any hope for the next day? And what would he be like if they did let him out at fifty-five? He'd be out of his head like Wacky Mike. A first-degree verdict would have been easier on him than this. Any man could die once, but Floyd Varney wasn't built to die every day.

Varney's throat suddenly became swollen. Why, why, his mind asked, had this disaster happened to *him*? As though he'd been cursed from birth! It made a man want to scream out at the universe, to say: "*Look* at me – I didn't deserve this!" Abruptly his mind went torpid again. He sat very still, the muscles of his neck slack and his head sagging down. Then, out of nothing, he began to think of his attorney, George Combs. Combs knew he hadn't gotten a fair shake, not in the jury decision, not in the judge's sentence, not any way around. What would Combs say when he read in the papers that Floyd Varney had killed himself? Combs would be sorry, of course, he'd be full of pity. It was kind of a mean thing to do to Combs after he'd been so decent and tried so hard – but what the hell, it wasn't Combs who'd spend the rest of his life in a stone coffin: it was him – *him*, wasn't it?

And Janey Welch would be sorry for him too: she'd cry herself sick. She hadn't lost her feeling for him. She'd been hurt, but she'd forgiven him. And if it had turned out the way he'd dreamt – the minimum sentence with parole* at the end of forty months – she'd have waited for him.

Varney's brain went spinning. "Oh, Janey, Janey," his heart cried, "help me do it – I can't take it, I need to die!"

Now his mind became feverish again, his thoughts racing and tumbling. If only he could get hold of a razor blade, it would be so easy that way. Wasn't there anything else – something sharp that would cut?

A piece of glass? There were no drinking glasses in any of the cells, and no mirrors. The tin cups weren't any good: they were too thick. The spoons were watched. A fountain pen? That would be the same as the toothbrush. Could he confide in a man like Quinn, ask his help? Quinn wouldn't talk. He might have – *Christ*, Varney thought, Quinn always carried his cigarettes in a tobacco can! He could rip off the top and flatten out the sides. The tin in a tobacco can was thin: he could sharpen it easily – he'd have a knife blade then. Why hadn't he thought of it when Quinn was talking to him earlier?

Varney jumped up, went to the open doorway of the cell and peered down the runway. He saw Quinn and Lauter halfway down the line, too far to call without risking trouble with the guard. Quickly he rapped on the wall of 122 and asked for word to go down that Varney wanted to see the Barber. He waited, twisting the toothbrush in his hands. Then, with a surge of anger, he saw Quinn turn to confer with Lauter and both men start towards him together. It was clear that Lauter had stooled on him. The two were old pals – it was certain whose side Quinn would take. With intense bitterness he told himself that *everyone* was against him, *everybody* was messing into his private business.

"You wanna talk to me, Floyd?" Quinn asked softly.

The reply was harsh, but kept to a whisper. "Yeah. Alone!"

After a moment Lauter said bluntly: "No dice, Floyd! I've told him what's on your mind, and what's on mine too."

"You an' your big mouth," Varney exclaimed bitterly. "I suppose you told the screw too?"

"No, he hasn't," Quinn whispered. "Nobody's tellin' nothin' – provided you don't stop Johnny from goin' home."

"I told him I'd keep him in the clear."

"That's all we want," Quinn responded. "But a man in your state of mind ain't predictable. So we're gonna make sure of it."

"What's that? How?" Varney snapped.

"We don't have to talk about it right now," Lauter interrupted. "What's on your mind?"

Varney hesitated. "Gimme that tobacco can you got, will you, Barber?"

Quinn and Lauter exchanged glances.

"For Chrissakes," Varney said in a beseeching tone, "be human, will you? Gimme a break! I'm washed up, finished! I'll keep Johnny in the clear, but let me handle it as easy as I can."

"OK, Eddie," Lauter said with a sigh. "You can let him have it."

"I wouldn't wanna have anything pinned on me, neither," Quinn muttered.

"How could it be?" Varney asked impatiently. "Anybody can buy tobacco in canteen. There's other guys on this tier with tobacco cans, but I don't wanna ask 'em."

"All right," Quinn muttered, "but you hadn't oughta be doin' it, Floyd. You haven't even taken your appeal yet." He turned around so that his back was facing the front of the tier. He emptied the cigarettes into his shirt pocket, then carefully wiped the can with his handkerchief. Handing it to Varney, he said sorrowfully: "You ain't doin' right to yourself."

Varney took the can without replying and walked to the rear of the cell. "Let's go," Quinn said quickly, "let's get away from here."

At about this hour in the afternoon a number of messages were being dispatched from the central offices of the jail to the tier guards of CB1. These, delivered by hand in sealed envelopes, informed the guards that the inmates listed by name and number would be transferred on the following morning to a series of different correctional institutions and penitentiaries. It was the duty of the tier guards to see to it that all transfers had a shower and a shave, and that their personal clothes were removed from their cells or from storage and sent to the tailor shop for overnight pressing.

More or less at the same time as these messages arrived, a member of the permanent jail population, known as Newsboy, appeared at CB1 with the afternoon newspapers. He was admitted to the first tier by Mr Jonas, and he went down the line with his checklist of subscribers. When he reached Eddie Quinn, he said "Hi, chum", and then in a whisper:

"Transfers tomorrow – I put you a list between page ten an' eleven."*
Quinn nodded his appreciation, nudged Johnny Lauter and murmured:
"Come into my cell a minute."

Since any man summoned for an evening shower would know that he
was scheduled for transfer, there never was any great practical purpose
to this particular aspect of inmate espionage. Nevertheless there were
other motives: personal pride and convict ethics. The inmate clerk who
had typed out the list of transfers received both moral and ego satisfaction from communicating restricted information in advance. By making
a series of duplicate lists, he was able to let transfers know almost a day
ahead of time the name of the institution to which they would be sent.
To him, and to Newsboy, there were satisfactions in this that outweighed
their fear of punishment if they were caught.

Quinn said suddenly to Lauter, as they scanned the list: "Oh, balls,
I'm on it for Lorton! Now I'm sunk – my whole plan's gone down the
drain."

"What plan?" Lauter enquired absently.

"Don't you remember? To get a cure from those doctors at the Yale
clinic."

"Oh, yeah."

"Ain't that real sour luck?" Quinn asked unhappily. "Just look... George
Trisler – Danbury. Why him? They hardly ever send guys from here up
there."

"He worked for the Treasury – maybe that's the reason: some big shot
spoke up for him. Listen, Eddie—"

"Christ, why couldn't it've been me?" Quinn interrupted unhappily. "It
was my big chance to get cured."

"Listen, Eddie," Lauter said impatiently, "you can ask for a transfer
when you get to Lorton. Now look—"

"Hell, that warden there won't do that for me. I know him. Tell me to
join Alcoholics Anonymous – little good that's ever done me."

"Eddie, for Chrissake, there's nothin' you can do about it right now, so
listen to me a minute, will you?"

"Sure. What's got you so hot?"

"These transfers – it means showers tonight. That can put me in the
clear with Varney."

"How do you mean?"

"If he really intends to knock himself off, that's when he can do it.
There's twelve guys on that list. It'll take twenty minutes – maybe half

an hour till you an' me finish up. I'll be out of the cell all that time, right under the eye of the screw."

"That's right. Hey, that's good! What do you think then – should I still ask him for the shiv after supper?"

"That's what I'm wonderin'. If you take it, how do we get it back to him? God Almighty, what a conversation – us talkin' how we can help a guy kill himself."

"Yeah," Quinn agreed, "but it ain't us who's crazy: it's him, the poor jerk."

"I'll talk to him, that's what," Lauter decided. "I can't help bein' on his side."

"Keep your mind on yourself," Quinn warned. "He's wacky enough to play tricks."

They left the cell, Quinn moving down the line to spread the word of the transfers, and Lauter walking slowly to his own cell.

Varney jumped up from the wall seat as Lauter entered, and then slumped with relief. He said angrily: "I thought it was the screw!" He was holding one hand behind his back.

Lauter sat down on the lower bunk. "Floyd," he began softly, "I've got somethin' to tell you." Varney gazed at him in silence, and with disinterest. "Pay attention, will you? There's gonna be transfers tomorrow. You listenin'?"

"Yeah."

"That means there'll be showers tonight. I'll be out of here for half an hour maybe. You'll be locked up alone."

"Showers?" Varney asked. Then he nodded with understanding. "That gives you a solid alibi, huh?"

With determination, yet with a sickening distaste for what he was saying, Lauter continued softly: "That's right. I sure hope you won't go through with it. But you've been sayin'... how you just had to do it tonight... so here's your chance to play square with me."

"OK," Varney replied firmly. "That's a break all around – that's when I'll do it!" It seemed to Lauter as though, in that moment, Varney's eyes had become more feverish, his face a more cadaverous grey. Suddenly he held out the hand that had been behind his back. "Will you help me out, Johnny?"

In Varney's hand was a strip of metal from the tobacco can. He had tried to rip the can apart at the vertical seal along one side, but instead the tin had torn on a curving line. To a degree he had got more or less what he wanted: a strip of metal that could be turned into a cutting blade. It was shaped somewhat like a large butterfly wing, and the upper edge, being rounded, could be grasped firmly. Nevertheless the lower, curved edge was not what he had expected. Unlike the tin of a coffee or fruit can, this had a thickness to it.

"I gotta sharpen this," Varney said feverishly, "an' I ain't got too much time. I'll hafta go to chow, or they'll start askin' questions. If I rub it on the floor slow, it wears down too slow. If I rub it fast, it makes too much noise. I'm afraid the screw might come along for some reason an' hear it. Stay out there an' watch for me, will you?"

"Guys next door might hear it an' ask questions," Lauter replied slowly.

"You can handle 'em – you can make up somethin'."

"I guess so."

"The screw's the only one I'm worried about. Will you keep watch for me?"

"Yeah," said Lauter heavily. "I'll do it."

He gazed at Varney for a moment, and then walked out of the cell. He put his fingers through the steel mesh of the runway screen and stared at the outer wall of the cell block. The opaque yellow windows high up in the wall were tinted now by the afternoon sun. They spoke of the out of doors, of the tranquillity of nature, of the free world. Behind him he heard the low metallic scrape that said Varney was already at work on his knife blade.

Eddie Quinn, appearing at his elbow, asked: "What did he say?"

Lauter nodded without looking at him.

"So what do you want me to do about the shiv at lock-up?"

"Nothin'. We'll let him have it. He wouldn't have any reason to cut himself before shower time."

"He's off his head – he's unpredictable."

"I'll trust him that far."

"You think he really means to go through with it?"

"I don't know – I think so."

"Maybe you can go to work on him – change his mind?"

"I'm gonna try again after we're locked up." He added heavily: "In the pens I've been in I must've known a coupla dozen guys who knocked themselves off. But I never had to go along with it in advance like this."

"If I had ninety-nine years, I still wouldn't kill myself," Quinn said. "A man's only got one life. What the hell, I'd wanna live it out."

"Yeah," Lauter agreed.

"What's that noise?"

"He's sharpening up a piece of tin from your tobacco can."

"Oh Jesus!"

They stood side by side, listening.

A nightmare vision – of a man stalking him with a knife in his hand – awakened Huey Wilson from a fitful sleep. Instantly his mind asked: "Where am I?" The silence and darkness that engulfed him, the fearful image that still was vivid in his mind's eye, were utterly confusing. His body chilled, and his heart began to pound with elemental fear as he sought, almost in panic, to place himself.

He became aware that his arm was aching, and that he was lying on a cool stone floor. The answer came. Almost immediately he began to wonder what time it was.

He sat up, groaning a little from fatigue and physical soreness. The bedbug welts around his waist began to itch, and he scratched at them in a mechanical and unaware manner. He had no idea how long he had been asleep, but he concluded immediately that it must be late in the afternoon. On the one hand he had not been given the two pieces of bread that would be his supper; on the other hand he knew that he had been called down for discipline at about one fifteen. It was four or five, perhaps – it couldn't be earlier – and in that case there would be no hearing until the next day, and it would take place without McPeak.

For a little while he remained seated. He felt physically worn out, mentally depressed – and very bored. He reflected sourly that the bastards who had invented the Hole as a form of punishment had known what they were doing. It was a clean way of clubbing a man senseless.

Presently the bruised bone in his lower back began to ache, and he rose to his feet. Slowly, with outstretched hands,* he groped towards the rear of the cell and found the washbasin. He pressed down the water tap, drank thirstily and then lowered his head beneath the flow of water. It felt refreshing, and he turned one side of his face to it and then the other. Shortly he stood up, removed his shirt and dropped it to the floor. With the palm of his hand he washed the dry coating of calomine lotion from the welts around his middle. Waiting for his skin to dry so that he could apply some fresh lotion, he tossed water on his neck and chest and shoulders. Suddenly he stopped. From what seemed to be a far distance he had heard another water tap being pressed down repeatedly. He responded in the same manner, then waited. The other replied. They alternated several times – until there came a distant shout: "Shut up there! You guys cut that out, or you'll get more Hole time!" Huey swore under his breath and wondered for a moment if it would be possible to work out some form of communication without running into trouble. But the thought struck him that the man who had replied might be Ballou. And then came a further, most unpleasant thought: that he had no way of knowing if Ballou actually was in the Hole. It was quite possible that he had not been punished at all.

A flush of anger spurted through his body as this occurred to him… only to subside as quickly as it had come. He realized that it made no substantial difference to him if Ballou had been punished or not. He didn't expect equal justice in a white man's jail, and he had more important things to worry about.

Carefully, using the tips of his fingers, he applied the calomine lotion to his welts. He bent down, felt for his shirt and put it on. With one hand against the wall he began to circle the cell. A question came to his mind: "Why do I feel so damn hopeless about everything?" No answer came, and he circled the cell for a few minutes more with his mind blank. Abruptly there was another question: "Where's all my fight gone to?" and still another: "If it turns out I can't be a lawyer, why can't I go for something else? Why the hell do I have to feel as though my life's been smashed?"

He paused in his walk and leant against the wall. He was frowning in the darkness, thinking hard, trying to examine himself in a way he had not done before. The last words his father had spoken to him during their visit came to his mind: "You're a good boy, Huey. An' you're no weaklin', that's sure. Whatever happens, I know we'll be proud of the way you'll do in your life." When his father had said that to him, he had not paid it any great mind. It was the sort of thing a father said to a son in such circumstances. Yet now, somehow, the words were sharp with challenge. If he wasn't a weakling, why was he feeling so defeated? For years he had made a personal hero out of Frederick Douglass – so much so that on his first Sunday in Washington he had gone to visit the Douglass Home. But what was the lesson of that great life if not perseverance and refusal to accept defeat under any circumstances? How else had a slave escaped to freedom, educated himself, become an abolitionist leader, an adviser to Lincoln, a world statesman? How much real inspiration had he drawn from Douglass if a few harsh blows could reduce him to jelly?

Again his father's words came to him, and this time they burned: "Trouble's come to you now like it's come to a lot of us cullid. I expect you to stand up to it the way you should."

Huey's brain suddenly went hot with understanding. He had tried to make McPeak stand up to trouble because it was the moral thing to do, but what about himself in the mean time? On how many occasions during the day had he not found himself wishing that there never had been a picket line, or that he had been home sick? Now he could understand why! Deep down, in his heart and guts and bowels, he didn't really have his father's outlook on life: he still was a little boy who wanted the world to be easy for *him*. Only this morning he had told himself that he had no business whining because white oppression had singled him out in a special way as it had tens of thousands of Negroes before. He had felt very brave then because McPeak had not yet run out on him. But now, at the first hard push of adversity, he had gone to pieces like a helpless boy. Little Huey Wilson understood quite well that life might be rough on the ambitions of other Negroes, but he just couldn't bear the idea that it might turn rough for him. "I want you to be a lawyer too, if you kin," his father had said. "But more'n that, I want you to be a man, a real Negro man. I don't want you ever to forget whose name we give you."

"Christ!" Huey said to himself now, muttering it aloud in the intensity of his feeling: "What a weakling I am!"

He stood stiffly, staring into the darkness.

The hour being five o'clock, the men of the west wing were filing past the steam table for their supper. Since the mess officer at this meal was Mr Coe, there was none of the usual whispered talk, even of the most cautious kind. Mr Coe was a martinet who took pleasure in reporting men for discipline. Even Wacky Mike, up on the Death Tier, was quiet at this meal, although that was accidental.

Since the menu was macaroni, turnip greens and tea, most men said "Light." For some reason that the inmates never could figure out, the prison cooks, who prepared some dishes moderately well, invariably served macaroni that was soggy and tasteless, and turned out turnip greens that were as dry as garden weeds.

To Tom McPeak the meal was an intense strain. He had been waiting all afternoon for a summons from Detective Stoner, but none had come. The thought that he might be forced to spend a third night in jail out of his week's vacation was making him wild with resentment – although he could not have said for certain whether he was more angry at the police or at Huey Wilson or at himself. Just before supper, when the mess men had arrived on the eating range, he had called to one of them, a middle-aged, grey-haired man. "That young feller, Wilson," he had enquired (although he was sure of the answer), "how come he ain't with you?"

"He's in the Hole."

"You know how much time he got?"

"No." And then, before walking away, Isaac Reeves had asked softly: "You still a friend to Wilson? You gonna testify for him?"

McPeak had felt like spitting in his eye. He had said nothing, merely turned his back and walked to the rear of his cell, but he had been boiling. Everyone pushing him, pushing him, he had thought bitterly, and now the coloured mess men. They didn't give him credit for what he already had done for Wilson, they couldn't be satisfied with that – no, they wanted him to put in prison time also. So to hell with them and Wilson too!

Now, trying to eat the small portion he had taken for his supper, he felt as though his stomach had knotted itself up into a resistant ball. It was not merely the unpalatable food, but the whole miserable, unnatural feeling that came from sitting in a row of silent men, all of them caged in like zoo animals, all of them eating hogwash with a spoon. "I want out," McPeak told himself fiercely. "Let me git out of here." Not the least of his resentments, as it happened, was the inmate sitting beside him, who seemed to personify everything about jail life that McPeak could not bear. This man, who appeared to be about thirty, had the look of a walking corpse. The only thing he had taken for his supper was half a cup of tea, which he had not yet touched. He was sitting with a slumped figure, his hands slack in his lap, and he was staring at the steel table with a vacant eye. And while McPeak didn't know, or even care, what made his neighbour look this way, he was sure that he himself didn't belong in a place with men like that no more than a healthy man could bear to be in an insane asylum.

McPeak's neighbour, who was Floyd Varney, had arrived at a point in which the act of inwardly saying farewell to life was being accompanied by a sense of overwhelming self-pity. He had not been able to avoid the stunning thought that this was his last meal, and that he was sitting at a table for the last time. When morning came, the men around him would return for breakfast, but he would not. He knew what they would eat, he knew* what their day's routine would be – he even knew what they would say about him. It was inexpressibly horrible to visualize himself as a corpse, a senseless thing lying in a box. Yet, even so, the thought frightened him less than the only alternative – the cold horror of continued prison existence. He was alive, and therefore the thought of death was awful. But the thought of ten thousand drab, unchanging days, of a bleak animal survival behind walls – that was unendurable. How much more welcome was a grave. And perhaps, he was thinking, his suicide on the very night of his sentence would rot the days ahead for the woman who had betrayed him. There would be some satisfaction in that – like cold tea for a man's last supper.

"Here lies Floyd Varney," he told himself mordantly, "born in a charity ward, died in a prison, and in between a sucker!"

In a queer way the thought was satisfying.

Men might be angry, and men might be sad, but jail routine did not vary. It was now five fifteen; the first-tier men had been served, and the men from Tier Three were waiting at the foot of the staircase. Mr Coe gestured with one finger, and the line filed over to the steam table. "Pork chops tonight," Mr Coe said, because he enjoyed making little jokes upon occasion, and he grinned with good humour as a few of the men tittered. He was a lean, handsome man of thirty who always conducted himself in a slightly theatrical manner. For this reason it pleased him to make the men laugh, just as it did to catch them in breaches of discipline. The smile instantly left his face, however, as a commotion broke out at the steam table. He called out "What's the matter there?" and strode over quickly.

Foley, the burly inmate at the head of the line, was red-faced and very angry. He jerked his thumb towards Isaac Reeves, who was serving the macaroni. "He won't give me anythin' to eat."

Mr Coe stared at Reeves. "What's going on here?"

"I won't serve anybody who insults me," Reeves explained quietly.

"How'd he insult you?"

"He called me 'boy'. It happens I'm a man."

"Oh, for Chrissakes," Mr Coe exclaimed with irritation, "so we're off on that again?"

Mr Coe had been informed of the fight that had occurred between a Negro and a white inmate at dinner, and he didn't want anything of the sort while he was mess officer. While the administration knew that it was impossible to prevent quarrels between inmates, the record of an officer in squelching such affairs was of the utmost importance to his career in the prison service.

"All right, let's go now," he snapped in a loud voice. "I don't want to hear any talking* from anybody. You men from the third tier say 'light' or 'heavy' when you come to the steam table, but not another word. Start moving now!"

From the tail end of the line up on the staircase, where it would be hard to identify anyone, an aggrieved voice called out: "What's niggers doin' in our cell block anyway?"

With this it became clear to Mr Coe that the dinner-time quarrel was being continued by prearranged plan. This fact was no less clear to the mess men and to the inmates of Tier One. Mr Coe hesitated, and the eating range became very quiet.

Among the mess men there was great tension. There was not one of them who had any desire to have this proceed, as it had with Huey Wilson, to punishment in the Hole, and most had a particular, personal reason for wanting to avoid it. Eugene Finnerty immediately thought of his painful haemorrhoids, which needed daily hospital visits. Isaac Reeves, hoping for parole, knew that a mark against him would weigh heavily with the Board. With the others it was more or less the same – yet, within most of them, there was an unspoken resolve not to take this kind of white talk no matter what the consequences. It had started with the enmity between Ballou and Wilson, but now it was being pushed by others – and they simply would not stand for it. And if a man like Alfrice Tillman was weaker in the knees than some of the others, he nevertheless had made up his mind to act like the rest. He knew it would be a lot easier on him to go to the Hole than to welch – and then be beaten to a pulp by his tier mates.

Mr Coe's hesitation lasted for only a few moments. He walked quickly to the foot of the staircase. His good-looking face had turned very hard. Direct violation of orders on the part of an inmate, even in a small matter, was for him the deadliest of sins, and a personal insult as well. He asked loudly: "Any of you men got anything to say to me?"

No one had.

"I thought not," Mr Coe continued with contempt. "I didn't catch the wise guy who shot off his mouth a minute ago, and he's lucky I didn't. There'll be no more talk, you get it?"

From the first-tier men at the tables, behind Mr Coe's back, a voice said quickly: "He likes coons."

Mr Coe swung around in a fury – to swing back again as someone on the staircase made an obscene sound with his lips, which then was taken up by several men at the tables. In a manner that was intolerable to Mr Coe, his authority was going to pieces.

There were several ways in which an officer in this predicament could restore discipline. The first was to notify the central control office and have several other guards dispatched to keep order. But this would be an ignominious confession of weakness for Mr Coe, and the last remedy he intended to use. A second manoeuvre would be to announce that every inmate was responsible for keeping the mouth of his neighbour closed, and that if one man spoke out of turn the entire tier would be punished. This Mr Coe did not think of doing because he was too excited. What he did decide was to break the deadlock by starting the mess line moving.

"OK!" he said, striding up to the steam table. "Let's go now! Start serving."

"No, sir," Isaac Reeves replied quietly. He had stepped back from the steam table, and his hands were in his pockets. "I'm through servin' anybody but myself. Let somebody else serve me."

This, as Mr Coe realized instantly, was the break in the situation he had been looking for – the open defiance of an order by someone he could discipline. "I told you to start serving," he said flatly. "You going to do it or not?"

"Nobody temporary in jail *has* to work," Reeves answered. "I've done quit."

"Maybe you're quitting tomorrow," Mr Coe retorted with anger. "That's up to the administration. But right now you're wearing a mess jacket and it's your job to serve this meal. Yes or no?"

"No."

"Stand back by the wall!" He pointed a finger at Alfrice Tillman. "Start serving!"

Tillman shook his head.

"You like as well know we've done all of us quit," Ben Wellman volunteered. "We're on strike."

"And everyone of you is going to be written up right now," Mr Coe snapped as he pulled his notebook out of his pocket.

From the dining tables a voice burst out in intense anger: "If that ain't the most goddam, unfairest thing I ever seen, I don't know what is!"

Mr Coe wheeled around. "Who said that?"

"I did!" It was Tom McPeak, his pudgy face flushed, his jaw thrust forward belligerently. Whatever the consequences might be of this free expression of opinion in jail, McPeak had not weighed them, or even thought about them. His comment had been wholly spontaneous – and if, an hour from now, he would come to regret his conduct, at this moment he was commanded by his indignation. "Goddam it, you're writing up the wrong guys," he shouted angrily. "They didn't start this."

"You tellin' me how to run my job?" Mr Coe snapped as he advanced to the eating tables.

"I'm sayin' you're discriminaten agin those mess men."

"An' what right have you got to be talking at all? Didn't you hear me tell everyone to be quiet?"

"Sure, an' I also heerd a lot of mean talk that you ain't done nothin' about, nothin'!"

"What's your name?"

"Thomas McPeak."

"What's your number?"

"I don' know my number."

"Where's your commitment slip?"

McPeak fumbled in his shirt pocket and handed it over. Mr Coe scribbled in his notebook, returned the slip and snapped: "Go to your cell!" Stepping over the man on the aisle seat, McPeak said with anger: "An' this food ain't fitten for pigs, neither."

The comment was as irrelevant to the situation as it was true, and there was a roar of laughter on the range. A shout from Mr Coe brought it to an end. He took the name and number of each of the mess men and sent them upstairs. He then delegated the first five men of Tier Three to serve the others. From then on there was quiet.

For Tom McPeak there was not* time to cool down or to have any regrets. The cell door scarcely had closed on him when it opened again. He heard his name being called by the tier guard. He peered out, saw that he was being summoned and obeyed. Since he was unfamiliar with jail routine, he assumed that it was for discipline. Walking by the side of the guard, who had been sent by the Rotunda to fetch him, he carried on a lengthy conversation with himself, most of it obscene. He still was so furious that he was longing to speak a piece to Authority. It was with considerable surprise, therefore, that he found himself led into an office where he was confronted by Detective Stoner.

"Hi, there," the detective said in a friendly manner. "How you doin'?"

McPeak kept silent and stared angrily at the other man. Stoner was in his early thirties, a big man with rusty hair and a pink-skinned, freckled face. The guard had paused outside, and they were alone.

"I expected to see you a little earlier in the day," Stoner said genially, "but I got busy. Still and all, it gave you a little more time to think things over, eh?" He smiled. "That was what you said you wanted, didn't you, a little more time?"

McPeak remained silent, and Stoner, noticing the direction of his gaze, said: "Yeah, that's your suitcase. I got a bus ticket for you too. There's a bus leavin' for Detroit in about an hour. A pal of mine on the Detroit force will be waitin' for you. You pull in there like you should and all charges here'll be dropped. There won't even be an arrest marked on you." Stoner's blue eyes hardened a little as McPeak still maintained his silence, but he said amiably: "What's the matter, Georgia, you still want to put your neck out for that nigger?"

"I don' like bein' pushed aroun'," McPeak told him flatly. "I come here for a family git-together an' a weddin', an' I aim t'go to it."

"Now look, Georgia," Stoner said with a quick change into a policeman's voice and manner: "I've given you every chance to get out of this mess easy, so don't start talking about being pushed. When that nigger goes up for his hearing, you're gonna be out of this town. If you're not, we're gonna slap so many charges on you that you'll never know what hit you. You'll pull time, Mister, an' I mean time. We'll show you what pushing can be."

Of all the things that Detective Stoner might have said to McPeak, this was the least well calculated. Divided in mind and heart as McPeak was, it would have affected him considerably if Stoner had chosen to dwell on some of the other realities of the situation – the possible loss of his job, the hardship to his family – all of the factors that had been gnawing at him for the past twenty-four hours. As it was, what Stoner said inflamed that area of McPeak's feelings that was most explosive: his resentment of arbitrary Authority. This resentment went so deep, and was so complexly founded on experience, that even McPeak himself could not have traced the sources of it. It went back to his first job in a lumber camp, where every worker had to pay off to the foreman to keep his job – and did so because World War I had ended and there was a depression. It went back to his terrible experience in the building of Boulder Dam,* where the cave-in of a tunnel nearly killed him. When he quit the job, he was told that he would be given a small part of his accumulated wages in US dollars and the rest in company scrip – which could only be used as money in the town of Boulder itself. He had gone raging to the company offices, he had burst in upon the chief of police, only to learn that one was a partner of the other and he could get nothing from either. And perhaps his resentment never would have amounted to more than that if he had not had the experience of pinning a union button on his shirt and sitting down on a factory floor. From that had come the knowledge that an anonymous labouring man didn't always have to take it in silence – that he was stronger than himself because he was not alone, and that he had the power in extremity to say: "Crap to you! We strike!" From that also had come something infinitely more subtle: that resonance within his heart that could make him stir with pride when a group of strange Negro mess men stuck together in the face of Authority.

"So show me!" he burst out suddenly to Detective Stoner. His face had turned red with choler, his eyes were blazing, his chunky figure was set as though for a fight. "An' I'll show you a thing or two, I will! I'm a-goin' into that hearin' an' I'm gon speak the truth. I'm gon testify for that coloured boy an' I'm gon tell every last part of this lousy frame-up you're tryin' to pull. When I git through talkin', goddamn it, it ain't me who'll pull time, it'll be you. I'll—"

"You son of a bitch," Stoner broke in furiously. "I knew we should've worked you over in that precinct house, I—"

"An' that ain't all I'm a-goin' t'do," McPeak shouted. In this ecstasy of speaking out his feelings, his imagination had caught hold of a lie that was as big as it was satisfying. "You don't know who I am, you sucker! I'm the chief shop steward of my union, Local 600, UAW,* the biggest union local in the US, sixty-five thousand members, an' I just been elected for the third time. You wait till this case gits in the newspapers. Man, will your ass git hot! The whole CIO—"

The door opened, and the jail guard was there. He said sternly: "What's going on here?"

"Take this damn cracker out of here before I tear him apart," Detective Stoner said violently.

"You an' who else?" McPeak shouted. "You jus—"

"Quiet!" the guard interrupted. "C'mon you!"

On the way back to his cell, McPeak had many thoughts, all of them explosive in nature. But by the time the steel door had hammered shut before him, he had quieted a little. His first thought then was that all of this was simply terrible for his blood pressure. And his second thought was that now he really had cooked his own goose – he was in trouble now, but good. Nevertheless, he became aware that his headache had subsided for the first time in many hours, and that somehow he felt not too worried about what was to come. And all of it was strangely reminiscent of the time he had sat down on a factory floor yelling: "No, Freddie, no work."

Chapter 15

The Jailhouse Serenade

Whatever the reaction of the other inmates to the events at supper, the two occupants of 124 were concerned with other matters. Floyd Varney had gone to work the moment he reached the cell. With savage and unrelieved intensity he was converting the strip of tobacco tin into a knife blade. He had had only about ten minutes to work at it before supper time, and there was no telling how soon the order would come down for the next day's transfers to have their showers. Grey-faced, his pale lips set hard, he was working without pause. The blade was sharp, but he wanted it to be razor-keen. He had no fear that the scrape of the tin on the concrete floor would be heard, because the loudspeaker had come on with a programme of Viennese waltzes. His only other fear – that the tier guard might come down the runway and observe him – was allayed by the presence of Johnny Lauter. The latter was standing watch for him at the cell door.

Lauter had not volunteered to do this, yet he had not refused when Varney asked him. It was, in a way, the smallest part of this nightmare that he should play a helpful role in his friend's suicide. However incredible it seemed to him at some moments, he nevertheless had begun to accept the fact that this living, feeling human being beside him would be a corpse before several hours had passed. Varney was calmer than when he first had returned from court, and his eyes had lost their hot frenzy – or so Lauter felt. Varney listened to him, made occasional comments, was aware of his surroundings. What he communicated, however, was even more sinister: a fixed, sickly determination that would not bend. In the half-hour since they had been locked up, Lauter had tried every argument he could think of – with no effect at all. He even had gone so far as to point out that any man who wanted to kill himself was a fool not to wait until he was transferred to a penitentiary, because tools were to be had in a big pen that would make the job easy.

"You can just forget that," Varney had commented very seriously at this point. "I don't wanna bump myself off somewheres else. If I do it in Leavenworth or Alcatraz, nobody'll ever hear about it. I want that judge to read about it in the papers tomorrow. An' that Peterson woman! I'm gettin' some satisfaction outa that."

Here was the sickness Lauter could not reach, the life force already twisted out of shape. He recognized it for what it was because he had seen before this what despairing men will do. He was thinking of a youngster he had known on the Carolina chain gang, who had been assigned twenty lashes with a bull whip, and then the sweat box, for trying to run away. An hour before his punishment he had attacked a guard with the deliberate intention of being shot down. He was recalling also the reformatory boy who had been forced into perverse sexuality by a dozen of his barrack mates, and who had gotten up in the middle of the night, thrust his face into a toilet bowl and drowned himself. When men were wholly despairing, they sometimes did such things, he knew. Yet he himself never would under any circumstances. There was something in the very idea of suicide that he rejected. In Varney's place he would have been planning not suicide, but a jail break.

Standing at the cell bars, his eyes on the runway, Lauter had a need to express this thought to Varney in a last attempt to reach him. Yet it was not easy, he found, to summon the right words. He never had talked about it before, not even to his wife, and to make sense out of his strong feelings was difficult. "Floyd," he said, "I wanna tell you somethin'. You listenin'?"

Varney looked up briefly, half-nodded and returned to his work.

"It's like this... the average kind of guy, like you or me... he ain't born to very much. Some gets it harder than others – you for instance. But I didn't have it easy either. I told you once, I lost my ma when I was ten years old – she had TB. My old man was practically a stranger: he worked nights on the railroad. So I ran wild, an' they shipped me to the reformatory when I was twelve years old. You listenin' to me, Floyd?"

"Uh-huh."

"Goddamn that silly radio," Lauter snapped. "Why don't they give us somethin' decent? A man can't hear himself think... Anyway, what I'm trying to get after is this: I seen enough, an' I read enough books, to know that the twelve-year-old kids of rich men never get sent to reformatories – they just don't. Course, most of 'em don't get into as much trouble as poor kids. They got nice homes, they got spending money, they don't have to go stealing a bike an' other things like I did. But even when they get into trouble an' land in a juvenile court – what the hell, their old man says: 'Judge, I'll take him to a psychiatrist, I'll watch him good, I'll straighten him out' – so the kid gets probation."

"I never got into trouble when I was a kid," Varney muttered suddenly. "I took care of myself – I did fine. You should've heard the talk my lawyer made for me in court today. I…" he stopped, muttered an obscenity and went on with his work.

"That's just what I'm talking about," Lauter continued eagerly. "Look, just supposin' you were a different kind of a guy – not a cook in a hotel, but some kind of a big shot with money, your name in the society pages – so help me God, you never would've gotten a sentence like this." He waited for Varney to look up, but there was no response. "What I mean is… your case got all dirtied up with that rape charge. It hurt you. But if you'd been a society boy, that charge would've blown up. Everybody would've said: 'Hell, she layed for him.' Even the cops would've laughed when she claimed you carried a switchblade knife. And even supposin' you got hung with this second-degree rap… what the hell, the judge would've thought to himself that in your shoes he would've gone to bed with Mrs Peterson too – an' in self defence he might've killed the other guy like you did – so naturally he'd have handed you no more than the minimum."

"You tryin' to make me feel good?" Varney snapped with venom. "You ain't. Why don't you shut up?"

"No, listen, Floyd, I ain't explaining good… just listen to me. What I mean to say is that things are rigged. Like I read about in the old times in England… there was nine hundred crimes they hanged people for – like just stealin' a loaf of bread when somebody was starvin'. They hanged 'em anyway. Well, so they don't hang so much now, but it's still rigged. I remember a book I read in Atlanta – it pointed out that ninety per cent of the laws on crime have to do with protection of property. You realize what that means? I got sent up to the reformatory for doin' some petty stealin', but no big-shot landlord got sent up cos my ma died of TB. What I mean is, you don't get TB if you live in a good house an' have milk an' good food an' fresh air. That's been proved, Floyd, all the doctors know it."

"God Almighty," Varney muttered, "what a lot of yackety-yak. You're worse than the radio. Why don't you leave me alone?"

"But what I'm tryin' to explain," Lauter said helplessly, knowing that he was making a muddle of his ideas, "is that when things are rigged like this, it's wrong to give in to 'em. I mean a man shouldn't let anythin' make him give up. Cos in one way or another things are hard for most people. I mean, even if they were shippin' me right now to a rigged trial in Carolina, I'd wanna fight for my life to the last minute because—"

"I ain't even listenin'," Varney interrupted.

"So why don't you?" Lauter shouted with anger. "There's plenty of time to be dead – you ain't dead yet."

At this, both men became rigid. The last phrase, "You ain't dead yet", had been shouted at the exact moment that the radio programme had shut off without warning – the words had boomed out into sudden silence in the west wing. There was laughter from a number of nearby cells, and a voice down the line called out cheerily: "Maybe you ain't dead yet, buddy, but you sure will be."

"Quiet!" the guard called from the front of the tier. "Everybody quiet down there – we're starting to test bars."

Varney cursed. Quickly he sat down with the piece of tin hidden in the palm of his hand. He knew what was coming. Periodically there was a test of all cell bars lest time or ingenuity weaken their power of confinement. The by-product of this was a peculiar serenade.

Mr Coe, who had been mess officer at supper, was the performer. Commencing on the first tier, he strolled down the line at an even pace, striking all bars of each cell with a wooden mallet. Each bar replied with a slightly different tone – a resonant, metallic timbre that was crystal-clear and cold. The successive notes emitted by the bars of each cell formed themselves into a peculiar xylophonic melody that was repeated by the next cell and the next. Varney had heard this serenade quite a few times in the course of his half-year's residence in the west wing, and always had been amused by it. He was not now, since it meant a loss of time that was precious to him. "Why'd they have to pick tonight?" he muttered savagely.

Mr Coe tested the low bars of their cell and passed on, but Varney did not stir. Since all vertical bars were divided into three separate panels, Mr Coe would pass three times along the tier. Varney's thoughts became fiery as he listened to the melody – it evoked a buried memory that made him wild. He was recalling the time, when he was eight years old, that his mother had bought a second-hand Victrola* and two used records for the entertainment of her customers. At night he would be in the rear room of their two-room shanty, lying on a straw tick in the farthest corner. Whenever the Victrola began to play, he would know that Momma had a gentleman visitor. Oh, those records! – each stencilled into his heart night after night... the one she called "sweet" and the other she called "hot", bedtime lullabies for her son. Christ, that on his last night alive he should be forced to remember it!

After ten minutes Mr Coe completed his serenade on the first tier and climbed the staircase to the second. Varney returned to work. And now

Lauter left him alone. He had said all he could say, and said it ineffectively, and he knew there was no use trying any more. He stood at the cell door and watched the runway, and said to himself: "Tomorrow I'm home with Amy and the kids. Tomorrow I start livin' again!"

At this time of the evening Huey Wilson was lying on the floor of his cell, eating the last of two pieces of bread. Supper time had come and gone with singular dispatch – the eye slot in the door had been opened, dazzling him with a beam of light from the corridor, and a voice had called to him to come and get it.

He had been very hungry, and now, finishing the last morsel, he remained hungry. This first meal had made it clear that the darkness, the silence and the boredom of the Hole were not the most severe of its punishments. From now on his main antagonist would be hunger.

Nevertheless, it was not hunger that was preoccupying him, but a grave need to understand himself. A little earlier he had been thinking of his cellmate, Finnerty, and of Finnerty's reflections on the men of their tier: "We's all got weakness an' bad in us – we's all human, an' human means weak."

He had taken comfort from those words, yet he was not satisfied. He was serious about life, and he wanted to live it in a way that was creditable. He had standards and moral values – or so he would have said a few days ago – and he needed for his own self-respect to measure up to them. Yet what sort of man was he that at the first blows of adversity his courage should have gone to pieces as it had?

Huey asked himself this, and then began to think of something quite disconnected. His mind went back two years to a summer night in Charlottesville. It was during vacation, with the war still on, so that he had found a good job for a youth of sixteen: labourer in a small meat-packing plant. They were working overtime, and the white foreman, irritated at the night work, was getting drunk. When work was over, he addressed a rather classic question to his crew of four Negroes – did they know some clean little brown girl who would give him a night's fun? Huey replied for all of the men, doing so spontaneously, without waiting to see how any of the others might handle the situation. His answer was quite unclassic for a southern town: he said that he did not know, but did the foreman know where he could get a clean little white girl? At this insult to southern womanhood the foreman cursed Huey violently and obscenely – Huey cursed back, the foreman struck at him, and Huey, sidestepping the drunken blow, knocked him down. It was the finish of that good job, and for two weeks after his parents made him sleep away from home out of fear of one sort of reprisal or another, but he never regretted what he had done.

He realized now that the memory had meaning. Why had he spoken as he had instead of playing the Uncle Tom, or just keeping his mouth shut? If it was a genuine part of his code to fight back at white chauvinism, then why had he fallen apart like a rag doll at the notion that he never could become a lawyer? The picket line in front of the school had been more important than his retort to one white man.

"I have an idea you don't really know what your principles are as yet," Professor Herrin had said to him only that morning. Was that true? Had the old fox understood something that he himself wasn't aware of?

Thinking about it, thinking seriously and gravely, Huey reflected that any man's principles, whether he was conscious of them or not, were surely the guidelines of his behaviour. A man who valued money above everything else might cheat to get it. What, then, in the deepest sense, did he value? What *were* his principles?

He realized that he did not know – not when he put it to himself that way. And perhaps it was this that Professor Herrin had sensed. Only a few days ago he would have answered without hesitation. He would have said that he wanted to become the very best lawyer he could, and use his skill on behalf of his own people the way a man like Charles Houston did, or Thurgood Marshall. There was principle behind that, surely. But what about a comfortable living, which he also wanted? Or his dream that he might become a celebrated attorney?

It began to seem as though his principles and his dreams were mixed up in one stew pot. Yet one thing was clear: if he had been caught in a motor accident rather than a police frame-up – if he had been left blind or crippled – then his goals in life would require changing, but surely not his principles.

Provided he had them! The question remained: what was basically important to him in life?

Huey got to his feet. With an outstretched hand he groped for the wall, and then began to circle the cell. Suddenly, vivid in his mind's eye, he had an image of himself as a boy, seated by his father's side, turning the pages of their family Bible. It was much more than a Bible: a family history, an album of precious photographs, a recorder of contracts and deeds, that had been handed down from Wilson to Wilson since 1864. And now, thinking about it, Huey had a flash of insight about himself – that there *was* something he wanted more keenly than money or success or becoming a lawyer: he wanted to win a rightful page in that family history.

The moment he said this to himself, he knew it was true, and he knew why. Because it was a record of men and women who had looked at the world with brave eyes, who had struggled to win things from it and who had known how to meet adversity when it came.

What else but this had he learnt from the life of his great-grandfather, whose name he bore? The first Huey Wilson had been a chattel slave in New Orleans, hired out as a dock worker by his master. Twice he had run away and been recaptured. The first time he had been lashed and branded on the cheek, the second time an ear had been cut off. When the Union army had captured New Orleans, he had not merely accepted his liberation: he had fought for it. He had joined the first regiment of Negro troops raised in the city and had lost an arm in the Battle of Port Hudson.*

How many times, Huey thought now, had he not gazed at the faded tintype* of the first Wilsons without realizing the full majesty of it? There was Laura, his great-grandmother, who had been a plantation-field hand near Baton Rouge,* and had joined the Negro troops as a nurse when they passed nearby. The two of them holding hands, sitting stiffly erect and proud, his great-grandfather in uniform, one sleeve empty, one ear amputated, one cheek with the slaver's brand. It was so clear that theirs was a dignity born of struggle and suffering – had he never understood that?

And their son, Jacob, who had supported his widowed mother from the time he was fourteen, a skilled bricklayer fighting the new chains of the Black Codes* by wandering north from town to town, seeking a place, a work, a home. He had built more wells, more stone fences, more cellars than any man in Charlottesville. Untutored, he had designed a family house in the year 1890, worked seven years to buy a piece of land, worked five more for the money to build the one room and kitchen into which he moved his wife, his two children, his mother and himself. It was a house that was a monument to human courage and effort, with the plans still to be seen in the family Bible, so well conceived that each new room became an integral part of the whole – a second bedroom in 1906, a front parlour in 1910, an attic bedroom, later Huey's own, in 1920. And how much a part of the same struggle it was that when his brother returned from the army in 1944 he had used his severance pay to add the final crown to their grandfather's home: electricity, inside plumbing and a bathroom!

With excitement Huey also recalled the pages of another family book he had opened with fascination a hundred times: a history of the Negro troops in the Civil War, dated 1888, with the muster role of the thousands of ex-slaves who had struck for their freedom like his great-grandfather. How many were the times in which he and his brother had fought the Battle of the Crater before Petersburg,* cheered in triumph when Lee surrendered,* and marched through the streets of Richmond singing, "We'll hang Jeff Davis from* a sour apple tree"?* He had felt his kinship to everyone of these soldiers of the Black Phalanx – but had he never really paused to weigh what they had faced, what they had endured?

Perhaps not, he thought now. Pondering it seriously, and wondering seriously about himself, Huey began to perceive something else about his life. All at once, it seemed, he could understand his parents in a new perspective: that in the most simple and unassuming manner possible, they had been living with heroism for all of the years he had known them.

What else had kept the family whole and solid during the depression years? He could remember still the winter evenings they had sat in the kitchen making "coal". Jeff and his father would scour the town's trash cans for newspapers. At home, sitting in a circle, the family would wad each sheet of paper into a tight ball; each ball was then soaked in water overnight, then put out to dry – and that was a depression lump of coal for the Wilson family. Yet, somehow, how pleasant and friendly had been those hours of dull work in a badly heated kitchen – because his parents had made it so!

And what else but heroic were the daily labours of his mother that he always had taken for granted – keeping a house that always was bright and clean, scrubbing floors, chopping the kindling, cobbling the family shoes. And weeding the vegetable garden in the backyard, cleaning the privy, washing clothes for white students at the university – always without complaint, and always with love and energy left over to sew for the annual bazaar of the First Baptist Service Club! And his father, never strong, with an arrested case of tuberculosis, working ten hours a day, six days a week, as a presser in a tailor shop – and never, never complaining. Saying only: "Git an education, don't be no-'count – work, we'll help you all we kin."

Yet what was wrong with their son that even for a moment he could feel alone in the world, or so overcome by his troubles?

Huey laughed out loud in the darkness of his cell. The truth was that he no longer felt alone, or helpless, or so abused. Instead, by some alchemy, he felt that he had discovered himself in a way he never had before. Now he could say to Herrin that, by God, he did have a guiding principle in his life. A career would be fine, and fame would be exciting, and money in his pocket would be splendid, but the bottom thing he wanted was to be what his father called "a real man". Maybe this case would end for him in a prison sentence, and maybe he never would become a lawyer, but he was glad, glad, that he had walked on that picket line – and if the legal case of Huey Wilson would push segregation in the schools one inch closer to the garbage can, then he'd be earning a page in that family Bible.

Huey stopped walking and leant against a wall of the cell. Again he laughed. There no longer was any conflict in him over his situation, and he knew it. He would not have believed that a man in the Hole could be happy, but that was how he felt.

A few minutes earlier there had been a shout of "Tier Men". Their cell door had opened, and Lauter had departed. Almost immediately Varney's legs had become weak, his brain fuzzy, and he had felt as though all the blood were draining out of his body.

He was prepared, the time almost was at hand, yet life still was sucking at his will. The radio had come back on with a programme of noisy jazz, and the beat of the drum, the hot call of the clarinet, spoke of the outside world, of dancing with Janey, of not being dead. To dance with a woman – to feel that inner warmth as you moved to the music, her face so close to yours, to press your cheek to the smooth coil of russet hair! To lie side by side on the grass in the park and watch a hummingbird as it beat its wings and sipped from the heart of a flower! To gaze upon the night stars! To live, even if badly, even if alone, even in prison!

Varney started violently. Further down the line of cells a door was grinding open. A second followed, a third and fourth. The iron clamour beat through the wing and into his heart, saying twenty-five years of nothing but doors, bars, stone, steel.

"Goddamn it, no!" he muttered aloud. "I can't take it! That ain't livin'!"

"Floyd?" It was Lauter at the cell door. "They're comin' out for showers."

With an interest that surprised both of them, Varney asked: "Many guys bein' shipped?"

"Twelve on this tier."

"Where to?"

"Most to Lorton."

"They can have it!" Varney said in a spasm of rage. "They're never gonna ship me to one of their pens."

Lauter stared at the sick face, the sick eyes. Then he put his mouth between the bars so that he could whisper beneath the music. He had planned something – a final step for his own security – but it took all of his will-power to say it. "Floyd?"

Varney stepped closer.

"Will you… do somethin' for me?"

"What?"

"Dodson next door is goin' for a shower. *After* he goes, will you speak to Groves?"

Varney nodded. "Yeah, I'll do it, I know what you mean." But then his lips parted, and he began to breathe with effort, and a look of such torment came to his face that Lauter could not endure it. He wanted once more to plead "Don't do it", to say "Don't give up yet", but he couldn't. The blood was pounding in his temples, and he felt as though he were strangling.

"Tier men, let's go with those showers." The call was loud, and Lauter turned away from Varney. He took a step, hesitated, and then called hoarsely into the next cell: "Dodson? Let's go." A man stepped out of 122, naked except for a towel around his waist, and they walked down the runway.

Varney remained standing, the strip of tin in one hand. Presently he heard the cell doors closing all along the line. He rapped on the wall of 122. A fist rapped back. With his mouth to the cell bars Varney said feverishly: "That you, Groves?"

"Yeah."

"I just wanna tell you goodbye." It was said with mordant satisfaction. "I'm breakin' jail tonight."

"Oh, brother," the other replied, "don't we all wish we could? I'm sorry to hear what you pulled today, chum."

Varney spat on the runway. He walked to the rear of the cell, paused for a moment, then took off his shirt. With a hand on the upper bunk he paused again, thought, then turned around to reach for the toothbrush, which he had hidden on the cardboard shelf above the sink. He climbed up on his bunk, arranged his pillow so that he would be in a reclining position and lay back on it. Carefully he put the toothbrush to one side. He gripped the tin butterfly wing with the fingers of his right hand and raised his left arm. He stared at it, at the several surface veins in his wrist and at the faint blue shadow of a larger vein in the hollow of his elbow. Then he put his finger on his pulse, which marked the vulnerable artery beneath. Suddenly his body began to shake. His right hand trembled so violently that the butterfly wing slipped from his fingers. A film of sweat wet his chest.

He lay back, his heart* pounding. Despairingly he asked himself if this was how it would end – in being too scared to live and too scared to die.

The music coming from the loudspeaker was softer now, and he could hear, from the other end of the tier, the running water in the shower room. He told himself that he only had a few more minutes to make up his mind. There were twelve men – three razors for shaving and three showers – fifteen minutes and Lauter would return.

The trembling of his body subsided a little. He picked up the butterfly wing and stared at it. With desperation he thought: "It's razor-sharp. One cut'll do it – just one!"

Abruptly, startling him, a light flashed on the ceiling of the runway outside his cell, and then the lights came on in the eating range beyond. He began to curse without knowing why and lay back panting again, feeling exhausted. From where he was he could see one of the yellow-glassed windows in the outer wall of the cell block. The rays of the setting sun no longer were touching it, but he could judge that outside it still was light, the soft light of twilight. Suddenly he was out of his cell and free of the jail, and he was walking in the gentle light of the evening, seeing men returning from work and seeing children at play before supper, and seeing young lovers as they walked in smiling silence, waiting for darkness, for park benches and tree shadows where they would hold each other, tenderly embrace, press their lips and bodies together in the enchantment of their living natures.

Without consciously willing it, Varney cut himself. He had not said to himself "Now" or "This is the time to do it". As though someone else had made the decision for him, his fingers suddenly had tightened upon the butterfly wing. He had slashed his left wrist above the pulse.

For a surprised instant, for a fraction of a second, nothing happened. He saw the cut in his skin, and a small seepage of blood from a vein, but nothing else. Then, astonishing him, a thin geyser of blood spurted before his eyes, leaping a foot in the air and falling back to stain his arm and wrist and the palm of his hand with warm carmine. He had a triumphant thought: "I did it!" The geyser spurted again, and he watched in sickly fascination the leap and fall of his own bright blood, this* crimson fountain that was his life. But then, suddenly, he was shaking again, his whole body quivering uncontrollably. A part of his mind, like an enemy trying to beguile him, pleaded: "Stop it! Shut off the circulation!" Instantly he said to himself: "No! Do it again!" He jerked up into a sitting position. Violently he slashed the flesh on his forearm. There was a quick flow of blood from a vein, but once again the alien within him cried: "Stop it! Call for help!" He cut down at the hollow of his elbow. Pain and terror blinded him now, and he almost toppled from the bunk. He fell over on his side, his mouth wide open, the tendons of his neck protruding like wires. And then he felt it – a scream for help that was swelling within him, and that he could not control, and that would burst from his mouth. "Now stab yourself, end it!" he told himself wildly. He jerked to his knees, groped for the toothbrush and found it. The thought came instantly: "It won't strike your heart, it'll break against your ribs" – and, in mid-passage, he changed the direction of his swing and drove it into his abdomen. He screamed and fell unconscious.

The scream was heard, but also it was not heard. At that moment there was an advertisement on the radio, a blend of girlish voices singing the virtues of a breakfast food. In several cells nearby there were men who heard the scream, yet were not sure what it was. Groves in 122 thought about it, but then dismissed it as a piece of radio static.

So it was that some ten minutes more passed before Johnny Lauter returned from the shower room. The transfers already were locked up, Eddie Quinn had just entered 102, and Lauter was on the runway alone. His feet were leaden, his whole body was dripping with a cold sweat. He was five cells away from 124 when the tier guard opened the door for him. He felt as though he couldn't go any further, but he did.

In the doorway he stopped, then jerked back on the tier runway. Varney had crumpled after stabbing himself; he was lying in a twisted heap crosswise on the bunk, his head towards the wall. As in the cruellest of dreams, Lauter saw the bloody, bleeding arm and, protruding from the naked abdomen, the bristles of the toothbrush. He couldn't move, he couldn't speak, he couldn't think. At the front end of the tier Mr Jonas called out loudly, in order to be heard over the radio: "Lauter – into your cell." Still Lauter remained where he was. "Hey there – what's the matter with you?" Mr Jonas shouted.

Lauter turned. He began to walk, then to run towards the guard. Perplexed, Mr Jonas watched him. "What's wrong with you?" he asked with curiosity.

"Varney!" Lauter's sallow face was milky white. "In my cell... he's bumped himself off."

Mr Jonas was a junior officer in the prison service, but he was well trained. His first concern was for the security of the tier. Therefore, before doing anything else, he checked the wall panel to be sure that all cell doors, except 124, were securely locked. Since they were, and the likelihood of an inmate trap was thereby diminished, he admitted himself to the tier runway, locked the door behind him and immediately ran his hands over Lauter's body for signs of a weapon.

"Jesus!" Lauter burst out, "I'm tellin' you straight."

Mr Jonas began running. With a great jangling of the keys on the brass ring at his hip, he pounded down the runway to 124. He saw the twisted form on the upper bunk, but since there was no light in the cell, the face was in shadow. He jumped for the switch.

He saw at once that Varney either was dead or else close to it. His face, drained of living colour, had the waxen look of a corpse. The mouth was sagging open, the lids were only half shut over the glazed eyeballs. Mr Jonas felt for the heart – thought he felt its flutter, was not sure, but then, turning the bloody arm over, saw a wild spurt of blood from the wrist. Instantly he snatched a handkerchief from his pocket, tied it around Varney's upper arm and, using his fountain pen, made a tourniquet. He twisted the pen until the flow of blood stopped, and then called sharply: "Tier man... Lauter... c'm'ere!"

Lauter appeared in the doorway. He had followed Mr Jonas down the tier, but he had been unable to re-enter the cell of his own volition.

"Hold this pen. Just like I have it."

Lauter obeyed.

"Don't let go." Mr Jonas ran out of the cell. To the accompaniment of the news programme on the radio, he pounded heavily down the runway past the silent, inquisitive faces of every man on the tier. He unlocked the tier door, locked it behind him and telephoned the Rotunda. The control office, not unaccustomed to this type of emergency, immediately notified the senior officer on duty, and then telephoned the prison hospital ward with a description of the medical situation. At the ward the night intern, who was a civilian, ordered the operating room made ready and a surgeon called from the adjacent city hospital, Gallinger General. Then, directing an inmate orderly to fetch a rolling stretcher, he set out with him through the series of basement passageways that led to cell block B1.

The senior officer from the control office arrived at the tier very quickly. He was a burly, white-haired lieutenant in his middle fifties who, unlike Mr Jonas, had witnessed enough inmate suicides to be neither flustered nor overconcerned. As Mr Jonas admitted him to the tier, he asked: "How bad is he?"

"I don't know, sir. I didn't do any more than stop the bleeding in his arm and get to the phone. But he stabbed himself with a toothbrush too. It's 124."

"Where did he stab himself?"

"In the belly."

"You sure it was suicide, not a fight?"

"I think so."

When the lieutenant entered 124, he saw Lauter holding the tourniquet in place, but standing with his eyes shut and his head sagging. It had been a ghastly interval for Lauter to endure by himself. Even more than the sight of Varney, it was what he himself was doing to keep his friend alive that was terrible for him. Once, for an instant, under the feeling that he simply could not do it, that Varney had the right to die, he had let the fountain pen go slack. But then, unable to watch the flow of blood, he had turned the pen until the tourniquet was tight.

The lieutenant asked: "Is he alive?"

"I think so," Lauter mumbled.

"Have you felt a pulse?"

"Ain't tried."

The lieutenant stepped up on the lower bunk and reached over to Varney's right wrist. After a few moments he said: "I don't know if I feel anything or not."

"I saw him breathe a coupla times."

"Yeah?" The lieutenant was straightening Varney's legs. Feeling the moist coldness of the skin he jumped down to the floor and tore the blanket off the lower bunk. He covered Varney with it, grumbling the meanwhile: "Don't anybody know enough to keep a man in this condition warm?"

Pallid-faced, Lauter said: "Lieutenant... this smell of blood is killin' me. This guy was my cellmate. Would you let me go out on the range?"

"You just keep a clamp on that fountain pen," the officer replied sharply. "I got things to do." He began a survey of the cell. He had taken note already that Lauter showed no bruises, cuts or other signs of combat, and he noticed now that the normal arrangements of the cell were not disturbed. He asked: "What are *you* in here for?"

"A bum rap. It was dismissed by a judge this afternoon. I'm goin' out of here tomorrow."

"You wouldn't try lying to me, bud, now would you?"

"It's easy enough to check."

The lieutenant grunted. He was partially satisfied that the evidence pointed to suicide, but he wanted to find the instrument with which Varney had cut himself. He was looking for it, without success, when the contingent from the hospital appeared.

"Is he alive?" the intern asked.

"I think so, but he's sure lost a hell of a lot of blood."

"Only cut his arm?" the intern asked, as he looked Varney over with his quick glance. "That's the radial artery, not a very big one. You'd be surprised how much blood a man can lose before dying."

"He stuck himself in the belly, too."

The intern raised the blanket. At the gruesome spectacle of a toothbrush protruding from a man's abdomen, he muttered: "Jesus, what don't they think of!" He pressed back one of Varney's eyelids, then took a stethoscope from his bag. He listened for the heartbeat, frowned and said: "I guess he'll make it to the operating table anyway. How long has that tourniquet been on?"

"Do you know?" the lieutenant asked Lauter.

"About ten minutes."

The intern nodded, substituted a rubber tourniquet for the handkerchief and told the orderly to roll the stretcher into the cell.

"Listen," said the lieutenant, "handle that toothbrush as carefully as you can. If there are any fingerprints on it, we don't want to lose them."

The intern nodded.

When the lieutenant found the strip of tin with which Varney had cut his arm, he told Lauter to come along. In the corridor outside the tier, where Mr Jonas joined them, the lieutenant scrutinized Lauter for a long moment and then asked roughly: "You smoke a pipe?"

Pale and physically shaky, but in command of himself, Lauter replied: "No."

"Does he?"

"Varney? No."

"How'd he get hold of a tobacco can, then? You see this?" Holding the sides of the butterfly wing between thumb and forefinger, the lieutenant thrust it towards Lauter's face; stamped clearly on one side was the remnant of the trademark – the last three letters of the word "Prince", followed by "Albert".

"There's plenty around. Anybody can get one."

"You know this tin'll hold fingerprints good, don't you?"

"Sure."

"You know if *you* cut him, it'll show up?"

"You got my prints on file. Go ahead and compare."

Abruptly the lieutenant turned to Mr Jonas. "You got anything to say?"

"Yes, sir. We've just been having showers for transfers. Lauter here is tier man – he was in the shower room all the time. It was after the showers were over that he found Varney."

"Uh-huh – but did you see Varney before you started the showers?"

"No, sir."

"So for all you know he could've been cut up already?"

"Yes, sir."

"What was the last time you saw him in normal shape?"

Mr Jonas frowned. "I don't remember – maybe when he came back from court."

"When was that?"

"About three thirty... a little earlier maybe."

"Chow comes at five. Did Varney go to that?"

"I don't know."

"He went," said Lauter.* "I can point you out the man who sat next to him."

"You can?" the lieutenant asked with some sarcasm. "How come?"

"I happened to notice. You want to hear some facts from me?"

"Go ahead."

"Varney was in on second-degree murder. He got sentenced today. He got twenty-five to life."

The lieutenant grunted. He pursed his lips, thought for a moment, then asked: "He tell you he was gonna do it?"

"No."

"Well now," the lieutenant said reflectively, "if he only got sentenced today, then he probably didn't have any idea of killing himself until after he found out what his sentence was. That means he started preparing for it *after* he came back from court. That means it took him some time to file down this piece of tin. It means he went to work on his toothbrush too. You can't stick a toothbrush into your belly unless the end is sharp, can you, bud? Now, where the hell were you while he was doing all this?"

"In the first place," Lauter told him deliberately, "there's no law I ever heard of says a man has to be a stool pigeon. In the second place, I'm a tier man. Until chow was over I had work to do, or I was walkin' up and down the runway chewin' the fat. So I wasn't in the cell to know what

Varney might be doin'. Hell, I'm goin' free tomorrow. I wasn't hungry to spend any time with a guy who just got twenty-five years."

"OK, buster," the lieutenant said with a dry chuckle, "you're not fooling me. You knew damn well he was going to cut himself. But don't worry, I won't hang anything on you because you didn't squeal. If your prints aren't on this or on the toothbrush, you're clear."

Lauter sighed a little. "Lieutenant?"

"What?"

"Can I get moved to another cell for tonight?"

"You got space?" the lieutenant asked Mr Jonas.

"Yes, sir."

"You can move him... Don't clean up that cell till I call you." The lieutenant strode off.

Tom McPeak was standing at the bars of 130 when Lauter appeared before the door carrying a pillow, a blanket and a mattress cover. The door ground open, Lauter entered and the door slammed* shut.

Wearily Lauter tossed the bedclothes on the lower bunk, sat down on the wall seat and lit a cigarette.

McPeak said, pointing to the far corner of the cell: "From where I was standin' I saw a guy carried out on a stretcher. Somebody get sick?"

Before Lauter could reply there came a banging on the cell wall by someone in 128. McPeak called: "What you want?"

"We wanna know from Johnny what happened."

With a sigh Lauter walked to the front of the cell. "Varney tried to kill himself when I was out in the shower room. He cut his arm to ribbons with a piece of tin, and he must've made a shiv out of a toothbrush. He stuck himself in the belly with it."

"Is he dead?"

"No, but he's bad off. They've taken him down for an operation. Don't ask me no more questions now, will you? I'm dead beat."

He returned to the wall seat, rested his elbows on the table and supported his head with both hands. McPeak, chewing a match, listened to the low pounding of fists on steel as the news was passed on. There was no programme on the radio now, and the buzz of men's voices rose in the wing. Presently McPeak said: "You feel like sleepin', I'll be glad to fix up your bunk for you."

Lauter shook his head. "I couldn't go to sleep now any more'n I could fly."

"What made him do it?"

Lauter ran a hand over his pallid face and sighed a little. "He got sentenced today... twenty-five to life. Look, I don't feel like talkin' about it any more. I liked that boy. I wanna get him off my mind."

"Sure, OK."

There was silence between them for a moment, and then Lauter said heavily, in an obvious attempt to find some conversation that would distract him: "You got yourself in a little trouble at chow tonight, huh?"

McPeak laughed. "Guess I did. I'm all the time losin' my temper. You think I'm gonna git disciplined out of it?"

"Could be. Inmates ain't supposed to talk to a screw the way you did."

"Send me to that there Hole?"

"I don't know. Maybe just take away some privileges."

"You think those coloured fellers'll git sent to the Hole?"

"Don't know that either. But the way they handled themselves an' stuck together, I don't think too much'll happen to 'em. When a whole bunch of guys put up a beef, the top screws get worried. If they put all those mess men in the Hole, they gotta start worryin' about what the rest of the coloured fellers in the whole jail will do."

"That's good. Glad to hear it about them, an' about me too."

"How come a cracker like you ain't down on coloured people?" Lauter asked with frank curiosity.

"Usta be, but I changed. I learnt things. I'm agin this discrimination."

"Yeah," Lauter said with sudden intensity, "people change." He stood up and began to pace the cell. "That's what this damn prison system can't do. It ain't set up to make guys any better. Hell, it just twists most of 'em more outa shape. There ain't anybody so bad he don't have some good in him. I've been watchin' my own kids grow up. They're good kids, wonderful – but don't nobody tell me they couldn't end up in a reform school like I did. All it takes is to handle 'em bad, nobody carin' what happens to 'em."

"I got kids too," McPeak said fondly, "a boy an' a girl. I—"

He was interrupted by the loudspeaker telling all officers to make their seven-thirty-five evening count.

"The count is clear," Lauter erupted bitterly. "One more guy dyin' or dead, and who cares?" He stopped pacing, climbed up on the top bunk and stretched out on the mattress.

"This ol' world sure needs a lot of fixin', don't it?" McPeak said philosophically. "I look to the labour movement to do a big part of it, too. Economics an' politics – them's at the bottom of everythin', I believe."

"Maybe so," Lauter responded, and closed his eyes.

Chapter 16

The Firefly

On the fourth tier, among the Negro inmates, there was no knowledge of Varney's attempt at suicide, and the men were preoccupied with other matters. Reeves, Tillman and Finnerty were due to be transferred the next morning, and all three were jubilant. They were in the shower room at the moment, and the worries they had brought with them* from supper were being dissipated by George Benjamin. "I know what I'm talkin' about," Benjamin was saying in an authoritative manner. "They's gonna forgit what happened at chow. Cos when the Bureau of Prisons orders 'em to move inmates, they gotta do it. Ain't none of you fellers gone t'be kept here for discipline on that kind of charge."

"You think it'll stay as a mark against us, though?" asked Reeves. "I mean for parole or good time?"

"I doubt it – ain't serious enough. You'll start fresh in the pen you git sent to."

"What about you an' Spaulding an' Wellman?"

Benjamin grinned comfortably. "You fellers movin' out is good for us, too – especially you, ol' man. You was the ringleader of our revolution. I don't expect they'll do much to us."

Reeves laughed with sudden pleasure as he soaped his sinewy body. "I don't recollect as I ever was a ringleader of anythin' before, but I liked it."

"Goddamn!" exclaimed Benjamin. "We sure told that Mr Coe off. I hate that man. He's the meanest screw in the joint."

"He don't like us neither," said Finnerty.

"What about some of those third-tier men?" Tillman put in. "They're real Ku Kluxers. I'd like to shoot them dead. Like to get 'em in front of my army Garand.* Bam! Bam!"

"The one I kaint figure out is that McPeak," said Finnerty. "He put hisself way out on a limb talkin' up for us. But if'n he feels that way, why ain't he honest enough t'stand by Wilson?"

"People got all sorts of things in their hearts," said Reeves thoughtfully. "Good an' bad, strong an' weak – we don't know that man good enough to know why he's like he is. All I know is he's a white man I'd be friends with any day. Say, listen, Benjamin, how come the guard didn't tell you where we was goin' tomorrow? Don't he know?"

"Maybe he knows, maybe not, but he didn't tell me."

"I sure hope it's Lorton," Reeves exclaimed fervently. He turned on the water in his shower and raised his voice so that he could be heard above it. "If I pull Lorton, my wife an' my boys can visit me every month. That way I can talk over business with 'em, keep my hand in things."

Benjamin suddenly adjusted his eyeglasses on his stubby nose and gazed at Reeves in a sorrowful manner. He said: "I got bad news for you, ol' man. Thought I wouldn't tell you the truth just yet, felt sorry for you, but now I guess I may as well. Tillman an' Finnerty are goin' to Lorton, but you ain't!"

"What?" Reeves shut off the water. "What's that?"

"You got a bad deal for an ol' man. They're sendin' you to a rough place – far away, too."

"Don't 'ol' man' me, an' don't feel so sorry for me," Reeves told him. "Just let me know where I'm goin'."

"Real far, where your family kaint visit easy."

"Ashland, you mean?"

"Nooo! Ashland's on'y in Kentucky. They're sendin' you real far."

"Well where, dammit – Texarkana?"

"Noooo – Texarkana's on'y Texas. You're really gettin' shipped – you got the finger. I guess the govinment's startin' t'get tough with you income-tax boys."

"Well, goldarn it, there ain't no other place they can send me. I've done covered every place for a short-timer like me."

"Three years may be short, but the govinment don't like income-tax criminals."

"Benjamin, damn your heart, you gonna tell me *where* I'm goin' or ain't you?"

"I was aimin' to tell you," Benjamin retorted in a waspish manner, "but if you're gonna cuss me out, then the hell with you." He left the shower room.

Reeves, utterly exasperated, started to follow him, then stopped as he realized that he still had soap on his body. "Now, ain't that the dirtiest deal you ever heard of?" he complained to the two others as he turned on the water. "Knowin' where a man's goin' an' not tellin' him! What other place is there?"

Tillman, drying himself, responded carelessly: "You forgot Alcatraz."

"*Alcatraz?* That's for real *convicts.*"

"What the hell do you think you are, a lil ol' violet?"

"I'm not *that* kind of criminal. I never been in trouble in my life before this. I tripped over my income tax, but Alcatraz ain't for men like me. Why, I got my own business, I got my sons workin' with me, I own my house, I'm a deacon in my church…" He stopped as Benjamin suddenly stepped back into the shower room. Reeves shut off his water, stepped up to the little tier man and seized him by the shirt. "Man, tell me the truth now – they sendin' me to Alcatraz?"

"Nooo," Benjamin replied sombrely, "you got a worser deal'n that. Alcatraz ain't so far, on'y in California. They're shippin' you to a new pen in Alaska."

Reeves stood with mouth agape.

"It's a brand-new pen," Benjamin continued, "jus' for income-tax boys an' fairies. You ever heard of it, Tillman?"

"Sure. Jus' las' week I read about it in the paper. That's the place they feed you frozen fish an' nothin' else, ain't it?"

"That's right! Call it 'Cold Can Reformatory'," said Benjamin, doubling over with laughter. "Poor ol' man, I feel sorry for you."

A sheepish grin came slowly to Reeves's face. "My," he said, "I sure swallowed that one."

"Cold Can Reformatory," Benjamin repeated with delight.

"Hey, in there," came the voice of the tier guard, "finish up an' get out."

"All of us be out in a minute," Benjamin sang back. "There's one ol' man still wet behind the ears."

At about this time in the evening the prison hospital put through an emergency call to the central office in the Rotunda. In turn, the Rotunda advised all tier guards in all cell blocks that a transfusion of whole blood, type O, was needed at the hospital. The officers were instructed to find out at once if there was a type O among the inmates in their charge.

As Mr Losey, the guard in charge of Tier Four, passed down the line, he found, as the other guards also were learning, that very few of the inmates knew their blood type. In 428, however, Alfrice Tillman answered immediately: "That's me – O… I'm universal."

"You sure?"

"I been sellin' my blood on the outside ever since I got outa the army. I can be used for everybody. I'm what they call an ORh negative."

"You willing to give a transfusion to a man in the hospital?"

Tillman thought about this for a moment and then answered readily enough: "Sure."

Mr Losey consulted the scrap of paper in his hand. "You ever had malaria?"

"Nope."

"Infectious hepa..." he hesitated over the pronunciation, and Tillman supplied it: "Hepatitis – they always ask that. Nope."

"OK. I have to report back. If your cell door opens, come right down front."

Mr Losey departed, and Reeves said with feeling: "That's a Christian thing to do, Tillman. I'm proud of you."

Tillman burst out laughing. "You got me wrong, Deacon. I never yet put a dime in a church collection box, an' I never will."

"Maybe you ain't a churchgoer," the old man responded earnestly, "but you can be a Christian anyway."

"Now look, get your feet on the ground," Tillman said with a grin. "You know why I'm willin' to give blood? Cos maybe they'll give me some extra good time in exchange. If I knew right now they wouldn't, I wouldn't even give 'em my piss."

Reeves was silent for a moment, obviously shocked. Then he said reproachfully: "You don't really mean that, do you? Suppose that man in the hospital would die?..."

"Now, wait a minute," Tillman interrupted. "I know this racket: it's a cash business. All the big hospitals buy blood an' store it up. Suppose you get sick an' need a transfusion? If you got any money, they soak you for it plenty, believe me. This jail could get type O in five minutes from Gallinger or any city hospital, but it would be charged up against them. That's why they're askin' for volunteers, they..." Tillman stopped in mid-sentence. A thought had brought an intense frown to his good-looking face. "Hey," he muttered softly, "suppose it's an ofay?" He jumped to his feet in perturbation. "I'll give blood to a damn dog if I get something out of it, but I sure won't give my blood free to no goddamn white man. Why didn't I ask that guard?"

"It's too late now, ain't it?" Reeves pointed out quietly. "You volunteered. They want you, you gotta go through with it."

"The hell I do! Let 'em pay off. I won't give no free blood to a damn peck – I'm tellin' you that right here an' now!"

"You mean to say you'd let any man die, even a white man?"

"Let 'em pay me off, that's all I say!" Tillman replied passionately. "Suppose it's some bastard like that Ballou. What do I wanna save *him* for? I'd like to see him dead!"

"But you don't know *who* it is. Suppose it's another kind of man – like McPeak?"

"Jesus Christ," Tillman exclaimed naively, "what'd you have to bring him up for? Now I don't know what to do. Sure, I'd help a man like him, but I sure wouldn't wanna give my blood to some white man who thinks I'm dirt."

"Sometimes a Negro man needs to put his hand out *first* to a white man," Reeves said earnestly. And then, with severity, "I'll tell you some-thin', Tillman. You can be as unchristian as you want, but there's no bigger truth in the whole world than 'do unto others'.* If a white man who never did you any harm is dyin' an' you put a price on savin' him, then I say you'd put a price on a coloured man too. It ain't his bein' white that's stoppin' you: it's that you ain't got no feelin' for anybody outside yourself, white or black."

The door to their cell jarred, then ground open. In silence, not gazing at Reeves, Tillman walked out.

Officer Coe, who had been dispatched from the Rotunda to conduct Tillman to the hospital ward, smiled a thin smile when he saw that the volunteer was one of the mess men. Tillman saw the smile and thought to himself "Screw you, bud", but his face remained uncommunicative. Nevertheless, as they walked swiftly through the underground corridors, Tillman asked: "Mr Coe – you know who this transfusion's for?"

"No. Why?"

"Jus' wonderin'."

"Does it make any difference to you?"

"Thought I might know him."

At the hospital, where the intern immediately drew blood from Tillman's ear lobe in order to confirm his type, Tillman asked: "Can you tell me who this transfusion's for, doc?"

"Man named Varney," the intern replied. "He had a transfusion a little while ago, when he was on the operating table, but now he needs another one and we're out of blood." He ran out of the room with the sample.

"Since it's Varney, he's a fellow from your wing," Mr Coe volunteered. "He tried to kill himself tonight."

"Uh-huh."

"Do you know him?"

"Ain't sure."

"Tier One... a white man."

"Uh-huh."

"Isn't that what you've been trying to find out?"

Tillman stiffened. "I didn't say anythin' like that, did I?"

"No, but you looked it."

Tillman said nothing.

Mr Coe smiled. It was not a good smile: it was the Uncle Charlie smile, as Tillman had learnt it early in life – contemptuous, superior. With cold amusement Mr Coe said: "How come you haven't asked me what you'll get out of this?"

"It ain't been on my mind."

Mr Coe smiled. "You might be thinking you'll get some extra good time, but you won't. The administration doesn't do that."

Tillman said nothing.

"I've got two packets* of cigarettes in my pocket," Mr Coe continued. "That's all the pay-off there is. Maybe you don't want to do it for that?"

"I don't smoke," Tillman answered softly.

The intern ran in, beckoned and called: "OK, let's go."

"Sure," Tillman said, and strode out.

A bed had been rolled into the isolation room where Varney lay. There was an unpleasant smell of ether in the room, and the sound of Varney's breathing – harsh, stertorous and unnatural – was upsetting to Tillman. He lay on the auxiliary bed with his left arm stretched out, his muscular, healthy arm with a needle in it, his husky brown arm sending blood through a rubber tube into the white arm of a stranger who had tried to commit suicide. The white intern was standing by Varney's bed, watching his face, counting his pulse. Between the two beds a white nurse was operating the transfusion apparatus. On a small table before her was a control valve and, attached to it, a large syringe, the latter strapped to a board. A rubber tube ran from the syringe to a bottle of citrate beneath the table. From a second outlet of the valve another tube ran to the needle in Varney's arm, and from the third outlet still another to Tillman. Quietly, efficiently, the nurse filled the syringe, turned the lever of the valve, then slowly pumped the bright fluid into Varney. The process was familiar to Tillman, and he paid no attention to it. His eyes were half closed, and he was thinking. He had seen Varney's face when he entered the room; if he cared to turn his head, he would be able to see him now in profile, but he didn't want to see that face any more. He never had spoken to Varney, but he remembered the healthy face from Tier One, and he knew how sharply it had changed. A sunken, drained-out, cadaver's face that said: "I've suffered" – a face that spoke to him with a poignancy that surprised him, and that he was trying to understand. Why was he feeling sorry for an ofay he didn't even know?

Tillman was not a reflective young man, and very little of his life's experience had been calculated to induce compassion for white men. In the back alleys of Washington, where so much of the coloured population lived in squalor, a boy learnt his social catechism early: that the white man had it good and the coloured man had it bad; that the law was a white man's law, and democracy was a whore with one blind eye. Yet now, somehow, he was sensing the inner heart of this white man with the cadaver's face. Varney's face said "I've suffered much" – and he might be white, he might be a stranger, but his suffering brought kinship. It made Tillman wonder what Varney's life had been like, and what had made him want death. It made him wonder by what right they were interfering this way, trying to bring back to life a man who had tried so hard to die. It brought to his mind an odd, bedevilling notion: that somewhere along the line this white man had been lynched no less than many a coloured man.

"You feel all right?" the nurse suddenly whispered to him.

He opened his eyes and nodded.

"We're more than half through."

He nodded again. Then he said: "Mr Coe… what happens to a guy who tries suicide… if he lives, I mean?"

"He gets in trouble," the guard replied. "He gets solitary for a long time. Of course," he added with a faint grin, "he can always try it again."

"Very funny," Tillman thought. He closed his eyes and told himself that he was sorry he had volunteered for this.

Time passed. He was beginning to feel, as he always did, a bit weakened by the loss of blood. Then he heard the intern say: "Nurse – hold it." He looked over at the other bed. The intern had his stethoscope to Varney's chest. "I don't get any heartbeat – stop the transfusion!"

Quickly the nurse drew the needle from Tillman's vein, placed some cotton in the hollow of his elbow and flexed his arm. The intern said: "Adhesive." He had removed the needle from Varney's arm and was pressing cotton to the puncture. He snatched the strip of adhesive from the nurse and said: "Ten minims of adrenalin for an intracardiac." As the nurse ran out of the room, he taped the cotton over the puncture and instantly began artificial respiration, raising and lowering Varney's arms in the rhythm of normal breathing.

Mr Coe, at the foot of Varney's bed, asked "Anything I can do?", but the intern only grunted in reply.

Tillman was sitting up, sweating. As the intern moved forwards and back, he kept catching glimpses of Varney's face. His eyes were riveted on that sorrowful face, waiting to see if the set mouth would open, hoping that it would not. This was too much like the torture he always had feared for himself in the still of the night – the heartless white mob bent upon a lynching. A man wanted life, but they killed him; a man wanted death, but they forced him to live.

The nurse ran in carrying a syringe, the needle topped with cotton. The intern pulled away the blanket covering Varney and raised the short hospital gown to expose the chest. Quickly his fingers palpated downwards from the collar bone, then moved to the left and pointed. He took the syringe from the nurse and checked it with a quick glance while she swabbed the spot with alcohol. With care and neatness, he drove the two-inch needle into the still chest.

Tillman groaned.

"Quiet," the nurse whispered to him. "Lie down."

He paid no attention. He watched as the needle was withdrawn, the puncture swabbed, the chest and bandaged abdomen hidden again by the olive blanket. Once again the intern began artificial respiration, moving forwards and backwards, breathing a bit heavily himself as he worked to make Varney breathe.

They waited, and when ten minutes or ten years had passed, the intern stopped. He pressed his stethoscope to Varney's chest, and then pressed back one eyelid, and then stood up. He made a clicking sound with his tongue and said: "Well, he's dead." To the astonishment of the others Tillman cried out: "That's fine! He on'y got lynched once."

At ten minutes before nine o'clock Mr Jonas, on duty at Tier One, stepped up to the wall panel that controlled the lights of the west wing. He was humming a popular song as he reflected with pleasure that in a little more than two hours he would be on his way home. Like a clerk operating an adding machine, he pressed a series of buttons in the wall panel. In rapid succession the lights on all tier runways went dark. Mr Jonas jabbed at a second row of buttons and turned off all but the dim night lights of the eating range. Then, still humming, he returned to his desk in the corridor where he was censoring the outgoing mail.

Now, in the entire wing, men began to prepare for bed, lighting up a final cigarette as they removed their clothes. The rustle of conversation rose higher because, after nine o'clock, talk would be forbidden.

Several floors below, in the darkness of the Hole, Art Ballou was lying at rest, waiting for sleep. The hard mattress which he had been given a few minutes before felt wonderfully comfortable after the hours of concrete floor. Nevertheless he would not sleep well on this night. Hunger would awaken him and make his rest fitful, and he would know better by morning what it meant to be sentenced to the Hole. It would not teach him anything significant, however: although he was only eighteen years old, he already was as formed in his character as a stone.

Three cells away from him Huey Wilson was thinking of the day just passed, and of the days to come. He was not thinking of himself, but of his mother, and of the millions upon millions of Negro women like his mother, who were so decent in heart, and so patient, and so hardworking – and who received so little. Mothers like his with swollen legs from overwork; mothers with sorrow in their hearts for sons who had ended up like George Benjamin; mothers who held a crying child to their aprons and tried to explain man's inhumanity to man. Surely the day would come when such women would come into their own, when their daughters could gaze smiling at their own dark faces in a mirror, and when their sons could freely aspire in a land of brotherhood.

As for himself, he felt at ease in this dark Hole. He had no regrets, and he was not afraid.

In 102 of the west wing Eddie Quinn was washing his dentures under the faucet, and wondering whether he would have any luck at Lorton, and whether it would be worthwhile talking to the warden about a cure for his drinking. At the other end of the tier Johnny Lauter was explaining to Tom McPeak what the procedure was in a preliminary hearing – and three tiers above them Alfrice Tillman, rather hesitantly, was trying to tell Isaac Reeves why he had felt so much compassion for a white stranger.

So men talked their tag-end talk on this warm October night in the year 1946 – until the minute hand reached the hour of nine and Mr Jonas stepped up to the wall panel, and all cells on all tiers went dark. With darkness came quiet. Men lay in loneliness, and now one coughed and one began to snore, and another wept.

Yet there was to be one more moment to this day for the men on Tier One. Johnny Lauter, staring out at the darkened eating range, saw a winking light near his cell. In all of his years in prison he never had seen anything like that, and he sat up to watch it. The light vanished towards the floor, winked suddenly farther out on the range, disappeared and winked again. He realized that it was a firefly. Quietly he got down from his bunk, nudged McPeak and walked to the bars. Standing side by side, smiling, the two men watched the tiny cold-green light. Winking and floating it moved through the cavern of the wing. All along the tier there were others who saw it and who sat up or left their bunks to gaze with wonder and amusement at this pretty thing. There was strange relish to this sight of an insect floating gay and free in a prison for men. But then, in the heart of more than one man, there was a burst of sadness. And a question came to mind that they could not answer. For the firefly was free while they were behind bars; the firefly was fulfilling its nature in this gentle, easy, winking flight, while they were unfulfilled and their lives had no free flight in them, and nothing was easy or glowing in their days or nights, their pasts or their futures. And what was man, that so often he did not fulfil himself, not even as well as an insect? They did not know, but there was no one among them who did not think back to the years of his childhood, when the future had held nothing but radiance, and when it had been his pleasure to run through a meadow or city lot to catch these odd insects and hold them prisoner, and gaze at them with delight.

They watched, and for a few moments were children again, returning to the childhood of soft grass under bare feet, of moonlight on cornfield or tenement roof – until the firefly passed through the steel mesh at the end of the wing and vanished from their sight. Then, with longing and nostalgia, they returned to their bunks.

The jail was quiet. Men slept – these men who were sinners. A long day in their short lives had passed, a short day in the history of humankind. Another day would come.

Note on the Text

The text is based on the first edition of the novel published in April 1957 (London: John Calder), which preceded the American edition (New York: International Publishers) by about two months. The UK and US publishers appear to have been working from the same typescript, but chose (slightly unusually) not to share the pagination costs, making several corrections to the text before publication independently of each other. Apart from keeping all Americanisms, the International Publishers edition chose to present colloquial speech without elision marks, for example "comin", "goin", etc. The Calder edition Anglicized the spelling throughout and changed some of the American words to their English equivalents. A few grating changes made by Calder (such as the replacement of "movie" and "movies" with "cinema" or the occasional toning-down of a swearword) have been restored according to the reading of the American edition, and the corrections indicated in the notes. Both publishers picked up a number of errors in the original script (the Calder edition being generally more accurate), which have been silently corrected in the present text. The most significant variants between the two editions have been indicated in the notes. The spelling and punctuation have been standardized, modernized and made consistent throughout. Some commonly known authors and fictitious references have not been annotated.

Notes

p. 7, *In the centre of all... indirectly tend*: From 'A Backward Glance o'er Travelled Roads', a prose epilogue to Walt Whitman's (1819–92) poetry collection *Leaves of Grass*, in which the author talks about his influences and his aims in the composition of the book.

p. 7, *You got a right... to the tree of life*: From the Negro spiritual 'You Got a Right' (ll. 1–2).

p. 12, *second-degree murder*: Murder with malicious intent but not premeditated.

p. 12, *In the dream... defend himself*: Floyd Varney's dream adumbrates the story of Prometheus – who, punished for stealing fire from the gods, is fettered to a rock, where an eagle (the embodiment of Zeus) is sent to eat his liver.

p. 18, *commodes*: American Edn: "toilets".

p. 20, *pegs*: American Edn: "pins".

p. 21, *have*: American Edn: "do".

p. 24, *a car*: American Edn: "an auto".

p. 29, *round*: American Edn: "around".

p. 29, *Gruen*: One of the largest watch manufacturers in the USA, active between 1894 and 1958.

p. 29, *packet*: American Edn: "package".

p. 31, *snotty*: Despicable.

p. 31, *gone to the movies*: Amended from "gone to the cinema", based on the American Edn.

p. 32, *pavement*: American Edn (here and passim): "sidewalk".

p. 32, *movie*: Amended from "cinema", based on the American Edn.

p. 33, *peckerwoods*: Unsophisticated, rustic white men.

p. 33, *the Ford Company*: The Ford Motor Company, a car manufacturer based, at the time, in Detroit.

p. 34, *round*: American Edn: "around".

p. 34, *suitcase*: Amended from "suitcases", based on the American Edn.

p. 34, *sent*: American Edn: "send".

p. 35, *tail bone*: The coccyx, the small triangular bone at the base of the spinal column.

p. 36, *fitted*: American Edn: "fit".

p. 36, *Frederick Douglass*: The American abolitionist and social reformer Frederick Douglass (c.1817–95).

p. 36, *on*: American Edn: "at".

p. 37, *"Dónde... paises, en..."*: "Where is Spanish spoken?" "Spanish is spoken in many countries, in..." (Spanish).

p. 38, *an ofay*: A white person (slang).

p. 41, *somewhere*: American Edn: "somewheres".

p. 41, *separate*: American Edn: "separated".

p. 43, *your*: American Edn: "yor".

p. 43, *'em*: American Edn: "them".

p. 45, *would be shy his rent money*: "Would be short of his rent money."

p. 51, *relief*: Food-bank assistance.

p. 51, *this man*: American Edn: "this new man".

p. 52, *attraction*: American Edn: "attention".

p. 52, *Jim Crow*: Racial discrimination (from the name of the eponymous black character in 'Jim Crow', an early nineteenth-century plantation song of the American South). "Jim Crow laws" were a series of state and local laws introduced in the southern United States in the late nineteenth and early twentieth centuries that enforced racial segregation.

p. 52, *Charlie*: Black slang term for a white man.

p. 54, *those*: American Edn: "these".

p. 56, *twenty*: American Edn: "twenny".

p. 56, *amazed*: American Edn: "amused".

p. 56, *feller*: American Edn: "fellow".

p. 58, *swung into*: American Edn: "swung out into".

p. 58, *perty*: Pretty.

p. 59, *white lightning*: Inferior or illicitly distilled whiskey.

p. 59, *in the Battle of New Georgia*: There were a series of battles on New Georgia, the largest of the islands in Western Province, Solomon Islands, between the Empire of Japan and the Allied forces of the United States, New Zealand, Australia and the British Solomon Islands from 30th June to 7th October 1943, resulting in a victory for the Allies.

p. 60, *round*: American Edn: "around".

p. 63, *nodded his agreement*: American Edn: "nodded in agreement".

p. 63, *took the slices*: American Edn: "took the two slices".

p. 65, *his*: American Edn: "this".

p. 67, *as*: American Edn: "and".

p. 67, *mass*: American Edn: "mess".

p. 68, *potato*: American Edn (here and l. 6): "potata".

p. 68, *That —— Ballou*: American Edn: "That —— —— —— —— —— Ballou".

p. 68, *Spaulding laughed at the rhyme*: American Edn: "Even Spaulding laughed over the rhyme".

p. 68, *rather*: American Edn: "ruther".

p. 69, *hempen justice*: Lynching ("hempen" referring to the hangman's halter).

p. 71, *way station*: Intermediate stop.

p. 71, *railway*: American Edn (here and passim): "railroad".

p. 71, *baloney*: Bologna sausage.

p. 72, *hid*: American Edn: "hid good".

p. 75, *lay*: "A woman who is readily available for sexual intercourse" (*OED*).

p. 75, *Mount Vernon*: The plantation residence of George Washington and his wife Martha.

p. 76, *Gurkha knife*: A kukri, a short sword with a curved blade used by soldiers of the Gurkha regiment.

p. 82, *in their hearts*: American Edn: "in their own hearts".

p. 84, *packet*: American Edn: "pack".

p. 86, *Uncle Tom*: A black person considered submissive or servile to white people.

p. 86, *rewarded*: Amended from "regarded", based on the American Edn (see also later on, in Chapter 6: "to the reward of Huey's laughter").

p. 87, *called*: American Edn: "called out".

p. 90, *tony*: fashionable; "swell".

p. 90, *pecks*: "Peckerwoods" (see first note to p. 33).

p. 90, *handkerchief head*: A black man who is servile to white men, an "Uncle Tom".

p. 91, *movies*: Amended from "cinema", based on the American Edn.

p. 91, *if you was to move out of here*: American Edn: "if they was to move you out of here".

p. 92, *"R" and "B"*: For "Red" and "Black". Reeves and Tillman are playing a game of draughts ("checkers" in American English, as it is called later in Chapter 6).

p. 92, *whirled by a tornado... he always had loved*: Probably a reference to *The Wonderful Wizard of Oz* (1900) by L. Frank Baum (1856–1919), in which the young Dorothy and her dog Toto are caught up in a cyclone and transported to the magical land of Oz.

p. 93, *could*: American Edn: "would".

p. 93, *thoughts*: American Edn: "thought".

p. 95, *them*: American Edn: "him".

p. 96, *NAACP*: The National Association for the Advancement of Coloured People, a civil-rights organization formed in 1909.

p. 97, *so*: American Edn: "this".

p. 98, *two or three days*: American Edn: "two, three days".

p. 99, *round*: American Edn: "around".

p. 99, *get at that time of night*: American Edn: "get that time of night".

p. 102, *a car*: American Edn: "an automobile".

p. 102, *round*: American Edn: "around".

p. 102, *Georgia cracker*: A name given to the native whites of Georgia (originally a contemptuous name given to the poorest whites in the southern United States).

p. 102, *moonshiners*: Distillers of illicit liquor.

p. 104, *my*: American Edn: "the".

p. 105, *have*: American Edn: "let".

p. 106, *We went to a movie, the girl and I. After the movie*: Amended from "We went to a cinema, the girl and I. After the cinema".

p. 106, *movies*: Amended from "cinemas", based on the American Edn.

p. 107, *same day that there was a race riot*: American Edn: "same day there was a race riot".

p. 107, *But we know there have been*: American Edn: "But we know that there have been".

p. 109, *fee*: American Edn: "fees".

p. 109, *eat so high on the hog*: Live in such an extravagant or luxurious way.

p. 110, *two or three years*: American Edn: "two, three years".

p. 110, *give*: American Edn: "gives".

p. 113, *it*: Amended from "you", based on the American Edn.

p. 114, *At*: American Edn: "An".

p. 114, *He had a suitcase with clothes*: American Edn: "He had a suitcase".

p. 114, *I doubt if anybody*: American Edn: "I doubt anybody".

p. 114, *round*: American Edn: "around".

p. 114, *you'd*: American Edn: "you".

p. 115, *the Phui fraternity*: A non-existent fraternity. "Pfui" is an expression of disgust or cursory dismissal. The Greek letter "Phi" (Φ), on the other hand, appears in the name of many American college fraternities.

p. 117, *genius who ever lived*: American Edn: "genius ever lived".

p. 118, *The Sea-Wolf*: A 1904 adventure novel by Jack London (1876–1916).

p. 119, *It's give*: Sic.

p. 120, *very drunk on the night*: American Edn: "very drunk the night".

p. 121, *Resurrection*: An 1899 novel by Leo Tolstoy.

p. 121, *of*: American Edn: "in".

p. 121, *There was one there*: The Tolstoy story referred to is 'How Much Land Does a Man Need?' (1886).

p. 122, *retorted with a guffaw*: Amended from "retorted with guffaw", based on the American Edn.

p. 122, *grapple it*: Amended from "grapple with it", based on the American Edn.

p. 123, *round*: American Edn: "around".

p. 125, *car*: American Edn: "auto".

p. 127, *garage*: American Edn: "gasoline station".

p. 129, *could best be settled*: American Edn: "could be best settled".

p. 131, *aeroplane*: American Edn: "airplane".

p. 131, *than for his father*: Amended from "than his father", based on the American Edn.

p. 134, *'stir simple'*: "Stir crazy"; a person who is psychologically disturbed as a result of being confined in a prison for a long time (from "stir": "prison").

p. 137, *chittlins*: Chitterlings, the smaller intestines of a pig cooked as food.

p. 140, *car*: American Edn: "auto".

p. 141, *hooey*: Nonsense.

p. 141, *movie*: Amended from "cinema", based on the American Edn.

p. 143, *Outside the bull pen*: American Edn: "Outside of the bull pen".

p. 145, *packet*: American Edn (here and in the following sentence): "pack".

p. 145, *get you out in about three years*: American Edn: "get you out on parole in about three years".

p. 146, *the*: American Edn: "that".

p. 148, *pulled boners*: Made a mistake; got it wrong.

p. 150, *Joe*: Fellow; guy.

p. 152, *get*: American Edn: "git".

p. 152, *heerd*: American Edn: "heard".

p. 152, *discriminashun*: American Edn: "discrimination".

p. 153, *Carter's*: American Edn (here and passim): "Carters".

p. 154, *and three or four*: Amended from "and, as well, three or four", based on the American Edn.

p. 155, *Dixie*: A nickname for the southern United States.

p. 158, *Bohn Aluminum*: Bohn Aluminum and Brass Corporation, a manufacturing company based in Detroit.

p. 159, *for both of us*: American Edn: "for us both".

p. 161, *Your*: Amended from "You", based on the American Edn.

p. 166, *Joe Louis... heavyweight champion of the world*: The American boxer Joe "Brown Bomber" Louis (1914–81) was world heavyweight champion from 1937 to 1949.

p. 167, *Jackie Robinson*: Jackie Robinson (1919–72) was the first African-American to play in Major League Baseball.

p. 167, *Brooklyn Dodgers*: A Major League Baseball team founded in 1883, which moved to Los Angeles in 1957, becoming the Los Angeles Dodgers.

p. 167, *have*: Amended from "had", based on the American Edn.

p. 168, *U Street*: The heart of the black community in Washington, DC.

p. 168, *Ford... DuPont*: The American industrialists Henry Ford (1863–1947) and Pierre S. du Pont (1870–1954).

p. 168, *Rockfeller*: American Edn: "Rockefeller". The reference is to the business magnate John D. Rockefeller (1839–1937).

p. 168, *Sears Roebuck*: Sears, Roebuck and Co., an American chain of department stores founded in 1892.

p. 169, *altogether*: Amended from "all together", based on the American Edn.

p. 169, *at the surrender*: Following their Second World War defeat, Japan's surrender was announced by Emperor Hirohito on 15th August and ratified on 2nd September 1945.

p. 169, *fluoroscope*: "An apparatus used to obtain an instantaneous X-ray image of an object" (*OED*).

p. 170, *the Scottsboro Boys*: A reference to the famous trial of nine African-American teenagers accused in Alabama of raping two white women in 1931.

p. 171, *Isaac Woodward*: On the day (12th February 1946) he was honourably discharged from the US army after serving in the Pacific during the Second World War, the African-American Isaac Woodward (1919–92) was viciously attacked by South Carolina police while still wearing his uniform. He was left blind as a result of his injuries.

p. 172, *billy*: A "billy club" (that is, a baton).

p. 172, *Willie McGee waitin' right now in Mississippi*: The African-American Willie McGee (*c*.1916–51) was controversially convicted for the rape of a white woman in November 1945. He was eventually executed on 8th May 1951.

p. 172, *seven poor boys… Martinsville, Virginia*: A reference to the "Martinsville Seven", a group of seven African-American men from Martinsville, Virginia, who were executed in February 1951 after being accused of raping a white woman.

p. 172, *CIO*: The Congress of Industrial Organizations, a federation of workers' unions.

p. 172, *where we never could join a union*: American Edn: "where we never even could join a union".

p. 172, *Civil War time*: The American Civil War lasted from 1861 to 1865.

p. 173, *f—— leech*: Amended from "b—— leech", based on the American Edn.

p. 175, *increasing*: American Edn: "increased".

p. 176, *time*: American Edn: "while".

p. 176, *Detective*: American Edn (here and passim): "Sergeant".

p. 176, *four*: Amended from "three" (error of continuity).

p. 177, *General Motors*: The General Motors Corporation, a car manufacturer based in Detroit.

p. 177, *car*: American Edn (here and in the following sentence): "auto".

p. 178, *pellagra*: A skin disease caused by a diet lacking in the vitamin niacin.

p. 178, *car*: American Edn: "auto".

p. 178, *in the winter of 1936… on strike*: There was a series of strikes affecting the car factories in Detroit and other American cities in 1936, which were resolved only in February 1937.

p. 179, *stool pigeons*: Informers.

p. 180, *four*: Amended from "three" (error of continuity).

p. 181, *whichever*: American Edn: "every which".

p. 181, *snot-nosed*: Contemptible.

p. 182, *he never had met before*: American Edn: "he never even had met before".

p. 183, *their dirty stories*: American Edn: "their stories".

p. 184, *heels*: Dishonourable or despicable persons.

p. 186, *the Mann Act*: According to the Mann Act, passed by the US Congress on 25th June 1910, it was a crime to engage in interstate or foreign-commerce transport of "any woman or girl for the purpose of prostitution or debauchery, or for any other immoral purpose".

p. 187, *a law*: American Edn: "the law".

p. 188, *versus*: American Edn: "vs.".

p. 192, *a WPA job*: The Works Progress Administration (WPA) was a federal-government agency formed in 1935 and dissolved in 1943 that employed jobseekers to carry out public-works projects.

p. 192, *YMCA*: The Young Men's Christian Association, an international youth organization founded in 1844 by the English philanthropist George Williams (1821–1905).

p. 192, *Purple Heart*: A decoration awarded to a serviceman wounded in action.

p. 192, *a GI school*: A school for active or former members of the US armed forces.

p. 195, *had*: American Edn: "has".

p. 198, *a cigarette*: American Edn: "cigarette".

p. 198, *packet*: American Edn: "pack".

p. 201, *a hophead*: A drug addict.

p. 203, *twenty*: American Edn: "thirty".

p. 204, *a lift*: American Edn: "an elevator".

p. 204, *it somehow… because*: American Edn: "it somehow was different because".

p. 204, *both of his legs*: American Edn: "both his legs".

p. 205, *turned his back*: American Edn: "turned back".

p. 205, *you f—— nigger*: Amended from "you b—— nigger", based on the American Edn.

p. 206, *and a haste*: American Edn: "and haste".

p. 206, *breeches*: American Edn: "britches".

p. 206, *sentiments*: American Edn: "sentiment".

p. 207, *feelings*: American Edn: "feeling".

p. 207, *To no purpose whatsoever*: American Edn: "To no purpose".

p. 207, *of*: American Edn: "to".

p. 211, *at all*: American Edn: "at all, not at all".

p. 212, *glaze*: American Edn: "daze".

p. 212, *I'll go and see*: American Edn: "I'll go see".

p. 216, *army stockade*: Army prison.

p. 216, *before Pearl Harbor*: That is, before the Japanese attack on the US naval base at Pearl Harbor, Honolulu, on 7th December 1941. The attack prompted the entry of the United States into the Second World War.

p. 219, *the Valley of Death*: The allusion is to Psalms 23:4: "Yea, though I walk through the valley of the shadow of death, I will fear no evil: for thou art with me; thy rod and thy staff, they comfort me."

p. 219, *greeting*: Amended from "greetings", based on the American Edn.

p. 219, *A dirty trick*: American Edn: "A real dirty trick".

p. 219, *on the level*: Honest; reliable.

p. 219, *in that position*: American Edn: "in his position".

p. 224, *When all those other boys*: American Edn: "When all those other boys and girls".

p. 225, *no-'count*: "No-account"; worthless; disreputable.

p. 225, *Cox's Row*: A slum area of Charlottesville, Virginia.

p. 226, *got*: American Edn: "gotten".

p. 234, *owns*: American Edn: "own".

p. 235, *McCormack*: American Edn: "McCormick".

p. 235, *DC*: Washington, DC.

p. 235, *garage*: American Edn: "gas station".

p. 237, *worn*: American Edn: "wored".

p. 239, *there would be men*: American Edn: "there would be men here".

p. 241, *a family of sharecroppers*: A sharecropper is "a farm labourer who receives crops, board, etc., as wages in exchange for work performed" (*OED*). Sharecropping was widespread in the southern states in the century following the American Civil War. "Sharecroppers typically lived in poverty, and sharecropping arrangements were one of the ways in which African-American labour continued to be exploited following the end of slavery" (*OED*).

p. 241, *syphilitic paresis*: Inflammation of the brain in the later stages of syphilis, causing progressive dementia and paralysis.

p. 241, *Terra Haute*: Terre Haute, Indiana.

p. 242, *afterwards*: American Edn: "atterwards".

p. 246, *from less harsh*: American Edn: "from the less harsh".

p. 247, *feeling already there was*: American Edn: "feeling already that there was".

p. 248, *snotty cur*: American Edn: "snotty one". For "snotty", see first note to p. 31.

p. 249, *and fourth*: American Edn: "and a fourth".

p. 250, *indeedy*: Amended from "indeed", based on the American Edn.

p. 252, *f—— nigger*: Amended from "b—— nigger", based on the American Edn.

p. 254, *on*: American Edn: "in".

p. 255, *from the wall*: American Edn: "from wall".

p. 255, *was always*: American Edn: "always was".

p. 258, *The music came back on again*: Amended from "The music came back again", based on the American Edn.

p. 259, *round*: American Edn: "around".

p. 259, *round*: American Edn: "around".

p. 260, *movies*: Amended from "cinema", based on the American Edn.

p. 262, *round*: American Edn: "around".

p. 262, *Yet it*: American Edn: "It".

p. 263, *to*: American Edn: "and".

p. 263, *round*: American Edn: "around".

p. 264, *four-flusher*: Bluffer (from "four flush", four cards of the same suit and one of another – a hand of no value in the game of poker).

p. 264, *round*: Amended from "rounds", based on the American Edn.

p. 265, *he had kept*: Amended from "he kept", based on the American Edn.

p. 267, *without*: American Edn: "unless you had".

p. 268, *A couple of days*: American Edn: "A couple days".

p. 271, *movie house*: Amended from "cinema house", based on the American Edn.

p. 271, *the*: American Edn: "that".

p. 273, *George Washington Carver*: The African-American agricultural scientist and inventor George Washington Carver (c.1864–1943).

p. 273, *Carter Woodson*: The African-American historian and journalist Carter G. Woodson (1875–1950).

p. 273, *Dr Du Bois… Charles Houston*: The African-American sociologist and civil-rights activist W.E.B. Du Bois (1868–1963); the African-American bass-baritone Paul Robeson (1898–1976); the African-American contralto Marian Anderson (1897–1993); the African-American lyric tenor and composer Roland Hayes (1887–1977); the American civil-rights activist Walter White (1893–1955), who led the NAACP between 1929 and 1955; the African-American lawyer Charles Hamilton Houston (1895–1950).

p. 273, *Thurgood Marshall*: The African-American civil-rights lawyer and jurist Thurgood Marshall (1908–93).

p. 274, *Briggs Meldrum*: That is, the Meldrum Avenue plant of Briggs Manufacturing Company, a Detroit-based manufacturer of car bodies for Ford Motor Company.

p. 274, *run*: American Edn: "rush".

p. 274, *of several*: American Edn: "of the several".

p. 275, *to*: American Edn: "for".

p. 275, *movement*: Amended from "moment", based on the American Edn.

p. 276, *for high*: American Edn: "for his high".

p. 278, *white mule*: Illicitly distilled whiskey.

p. 278, *Perfessor*: Amended from "Professor", based on the American Edn.

p. 279, *you*: American Edn: "you'll".

p. 282, *with parole*: Amended from "with a parole", based on the American Edn.

p. 284, *eleven*: American Edn: "eleven of your newspaper".

p. 287, *hands*: American Edn: "hand".

p. 290, *he knew*: American Edn: "and he knew".

p. 291, *any talking*: American Edn: "any more talking".

p. 294, *not*: American Edn: "no".

p. 295, *Boulder Dam*: Now called Hoover Dam, built between 1931 and 1936 on the border between Nevada and Arizona.

p. 296, *UAW*: United Auto Workers, an American workers' union.

p. 300, *Victrola*: A brand of gramophone.

p. 303, *the Battle of Port Hudson*: Usually known as the Siege of Port Hudson (22nd May to 9th July 1863), this was the final engagement in the Union campaign to recapture the Mississippi River during the American Civil War. It resulted in a victory for the Union army.

p. 303, *tintype*: A photograph taken as a positive on a thin tin plate.

p. 303, *Baton Rouge*: An area of south-eastern Louisiana and the site of a battle (5th August 1862) during the American Civil War which resulted in a victory for the Union army.

p. 303, *the Black Codes*: A series of laws passed by some states after the end of the American Civil War restricting the rights of African-American people.

p. 304, *Battle of the Crater before Petersburg*: The Battle of the Crater (part of the Siege of Petersburg, a series of battles around Petersburg, Virginia, that took place between 9th June 1864 and 25th March 1865) was fought on 30th July 1864.

p. 304, *when Lee surrendered*: The Confederate forces under the command of General Robert E. Lee (1807–70) surrendered to the Union army led by Ulysses S. Grant (1822–85) after their defeat at the Battle of Appomattox Court House (9th April 1865) in Appomattox County, Virginia, which brough the American Civil War to an end.

p. 304, *from*: Amended from "on", based on the American Edn.

p. 304, *We'll hang Jeff Davis on a sour apple tree*: A line from 'John Brown's Body', a famous Union marching song of the American Civil War. The original song says "They will hang Jeff Davis to a tree!", but another variant has "They will hang Jeff Davis to a sour apple tree!" and an African-American version is recorded as "We'll hang Jeff Davis from a sour apple tree!" Jefferson Davis (1808–89) was president of the Confederate States from 1861 to 1865.

p. 307, *back, his heart*: American Edn: "back with his heart".

p. 307, *this*: American Edn: "the".

p. 312, *said Lauter*: American Edn: "Lauter said".

p. 313, *slammed*: American Edn: "hammered".

p. 315, *brought with them*: American Edn: "brought back with them".

p. 315, *my army Garand*: The service rifle of the US Army during the Second World War.

p. 319, *'do unto others'*: "Do unto others as you would have them do unto you" (from Jesus's Sermon on the Mount – see Matthew 7:12; Luke 6:31).

p. 320, *packets*: American Edn: "packs".

ALMA CLASSICS

ALMA CLASSICS aims to publish mainstream and lesser-known European classics in an innovative and striking way, while employing the highest editorial and production standards. By way of a unique approach the range offers much more, both visually and textually, than readers have come to expect from contemporary classics publishing.

LATEST TITLES PUBLISHED BY ALMA CLASSICS

www.almaclassics.com